Praise for the Crime of Fashion mysteries

"Devilishly funny. . . . Lacey is intelligent, insightful, and spunky . . . thoroughly likable." —*The Sun* (Bremerton, WA)

"Byerrum spins a mystery out of (very luxurious) whole cloth with the best of them." —Chick Lit Books

"Fun and witty . . . with a great female sleuth." —Fresh Fiction

"[A] very entertaining series." —The Romance Reader's Connection

Hostile Makeover

"Byerrum pulls another superlative Crime of Fashion out of her vintage cloche. . . . All these wonderful characters combine with Byerrum's . . . clever plotting and snappy dialogue to fashion a . . . keep-em-guessing-'til-the-end whodunit." —Chick Lit Books

"So much fun." —The Romance Reader's Connection

"The read is as smooth as fine-grade cashmere." —*Publishers Weekly*

"Totally delightful . . . a fun and witty read." —Fresh Fiction

continued . . .

Designer Knockoff

"Byerrum intersperses the book with witty excerpts from Lacey's 'Fashion Bites' columns, such as 'When Bad Clothes Happen to Good People' and 'Thank Heavens It's Not Code Taupe.' . . . Quirky. . . . Interesting plot twists." —*The Sun* (Bremerton, WA)

"Clever wordplay, snappy patter, and intriguing clues make this politics-meets-high-fashion whodunit a cut above the ordinary."
—*Romantic Times*

"Compelling. . . . Lacey is a spunky heroine and is very self-assured as she carries off her vintage looks with much aplomb."
—The Mystery Reader

"A very talented writer with an offbeat sense of humor and talent for creating quirky and eccentric characters that will have readers laughing at their antics." —The Best Reviews

Killer Hair

"[A] rippling debut. Peppered with girlfriends you'd love to have, smoldering romance you can't resist, and Beltway insider insights you've got to read, *Killer Hair* adds a crazy twist to the concept of 'capital murder.'" —Sarah Strohmeyer, Agatha Award–winning author of *The Secret Lives of Fortunate Wives*

"Ellen Byerrum tailors her debut mystery with a sharp murder plot, entertaining fashion commentary, and gutsy characters."
—Nancy J. Cohen, author of the Bad Hair Day mysteries

"Chock-full of colorful, often hilarious characters. . . . Lacey herself has a delightfully catty wit. . . . A load of stylish fun."
—Scripps Howard News Service

"Lacey slays and sashays through Washington politics, scandal, and Fourth Estate slime, while uncovering whodunit, and dunit and dunit again."
—Chloe Green, author of the Dallas O'Connor Fashion mysteries

"*Killer Hair* is a shear delight."
—Elaine Viets, national bestselling author of *Murder Unleashed*

Raiders of the Lost Corset

A CRIME OF FASHION MYSTERY

Ellen Byerrum

A SIGNET BOOK

SIGNET
Published by New American Library, a division of
Penguin Group (USA) Inc., 375 Hudson Street,
New York, New York 10014, USA
Penguin Group (Canada), 90 Eglinton Avenue East, Suite 700, Toronto,
Ontario M4P 2Y3, Canada (a division of Pearson Penguin Canada Inc.)
Penguin Books Ltd., 80 Strand, London WC2R 0RL, England
Penguin Ireland, 25 St. Stephen's Green, Dublin 2,
Ireland (a division of Penguin Books Ltd.)
Penguin Group (Australia), 250 Camberwell Road, Camberwell, Victoria 3124,
Australia (a division of Pearson Australia Group Pty. Ltd.)
Penguin Books India Pvt. Ltd., 11 Community Centre, Panchsheel Park,
New Delhi - 110 017, India
Penguin Group (NZ), cnr Airborne and Rosedale Roads, Albany,
Auckland 1310, New Zealand (a division of Pearson New Zealand Ltd.)
Penguin Books (South Africa) (Pty.) Ltd., 24 Sturdee Avenue,
Rosebank, Johannesburg 2196, South Africa

Penguin Books Ltd., Registered Offices:
80 Strand, London WC2R 0RL, England

First published by Signet, an imprint of New American Library,
a division of Penguin Group (USA) Inc.

First Printing, July 2006
10 9 8 7 6 5

REGISTERED TRADEMARK—MARCA REGISTRADA

Printed in the United States of America

PUBLISHER'S NOTE
This is a work of fiction. Names, characters, places, and incidents either are the product of the author's imagination or are used fictitiously, and any resemblance to actual persons, living or dead, business establishments, events, or locales is entirely coincidental.

The publisher does not have any control over and does not assume any responsibility for author or third-party Web sites or their content.

ACKNOWLEDGMENTS

Writing a book is an amazing journey, and it never ceases to amaze me how generous people have been to me with their gracious support and special knowledge. And if I have taken that information and twisted it to my own ends, it is not their fault; it's mine. It's just fiction.

I want to express my appreciation to Inara Apinis, Alex Braguine, Regina Cline, Jack French, Lloyd Rose, and Pat Ware, all of whom shared much information over many lunches. Rip Claassen at Backstage Books in Washington, D.C., gave me his time and insight into the costumer's art, for which I am truly thankful.

Many thanks go to Don Maass, Cameron McClure, and Rachel Vater at the Donald Maass Literary Agency for their support. I would also like to thank Martha Bushko, my editor at Signet.

My thanks as well to the city of New Orleans and its friendly and helpful inhabitants. This book reflects a little of the gracious Crescent City as it was just before Hurricane Katrina, and as it will someday be again.

This book would not have been written without the complete support and help of my husband, Bob Williams, who will no doubt want to sweep me off to Paris (again) after reading this acknowledgment.

chapter 1

"Find the corset!" the old woman gasped.

Magda Rousseau was never more enigmatic, Lacey Smithsonian thought, than with death at her door. She lay draped in a profusion of gaudy jewels on her tattered old sofa, one of its broken legs replaced by several large books.

The jewels were fake, of course. Anyone could see that. Yet the ropes of faux pearls and necklaces of rubies, emeralds, and diamonds gave the old Frenchwoman the air of regal hauteur she sought in life. Magda had a glazed look in her eyes, a half-smile playing on her lips, and a secret she refused to divulge: Who killed her—or rather, who had *tried* to kill her. After all, Lacey realized, Magda wasn't dead yet. Perhaps there was still time to save her life. But all Magda cared about was the corset.

"Magda, what happened to you?" Lacey reached for her cell phone. She dialed 911 for an ambulance. With her free hand she touched the woman's forehead. A string of fake sapphires came loose and fell to the floor with a clatter.

Magda's skin was cool, her face looked waxy, and her breath was shallow. She kept smiling, arrayed in her false glamour. She was still alive, though barely, when Lacey arrived at Magda's little theatrical costume and corset shop, Stays and Plays.

The woman shook her head as if trying to clear her thoughts. "Poison."

"Poison! You were poisoned? How? Who?"

Magda stared at Lacey, her brow wrinkled in concentration. "Don't drink—the wine, Lacey. It seems to be a very—*bad* vintage. And it is not French." Lacey saw the nearly empty wineglass tilting out of Magda's loose grasp, its remaining red drops staining the pale pink rose of the sofa. She let go of the glass, but it stayed in position, held fast by the tangle of false gems.

So that's where the poison was, Lacey thought. Who would poison the eccentric old woman, and why? "Please try to conserve your strength," she pleaded. "Help is on the way."

The dispatcher came back on the phone, urging Lacey not to hang up, reassuring her that paramedics were en route. Lacey feared it would be too little, too late. Could the paramedics make it in time? She heard an ambulance wailing in the distance, but in Washington, D.C., that was an ever-present background noise. It might be headed anywhere.

"Do you know what kind of poison?" Lacey asked.

Magda managed a wry smile. "The fatal kind."

"Let me get you some water; maybe it will dilute the poison. We have to do something." Lacey reached out to take Magda's hands. "Come on, I'll help you to the bathroom."

"I can't, Lacey." She didn't move. "He has my feet."

"What are you talking about?" She looked down. Magda was barefoot, the large purple veins contrasting with her bluish-white skin. Lacey knew she preferred to work in her bare feet and often kicked off her scruffy black shoes. "Who has your feet?"

"Him. *L'Ange de la Mort.* Death, with his icy hands." Her French accent became thicker. "My feet are already gone. He has taken them. I can't feel them anymore." Lacey put the phone down on the coffee table and grabbed a bolt of soft blue flannel. She knelt to cover Magda's feet with the material. "So this is how he comes, the angel of death. He starts with the feet and puts them in ice."

"Good God, Magda, stop being so drearily European about this." Lacey rubbed Magda's feet vigorously to jump-start her circulation. "This is America. Dying is a last resort here. Try a little optimism. Concentrate on fighting this. There's an antidote. Usually. Maybe." Lacey's efforts weren't helping, and the chill was seeping into her hands. "You really must wear your shoes and socks. Warm socks. Or your slippers, Magda. Do you have any slippers? I'll get them for you—"

Lacey realized she was babbling out of fear and concern, and in any case, her advice was useless: Magda Rousseau seemed to be intent on taking the train to eternity with the icy angel. Lacey could feel the woman slipping away, but she carefully tucked the warm flannel around Magda's feet. She was furious there was so little she could do.

"Who brought the angel of death here? Who did this to you?" Lacey shouted. Magda was fading. The Frenchwoman merely shook her head. "We have to find a way—"

"No!" Magda struggled for breath. "Find the corset! You promised me." Lacey barely understood her slurred and accented speech. "The corset is more important than my feet. Find the corset!" she croaked in her thick French accent, running out of breath. "Promise me!"

"I promise. Please, Magda. Hold on, they'll be here soon." Lacey realized she had done everything she could do. Now she could only wait. She held Magda's icy-cold hands.

Magda Rousseau was a master corsetiere, one of the last practicing the not-quite-lost art of accentuating (or creating) the alluring curves of the female form with laces and stays. She created exotic special-order corsets and other fine and fancy underpinnings for an interesting set of characters, including Lacey's brassy hairstylist, Stella Lake, the numerous local corset fetishists, and a select group of high-priced call girls. She also put her needle to work making costumes for Washington, D.C.'s theatrical community. Her work had graced elegant costume dramas at many of the finest theatres in the Nation's Capital.

The jewels covering Magda were just flashy baubles meant for costumes of kings and queens, jesters and fools, to make the illusion glitter in the footlights. The effect was startling, as if someone had emptied the shop's entire inventory of junk jewelry over her, as if it were a set piece in an absurdist play, or a topsy-turvy robbery in reverse. Had she really been poisoned? Was she attacked by an enraged thief who didn't find what he was looking for? And what was her assailant really after? Lacey didn't want to take her eyes off Magda, but she glanced away quickly to take in the room. It was a disaster. Even at the best of times, she reflected, it was barely controlled chaos, but today it was chaotic even by Magda's standards.

Lacey glanced up uneasily at a row of wig heads that stared at her with sightless eyes under elaborate curled hairdos. *No wonder I feel like someone's staring at me.* The workshop where Magda made her living occupied the second floor of a converted town house in Washington, D.C.'s Eastern Market neighborhood, over a storefront on the ground floor. Magda's apartment was on the third floor, one of two tiny apartments. Near the sofa where Magda lay, Lacey saw the large antique oak notions cabinet, its many glass-front drawers open, their contents spilling out, a treasure chest of faux jewels, bits of gold braid, and chains like the ones that decorated her still form.

A nearly finished corset in sassy pink satin with black lace trim was provocatively positioned on a dressmaker's dummy, next to another dummy displaying a purple velvet Elizabethan corseted gown for *The Merry Wives of Windsor.* A third dummy, with a drape of blue silk for a fancy bustier, had fallen or been thrown to the floor. A profusion of corsets and bustiers in silk and satin and brocade in every stage of construction were strewn about. But Lacey knew that none of these was the corset Magda was talking about.

"A corsetiere knows all your secrets," Magda had often said to Lacey with a wink. "The secrets you keep and the secrets you give away, all the secrets you hide beneath your clothes." But clearly she wasn't parting with any secrets today. Perhaps, Lacey thought, she could keep Magda among the living by engaging her, by simply refusing to let her go.

Keep her talking, she thought. *She's such a storyteller, maybe she'll get started on a story and forget to die.* "What's with all the baubles, Magda?" she said. "You couldn't decide what to wear tonight?"

The old woman shook her head. "The corset! Nothing else matters. You must talk to my cousin—" The words were gasps of agony between shallow breaths.

"Forget about the corset! Someone tried to kill you," Lacey shouted, trying to get through the woman's fog of pain.

Magda wasn't listening. Even while losing her grasp on the material world, dreams of a treasure beyond imagining were never far from her mind. "At first, you know, I thought my grandfather had stolen a Fabergé egg, not a bloodstained corset. Did I tell you about all this?"

Lacey could see her struggle for air, and for her thoughts. "Your grandfather, I know, the corset, you told me. But who did this, Magda? And why?"

Magda summoned the last remnants of her strength and clarity and fixed her gaze on Lacey. She said very distinctly, "Promise me you will find the corset!" Then she closed her eyes.

Oh, no, Magda, you can't die, Lacey thought irrationally, *you still have stories to tell!* And it was so like Magda to hold a hasty promise over Lacey's head as she died, to haunt her with this peculiar pipe dream. And where on earth were the D.C. paramedics?

Find the corset. A spectral command. "Yes, the corset! Magda, whoever poisoned you, were they after the corset? Tell me, Magda!"

It wasn't just any corset, Lacey knew. It was a corset of rumor and legend, a corset that would be worth millions, a corset of infamy sewn with hidden imperial jewels, lost for most of the twentieth century. *More than enough motive for murder.* That is, if Magda were to be believed. Lacey was never sure how much the old corsetiere might have embroidered her stories. Quite a lot, Lacey suspected, which would be appropriate for an expert seamstress. Perhaps some tales were even made up out of whole cloth. But the mythical corset was a treasure that Magda Rousseau had intended to recover, with fashion reporter Lacey Smithsonian of *The Eye Street Observer* at her side to document the search. It was a lunatic idea, which made it appealing to both of them.

"Magda?" Lacey said. "Magda Rousseau!" There was no answer this time, and Lacey knew she was dead.

What once was Magda sat on the faded floral sofa in the middle of her workroom, her head leaning back, her fingers still touching the poisoned glass of wine. Her purple shirtwaist dress was old, clean, and well tailored, but the top button was missing. Her short curly brown hair, shot through with gray, perpetually resisted all her attempts at taming it and was now sticking straight up. Oddly, Magda looked at peace, the jumble of jewels and all.

Magda was probably between sixty and seventy, but looked older. *It isn't the years, it's the mileage,* Lacey thought. Magda's upturned cat eyes had always sparkled with a bit of humor, as they did even now. Her lips bore traces of coral lipstick and her ghastly white cheeks sported two bright spots of rouge, and her love of wine and vodka showed in the broken capillaries across her cheeks. Lacey stared at the dead woman, hoping vainly that her friend's death was just an illusion and she might soon rouse herself and say, "All a joke, Lacey! A good joke, no?"

The sun was sinking lower beyond the room's one large window. The golden afternoon light glinted on the paste jewels and reflected from dust floating quietly over the scene. It had started out a fine November day, with a hint of warmth in the air, but darkness would come soon enough and a chillier air would seize the night.

Lacey remembered the cell phone and picked it up from the coffee table to hear a voice.

"Ma'am, are you there?"

"Why the hell aren't you here?" she shouted, her frustration taking over.

"They will be there soon, ma'am. Please stay on the—"

Lacey clicked off the phone. She didn't want to talk to the voice anymore. The heaviness of death settled on her shoulders, leaving her with a melancholy that bore into her bones. She knew she would cry later, in private. But she called on her reporter's hardness, woven through with cynicism, to help her through the next few hours. She would wait for the ambulance. And the police. She wanted to see Magda through to the bitter end.

Mac isn't going to like this, Lacey told herself, and then she thought of all the people who wouldn't like it. Her editor, Mac, was just one, her erstwhile boyfriend, Vic Donovan, was another, and she put herself at the top of the list.

"This isn't the way it's supposed to go," she said aloud. She pulled out her cell phone again to dial Tony Trujillo, police reporter at *The Eye,* but she hung up. It was past today's deadline. *Let Trujillo find his own news.* Lacey was tired of being in the center of bad news. The small shop would become a circus-like scene soon enough. She saved that conversation until later and put the phone away.

Feet pounded up the steps to the second-floor workshop. Paramedics stormed through the unlocked door and advanced on Magda, even though Lacey said, "You're too late." They paid no attention to her. Lacey gazed at her friend one last time before the old woman was subjected to their indignities. Magda's strong, dexterous fingers still bore multiple rings, each holding a sentimental memory. She leaned in to take a closer look.

"That's funny," Lacey said aloud, realizing that it was absurd that she would notice anything amiss under Magda's gaudy garlands of costume jewelry.

"What's funny?" a booming baritone voice bellowed behind her.

Lacey knew that voice.

chapter 2

Detective Broadway Lamont of the D.C. Metropolitan Police Department filled the doorway.

Oh, no. Not Broadway "the Bull" Lamont.

"Lacey Smithsonian. Good God almighty. What are the damned odds?" His brown face glowed with sweat. He didn't look pleased to see her either.

A man and a woman in dark blue uniforms were performing CPR on Magda. As they repositioned her body, blue, green, purple, and red rings, bracelets, and bangles scattered and streamed to the floor, clinking and pinging against one another.

"Talk to me," Lamont ordered in that threatening way Lacey had come to know and appreciate. She imagined suspects who faced the huge African-American detective were duly cowed. She felt a little cowed herself, but she wasn't about to let him see that.

"Nice to see you again too, Detective."

"You call this in?"

"Yeah."

"Yeah, and—? Don't make me cranky, Smithsonian." He looked like he was already cranky. "Who's the Christmas tree?"

"Her name is Magda Rousseau."

"They said it was poison. You tell 'em that?"

"That's what she told me when she was still talking."

Lamont loomed over the sofa and bent his head close to the busy paramedics to take a good look at the victim. He snorted. "Poison, huh? She got a knife stuck in her, she tell you that? There, right between her ribs."

"What!?" Lacey followed his look. With the blanket of faux jewels cleared away, she could see a petite amethyst-and-emerald-handled knife protruding from Magda's ribs. It looked like a prop dagger, something in a costume drama. A little blood seeped around the wound, staining the purple dress darker. Lamont pulled her away. "My God, I swear I didn't see that," Lacey said. "There was so much stuff on her—"

"Where I come from, we call that a clue, Smithsonian. A big fat clue."

"She didn't say anything about being stabbed. Just poisoned. I was rubbing her feet." Lacey choked back a sob. "She said they were cold."

"Don't fall apart on me just 'cause you didn't see it." His baritone softened ever so slightly. "You're no detective is all. Or else you'd have noticed there's something wrong with this picture. A poison victim with a knife stuck in her? What's up with that? And there ain't much blood for a stabbing. Ought to be more blood, you know. And what the hell kind of voodoo shop is this place?"

" 'Bloody thread, knock 'em dead,' " Lacey said in a whisper. Lamont looked at her sharply. She quickly explained, "She's a corsetiere, a costume maker. For the theatre, among other things. 'Bloody thread' was an expression of Magda's, a backstage theatre expression, she said, a superstition. Like saying 'break a leg' to an actor."

"Yeah? Impress me with your backstage theatre knowledge."

"She said costume makers believe if they prick their fingers while they're making a costume, it means they're putting their blood, their soul, into the work and it's bound to be a good show. At least that's what Magda claimed."

"This ain't my idea of a good show. Poison *and* a knife. Doesn't add up. I don't like it, not a damn bit." He looked even crankier than before, if possible. "Especially with you in a starring role." He lifted his chin toward the deceased. "Knives are your specialty, aren't they?"

"Hey! That was self-defense and you know it." Lacey didn't like the look on his face. *What was he implying?*

"More than once, Smithsonian."

"If I'm going to skewer someone, Lamont, it's going to be in self-defense." He scowled, but he backed up a step. "Magda was my source. My friend. I was trying to save her life. I had an appointment with her. We were working on a story. A *fashion* story."

"Oh, God, here we go again." Broadway Lamont's eyebrow lifted. "You gonna start telling me about fashion clues?"

"I'd rather not."

"Just as well. Looks stupid on my report." He snorted. "So how do you get involved in these messes? A pretty woman like you should have better things to do. And you're supposed to be sort of smart, aren't you?"

"'Sort of smart'?" She could feel her own eyebrow lift involuntarily.

"If you were really smart, you'd keep your ass outside the crime scene tape."

Lacey sighed. "Point taken." She couldn't argue with that, and she was determined to stay out of the way, out of trouble. This time.

"This corset-maker of yours, this Magda Rousseau," he said, "she work here alone?"

"No, she has a partner." He waited for more. "Analiza Zarina. She's usually around, but she doesn't seem to be here today."

"'Anna Lisa'?" Lamont asked, his notebook and pen poised. "She a foreigner too?"

"It's Latvian." Lacey spelled the name for him. The co-owner of the shop was in her mid-forties, a flighty woman who never seemed to stand still. Analiza's tumble of curly strawberry-blond hair bounced as she fluttered through the workshop like a nervous sparrow. Analiza sewed at top speed, Lacey remembered, racing her seams through the madly beating machine, the needle clacking up and down. Her sewing machine was quiet now, a length of bright red material draped over it waiting to be turned into a cape, perhaps for a Little Red Riding Hood in a school play. A beaded black sweater hung across the back of her chair; Analiza always complained of the cold. Magda was always the calmer one, the know-it-all, the boss.

"Any tension between the two of them?" Lamont interrupted her reverie.

All the time, Lacey thought. The women were always sniping at each other in a familiar, comfortable way. Magda grumbled at Analiza for wasting expensive material; Analiza groaned that Magda would worry about the price of air, if she could. They even argued over that costumer's saying of Magda's, "Bloody thread, knock 'em dead." Analiza insisted it was "Bloody stitch, all get rich." "Just general coworker kind of tension," Lacey told Lamont. "Like siblings."

"The kind that ends with a knife between the ribs?"

"I don't know. I wouldn't have thought so, but—" She shrugged.

"So, what's so 'funny,' Smithsonian? That's what you said when I came in."

"There's nothing funny here anymore, Broadway." Lacey tried

to get a glimpse of Magda, but her view was blocked by the medical team. They were still in a flurry of activity, but they seemed to be losing enthusiasm. Faux jewels covered the floor like colored raindrops in a pool of fading sunlight. "There was a pin, a broach she always wore, but she's not wearing it now. I thought it was funny that it's missing. It's hard to ignore, it's so gaudy."

"Gaudy? In this mess? How could you tell?" Lamont glowered. Lacey realized the statement sounded ludicrous considering the outrageous bejeweled mess covering the sofa and spilling onto the floor. She looked again, but the pin was not among the scattered plunder.

"Sarcasm from Broadway Lamont. Who would have thought?"

He grunted. "Sarcasm's cheap; take all you want. This broach thing valuable? Something someone would kill for? Or maybe this scene started in a robbery, ended in something else?"

"I never saw her without it. That's all. Maybe it wasn't so cheap after all. Maybe someone took it. Or maybe she just wasn't wearing it today, didn't go with her outfit."

"So this is one of your so-called 'fashion clues,' huh?"

She shrugged and the detective rolled his eyes. Lacey felt a chill in the air. She crossed her arms and leaned back against the sofa where Magda still lay. "Hey hey hey! Crime scene!" Broadway yelled and she jumped up involuntarily. "Keep off the furniture."

She moved and silently urged her nerves to calm down. "I didn't say it was a fashion clue. I just noticed it was missing."

"Yeah, yeah. Killer takes a souvenir. Something pretty to pawn, maybe. I'll need a description of this whatchamacallit from you, Smithsonian." He took out his notebook again.

"Maybe she left it in her room," Lacey continued, "in a jewelry box or something." He looked perplexed. She pointed up. "Magda lives upstairs. She keeps her key ring on a peg near her sewing machine." Lacey walked quickly to the sewing machine and pointed but did not touch. The keys were hanging there. Lamont looked a little happier.

"Now that's more like a real clue. Let's go, Smithsonian," Lamont said. He snapped on latex gloves and grabbed the keys with his big right hand. "Probable cause for a search. You better show me the way."

Chapter 3

Lacey ushered Detective Lamont past a hanging rack of brightly colored velvet and satin costumes to the back of Magda's workshop and through a door propped open by a small bust of Shakespeare. She led him up a dim narrow staircase illuminated by a bare forty-watt bulb. At the top of the stairs two front doors with chipped white paint were angled across from each other. On the right, Magda's door led to the rear of the building, her apartment facing the small backyard and alley. From the other door the tantalizing aroma of baking bread hovered in the air.

The workshop and apartments were located in an older house in the Eastern Market section of D.C., east of Capitol Hill, in an area where gentrification had turned the neighboring houses into stratospherically priced homes for the well-to-do and into chic storefronts. It was only a matter of time before this one too would receive a stylish makeover that would displace the remaining residents, one of whom had just been displaced by death.

Lamont opened the door. Magda's apartment wore an air of proud but shabby gentility. The paint was old and chipped above the doorjamb and there were cracks running down the walls. An ancient Aubusson carpet covered the floor with flowers in faded shades of ivory, blue, and rose, worn and threadbare in places. Still, it had a certain *je ne sais quoi,* as Magda would say.

Lacey's visits had been restricted to the minuscule living room where she and Stella often shared strong coffee with Magda after fittings. Lacey remembered mismatched china cups and plates that held croissants and jam perched on the marble-top coffee table. Now it was full of sewing and pattern magazines and a travel magazine about France.

Lacey had never seen Magda's bedroom, but Lamont beckoned her to it, flipping the light switch. It still held a lingering trace of

Magda's distinctive perfume and of the sachet in her chest of drawers and closet. A single bed, neatly made with a yellow daffodil-patterned spread, was flanked by small white wooden end tables. On the tables were twin lamps, dancing ballerinas holding up the white and yellow shades. Magda must have loved the ballet, Lacey realized; there was a large painting of ballerinas above the bed. Next to a small window, a plain white dresser was topped by a white leather jewelry box. When Lamont opened the lid, a ballerina sprang up, dancing to a tinkling music box air from *Swan Lake* in front of pink satin lining.

This is a little girl's room, Lacey thought. She wondered whether Magda had ever had a man in her life. Lacey had vaguely thought of her as a widow, but she realized she had never mentioned a husband, deceased or otherwise. Besides the daily demands of her costume business, she seemed to have only one ambition—to find the lost corset.

"Come here." Detective Lamont motioned Lacey over. He gently poked through the jewelry box with a pen from his pocket. "You see it in here, that broach thingy? Maybe the perp never made it up here."

She gazed at the pieces. A couple of necklaces, faux pearls, earrings. "No. It's not there."

"What did the thing look like? Can you draw me a picture?"

"Would now be a good time to tell you I got a D in eighth-grade art? I barely mastered circles and stick figures."

"You're hopeless, Smithsonian. Can you at least describe the damn thing?"

"Yeah, I can describe the damn thing. It's a round pin with a fluted edge, about the size of a golf ball, silver with lots of colored stones, red, blue, and green."

Lacey was no authority on the life and dreams of Magda Rousseau. She'd probably met her no more than a dozen times crowded together in the last few months, often in the company of the inimitable Stella, the hairstylist they had in common. But every single time, Magda had worn the gaudy pin. She said it "went with everything."

"Maybe it had sentimental value," she said, thinking it might have been a gift from a man, a lover. But the room wasn't talking. There weren't even any photographs of Magda, or of anyone else.

"We'll let Forensics poke around up here. When they get here. Let's you and me go have a chat, Smithsonian." He sighed loudly and followed her back to the living room and down the stairs to the costume shop. With his lumbering gait he reminded her of a big bear. *A big bear who also happens to be a big drama queen,* she thought.

The paramedics had given up and were standing by amid the uniformed police. Magda lay on the sofa now, her eyes half open in that teasing way, the weird smile in place, as if she were rather amused by the proceedings occasioned by her death. Lacey hoped she was.

Behind Lacey, Lamont said, "Top button's gone off the dress."

She turned and looked at the dead woman again. Magda's face looked chalky. "That's where she would have worn the pin. Maybe to hide the missing button." She pointed to a tiny rip, wondering if the same someone who spiked Magda's wine took the gaudy piece of jewelry. But was that the same someone who spiked her ribs with a gaudy dagger? And why try to kill her twice? Was it possible there were two killers?

"What did she tell you?"

"Not to drink the wine." Lacey indicated the bottle of Pinot Grigio sitting on the edge of Magda's sewing machine.

"We'll have it tested." He signaled to another cop to collect it and several other glasses scattered around. "She didn't tell you what kind of poison? Arsenic, rat poison, cyanide?"

"She just stared at me with that look."

"Dead people can be damned uncommunicative," he said. "But hell, that's what autopsies are for."

"Right. An autopsy. How are things going down at the morgue?" Lacey had heard horror stories about the D.C. morgue.

"It's a damn mess." Lamont rubbed his chin.

"How long will it take?"

"Do I look like I got a crystal ball on me? So how'd you meet this Magda Rousseau?"

"A friend. I met Magda through a friend." *It's all Stella's fault.* Lacey met Magda because Stella had a passion for exotic fashion, which included leather bustiers, sequined halters, and full-fledged boned and brocaded corsets. Because Lacey was the fashion reporter for *The Eye Street Observer,* Stella insisted Lacey should write a story about her friend Magda Rousseau. Stella had modeled Magda's latest laced-and-boned creation and promoted the old woman's craftsmanship and design sense as a subject for one of Lacey's "Crimes of Fashion" columns.

"What did I tell you? The woman is a total genius with underwear," Stella had said. "She's French, did I tell you? And her fancy underwear is like outerwear for the inner goddess, you know? You could use that in a column, huh? Give me credit if you use it, okay, Lace?"

Lacey shuddered at the idea of slipping racy French lingerie into her style columns for the staid, buttoned-down Washingtonian woman, but Stella persevered in her lobbying on behalf of Magda's talents. Lacey agreed that beautiful underwear deserved respect, as Magda said, and that the secrets under your clothes might be worth examining. Under duress, Lacey even conceded that corsets had a certain charm and a sexy retro panache. Indeed, many designers were incorporating them in their collections, notably in formal wear. But she had told Stella firmly that she should not, could not, *would* not write about kinky corset fetishes and call-girl couture in a family newspaper. Her editor, Mac, would have a heart attack.

"I will not write about kinky boys and girls in kinky underwear, do you understand, Stella?"

"Whatever," Stella had replied with a dismissive lift of her shoulders. "Don't knock it till you try it, babe."

Lacey's stylist had dragged her to the small shop where Magda worked, stitching custom underwear, corsets, and costumes, and where she bickered with Analiza Zarina, and Lacey and Magda had hit it off.

" 'A friend,' huh? You were working on a fashion story?" Broadway Lamont broke into her thoughts. "What's the angle? This old broad's no dish. Not like that fashion model that got herself gunned down in front of you in Dupont Circle a few weeks ago."

"Magda's not a fashion plate, she's an old-fashioned corsetiere. She makes corsets, fancy undergarments of all kinds, by hand, the way they used to make them. The corset renaissance is the fashion story. Or rather, *was* the story."

"You're writing about ladies' fancy undies? I thought *The Eye Street Observer* was a family newspaper. Corsets are more like *City Paper* turf, aren't they?"

"*The Eye* believes in the right to wear the underwear of your choice, Detective. Besides, you told me you don't read my newspaper."

"That's right." He nodded his large head. "It's third in line behind the other papers I don't read. *The Washington Post* being the number-one paper I don't read. Don't mean I don't know all about it. So what's the story?"

"Magda and I discussed corsets and cleavage, uplift and control, things like that. And besides all that, Magda was an interesting character, a real dynamo. And a storyteller."

In fact, Magda was even more persistent than Stella. "How can you write the story of the corset without your own corset? How will you know the *je ne sais quoi,* the feel, the experience?" She badgered Lacey until she gave in and ordered a custom-made corset of her own. Magda promised she would craft a corset for Lacey for only a little over the materials' cost. She promised she would not reveal Lacey's measurements to anyone, then loudly announced in front of several clients that Lacey's waist was nothing to be ashamed of. The ordeal had been excruciating, and Lacey knew that Broadway Lamont did not need every little piece of information her flirtation with fancy underwear might have uncovered. *He'll need a subpoena to get my waist size out of me.* Little by little, when Stella wasn't around, Magda had spun out her theory about the lost corset. She swore Lacey to secrecy. Lacey wondered at first whether this was just a ploy to whet her appetite for the story.

"Wake up, Smithsonian," Lamont demanded. "You been drinking that wine too?"

A puzzled female voice broke in behind them from the back door of the shop. "What's going on? Where is—" Then a strangled scream. "Magda!"

Lamont turned toward the voice. Lacey spun around to see a slim, attractive woman being restrained by a police officer. Lacey recognized her as Natalija Krumina, one of Magda's neighbors, whom she had met in passing once or twice. Aside from the fact that she was also Latvian and she pronounced her name "Natalie," Lacey knew little about her.

"Oh, no! My poor Magda! My God, what has happened? Was it her heart?" the woman asked Broadway Lamont. "She told me she had a weak heart. Is she—?"

"And just who might you be, ma'am?" Lamont asked politely.

Lamont was never that polite with her. But then Smithsonian bore the stain of being a newspaper reporter, a member of the Fourth Estate, a class merely tolerated if not downright despised by police and politicians alike in the Nation's Capital.

"Natalija Krumina. I live upstairs," she said with a tremor in her voice. She spoke with a slightly musical accent. "I was going to invite Magda over for some fresh herb and olive bread I just baked. She loves it." She approached Magda's still body and her eyes filled up with tears.

Natalija was probably Lacey's age, her early thirties, with chestnut brown hair that fell below her shoulders in one dark, silky wave. Her features were even and pleasing. She had large almond eyes in a distinctive shade of golden brown, now wet and glistening.

Oh, yeah. Lamont is no doubt a big sucker for tears, Lacey thought, running her fingers through her own hair, wondering what she looked like after the shock of finding Magda dying. Finding a dead body, no doubt, would be hard on the complexion, as well as the blood pressure.

The big detective asked Natalija a few questions, whether she remembered seeing anyone visiting Magda earlier, whether she had heard anything. Natalija swore she knew nothing, heard nothing, and had seen nothing.

"What about her favorite pin?" Lamont asked. "Seems to be missing."

Natalija went blank for a minute, gazing at the puddle of fake jewels on the carpet. The detective gestured to Lacey, who dutifully described it. Natalija grimaced. "That old thing? I don't know. Maybe she lost it." She looked over at Magda again and shook her head. "She's really dead, isn't she?"

Detective Lamont looked grim and Natalija burst into fresh tears. "Miss Krumina, do you happen to remember a theatre expression Magda Rousseau used to say? A good luck thing?"

"Why? Does it mean something?" She gazed up at him. "Ah, yes, you mean, 'Bloody dress, get good press'? She said that whenever she pricked her finger. She was funny that way."

Lamont lifted an eyebrow at Lacey. She shrugged back. It was yet another variant of the same phrase. Magda seemed to have more than one version of every story. Lacey wondered how many different versions of the corset legend she might have told as well.

"Maybe you should go back to your apartment, ma'am," he said to Natalija. "There's nothing you can do here."

She nodded, not moving, until Lamont pointed the way and a policeman ushered her out to the stairway to the third floor apartments.

"Should I leave too?" Lacey asked hopefully, edging toward the front door.

"Not so fast, Smithsonian. You and I are going to finish that chat. You can start with everything you know about Magda Rousseau, in that clear, concise journalistic manner that I know you're capable of."

Lacey took a breath and brushed the hair out of her face. She gave him a brief rundown, leaving out a few tiny details that would just muddy the situation, she thought, like the corset.

"Magda was French and Latvian and grew up in France. She came here years ago, never lost her thick French accent, particularly when she was excited. Even Analiza, her Latvian business partner, had trouble understanding her sometimes. Magda insisted that she always spoke perfect English with no accent at all."

"Do you know any reason anyone would want Magda Rousseau dead?"

Possibly. But there was no way Lacey was going to tell Broadway Lamont, the Metropolitan P.D.'s King of Scorn, the story that Magda had told her in confidence. Magda Rousseau was engaged in a long on-again-off-again search for a legendary jewel-filled corset worn by one of the Russian imperial princesses during the execution of the entire Romanov family in a dark basement in Ekaterinburg, Russia, in July 1917. A bulletproof corset that saved the princess from the initial volleys of gunfire. A blood-stained corset stripped from the princess's body by one of the Latvian guards who had refused to shoot the children of the Czar. The official accounts said that the jewels found hidden in the ladies' corsets and other clothing were all confiscated by the Bolsheviks and used to further the cause of the Revolution. But according to Magda, one corset had been stolen and spirited away amidst the chaos of that horrible, drunken, murderous night.

The Latvian guard who had stolen the corset, Magda had told her, was Juris Akmentins, her maternal grandfather, who had later emigrated to France and hidden the corset there. Magda wanted to mount a search for the corset, but she couldn't afford the plane ticket to France and the expenses of the adventure.

Magda had read Lacey's "Crimes of Fashion" columns and recent newspaper stories about her role in solving several crimes. She was also impressed by Stella Lake's slightly exaggerated tales of Lacey's encounters with murderers. Stella sang Lacey's praises as a fashion maven and amateur sleuth with a "nose for nuance." It was time, Magda had decided, to share the secret with someone crazy enough to believe her: Lacey Smithsonian, a fashion columnist who didn't take fashion too seriously and who had been involved in some unusual investigations. Magda had appreciated Smithsonian's curiosity, her unquenchable desire to know the end of the story. And the corsetiere used it to her advantage.

Convinced she knew where the corset was now hidden in

France, Magda had enticed Lacey, and in turn *The Eye Street Observer,* into sharing her fantasy of finding it. It was to be the story of a seamstress with a dream. Lacey wanted this story, she wanted the adventure of documenting the possibility of finding such a treasure. *Adventure with a capital A.* It didn't matter to Lacey if the Romanov corset proved in the end to be real or a chimera: It was a great story either way, though actually finding the legendary artifact would be wonderful. Lacey was resourceful and good at self-defense. What's more, Mac had promised her that the paper would fund the entire search in exchange for the exclusive rights to Magda's story. She was going to Paris!

Despite the fact that Broadway Lamont once told her he heard "crazy shit all the time," Lacey was afraid the tale would sound too insane, like the mutterings of a lunatic. To Lacey's knowledge, Magda was not a lunatic. But Lamont was waiting for an answer.

"Who would want Magda dead? I don't know, Broadway, it's not the best neighborhood here," Lacey told him. "Maybe someone thought she kept cash on the premises."

"It's not the worst neighborhood either, and this dump wouldn't be a prime robbery target. And we don't see a lot of drive-by poisonings in the District, if you know what I mean. Poison is personal and premeditated. It's a female method."

"Oh, really, Broadway. How gender-biased of you."

"Hell, yes. So is murder. A man uses a gun, a machete, his hands. Poison is like a woman: subtle, devious." He gave her the raised eyebrow. "Female. Like that girly little dagger you didn't notice sticking in the dead woman's ribs. And women are always in the kitchen cooking something up. Something like poison."

"I'll keep that in mind . . . when you drop by for a gingerbread cookie."

Lamont snorted and almost smiled. Lacey hoped he had exhausted his interrogation and intimidation routine. He gave Lacey a warning and his card. "In case you lost my card from our last encounter."

"I could never forget meeting you, Lamont." In fact, he had scared her during the interview. He still scared her a little.

"You do anything about a new car yet?" he inquired.

That was a sore point. Her beloved silver and burgundy Nissan 280ZX had been stolen the month before and, in the police phrase, "employed in the commission of a crime." What was left of it was now evidence in a murder case. It made her feel sad and vulnerable to lose it to a killer. She had offers of cars from friends, Brooke and Miguel to name just two, but she'd been too busy with this story to make a decision. In a way she felt getting a new car would be a betrayal of her poor lost Z.

"No, I haven't had a chance. Been taking the Metro."

"You think about the police auction, like I told you?"

"Good advice, Broadway." Lacey would never love another car the way she had loved the Z. Maybe it was better that way, she thought. *It would be easier to say good-bye to some clunker the next time some miscreant needed a getaway car.* "After all, who wouldn't want some drug lord's land yacht with a body in the trunk?"

"You take care, Smithsonian. You wouldn't want to run out of luck. How did that lucky saying of hers go? 'Bloody thread, don't get dead'?"

"Very amusing. I don't feel so lucky today."

"You're lucky as hell. You hang out with victims, you stumble over crime scenes, yet you're still here. In my book, that's lucky." He finally smiled a big ivory smile that lit up his face. "You think of any of those crazy fashion clues you like to come up with, you give me a call. Got it?" He favored her with one more suspicious look. "I doubt you will, but you could get lucky again."

"Don't worry, Broadway."

You can read all about in The Eye. *In "Crimes of Fashion."*

Chapter 4

"I've got some bad news, Mac." Lacey stood at the office door of her editor, Douglas MacArthur Jones. She remained standing so she could run away if necessary.

"Bad news, Smithsonian?" He looked up from a pile of newspapers. Reading glasses were perched on his nose above the bushy mustache that made him look like a stern black G. Gordon Liddy. "I thought you were gone for the day." Her editor scowled and reached for his bottle of Maalox. He waved it at her. "Do I swig now or later? The suspense is killing me."

"Magda Rousseau is dead. I just came from her apartment."

"Dead? Dead as in heart-attack dead?" He looked straight at her over his spectacles. "As in natural-causes dead? Please tell me she's dead because she was an old lady and her number came up and her heart gave out." His expression dared her to contradict him. He gestured for her to enter the office and sit down. "She was old, right?"

"Yeah, she was really old, Mac. Really, *really* old. About your age," she lied. Lacey slipped into the room, closing the door. She realized it was now or never to save this story—and her trip to Paris. She removed a stack of newspapers from one of the chairs. She piled them on Mac's desk, dusted the seat with her hand, and slid onto it. "Magda told me she was poisoned. Then she warned me not to drink the wine, which she had been drinking. I suppose she could have been kidding. Or wrong. She might have been stabbed, too. But just a little."

"She told you she was poisoned? She was alive?"

"Barely. And then she—" Lacey choked up, but she controlled it. "She died. And I didn't poison her, if that's what you're thinking." Mac glared at her. Lacey glared back at him.

"No, of course you didn't poison her! That would be too easy."

He slapped his desk with an open hand. Dust rose from the stacks of *Eye Street Observers* resting there. "Damnation, Smithsonian. I suppose this little tableau also included police, paramedics, yellow crime scene tape, all your usual fashion accessories. What is it about you?" he muttered. "It's been nothing but death, death, death, ever since you took over the fashion beat."

"Technically, that's not true," Lacey said, keenly attuned to the facts of her job situation. "It started well before me, with Mariah 'the Pariah' Morgan, our late and unlamented fashion editor. You remember, don't you, Mac, when she died in her chair and you stuck *me* with this beat? And how long did it take you to notice she was dead?"

"It wasn't that long. I thought she was taking a catnap."

"Eight hours! She was in full rigor mortis! They had to roll her out in her chair."

"It seemed like a good idea at the time. She loved that chair." Mac sighed and looked weary. "When are you going to let that go?"

"And then you tried to stick me with her damn chair! The chair of doom!" Lacey was surprised that detail could still rile her.

"That is a perfectly good chair. And Mariah died of natural causes."

"So you say. She probably died just to escape this beat—it seems to be the only way out of it." Mariah's chair was still floating around the newsroom, like Lincoln's ghost train. It was a favorite joke among the reporters to hand it off to interns, casually mentioning the connection to the dead former fashion editor only when the fledgling was firmly glued to his or her seat in Mariah's Death Chair under crushing deadline pressure.

Mac grunted. Lacey took a deep cleansing breath. It didn't work. "We both know fashion is a dangerous job, Mac. But I don't want to argue."

"There's a relief." He leaned back in his own chair, clasping his hands behind his head. "So what were you just doing if not arguing?"

She ignored this. "I want you to know I'll be on that plane to Paris this week." *Please Mac, whatever you do, don't take Paris away from me.* "It's still my story."

He shook his head. "No way. There is no story. Your source is dead. Maybe there's a murder story now, but that's Trujillo's beat, not yours."

"Look, if she was killed because of the corset—"

"Are you telling me she was murdered because of this mythical nonexistent bullet-riddled corset?" He and his chair snapped forward to full attention.

"Not exactly. I don't know why yet. But there's still a story in France and the tickets are already bought and paid for." She leaned toward him, placing her hands flat on his desk. "They're nonrefundable. Like my dreams, Mac."

"Don't start with me, Smithsonian. Your life is also not refundable." He rose from his seat. "No trip! If she was a murder target because of this crazy story, then you'd be a target, too. Besides, you need the Rousseau woman as a guide. And I cannot be responsible for what havoc you might wreak unchaperoned on foreign soil. Even though we don't officially like France."

"The story is still out there, Mac." She stood up and towered over him in her heels. "Think about *The Eye* bringing back the lost corset of the Romanovs. Imagine the headlines: EYE STREET REPORTER MAKES HISTORY! DISCOVERS PRICELESS REMNANT OF RUSSIAN IMPERIAL FAMILY, LOST FOR A CENTURY."

Mac rolled his eyes. "How about this one: EYE STREET REPORTER CREATES INTERNATIONAL INCIDENT. FRANCE CUTS OFF OUR CHEESE."

"But what if some other reporter's onto it?"

"Onto *what*? Even *you* don't believe there's a corset full of jewels, Smithsonian." He stared at her. "This is just a tall tale on steroids. It's got pathos. It's got dreams and heartache and history and human interest. And it would sell papers. But nobody believes there's a corset."

That's what he wanted to believe. Unfortunately for Mac, *The Eye*'s glamorous publisher, Claudia Darnell, took a special interest in the fashion beat and in Lacey, and she loved the whole idea of chasing the lost Romanov corset. Claudia had enthusiastically okayed the story (and the minuscule budget), agreeing that it would have to remain a secret from the other *Eye Street Observer* reporters until Lacey broke it. The secrecy would also keep expectations down if the story turned out to be a wild goose chase or a humiliating disaster. In that event, the story would detail the strange journey of an eccentric immigrant woman and her lost dreams of glory, and Lacey could cram it full of pathos, adjectives, and a literary gloss. And a possible sidebar on the corset renaissance on the Paris fashion runways.

"Why can't you just write about dresses and shoes?" Mac opened the bottle of Maalox and took a big slug. "I thought women were obsessed with shoes." His brows knit dangerously.

"I do write about shoes," she protested. "If you read my column you'd know that. Remember, Mac, *you* stuck me with this fashion beat. Besides, I never get to go anywhere good. Other fashion reporters get to go to Paris, Milan, New York. I go nowhere. This time I'm going to Paris." She locked eyes with him like a laser beam, daring Mac to look away first.

Tony Trujillo, the cops reporter, stuck his nose through the door. "Lost another source, Lacey? Rumor says you called in the murder and a force of nature no smaller than Broadway Lamont is on the job. So what's really up?"

"Drive-by poisoning. Go away. We're talking about shoes."

Mac leaned back in his chair, setting his feet on his desk, looking like the school principal. "What about the knife that was stuck in her?" Tony inquired.

"You didn't mention a knife," Mac growled.

Lacey looked from Tony to Mac. "I did too. It wasn't in very deep. It actually looked like a prop knife. The handle was covered with jewels."

"Jewels?" Tony said. "A jewel-handled dagger? Cool." She could see him turning the phrase around in his head as if it were the lead in the story. His story. *Good God*, Lacey thought, *this whole story is slipping right through my fingers.*

"Fake jewels, obviously. If they were real, the killer wouldn't have left it. Besides, she *told* me she was poisoned," Lacey said. "Kind of a dying declaration, you know?"

"Yeah." Trujillo smirked. "I hear that's becoming a real trend in D.C."

"Trujillo, go back to your beat." Mac drummed his fingers on his desk.

"I don't know, man, this is just beginning to get good. And this *is* my beat. My beat is cops, remember? Dead bodies? Poison? Jewel-encrusted daggers? My turf, Mac. I need to know." The handsome, black-haired Trujillo flashed his lady-killer smile, slid into the room, and shut the door. "Lacey's obviously trying to spin her way out of a hot spot. And onto my beat."

Lacey tensed for combat. "I resent that editorial comment, Trujillo. And it's my story. I was there, at the crime scene. Getting Magda's last words. Trying to save her life. Where were you? Getting your snakeskin boots polished?"

Tony's smile faded. "I'd have been there too—if you'd called me before it was all over."

Mac eyed Trujillo. "Don't you have some mayhem of your own to write about?"

"Not when her beat gets this good. All the mayhem is happening right here. So Mac, what's going on with Smithsonian? Why all the closed doors?"

"Hey! I'm in the room too, Tony." She shot him an icy look, but he shrugged it off. "Afraid I've got another scoop?"

"Not afraid, just interested. Tell me a story, Brenda Starr. You know we work better together than when we dance on each other's toes." He moved a stack of papers and sat down in the chair next to her. Mac sighed. Lacey waited on pins and needles. *Spill my big secret, Mac, and I'm telling Claudia. You'll be sorry.*

Mac weighed his words carefully. He and Lacey both knew how much their publisher disliked having her orders short-circuited by anyone. "You know Smithsonian was doing a fashion story with the old seamstress dame in France. Corsets in haute couture, past and present, something like that. Now the old lady's dead." Mac shrugged elaborately. "End of story."

"Ha. Somebody is dead and Smithsonian is involved? That is never the end of the story," Tony asserted, "only the beginning."

"Not this time. Smithsonian is not going to France now. No old lady, no source, no story. The old lady's death is just another D.C. murder story. You two split the byline. We're done here."

Lacey cleared her throat. "I am going to France. I am writing the story. And Magda Rousseau—um—wasn't that old." Lacey folded her arms to keep her fists from creating an incident that would be written up for her personnel file.

"Wait a minute, Mac," Trujillo said. "France is still there, still the capital of the fashion world, right? Corsets are still hot, even if the source got iced. But just because the old lady's dead, Mac, you're pulling the trip? I don't get it. Or do I? If you *are* pulling it, then the story's not tied up with fashion, it's tied up with the old lady. Am I right?"

Mac was silent. Lacey saw her opening. "I'm going, Mac, even if I have to take my annual leave to do it," Lacey said. "I've got the tickets, I've got the story. You've got Tony. I'll send you both postcards from Paris." She stood to leave. "See ya."

Tony jumped up and blocked her escape. "Spill it, Supergirl, what's going on?"

Mac chewed his mustache. He didn't want everyone in the newsroom badgering him for foreign travel budgets. And Trujillo could be a world-class badger. "Sit down, both of you. What's said in this room stays here. Got it?"

"Anything you say, boss." Trujillo looked like a cat with a stolen bowl of cream. Lacey threw a newspaper at him, which he caught in midair.

Mac turned to Lacey. "If she's dead because of this wild-goose chase you two were on, you're not going anywhere. It's too dangerous."

"Maybe she was kidding about the poisoning," Lacey said. "Maybe there's no connection; maybe she was killed in a botched robbery or something. We won't know unless I do the story, Mac. Is this a newspaper or what? Stories are what we try to find, right?"

"What's the story? What wild-goose chase?" Trujillo demanded.

"It's a wild-fashion-goose chase to find something that was lost a long time ago," Mac said. "Probably lost forever. Or never existed."

"What?" Trujillo pressed.

"A piece of clothing," Lacey said. "An unusual piece. A museum or two would be interested. And Magda Rousseau is still our source for this story, alive or dead."

"A murder, a mystery, and a scavenger hunt all in one? My favorite kind of story." Trujillo grinned. "I'm with Lacey here, let's give it a shot, Mac."

"Hey, hotshot, a woman is dead," Lacey growled. "Show some respect."

"We can't save her now; let's at least tell her story." Trujillo shrugged. "If she's got a story. I still don't get the big mystery."

Mac was clearly fed up with this tap dance. He gave Trujillo a brief summary of Magda's tale of the fabulous lost corset of the Romanovs. And he cautioned everyone in his office that if this story leaked out before it saw newsprint in *The Eye Street Observer*, Claudia Darnell would have all three of their heads on one platter.

"*Madre de Dios.* A bloodstained corset full of Romanov jewels?" Trujillo's eyes lit up. "What would that be worth on the open market?"

"It's anyone's guess," Lacey said, remembering that Magda was sure she would be rolling in millions one day, with plenty of time on her hands instead of handfuls of fabric and pins. "And it's my story."

"Even if it's a fool's errand, it's a hell of a story." Trujillo turned to Lacey. "What about Donovan? He's going to let you go off on a story like this on your own? Or do you have him tucked away in a little love nest in Paris?"

She looked away, feeling a quick pang of regret at hearing Vic Donovan's name. "We're not seeing each other at the moment, so he's not a concern."

"Whoa! What happened?" Tony's eyes opened wide. "You guys were just about to—"

"To what?" She flashed him a look that just dared him to continue.

"Nothing." He looked away. "I just thought things were going so well."

"They were. It's complicated," she said. It was almost inexplicable, even to her. Finally, after months of a stalled relationship, it looked like she and Vic were on the expressway to love, or at least something like it, perhaps with love just down the road. Then Vic slammed on the brakes. The last time he visited, he said he wanted to take a break. He didn't seem to be able to say why. Clumsy words between them escalated into a scene. What about Paris? she asked. She had been so looking forward to spending time with Vic in Paris after wrapping up Magda's story.

"I'm not going to Paris," he had told her. "I don't even like Paris."

"How could somebody not want to go to Paris?" she demanded.

He had a little list: They don't like Americans. They smoke, they smoke in restaurants, they let dogs eat in restaurants. They let dogs *smoke* in restaurants. He thought he was being funny, but she didn't think so. She insisted on his real reasons for not wanting to go with her. He gave her more comedy. She thought this little routine must be just a pathetic cover-up for breaking up with her. And it broke her heart that he couldn't tell her what he really meant, whatever that was; he had to make a silly joke out of it. It quickly turned into a full-scale fight.

"Good-bye then," Lacey had said. She led him to the door and pushed him out.

"I didn't mean forever," Vic said. "I just don't want to go to Paris."

"Fine." She spat the word. "But the next time you decide to play hardball with my heart, I won't be home. I'll be in Paris. Without you."

"Lacey, wait." Vic was as handsome as ever, a dark curl falling over his forehead, trouble in his jade-colored eyes, his strong jaw set.

Her last glimpse of him was at her apartment door, which she shut firmly. Lacey had waited for a full minute with her back pressed to the door while her heart sank in a sea of unresolved feelings. Then the tears came. He hadn't called since; nor had she. It had been over a week.

Take a break indeed, she thought. Vic was the one who complained they had waited for years to start their relationship, then they waited months to consummate it. Then it was over before it even began.

"It's complicated," she repeated to Trujillo. "But I'll always have Paris. All to myself."

"Sorry, Ms. Lane," Trujillo said, "sounds like Superman's succumbed to Kryptonite."

"Drop it, Jimmy Olsen."

"Hey, you two." Mac's voice brought them back to reality. "Do the comic book thing on your own time."

Trujillo rose from his chair. "Send me along, Chief. Lacey and I have tag-teamed before. And I've never been to Paris. Sounds great."

"You're not stealing my story," Lacey said. "This one is all mine."

"Double byline. *S* before *T*." He aimed the killer smile at her. It didn't work this time. She was over all of Tony's tricks. Mac was rubbing his smooth dome in pain.

"I haven't decided anything yet," Mac said. "I gotta talk to Claudia. Get out of here, both of you. You give me a headache."

"Just let me know whether I'm flying to Paris this week on *The Eye*'s time or on my own," Lacey said, standing to go. "You can run my backup columns while I'm gone." She tried to calculate whether she could afford the hotel room the paper had booked. The plane fare could be deducted in installments from her paycheck. She didn't care. Paris beckoned. The lost corset beckoned. She had a story to chase. She smiled in a last attempt to soften her editor. "It's a treasure hunt, Mac. Everyone loves a treasure hunt."

She slipped out of the office with Trujillo hard on her heels, but he was distracted by a phone call on his cell.

"No, no, I'll call you later, babe," he was murmuring into the phone under his breath. "No, later than that, sugar, I got a story—"

"Another blonde, Tony?" Lacey teased. He looked like he'd been caught stealing cookies. "Don't strain your brain, boy. With you they're always blondes."

Lacey left Trujillo with blonde trouble and made her getaway.

chapter 5

Lacey retrieved her file of information on the Romanov corset from her overstuffed desk. It included maps to the location in Normandy where Magda believed it was hidden, a letter of introduction Magda had written for her "just in case," and her own extensive notes. She had been documenting her conversations with Magda from the beginning, and the old woman had encouraged her to write everything down. *Maybe she had a premonition*, Lacey thought.

After the search for the corset had either born fruit or come up empty-handed, Magda had wanted to see an old friend of hers in Paris, the fashion center of the world. Paris was the icing on the cake for Lacey, whether the newspaper would pay for it or not.

Leafing through the contents, she found the plane tickets and Magda's own English translation of part of a diary written in Latvian by her grandfather, Juris Akmentins. Magda had learned Latvian from her grandparents as a child, and using dictionaries, she had painstakingly translated the diary into French for her own reference. She had written out an English translation of the relevant pages for Lacey, who had only this English version in her file.

"Oh, my God, the diary!" Lacey said out loud. Nobody bothered to look at her. Reporters regularly talked to themselves and read their stories aloud. At the newspaper, it didn't indicate mental illness, it was just part of the writing process.

The diary recounted the days surrounding the Romanovs' execution by the Bolsheviks, and Akmentins' own part in the whole gruesome affair. It was written as a memoir decades after he had allegedly taken the corset, decades after he took the surname "Akmentins." He had deliberately lost his original name somewhere along the way. Lacey had seen the slim brown leather volume only once.

Magda had assured her repeatedly that the original diary and the French translation were in a safe place, but Lacey realized they were probably just as safe as the keys to Magda's apartment, the keys that were kept dangling in plain sight above the sewing machine. Were they still in Magda's apartment now—or had her killer taken them?

Why hadn't her grandfather rid himself of the corset or sold the gems on some black market? Lacey wondered, and it bothered her. He had tried to sell it once, Magda said, but he failed and had nearly been caught by the Soviet authorities. He took that as a sign that there was no safe way to get rid of it and realize the wealth he had dreamed of. He had lived the life of a tailor in near-poverty with a hidden fortune in gems, a fortune too dangerous to try to make any use of.

Juris Akmentins' diary stated that he had no objection to shooting the Czar or the Empress, but he and the other Latvians had no stomach for killing the children. They were already frail from their captivity and illness, and would no doubt die soon anyway. No matter what crimes the Czar was guilty of, his children were innocent. But ultimately Akmentins' stand changed nothing—it didn't stop the others from slaughtering the entire family. As punishment for his reluctance, he was ordered to help strip the clothes from the battered and bloodied bodies after the execution.

Lacey skimmed through the English translation again at her desk. She could imagine the awful chaos of the scene that Akmentins described. After the first rounds of gunfire directed at the family, the Bolshevik executioners were amazed to find the Romanov princesses still alive in that smoke-filled hell of a basement. Their corsets, filled with layers of imperial jewels, had virtually become bulletproof vests. The jewels protected them from the first onslaught of bullets, but this brief respite from death simply ensured that more brutal means were employed to finish them off: bayonets, rifle butts, pistol shots to the head. Later, after it was done and the bodies were stripped, the drunken soldiers became obsessed with touching the bodies of the dead imperial family, perhaps to convince themselves they were really dead. They pocketed small souvenirs of their blood-soaked task. The executioners seemed torn between shame and pride in their deeds even before the bodies were cold in the ground.

The diary claimed that several corsets on the bodies of the imperial princesses were found to be filled with hidden jewels. Empress Alexandra wore a heavy pearl belt beneath her clothes. Each new discovery momentarily drew everyone's attention away from the other bodies. But Juris Akmentins paid no attention. He had also found a corset on the body of an imperial princess. He didn't know which one she was; the body was too disfigured. Blood-stained, torn by bullets, pierced by bayonets, her corset leaked jewels. Surrounded by greed and madness, Juris saw his chance and kept his mouth shut. He stripped the corset from the small body, and the Latvians looked out for each other. While the other assassins slipped and stumbled around him on the floor slick with blood, Juris shoved the garment deep inside his long coat, then made a show of tossing a petticoat and other garments from the girl's body into a pile of clothes growing in the middle of the floor. She wore no corset, he told them, adding he knew nothing of women's underclothes. The soldiers were threatened with execution if they stole anything from the Revolution. Frightened for their lives, several of them tossed small valuables into a pile, items they had taken from the bodies as souvenirs, a watch, a ring, a medal. Akmentins threw in a gold button he said he had found on the floor. They were not searched. The officer in charge was satisfied his threats had ended the stealing. But Juris Akmentins had seen so much slaughter that death had no power to frighten him.

A decade later, when he fled what was then the Soviet Union to emigrate to France, Juris wrapped the stained and tattered corset, its burden of jewels still intact, around his infant daughter beneath her dress and blanket. None of the border guards cared to inspect the squalling child's diapers, and they left her untouched in her parents' arms.

The corset eventually became a badge of shame and remorse for Juris Akmentins, a burden of sins he didn't know how to deal with. He hid the garment away, but he wrote about it obsessively, leaving clues to its whereabouts in the slim leather-bound book. Perhaps he hoped it would be cleansed of its shame by years and distance, and someone among his descendants might claim it with innocent hands.

The diary of Juris Akmentins came into Magda's hands after the death of her mother, Juris's daughter, who had unknowingly worn the corset as an infant. The diary's contents led Magda to believe the corset was hidden at a farmhouse still owned by a member of her family. If she was right, it was in France near Mont-Saint-Michel, several hours' drive west of Paris.

If someone knew the diary was the key to a treasure, Lacey thought, it was a more convincing motive for murder than Magda's cheap broach. Had Magda told anyone else about her grandfather's diary and the corset? She had assured Lacey that it was their secret, but Lacey had seen how much Magda relished telling a good story.

Broadway Lamont was right: There were no drive-by poisonings. She called the detective's cell phone and left a message. She didn't have to wait long for his call back.

"Yo, Smithsonian, you got it all solved, wrapped up in a big present for me? 'Cause I love listening to reporters tell me how to do my job."

"Thanks for calling back, Broadway." She ignored the jibe. "I just thought of something."

"Better be good."

"There's a diary. It belonged to Magda's grandfather. You might want to locate it. Should be in her apartment somewhere. She said it had information that was priceless."

"You want to be more specific?"

"Small brown leather-bound book. She showed it to me once," Lacey said, ducking the issue of exactly why that information might be priceless. "And it's in Latvian."

"Latvian." She could hear him snort. "I hear there's a hot market in Latvian diaries."

"I only know what Magda told me. She wouldn't want it to fall into the wrong hands."

"Yeah, I'll put it on the list. Missing ugly broach, missing Latvian diary. Anything else missing?"

My sense of humor. "There's a French translation of it too, in Magda's own handwriting in one of those school composition notebooks."

"Oooh la la, a French diary! Now that's really hot."

"You're a scream, Lamont. You got anything on the poison or the dagger or the cause of death yet?"

"Gimme a break, Smithsonian, it only happened a couple hours ago. Takes longer than that for the morgue to type up a toe tag." The detective hung up and Lacey breathed a sigh of relief. Now she couldn't be accused of not telling the police what she knew, or at least some of what she knew. She returned Magda's papers to her file drawer and locked it. Nobody paid any attention. She started to gather her things to go home.

Other reporters around her were still involved with their own stories, and a few were hanging around after hours. Lacey could see one determined reporter heading for the LifeStyles section of the paper right now. It was Harlan Wiedemeyer, *The Eye*'s reporter on the "death and dismemberment beat." He was headed her way, and it was too late for her to run.

"Exploding toads! Can you believe it, Lacey? In a pond in Germany. A thousand toads just exploded." Wiedemeyer's eyes gleamed with pleasure, not so much at the fate of the toads, but at the joy of a new and strange phenomenon to report, the weirder the better.

Lacey rubbed her head. She felt a headache coming on. Her head suddenly felt like an exploding toad. Wiedemeyer thrilled to impart news of the strange, the grotesque, and the gut-churningly disturbing. He filled his round cheeks with air, then expelled it quickly in the manner of an exploding toad, or at least his cheerful impression of one. "Kaboom! Ribbit!"

"Oh, Harlan, that's terrible," food editor Felicity Pickles cooed at him, with a love offering of freshly baked goodies. Felicity was a large woman with a face that looked innocent at first glance, big round blue eyes, porcelain skin, long auburn hair. She looked rather like a deranged china doll. Wiedemeyer, her love-struck suitor, was a round little gnome of a man with a receding hairline and a wide mouth. "Those poor little toads. Have a gingerbread man. Aren't they cute? "

"Poor little bastards," Harlan agreed. "Kaboom!" He took today's fresh baked carbohydrate bomb from his indulgent angel of the food beat. "Kaboom! Ribbit! Kaboom! Ribbit!"

Felicity had few social skills, but she knew how to cook. At *The Eye Street Observer*, that was enough to make her Miss Congeniality. Reporters of all stripes found a reason to hover around her desk across the aisle from Lacey's whenever Felicity was trying out a new recipe. This week she was testing desserts for an upcoming Thanksgiving section. Her fattening food of the day was spicy gingerbread men slathered in cream cheese icing with eyes and noses and buttons of crystallized ginger. More evidence to feed Lacey's theory that Felicity lived a secret life as a Gingerbread Witch, lurking deep in the forest in a gingerbread house with a fluffy cream cheese roof, tempting all who entered to eat a tasty shutter or two so she could fatten them up for her larder.

The zaftig food editor never liked the svelte fashion writer, and the feeling was mutual. But Felicity now found herself happily dating exploding-toad reporter Harlan Wiedemeyer, and it was all thanks to Smithsonian. Lacey had recognized telltale signs of infatuation in thc chubby would-be lovebirds hovering incessantly near her desk, admiring each other in love-struck awe, and she had found it unbearable. Wiedemeyer was also known to be the office jinx, but he made Felicity blush all the way down to her round little toes. And Felicity Pickles made Wiedemeyer lose the ability to speak coherently.

They were driving her crazy. Much to her own surprise, she had recently reached a breaking point and brazenly put the two of them together, face-to-face, hand in hand, brownie to doughnut, blowing the cover on their secret crushes on each other. Wiedemeyer thanked Lacey profusely nearly every time he saw her.

Lacey did not believe that Harlan was a jinx, exactly. However, as Mac had observed, "Bad things happen when Harlan's around." To blame the exploding toads of Germany on Harlan Wiedemeyer was probably going too far, but Felicity's minivan had been blown up outside the office by someone who mistook her for Smithsonian, and Felicity decided that having lost her transportation, there was nothing more to lose if she dared to date Harlan. Putting the two of them together had seemed to lift a mysterious cloud of misfortune from Lacey's shoulders. Coincidence? Lacey didn't think so.

Felicity politely offered a gingerbread man to Lacey. It looked delicious. Alas, Lacey had to be thin to enter France; it was a matter of French law. So she resisted. But Wiedemeyer dug in with gusto, gingerbread lighting up his pleasure centers. He and Felicity made little "um-um" noises at each other. Lacey had to turn away to keep her stomach from turning, only to see the gloomy visage of the paper's editorial writer, Cassandra Wentworth, morosely making her way from the staff kitchen. Cassandra held a steaming mug of herbal tea that smelled like swamp sludge. The terribly thin and careworn Cassandra said a world-weary hello to Felicity, then desolately lifted a fat piece of gingerbread onto a napkin to nibble on later at her desk. She eyed Lacey with reproof.

"I read 'Crimes of Fashion' this week, Smithsonian," she moaned. "All the misery in the world and you scribble on about clothes, clothes, clothes."

"That's my job," Lacey said, laughing. "Misery is your beat. But Harlan's got a great story about exploding toads. You'll love it."

"Exploding toads are an early warning sign of grim environmental disasters about to engulf the earth. Everyone knows this. You think everything's funny, don't you, Smithsonian?"

"Everything but pointed shoes. Nothing funny there. I think they're a travesty, a health hazard, and they're ugly." Lacey looked down at Cassandra's feet, encased in thick gray wool socks and Birkenstocks. "However, your shoes are eminently, um, sensible. No laughing matter there, either." The woman was also wearing rumpled mud-brown pants and a pilled pavement-gray sweater several sizes too large. Lacey refrained from commenting on the mismatch, or on the way the dreary, soul-destroying colors sucked the life out of Cassandra's face.

"You just don't get it, do you?" Cassandra's murky brown eyes almost seemed to gleam with a passion for disaster. "People are hungry. People are dying. Toads are exploding."

"Then I suggest you eat that gingerbread right now, before chunks of exploding toad come flying through the windows."

Cassandra averted her eyes in disgust. "Laugh while you can."

"And look on the bright side, Cassandra," Lacey said. "Maybe we'll all be wearing chic new toad-skin pumps. How big are those toads, Harlan? Big enough to make a ladies' size six sandal?"

"I wouldn't be a bit surprised. Giant exploding toads, Lacey! Ribbit! Kaboom!" he said with an explosive gesture. Cassandra was not amused.

"Writing about fashion is just a drain on humanity in these times of dire emergency. Clothes should be functional and protect us against the elements. And against deadly solar radiation from the hole in the ozone layer created by Western civilization's shortsighted reliance on fossil fuels. That's all."

"Sounds like an editorial to me." Lacey yawned extravagantly. "Will we see that in the paper tomorrow?"

"Being flippant. That's your little specialty, isn't it?"

Lacey smiled at her. Why the defiantly plain Cassandra particularly liked to rain on Lacey's parade was a mystery to her. There were other beats that were just as frivolous. "Why don't you go harass the sports section, Cassandra? They're big-time flippant."

"At least organized sports help keep dangerous felons off the streets during games."

"That's true. Most of the dangerous felons are *in* the game."

Cassandra took her storm cloud and her gingerbread man and left. The fashion pages apparently weren't keeping anyone off the streets. They were just a waste of newsprint in Cassandra's time of emergency.

Lacey looked down at her latest "Crimes of Fashion" column, clipped out neatly on her desk. It was entitled "What Were You Thinking?" and she wondered what on earth *she* was thinking. Not about her clothes, of course. Lacey was wearing a long emerald green skirt, matching blouse, and suede belt, an ensemble that complemented her expertly highlighted hair, her blue-green eyes, and her petite curves. She topped them with a green-speckled black wool jacket from the 1940s, with broad shoulders that meant business and a beautifully tailored waist that fit her own perfectly and combined business with pleasure. In the breast pocket, she wore an emerald green silk hanky secured with a vintage pearl pin. She also wore black leather boots, not too high and not pointed. No, her clothes were fine. She was thinking about her life.

There was a dead woman with a dream who had been a friend of hers, an unknown killer with unknown motives, mystery, and danger lurking all around this story, yet the thought of going to Paris to begin the search for the lost corset called to her like the Pied Piper luring children from the safety of their homes. She was mentally dancing down the street to the tune of "An American in Paris." Unlike nearly everyone she knew, Lacey had never been to Europe, and she wanted to go there so badly she could taste it. Her quirky Washington version of a fashion beat had made many unexpected little adventures possible, but it would never send her to Paris if it weren't for Magda's story.

Her disappointment with Vic and the puzzling end to their promising romance somehow made it all the more important now that she go to Paris, that she must have a wonderful time. If she happened to stumble upon a lost corset full of Romanov jewels that had been the stuff of legend for nearly a century, well, that would just be a delightful bonus. But Lacey *had* to go to Paris. Or else she thought she might as well just say to hell with everything and eat every last one of Felicity's gingerbread men until she exploded like one of Wiedemeyer's toads.

Paris. I must have Paris.

Lacey Smithsonian's

FASHION BITES

The Red Bra of Courage

Do you need a little something extra? Do you need the swagger of a sexy secret under your conservative suit? Do you need to tell the world, "There's more to me than this boring uniform"—without telling them *too* much? Do you need a jolt of pure physical confidence that comes from within (or pretty close to it)? *You need the Red Bra of Courage!*

Your boss, your barista, that weasel in Accounting, that cute new guy in Sales, they won't know why you suddenly have an extra bounce in your high-heeled step, why your mood is buoyant, your confidence unshakable. But you'll know. You may not sing and dance in your underwear like Tom Cruise in *Risky Business* or Madonna, the woman who almost single-handedly revived the bustier and corset as *oh-so-daring* outerwear. But clad in the cozy secret of the right underwear, you might just want to sing *hallelujah*. (Under your breath, of course.)

How does your underwear make *you* feel? Like running a 5K, putting on the Ritz, winning your case in court? Or like a five-pack of sturdy white cotton granny panties? Respectable enough to be caught wearing in case of a fatal accident, but about as exciting as eating oatmeal mush and wearing the box it came in? Do your undies make you feel strong and sexy? Courageous? Alluring? Or boring and dull, generic and suitable (barely) for everyday use?

A little-known (except by you, Stylish Reader) fact about underwear is that it can affect your mood, your confidence, your entire style. It is the secret language beneath your clothes. If it whispers to *you*, your confidence will shout to *us*. And there is more to that secret language than the mundane statements of a jogging bra and baggy granny panties.

When it comes to lingerie, one set does *not* fit all. Different clothes may require different undergarments, but you also have maximum freedom in what is most concealed—concealed to everyone except to you. High-cut panties, bikinis, thongs in cotton, nylon, lace, or silk are not just a personal comfort decision, they're a decision about your identity and attitude. Bras, whether strapless, underwire, eighteen-hour, racer-back, or pushup, not only cover but shape and uplift and determine how you look in that dress or blouse—and who you think you are. That's a lot to ask of such a small piece of fabric. Measured in *oomph* per ounce, your underwear can be more powerful than plutonium—or deader than the dodo.

Women in Washington, D.C., are accustomed to wearing business camouflage all day long, an endless array of gray and beige and black suits. One hopes their secret wardrobe beneath those suits is a little more exciting. Remember, underwear can say what your outerwear can't say, and nobody has to know it but you. Others will feel it in your attitude. Don't you just love keeping secrets? And isn't it even more fun to whisper them in the right ear?

- Is your ferocious inner feline just roaring to stalk the jungle, but it's caged inside your city-bound suit? Hunt down that leopard-skin spotted slip and matching bra and garters, and you *growl*, girl! *Grrrr.*
- Do you love that old-fashioned boudoir glamour, the silk nightgowns and robes you've seen in late-night movies, satin gowns cut on the bias that caress every curve, but despair of finding anything quite like it today? Check out vintage stores that carry exotic styles from yesteryear. Some even have "new" old lingerie, nightgowns, and robes from the Forties and Fifties with the original tags.
- Is all this beautiful stuff that no one but you will see too expensive? Wait for a sale—it's worth it. Everyone, including Victoria's Secret, has sales. Keep your eyes open and go early when the selection is the best, and you won't have to go manicured *mano a mano* with the satin-maddened crowds swarming around the $5 bra bins after work.

In the eyes of the world you might have to look like someone who wears a boring suit, a uniform, scrubs, sweats, even judicial robes. But underneath it all, you can be who you really want to be in your underwear. And maybe we'll even see it in the twinkle in your eye, and we'll wonder: "What's *her* secret today? Could it be . . . *The Red Bra of Courage*?"

chapter 6

Because the woman who had introduced her to Magda should not hear about her death secondhand, Lacey walked from the offices of *The Eye* to Stylettos at Dupont Circle, where Stella Lake held court with her scissors and shampoo bowl.

Lacey had spent the fifteen-minute walk trying to figure out how to tell her the awful news, but Stella took one look at her and cried out, "Oh my God, Lacey! Who's dead?"

"Magda Rousseau."

Stella dropped her scissors. "No! I just saw her last week. She looked totally healthy." Her eyes began to moisten. "You know, for an unhealthy crazy old lady. Was it her heart?"

"I'm sorry." Lacey hugged Stella's shoulders. "I found her. Can we talk somewhere?"

Stella stood still in the busy salon as her eyes filled with tears. Lacey couldn't stand to see her friend cry; she was sure she would be crying herself in mere moments. She handed Stella a tissue and waited while her spunky hairstylist dabbed at her eye makeup.

A young man whose hair looked like a dalmatian got up out of his styling chair and gave Stella a hug and a tip, oblivious to her tears. She had apparently just dyed striking black spots into his short platinum-blond flattop. "Thanks, Stella! Whoa. It's radical." He preened at himself in the mirror and was gone. Lacey glanced at Stella with an eyebrow raised. Stella's evenly dyed black hair looked positively conservative by comparison.

"Yeah, it's a pretty cool look, huh, Lace," Stella said, looking wistfully after her spotted handiwork. "I don't know why I didn't think of it first." Then she remembered Magda and sighed.

"Are you okay?" Lacey said.

"Yeah. I'm through for the day." She turned back to Lacey. "We need to do something in memory of Magda. Let's go get a drink.

Our own little wake for Magda," Stella said, stripping off her black Stylettos smock to reveal an eye-popping purple corset—no doubt a Magda Rousseau Original—over tight black capri pants. Her formerly bright red crew cut was growing out. She had dyed it jet-black and was wearing it slicked back and sleek like a seal. She reapplied her eye makeup and checked for imperfections in the mirror. Her eyes were lined with black kohl, her lips were red as blood and matched her long nails. She looked as exotic as if she were channeling a mutant mixture of Mata Hari and Rudolph Valentino. Lacey whistled softly at the new Stella.

"New look, Stella?"

"You like it?"

"I like it lots. It's you."

"Yeah, that's what I thought. Totally me. Makes me feel dangerous."

"Do you need to feel dangerous?'

"Duh, you bet I do. I need a man."

"What about Bobby Blue Eyes?" Stella had been crazy for months about a certain angelic-looking blond dude who loved motorcycles, erotic adventures, and Stella's very assertive twin peaks—"the girls," as she called them.

"You know. History. Down the road. Whatever."

"But I thought you guys were, um, cozy," Lacey said. Stella was grabbing her jacket and striding toward the front door. "A couple. Permanent. Or at least semipermanent."

"Permanents don't last forever, Lace. Life is like hair, you know, sometimes you just gotta cut loose, make a change. And I can't wait forever for a new man. I'm not like you." Stella threw her a pointed look that Lacey decoded as *You are so pathetic.* "A woman's got needs, you know."

Lacey ignored that. She followed Stella out the front door of the shiny Dupont Circle salon. She didn't want to get Stella started on what a woman needs. And she didn't want to get into a long discussion about whether what Lacey needed was Victor Donovan, the big dope who still made her heart race.

They chose a nearby bar that served trendy drinks to a nerdy crowd of Capitol Hill staffers who were trying to look cool. They sat at the bar, lost in their own thoughts, until their trendy drink specials arrived, a Pink Lady with a double shot of gin for Stella and blue champagne for Lacey. Stella took one big gulp of her Pink Lady, opened her eyes wide, and socked Lacey in the shoulder. Lacey spilled a little blue champagne.

"I know! Everyone can wear their corsets to the funeral! For Magda, you know?

Lacey blinked. "Corsets?"

"Yeah, you, me, my assistant manager Michelle, the rest of the salon. All those actresses she costumed. And I know some of her call-girl clients and that corset-kinky crowd." Stella took another gulp of the pink liquid. "We all got our corsets and bustiers from Magda. It would be one last great costume parade for the old doll."

Lacey couldn't imagine the refined Michelle, a gorgeous black woman, in a corset. If Stella had her way, the funeral would look like some sort of misguided Old West saloon gal musical number, or a corset fetishist's ball. Lacey was still trying to adjust to mourners showing up in their casual Friday clothes or their barest black cocktail dresses, just because they were black.

"Maybe we could all wear black ones. You know, like formal funeral corsets?" Stella looked so hopeful that Lacey didn't want to crush her spirit with a dose of conventional good taste. All Stella had learned from reading Lacey's columns was that if you wore clothes to express who you really were inside, you were in fashion and all was forgiven. Stella liked to broadcast her inner vixen through her clothes. Lacey realized that the "dress-to-express" side of her message resonated with Stella's rebellious little inner vixen, but the other side of the message, the "dress-to-respect" side, wasn't what Stella wanted to hear.

"Well, my own Magda Original corset is not exactly somber enough for funeral wear," Lacey pointed out. "It's baby-blue." She groaned inwardly for giving in to Magda's flattery and having a corset made in the first place. Where could she ever wear such a thing in Washington? And Stella couldn't possibly imagine that Lacey would really wear a baby-blue satin corset to a funeral, she thought. *Could she?*

"Michelle has three, Lacey, maybe you could borrow one."

That suggestion was even more alarming to Lacey. "Stel, it's not really done, wearing underwear to funerals. Not without wearing something over it."

"But it's for Magda! She'd understand."

"She's French. Heaven only knows what she'd think."

"She'd love it!" Stella waved her glass at the waiter for another Pink Lady. "She'd totally love it. *La Vie en Rose* and all that. It would be like a tribute to her life's work. Can't you just see it, Lace?"

Lacey sipped her blue champagne. She could see it all too

clearly. A chorus line of corset-clad women, all shapes and sizes and colors, rocking Magda's funeral like a late-night cabaret. They would be wearing berets and scarves and fishnet tights. Edith Piaf would be singing. Then Edith would toss them all top hats and canes and they would dance, like the Rockettes or the Folies Bergère. Would Magda rise up from her coffin and join the corseted chorus line?

"I just want to do something nice for Magda. Everybody's dying on me, Lacey. First poor Angie. Then that diva supermodel Amanda Manville. Now Magda!" Stella wailed. "What is it about me? I'm like some death magnet."

Lacey had asked herself the same question. "Don't be ridiculous, Stella, you had nothing to do with any of those," she said. "Coincidence."

"I can't believe Magda is dead." Stella gazed into her reflection in her fresh Pink Lady, as if to divine what fate it was that caused her friends and clients to die.

"It's not you," Lacey said, wondering how to avoid the subject of Magda's unknown cause of death. "She didn't live a healthy life."

"That's true," Stella mused. Although Stella was in the dark about the lost corset, she was aware that Magda and Lacey were working on some kind of fashion story. "So I guess the big trip is off? The big story, corsets in French couture or whatever?"

"No. France is still there. I'm still going and I'll write some kind of tribute to Magda."

"Aw, that's so sweet of you." She downed some more of the Pink Lady. "Hey! I know. I could go with you!"

"Uh, right. Okay." Stella in her corsets and her sleek new look would no doubt dazzle them in Paris. *Think fast, Lacey.* "So, Stella, do you have a passport?"

"Oh, hell, a passport! I knew there was something I've been meaning to do. Guess it's a little late now."

"This time, yeah." Lacey wasn't about to tell Stella how to get an emergency passport application expedited. "But thanks for the offer. Next time."

Stella clinked their glasses together. "Deal, Lacey. Do you know how the old girl died? Stroke or something?"

The question she had been trying to avoid now hung in the air. She had only Magda's word for how she died, though that dying word was "poison." Lacey had learned the hard way that anything she told Stella would soon be broadcast wider and faster than CNN could ever do it. Even more distressing, Stella would take any of Lacey's half-formed speculations as the absolute truth.

"Um, the police came. It was a pretty confusing scene. I don't think there's an official determination yet."

"Poor Magda. I'm so sorry you had to find the body, Lacey. As you are all too aware, I know exactly what that's like," Stella said, wiping a single tear away with one daggerlike fingernail. They were silent for a moment, remembering poor murdered Angie Woods, the hairstylist Stella had found dead in her own salon last spring. "Wow, we're like totally maudlin here. Tell a joke or something."

"Sorry, Stel, I can never remember the punch lines." Lacey paused for a moment, studying the pretty glass of blue liquid. "Stella, did Magda have any enemies?"

"Nah. She was a doll. You know what a sweet old lady she was."

"But some of her clients were a little, um, weird." Lacey sipped her champagne.

"You talking about the leather lads or the high-priced hookers?"

"Both. And anyone else unusual you can think of. I need to know everything interesting about her. For my story. You know."

"Don't think so." The slim and handsome waiter returned with Stella's third Pink Lady and set it down. "You know those guys who are into the kinky underwear? When they go crazy, they just kill each other."

"Don't I know it, honey!" the waiter interjected, and winked before moving off.

"What about the call girls and the hookers?" Lacey asked. "Anybody dangerous there? Haven't they've all been arrested one time or another?"

"Some of 'em. Cost of doing business," Stella said. "Sweet girls, the call girls, once you get to know 'em. In fact, Jolene, the really pretty blonde, did you ever meet her? No? She's a client of mine, I do her highlights. She's the one who introduced me to Magda. And her girlfriend Sylvania. They wouldn't hurt Magda, they all love her! Besides, hookers only want to kill their johns. Or their pimps." She slurped more of her Pink Lady and then choked on it. "Whoa! Wait a minute, Lacey! Are you saying what I think you're saying? That some bastard knocked her off?!"

"I don't know yet, Stel! Like I said, the police haven't made a determination." Stella gave her a look that demanded the truth. Lacey looked away. "But yes, it's probably murder."

"Oh, God. But why? Why Magda?" Lacey had no answer for her. "Damn it. Damn it all to hell. Well, don't you worry, Lacey."

Stella's voice rose and Lacey put her finger to her lips. Stella lowered her voice to a stage whisper. "Don't worry, 'cause I'm going to help you this time. I'm going to help you catch the bastard."

"No, Stella. I'm not getting involved this time." Lacey put down a bill to pay for the drinks and slipped her jacket on. *Not again*, she thought, *never again.* Besides, Magda didn't ask Lacey to find the killer, only the corset. "Let the police handle it. There's no way they can call this one a suicide. Let them do their job, Stella, we are not detectives."

"Broken record. Like it's your number-one hit song. 'Not gonna do it, not gonna do it, not gonna do it.'" Stella smiled. "That's what you always say. And then you do it anyway. You know you're gonna. And I'm gonna be there with you. Just remember, this is Stella you're talking to. I'm your stylist. I know all your secrets."

That was exactly what Lacey was afraid of.

Chapter 7

Brass buckles clicked beneath her fingers as Lacey opened what she considered her greatest treasure: Aunt Mimi's trunk. The leather bands were beginning to stiffen and crack, even though Lacey tried to keep them well oiled. The trunk served as her coffee table, her center of calm, her secret refuge. She had inherited the trunk from her favorite great-aunt, and she sought out the familiar security of its contents whenever she was fatigued, worried, and lonely. At the moment, she was all three.

Magda's murder and Stella's pledge to help find the killer were alarming enough, but Lacey felt an empty ache inside that had nothing to do with hunger or danger or blue champagne, and everything to do with Vic Donovan. The Aimee Mann music she was listening to didn't help, but the mournful melodies and sad stories fit her mood. She had hoped Vic would meet her in the City of Light after the big corset hunt. That wouldn't happen now. She wondered if she would ever see him again. She forced him from her thoughts and concentrated on Mimi's treasure chest.

The trunk was filled with Mimi's treasured collection of vintage patterns, suits, dresses, and gowns of every description, mostly from the 1940s. Many were still attached to the fabrics Mimi had selected for them but never made. Some were partly made but not finished. They were beguiling. Some were more than half completed, some had photos clipped of movie stars outfitted in similar attire, all were intriguing. Lacey was slowly having some of the stunning outfits made for her. It was an expensive luxury, but worth every penny. Grateful that she and Aunt Mimi had the same taste and style and were the same size, petite with real women's curves, Lacey loved to imagine where she would wear such beautiful clothes. The trunk brought her closer to Mimi and it contained more than its share of mystery in old letters, photos, fabrics, and memories, a time capsule from Mimi's adventurous life. Even a short trip through the trunk left Lacey feeling better, as if she had stepped through a door into another time and place, and right now she had to get the sight of Magda's amused dead eyes out of her mind.

Reminding her of a pirate's treasure chest, the trunk added just the right panache to her shabby-chic living room. Lacey lifted the heavy lid and steadied the top. A whiff of decades-old lavender sachets wafted up delicately and tickled her nose, evoking her Aunt Mimi. She wondered what Mimi would do. Would she abandon Paris as a lost cause, or grab this once-in-a-lifetime chance with both hands?

Go, girl, trust your instincts. That's what feminine intuition is for, isn't it? Lacey imagined her saying. *Don't forget your war paint!*

Of course Mimi would be on her side. Lacey lifted out a black-and-white photograph of Mimi in her early thirties. She was a beauty who never married, although she had plenty of boyfriends and one long-term romantic relationship that the family wasn't supposed to know about. Lacey looked quite a bit like Mimi with her high cheekbones and expressive green-blue eyes. But while Mimi's hair was a vibrant auburn, Lacey's was a light brown with subtle highlights, courtesy of Stella.

Lacey set aside the photo and lifted a special garment left to her by Aunt Mimi, a tarty black lace and satin number with seven stays and twelve hooks and eyes. A corset in the style known as a Merry Widow, it was wrapped in tissue tied with pink ribbons. Lacey couldn't imagine how women in the Forties and Fifties had worked up the nerve to buy such things. She had nearly died of embarrassment being fitted by Magda for her new blue satin corset, and Mimi's Merry Widow was at least as racy. It sucked in the waist and ended at the top of the hips. Lacey had worn it several times under a couple of her vintage outfits to get just the right hourglass silhouette. Literally it was breathtaking, and with the garters and stockings attached, it made her look like Bondage Barbie. Only the whip was missing.

Lacey thought of the baby-blue satin confection of a corset Magda had insisted she needed and which Stella thought was appropriate funeral attire. While Stella was interested more in the naughtiness factor, heavy on red and black and *va-va-va-voom*, Lacey's custom corset was delicate and pretty. With the right skirt, it might even be appropriate evening wear. Corset tops were everywhere these days and Stella was right, underwear had somehow become outerwear. Lacey had even attended a wedding where the bride's gown was a corset top paired with a full satin skirt. It was demurely sexy and romantic, and it had also succeeded in giving the petite bride actual cleavage, a dream come true.

Lacey went into her bedroom and pulled the slim box from the top of the closet. She lifted the lid and carefully removed the blue tissue paper covering it and appreciated the sexy garment. It was truly one of a kind. Lacey loved pockets and Magda happily complied with her whim for a secret pocket stitched into the corset. It was so slim that only a folded bill or two would fit inside.

She and Magda had discussed how jewels could be sewn into a corset without the agony of bumps and bulges gouging into the wearer's skin. Lacey didn't see at first how it could be done. But it was possible, Magda said, if there were layers built into the corset, perhaps a quilted layer with the jewels laid flat, then more layers sewn on top or inside. She had thought about it for a long time; she told Lacey the comfort level also depended on how tightly laced it was. If the Romanov girls had been losing weight in their long captivity by the Red Army, there would be more room in their clothes to hide jewels. It sounded mad, yet plausible.

With Magda gone, Lacey was now seized by a sudden fierce desire to tell the whole story, legendary lost corset and all, to someone. She felt as if she might burst. Lacey rationalized that if she were in Paris alone and danger reared its ugly head, someone ought to know, someone who would understand the situation and could be reliably sworn to secrecy, unlike Stella. Someone who was bound by attorney-client privilege, and not by the gossipy soapsuds of a shampoo bowl. She had to speak to Brooke Barton, Esquire, her friend and occasionally her lawyer. Lacey lifted the receiver and dialed.

"You can't go alone, Lacey. It's simply not safe." Brooke's voice was tense, but Lacey knew it wasn't fear but excitement that it betrayed. "I'm going with you! When do we leave?"

Brooke had raced right over to Lacey's apartment overlooking the Potomac River upon hearing the news that Magda Rousseau was dead and possibly murdered. She was still in her attorney-gray suit of the day, her blond braid coming loose. She kicked off her shoes and inquired whether there was anything to eat or drink.

"Wait a minute, Brooke," Lacey said, checking her nearly empty refrigerator. "How can you just take off for Paris at the drop of a corset stay? Aren't you a hard-charging young barrister with a full plate of important clients?" She reached into the fridge for Brie, wine, and baguettes. Nothing like setting the mood, she thought. And the only other food in her kitchen was popcorn.

"Oh, please, *quel* bore. My current clients would put an insomniac in a coma. We are talking about adventure and murder and Romanovs. And a century-old secret. And Paris."

"Actually it's supposed to be in a farmhouse somewhere near Mont-Saint-Michel."

"I love Mont-Saint-Michel! And Paris, and the lost corset of the Romanovs. I love everything about it, and I love you for calling me. This adventure calls for teamwork, Lacey." Brooke had forgotten the boring brief she had written that afternoon and was mentally soaring on the heady fumes of a good story. "We make a great team. Your instincts, my legal know-how. And Damon's—"

"Damon can't come," Lacey insisted. "Just you and me. Attorney–client privilege." She sliced the bread and Brie, placed it on a tray, added a bunch of grapes, and handed Brooke a plate.

"But he's—"

"He's a sweet boy, Brooke, and your boyfriend *du jour*, I know, but he's a madman masquerading as a journalist."

"I know he has a reputation, but you're wrong," Brooke pleaded. "He can be trusted."

Trusted was the last thing that Damon Newhouse could be, Lacey thought. "He likes to mock me, to ruin my reputation. In print." Lacey remembered the many times Damon had made sport of her on his Web site, Conspiracy Clearinghouse, a.k.a. DeadFed dot com, the notorious repository of all things related to Washington conspiracy theories and every kind of unsubstantiated rumor and speculation with which the Nation's Capital was so rife.

"Oh, no, DeadFed is a mission for Damon, an important one. And he has nothing but respect for you." Brooke grabbed a piece of cheese. "The truth is out there."

"No, the truth is subjective, and there are a thousand and one fantasies out there. Anything you like. Damon stocks a veritable grocery store of tall tales."

"You say that now." Brooke chewed merrily.

"I know you love him." Lacey tried to be gentle. "He's a doll, but—"

"Okay. Forget Damon for a moment," Brooke said, licking her lips. "Are you sure you don't want Vic there?"

"It's over." Lacey settled in on her velvet sofa, balancing the Brie and a baguette, and leaned her head back.

"No more Vic? No! I don't believe it."

"My heart is not a football," Lacey said. Even so, her heart said she was a fool. She would just have to teach it a lesson.

"I could have Damon talk to him," Brooke offered.

"Keep Damon away from Vic!" Lacey sat up straight. "He'd try to convince Vic I was kidnapped by, I don't know, android congressional pages and held ransom for the plans to a top-secret new hybrid vehicle run on tidal energy from the full moon. Or something."

"Android congressional pages? Could be true, I've seen those pages. Not human, the lot of them." Brooke sipped her wine. "But do you think the man-to-man thing might work? We could try it."

"Thanks, but no. If Vic Donovan can't work up the gumption to see me himself, I don't want an intervention. After all, there are men in Paris. Frenchmen. I've heard stories."

"Yes, but Frenchmen are only fling-worthy, and you don't believe in flings. I really think Damon and I could help. And if Damon came with us to Paris—"

"No, no, no. I know you mean well, but you and Damon together are nuclear. Radioactive."

"Well, certainly between the sheets. Did I tell you about the time we—"

"Too much information, Brooke. And we're starting with one dead body already."

"Ha. You're a fine one to talk about being nuclear. Look at you, another dead source!"

"Hey, it's not like I knock them off myself. That's poor form for a reporter."

Brooke broke off a piece of baguette and gestured with it. "My point is that they are dead. This time, you're way more involved. You're privy to the murder victim's secrets. You were the last one to see her alive. You may have gotten there mere minutes after the killer left. He, she, whoever it is, may have seen you and thinks you saw them. You're in danger."

"Of course I'm in danger, I live in the D.C. metropolitan area. Anthrax, terrorists, snipers, cabdrivers, the Beltway, the Virginia Department of Transportation. But this is an adventure and I want it."

"Rousseau's killer might go after you next."

Lacey lifted her wineglass. "In that case, I'm going to Paris before I die. Just remember, you might be in danger too," she said. "You can reconsider the trip."

"It's a chance I'll have to take." Brooke's eyes glittered.

"Stella volunteered to come too."

"Good God! No!" Brooke and Stella didn't get along. "That blabbermouth would get you killed for sure. Stella knew Magda, didn't she? Does she know about the Romanov corset?"

"Not yet. Or else the story would be everywhere, swapped among customers between the highlights and the haircut. If Stella knew, it would be on the Web by now. Damon would be all over it." Lacey moved to the French doors to her balcony overlooking the Potomac. The view of the river was her favorite part of the apartment. "I'm not sure who knows what about this thing. Magda said I'm the only one who knows, but I'm not sure. Leaving the body covered in cheap jewels doesn't sound like just a coincidence to me."

"Obviously a message," Brooke said. "But what?"

"I'll still be writing the story for *The Eye.* But I'm telling everyone I'm on vacation."

"Good idea. That's what I'll tell everyone too. You're heartbroken and I'm going to help cheer you up by going to Paris with you to help you pick up hot Frenchmen."

"Ease up on the sympathy angle, would you?" Lacey returned to her sofa.

Brooke breezed on. "I have tons of vacation time coming that I never get to take." She wiped her fingers delicately on her napkin and poured herself more wine.

"Your boss can spare you?" Lacey asked archly.

"Daddy?" Though she sometimes felt constrained working in the family law firm, Brooke Barton found there were many advantages in being associated with the firm of Barton, Barton & Barton. "Oh, I think so. There's nothing I can't fob off on the junior partner."

"Your brother Benjamin?"

"Of course." Brooke laughed.

Lacey handed her a copy of the itinerary. "You can take Magda's room at the hotel. We're on the same floor. *The Eye* is cheap, but there was no way I was going to share a room."

"Cheap! You're in a two-star hotel. *The Eye* is so cheap it squeaks!" She refilled her wineglass.

"Big deal. Who wants some big, anonymous American-style hotel? If you want to stay at another hotel, be my guest."

"No way. We need to stick together, babe. I can rough it for once in a mere two-star." Brooke leaned back into the sofa cushions and stretched like a contented cat. "What do you think is hidden in the corset? Diamonds, rubies, emeralds? The diamond-studded imperial back-scratcher?"

"All of the above. They had ungodly amounts of jewels," Lacey said, remembering the remnants of Romanov wealth she had seen on display at Marjorie Merriweather Post's Hillwood Museum in D.C. "You should see the crown the Empress Alexandra wore at her wedding. It's just solid diamonds. A hundred or more. At least one carat each. Looked like it came out of a giant gumball machine."

"Whose corset do you think it was?"

"I assume you mean if it really exists and it isn't some figment of Magda's fevered imagination?"

"Yeah. That's it. Whose was it? Out of four daughters and one empress, whose?"

"The latest book I've read on the Romanov execution said that no valuables were found on Princess Marie. No corset on her, supposedly. The author—a man, wouldn't you know it—theorized that her family was mad at her for flirting with a Bolshevik guard and withheld her fancy underwear." Lacey cleared away the dishes. "Yeah, that makes a lot of sense. I can hear them: 'Now you've done it, Missy, we're hiding your underwear! No corset for you, my girl.' Remember, these were very reserved people. Practically Victorian. It's not like they're going to let a teenage girl go braless. Not even with the noose practically around their necks."

"Absolutely," Brooke agreed. "Only a man could come up with such a ridiculous premise. More likely they'd make her wear *two* corsets. And a chastity belt."

"Maybe she was thought to be corsetless because someone had already found her corset and spirited it away," Lacey continued. "Someone like Magda's grandfather, Juris? And maybe his Latvian buddies helped or covered for him. After all, the scene was total chaos. Drunken slaughter. Horrible." A silence fell over them for a few moments while they pictured the victims' awful final moments amid the pandemonium that set in among their executioners.

"So it was Princess Marie's corset," Brooke said. "Maybe."

"It's a theory." Lacey shrugged. "Or maybe it's Magda's dream-weaving, or her grandfather's lies. My money's on the latter. Grandpa Juris is dead: Dead men tell tall tales."

"Some people think such an object would have almost magical powers." Brooke's eyes took on a glow with the intoxication of a lovely conspiracy theory. "A holy relic of the Romanovs' martyrdom.

Sort of like the lost Ark of the Covenant. Obviously there are those who might want it destroyed, and those who would kill to get their hands on it—"

"Hold on, counselor, you are a confirmed 'conspiromaniac.' Step away from the corset, ma'am."

"Even if the corset doesn't have supernatural properties, it would be worth millions. Millions and millions."

"We have to play it very cool," Lacey warned, wondering if it was such a good idea to have told Brooke after all. "And we can't discount the possibility that someone unrelated to the corset killed Magda. Her clientele also included hookers and kinksters. And those crazy theatre people. Perhaps someone wanted to kill her with a theatrical flourish."

"An actor?" Brooke said. "But you'd never kill your seamstress, your stylist, or your attorney, right? No matter how often the thought might cross your mind. Especially an actor. It would be bad karma."

"We'll play it cool, Brooke. Fun, frivolous, female. We're just two crazy American chicks on vacation, remember?"

"Right on, chica." Brooke stood up and retrieved her shoes and purse. "I'll make a list of what I need to take. Camera, recorder, cell phone, laptop, GPS, BlackBerry, iPod, blow-dryer, battery chargers, outlet adapters—"

"Don't you think we should travel light?"

"It's all light." She fumbled her keys out of the bottom of her large plaid Burberry bag. "Don't let me forget my night-vision goggles."

"The essentials, Brooke. Don't pack the whole spy store."

"Not to worry, Lacey, it'll be such fun. It'll be an adventure, a mission to seek out the truth, a raid on the secret of the century. Raiders! That's it, we'll be the Raiders of the Lost Corset!"

Lacey let Brooke out, then sagged against her door. She wondered if she should have decided to go alone. *Raiders of the Lost Corset indeed. Have I lost my mind?*

chapter 8

The following morning, the security guard at *The Eye* called a still-groggy Lacey Smithsonian to the front lobby to meet a visitor. This was odd, as she didn't generally have surprise guests. On the fashion beat, her sources usually were preceded by publicists waving glossy photos.

As she stepped out of the elevator in the lobby, the surprise visitor was a woman with a mop of strawberry-blond curls and a flapping khaki raincoat. She hurled herself toward Lacey.

"She's dead!" Analiza Zarina grabbed Lacey's arms. "Why? Nothing bad ever happened to us until Magda started talking to *you*, and now she's dead!"

"Wait a minute, Analiza, I only found her. That's all."

"I don't believe you! This is all your doing!" Analiza's Latvian-accented voice rose to a shriek. The guard came rushing over.

"Everything okay here, ladies?" he asked. Analiza released Lacey and stepped back, glaring.

"Maybe we could get out of the traffic here. Somewhere we can talk." Lacey and the guard ushered the distraught woman into an empty break room and Lacey poured black coffee into two paper cups. The guard left them alone, with a word in Lacey's ear to call if she needed help. Hot coffee could be a good defensive weapon, Lacey decided, if Analiza went ballistic and leapt for her throat. The woman still had a manic look in her eyes. Her reddish tousle of curls was as slapdash as her makeup, with a streak of blush across her cheeks and flecks of mascara below her lashes. She was usually quite attractive in a disheveled and distracted way, but she wasn't living up to her potential today. They sat nervously across from each other at the coffee-stained table.

"You didn't kill her?" Analiza glared suspiciously at her.

"Don't be ridiculous, Analiza! She was barely alive when I got there. I called 911, but she died before they arrived. I don't know who killed Magda. She wouldn't tell me. Or couldn't."

Analiza choked on her coffee. "She was alive when you got there?!"

"Alive. And where were you, by the way?"

"Out buying red thread. For the Red Riding Hood costume. How we ran out, I don't know. We always have thread, but not the red, not yesterday. Why, what do you think?"

"Just asking." Lacey raised an eyebrow. "Didn't the police talk to you yet?'

"Of course they did. Stupid men. What did Magda tell you?"

"She told me she was poisoned."

"Poisoned?" The woman's hands shook.

That information was already in Lacey's story posted on the paper's Web site. The printed version would appear the next day. "Magda warned me not to drink the wine. But she didn't say who gave it to her."

Analiza considered her coffee, then took a sip. "That's ridiculous, why wouldn't she tell you who it was?"

"I don't know," Lacey said, thinking that if Magda had only told her, it would have made everything so much simpler. "Maybe she didn't know. What do you think?"

"I think she was crazy, but she didn't deserve to die. You two were going to France on some wild adventure." It was an accusation. "I'm sure she told you some crazy story." Analiza looked at her hands and began to pick nervously at her remaining nail polish.

"It was a fashion story. A corsetiere returns to her beloved Paris. Corsets in haute couture."

"I know better than that," Analiza said. "Magda liked to run her mouth. It was more than that."

"Like what?" There was no response. "Yes, she liked to talk. She was full of stories."

Analiza seemed to make up her mind about something. "I'm her business partner, you know. I inherit everything."

"The shop, you mean?" Perhaps a motive for murder, Lacey thought, if the shop were a real money maker. Magda had confided that it was a living for the two of them, but not much more.

"Everything. If you have anything of Magda's, you must give it back to me."

"What would I have of Magda's?" Lacey asked, thinking of the secret diary. *But I don't have Magda's diary,* Lacey thought, *I only have my own English version. She made that for me. And Analiza will have to ask for it by name before we're having that discussion.* Analiza silently studied her coffee. "I don't know who killed her, Analiza. I'm sorry."

Analiza drummed her fingers on the table. "You have a reputation for getting involved in other people's business. Too involved. But Magda thought you were smart. So are you going to look for Magda's killer?"

"I'm not a detective. I wouldn't know where to start."

Analiza set her cup down. "That's good. The police should do their job for a change." She put her hand in her coat pocket and pulled out a crumpled piece of paper, which she thrust at Lacey. "She liked to read your column. Here. It's an obituary. Can you get this in the paper?"

Lacey smoothed the paper out. There was a scant handwritten paragraph on Magda Rousseau. Birth date. Death date. A corsetiere, born in France, moved to America, settled in D.C., well-known in her trade. "So few words for an entire life."

Analiza shrugged. "It's enough. The memorial is tomorrow."

"So soon?" Lacey wondered about the autopsy and toxicology tests. The D.C. medical examiner's office was not known for such speed and efficiency. "Have they released the body?"

"No. They won't tell me when. By the time they are through with Magda Rousseau, no one will remember her."

"I'll be there," Lacey said.

Analiza stood up and walked out of the room without saying good-bye.

Lacey ran her hands through her hair and sighed. "Nice way to start a day."

Trujillo popped his head into the break room. "Fan of yours?"

"Eavesdropping, Tony?"

"News gathering, Smithsonian. It's in the job description, you know." He smiled a very bright smile for so early in the morning, moved the rest of his fit and muscular body into the room, and poured himself a jolt of java.

"What did you hear?" Lacey asked, grimacing at a swallow of her bitter coffee.

"You mostly, trying to smooth some ruffled feathers. You look a little ruffled yourself." Trujillo reached out and smoothed back a lock of her hair. She swatted his hand away.

"I don't need a bodyguard."

"Don't worry, no charge." He leaned in closer and lowered his voice. "So, speaking of bodyguards, I'm trying to convince Mac to let me go to Paris to keep you out of trouble."

"Butt out! You cause me enough grief here, much less in Paris."

"You always get into trouble. And it's Paris, man. Expense account time."

"The stripped-down version of an expense account. Standard per diem. *The Eye*'s per diem. You know what that means. Starvation. A zero-star hotel. The Métro instead of cabs."

"You don't look too upset about it."

"I'm going to Paris, Tony." She smiled at him wickedly. "You're not."

"I want a piece of it. Besides, what if you run into a killer? I always miss the important stuff. I could use a little of that hero stuff on my résumé."

"You want to fight off the bad guys, Tony? I thought you liked to let me do the dirty work. And then you ride in late and lasso the byline." Lacey stood up and tossed her cup in the trash. "Never thought I'd see the day you're jealous of me."

"A little professional rivalry, that's all," Tony said. "I'm the cops reporter, yet you're the one always hanging around with cops."

"I'm done with cops." She smiled widely and waltzed out the door. "And just for the record, I'm done with killers."

Passing Mac's office door on the way back to her desk, Lacey halted when he waved her in. "Shut the door," her editor ordered. She did, but remained standing. "This is the deal," Mac said. "Our publisher has spoken. Claudia says you are to use your own best news judgment on this story. I told her that was a mistake, your best news judgment always leads you astray. And me to a nervous breakdown."

"I have a nose for news," Lacey protested.

Mac glared under his bushy brows. "Trujillo wants to go. I'm not letting him."

"Good. My byline is secure. Tony doesn't understand fashion, he doesn't care about the story, he's just jealous. And I've found someone to come with me. She'll pick up the cost of Magda's room and pay her own way."

Mac looked interested. "Who is it?'

"Brooke Barton, my lawyer."

"That conspiracy nut? Isn't she a little scary?"

"More than a little. That's why she'll be the perfect companion."

He grunted. "Just remember, the French believe you're guilty until proven innocent."

"Who says I'm going to get in any trouble?"

Mac reached for his blue and white bottle of Maalox, and Lacey reached for the door. "I didn't have ulcers before I met you."

"Sure you did, Mac. You were born with ulcers."

"I don't need any more. Get out of here."

She smiled and strode back to her desk to read the crumpled piece of paper that Analiza Zarina had given her. She took Analiza's basics and added a couple of paragraphs of her own, then printed it and she sent it to Obituaries by e-mail and in hard copy with a note, a personal plea that it be included in tomorrow's paper, even though it had missed their deadline. She added one of Felicity's treats *du jour*, a strawberry cheesecake mini-tart wrapped in a napkin. It was the least she could do. *Pays to be nice to the Obit beat,* she thought, *you never know when they'll be writing yours.*

There were too many things to do to prepare for the trip; her mental notes were piling up. She had to clean and pack and organize, she had to sort her maps and guidebooks and make phone calls, she had to attend Magda's memorial service, she had to discreetly stay on top of Detective Broadway Lamont's murder investigation without stepping on Trujillo's toes. She had to not get killed by whoever killed Magda. And on top of all those things, she had to field the weekly phone call from her mother, which came later that night.

"But Lacey, why can't you come to Denver for Thanksgiving?" Rose Smithsonian asked, and Lacey tried to think of just how to phrase her many reasons. "We always have such a good time. You can invite that handsome Victor Donovan. He seems awfully nice."

"It's just not a good time right now, Mom." Since her mother had met Vic on her recent visit to D.C., Rose Smithsonian had become way too interested in Lacey's relationship with him. She had even offered Lacey her personal meatloaf recipe, which Rose noted men always loved. In her mother's world, Lacey knew this was tantamount to a mother passing down to her daughter their tribe's time-honored secret love mojo, the Kama Sutra of the Colorado kitchen. But Lacey hated meatloaf. She had sworn she was never going to make meatloaf for anyone, not even Vic Donovan. Especially not Vic.

"There's nothing wrong, is there?" Her mother's voice edged into maternal concern.

"Don't be silly, what could be wrong?" Lacey fiddled with the pencils in her desk. She didn't know why she had pencils: She never used them; she preferred her fountain pen.

"You're not tangled up in some scary investigation, are you? Some killer, there in Washington?"

"No, nothing like that." The pencils spilled out of her hands. Rose could be spooky.

"Because your sister and I could come out and help you. Like we did the last time."

Wonderful. Rose had decided after her daughters left home to resume playing tennis, to take up golf, and now to start a career as a freelance righter of wrongs. All because she happened to be in town last month, and she and Lacey's sister, Cherise, had actually been able to help Lacey out in a tight spot. In a rare show of solidarity, the family Smithsonian had brought down a killer. And Cherise had found a good target for her killer cheerleader kick: a killer's chin.

Rose wasn't about to let her forget it. Lacey had to do something to stop their latent crime-fighting (and life-making-over) urges. They were back in Denver, safe and secure, and she was intent on keeping them there.

"I have orders from Detective Broadway Lamont to keep my posse out of town."

Her mother laughed merrily over the phone. "That big detective of yours? He really didn't say that."

"Oh, he really did, Mom. He did. But with the holidays coming, I'm sure you're busy."

"Everything's organized. The turkey's ordered. You know, fresh, corn-fed, no hormones."

"I'm sure it will be perfect. And besides, um, remember I'm going to Paris for a week. On a story."

She heard her mother puttering around in the kitchen, pots and pans clanging about. "You did mention something about that. I wanted your father to take me to Paris once before you girls were born, but he had this fishing trip planned, and, well, my high-school French is a little rusty, so we just went to Steamboat Springs instead and we stayed at one of those cute little fishing cabins and I cleaned all his trout and we had a simply wonderful—"

"Sounds great, Mom. And I'll be really tired of plane travel by the time I get back, so—"

"You're sure, Lacey? It would be such fun."

"And I have plans," Lacey said, thinking that sleeping for a few days solid over Thanksgiving was a good plan.

"Plans with Vic Donovan?" Her mother sounded hopeful. "And his family?"

"Um, I really can't say yet. Vic's pretty busy these days."

"Well," her mother said, "I suppose we wouldn't want to scare him off with one of our big family gatherings so soon. You two lovebirds need some time alone, don't you? Have you tried my special meatloaf yet?"

Lacey couldn't tell her mother she had already scared Vic off all by herself, without any help from her family. Or the special meatloaf. "Thanks for being so understanding."

"It's not too early to think about Christmas," Rose said, in that way that all mothers have.

"You'll have to take that up with my editor."

"Oh. Mr. Jones? He seemed nice. Do you have his number?"

Lacey finally got her mother off the phone, then made a stab at packing. It was useless, she decided. The phone rang and Lacey picked it up, thinking her mother had forgotten something, some secret aphrodisiac to give the special meatloaf a little more zing.

"Hello," she said. There was a pause, a clicking sound, then someone hung up. She noticed that her phone machine was blinking. Three hang-ups, no messages. *Someone wants to know if I'm home*, she thought. *But they don't want to talk to me.*

Chapter 9

Analiza Zarina hosted the memorial for Magda Rousseau at their shop, Stays and Plays, where Magda had died. She had set the time for late morning on the following day. Once the body was released, there would be a funeral mass at the local Catholic church, but no one could predict when that would happen.

The obituary from *The Eye* was taped to a poster and hung on the street-level door that led up the stairs to the shop. When she saw it, Lacey was glad she had added some thoughts to the sparse facts supplied by Analiza. She even had managed to come up with a photograph of Magda for the obit. The paper's head photographer, Todd "Long Lens" Hansen, had found in his files a shot of Magda fitting a local actress in a period costume, taken for a feature story on the theatre. The photo, which never ran in the newspaper, had neatly captured Magda's gaze of intense concentration when she was involved in a project. It was a gaze Lacey remembered well. It was lucky, she thought, that Hansen kept voluminous photo files and had a near-photographic memory for his work.

Analiza's handmade poster issued an invitation to all of Magda's friends to attend the memorial. The small room was full when Lacey arrived. The racks of costumes had been pushed to the walls under the unseeing eyes of the wig heads, and five rows of folding chairs had been set up in the middle of the shop facing a tiny podium borrowed from a theatre. They weren't enough; the crowd of clients, neighbors, and friends jammed the place shoulder to shoulder.

Lacey stood in the back, wearing her black Bentley suit from the 1940s, one of her most treasured vintage outfits from Aunt Mimi. Magda had admired the suit's amazing lines and tailoring. Lacey could not bring herself to wear the corset, not even underneath the suit, no matter what kind of guilt trip her corset-loving stylist tried to induce. She spied Stella across the room, wearing her idea of a compromise, a black leather jacket and skirt ensemble worn with a scarlet corset. She was flanked by Stylettos' assistant manager, Michelle, and another stylist, both in similar get-ups. More people arrived as a young woman Lacey didn't recognize strummed a guitar and started to sing something she said was a Latvian folk hymn.

Magda would be pleased to see how many people showed up, Lacey thought, but she wondered what the deceased would make of her motley crew of mourners. Analiza was in black, wearing what looked suspiciously like a costume from the "what to wear to a funeral if you're *theatrical!*" collection. Magda had often complained that Analiza "wore the inventory," adding to the wear and tear on the costumes they rented and sold for a living. But today, the woman looked sadly charming, if rather lost, in a flowing black dress with a fitted bodice that laced up into a modified corset. It had a romantic handkerchief hem and long, dipped sleeves. She wore her tangle of red curls loose, restrained only by a black silk orchid behind one ear. The full effect of Analiza's outfit, Lacey thought, was rather like a slightly deranged Ophelia attending Hamlet's funeral; that is, if Shakespeare had seen fit to let her live to the end of the play.

Looking like she was channeling a *Breakfast at Tiffany's* vibe, Natalija Krumina turned heads in a sleek sleeveless black dress. She rushed toward Analiza and embraced her like a sister. Lacey noticed both women's eyes were dry. She sat down to listen to the service.

The first speaker was a very grand local actress of a certain age, wearing one of Magda's elaborate Victorian gowns from her role as Lady Bracknell in a Washington production of *The Importance of Being Earnest.* She gathered up her voluminous skirts and declaimed for the mourners a selection of famous theatrical quotes and comments on costume, clothing, and fashion, concluding with several epigrams from Oscar Wilde. "Fashion," she quoted the great Irish playwright, "is what one wears oneself. What is unfashionable is what other people wear." Furthermore, as Wilde said, "One should either *be* a work of art, or *wear* a work of art," and she noted to general laughter that "while many of Magda's clients might not be themselves great works of art, at least they could wear them, courtesy of dear Magda."

The other mourners included a woman Stella introduced to Lacey as Jolene Franklin, a strikingly well-tended blond beauty.

Stella had described Jolene privately to Lacey as a very high-priced Washington call girl who thought nothing of special-ordering five-hundred-dollar corsets from Magda, sometimes three or four at a time. She looked as regal as an expensive trophy wife. In her mid-thirties, Jolene Franklin was studying to be a stockbroker under her real name, whatever that was. Even Stella, the gossip bureau for the Dupont Circle hairstyling world, didn't know. She also had some Latvian connection, Stella said, but she couldn't recall what it was. Lacey admired the warmth and solidarity of Magda's ethnic community. The Latvians, it seemed, had hung together after emigrating to America. Although Magda grew up in France, had spoken French from birth, and considered herself a Frenchwoman, her Latvian ties seemed stronger.

The stunning black woman who went by the name Sylvania was another top-drawer call girl. She and Jolene often worked together, Stella said, entertaining lobbyists, diplomats, and politicians. Sitting together cozily, they presented an elegant salt and pepper set, the blond Jolene dressed all in black, and Sylvania, her chromatic opposite, wearing a tailored suit as white as the driven snow. Lacey wondered whether this appearance fell under the heading of advertising, or perhaps they were off to a joint assignation after the service.

Lacey also recognized several other actors, including two young women who had each been nominees for the Helen Hayes Award, Washington's version of the Tony Award. Magda had fitted them for costumes while Lacey watched, marveling once again at how some actresses could transform themselves into fabulous creatures on stage and yet be content to look like an unmade bed offstage. They wore no makeup and shambled into the shop in black jeans and Doc Martens, T-shirts and flip-flops. Even though it was November and the temperature a scant 60 degrees, they apparently weren't giving up their offstage casual wear for a mere memorial service. No doubt that was fine with Magda, Lacey reflected, who often saw her clients at their most vulnerable. She worked her costumer's magic to cover up their inadequacies with just the right undergarment, just the right perfectly turned-out gown or costume.

"See how they need me," she might say. "You are what you wear, eh, Lacey?" If she were here, she would be thinking how to costume them properly for this very event. Lacey smiled at the thought.

Detective Broadway Lamont sidled his bulk up to Lacey. "Any

fashion clues I should know about?" he asked with his big deadpan face.

"Only fashion crimes," she said. "Lots of them. Are the toxicology tests in? What about the dagger?"

"What world you live in, Smithsonian? Does look like poison, though. Don't know which one yet."

She nodded. The room had grown quiet for the next speaker. Analiza Zarina stood at the podium and launched into a long, rambling reminiscence about her late business partner Magda and the various shows they had costumed and the local celebrities they had supplied with custom-made gowns and corsets. "We were as close as sisters," Analiza said. "Closer." None of the familiar siblinglike banter that Lacey had witnessed was apparent in her words today.

Lacey had brought a copy of her latest column to give to Analiza, the one about Magda, but she was unprepared when the woman called on her next to say a few words about the deceased.

Stella dragged Lacey up to the podium. "Go up there and tell all these people about Magda, Lace, the way only you can." A genius at mixing guilt and flattery, Stella uttered a few words of her own and then turned to Lacey. Thankful at least that Stella had passed up the opportunity to show the gathered crowd all the intimate intricacies of corsetry using her own ensemble as an instructive example, Lacey cleared her throat, took a deep breath, and called on her long-ago college acting experience. She spread her column on the podium and read from it.

CRIMES OF FASHION

Behind the Seams: Corsetiere Magda Rousseau Slain

By Lacey Smithsonian

"Bloody thread, knock 'em dead." Everyone who knew Magda Rousseau has heard her say that. The saying comes, she said, from an old tradition among theatrical costumers, a belief that if the seamstress accidentally pricks her finger and spills a drop of her blood on a costume, the show will be a hit. "Bloody stitch, all get rich" is another version of the same saying. "Prick a finger," Magda told me, is to a costumer a good-luck wish akin to telling an actor to "Break a leg."

Magda pointed out that it was impossible, of course, not to prick your fingers while sewing so many elaborate costumes under the short deadlines of the theatre world, so nearly every costume holds a tiny good-luck drop of the seamstress's blood. And along with that drop of blood, Magda always poured her heart and soul into her work. She died this week in her costume shop in the District, still pouring her heart and soul into her work.

Our community is diminished by the loss of Magda Rousseau. You may not have known her, but if you attend Washington theatre, you have seen her work on stages around town for many years. An artist with a needle, a poet in fabric, a corsetiere of the old school with a loyal clientele, Magda was also a stern taskmistress and a loving friend who . . .

Lacey finished her reading and sat down to appreciative murmurs from the other mourners, only to be corrected by another costumer. A large woman in a black corset bodice gown stood up to lecture her that the correct saying was actually "bloody dress, good press," a play, she elaborated, on a phrase that actors say but don't really believe, "bad dress, good press," referring to a show's dress rehearsal. If that rehearsal is dreadful, she said, it's thought to predict that the press notices for the show will be glowing. The woman then went on to lodge a vociferous complaint about the new theatre critic of *The Eye,* whom she called "the Butcher of the Beltway," one of Mac's new hires whom Lacey hadn't even met yet, but whose assaults on local theatre were apparently all Lacey's fault as the Voice of *The Eye.*

This was a good time to exit, Lacey decided. She slipped into the crowd and out the shop door while the large costumer was still haranguing the other mourners. While she was reading from her column, Stella and the other stylists had rushed back for their afternoon shift at Stylettos, leaving Lacey without a ride to *The Eye.* Now she stood on the sidewalk and pawed through her purse, looking for her MetroCard, resolving fervently to buy another car soon, very soon. Lacey barely registered that the November day was heartbreakingly beautiful. Colors exploded on maple trees and the sky was Queen of Heaven blue. She finally extracted a crumpled Metro card from the outside pocket of her purse and turned to go.

"Lacey Smithsonian?" someone asked in an elegant British accent.

Chapter 10

Lacey looked up at the man standing in her light. His silhouette was tall and thin, and he was wearing a khaki trench coat over a charcoal V-neck sweater and gray slacks. She didn't know him.

"You are, of course, the famous Lacey Smithsonian." He flashed a smile. His teeth were good, she thought, for a Brit. She sighed. Someone with a complaint about her column, she assumed.

"I'm afraid I'm the only Lacey Smithsonian, famous or not."

"Lovely tribute to our dear Magda. Your piece went over well. You have a beautiful voice, by the way."

" 'Our' dear Magda? I didn't see you up there. And who are you?"

"Pardon me." He offered her his hand. Good handshake, she thought. For a Brit. "Griffin."

"Griffin? Mythological beast? Half lion, half eagle?"

"Two beasts for the price of one." Griffin was very nice looking in a well-bred, understated English way, with short light brown hair and hazel eyes. "Forgive me, Lacey, may I call you Lacey? Smithsonian is such a mouthful. We must talk. Would you mind having coffee with me?" She hesitated. "I see your friends have all left. That leaves me. A poor substitute, I'm afraid, but I am a mythological being, after all. Shall we?"

Lacey had been in Washington so long she couldn't tell whether he was flirting or not. "Why?" Was he some kind of cop? Detective Broadway Lamont had disappeared too, so probably not. He didn't look or talk like a cop. "What about?"

"You knew Magda," he began. "She must have mentioned—I need to ask you about—" He didn't seem to know what to say for a moment. Lacey's defenses went on alert. Maybe he was worse than a cop. Maybe he was another reporter, a competitor, even a hack for Damon Newhouse's Conspiracy Clearinghouse. If so, he wasn't getting anything out of her.

"What do you do, Mr. Griffin?"

"Nigel, please. Nigel Griffin. And what do I do? It's fascinating. Let me buy you coffee. You must be curious. I know I am."

"Five minutes. I choose the place. I leave when I'm ready to leave."

"You don't trust me?"

"Would *you* trust you?"

"Well, no, but that's just me. I'm suspicious by nature. But to allay your dark suspicions, Lacey, I'll get to the point. Just between us, it's about the jewels."

Lacey's heart lurched. *Oh, God, what does he know?* "Jewels?" She tried to look appropriately clueless. *So he isn't flirting. Had Magda told everyone?* Or had he read that the body was covered with fake jewels? That detail was in the paper. "I haven't the slightest idea what you're talking about. But I will let you buy me coffee and a pastry and you can tell me." *He won't be the first to assume I'm just a dumb reporter. Especially if he's a dumb reporter too.*

Nigel Griffin frowned momentarily, scanning what was left of the crowd dispersing from the memorial, as if there might be someone there more interesting, who might have more promising information. But then he brightened. "Of course. Lead on, please, Lacey. Your choice."

They walked down several blocks without a word and found a coffee shop that wasn't part of a chain. She ordered a latte and a pricey piece of cheesecake. He did the same, and they found a table near the window where she could look out on Pennsylvania Avenue. Lacey was careful to take the seat nearest the door.

Griffin stretched his long legs under the table, almost reaching Lacey's feet. She adjusted her chair to make sure there would be no playing footsie. He laughed.

"Don't play the coy one with me, Smithsonian. I know all about you."

"I doubt that." She busied herself with putting sugar in her coffee.

"Oh, but I do. From your news clippings. And that Web site. What's the name of it?" He paused while she waited for the inevitable mention of Conspiracy Clearinghouse's Web address. "DeadFed dot com. That's the one," he said triumphantly. "You're so often their star attraction."

She set her coffee cup down. "Are you sure you don't work for them?" Her name had been splashed in too many headlines by Damon Newhouse, Brooke's crazy co-conspirator.

"Me? No. Might be fun, though. If I could write, which I can't.

That is, I can read and write, of course—I'm quite an educated fellow—but I'm not a writer. And DeadFed makes you sound positively like a wild woman." He looked at her carefully. "I must say I'm surprised to find you so— Ah, what's the word? Demure. You look as if you're having tea with the queen."

"You do know DeadFed is all crap?"

"Surely not all crap. I gather your speciality is stabbing people," Griffin continued, waving his plastic knife at her. "But can your sister Cherise really knock a man out with a cheerleader's kick?"

Leave my sister out of this! "Would you like a personal demonstration?"

"Tempting, but no thanks." He paused. "As I was saying, you must know about the treasure old Magda had in her sights. Worth a king's ransom, you know." He slurped his coffee.

"A treasure?" Lacey let her eyes light up facetiously, even as her stomach sank. "Ooh, tell me about her treasure. Was that why she lived like a queen?" *Damn it, Magda! Who else did you tell? What did you say? Does the whole damned world know by now?*

"The act's not funny, Smithsonian. You know what I'm talking about."

She took a bite of cheesecake. Analiza was hosting a small private luncheon after the memorial, to which apparently neither she nor Nigel Griffin had been invited, and she was hungry. "No, really, what treasure? Tell me." She leaned forward eagerly. "I'm dying to know."

"I don't believe you." He folded his arms grumpily. "Don't play with me."

"What kind of treasure? Did she keep cash under the mattress? I'd love to know."

He shifted in his seat. "If you know nothing about the treasure, what were you doing with Magda?"

"My job, of course. The fashion beat. I was documenting the nearly lost art of the old-school corsetiere." Lacey forked another bite of cheesecake. "Writing a feature story on a brilliant seamstress."

"That's all? You visited her on numerous occasions. Deep into the night."

"Is that right? Have you been stalking me?"

"Stalking is such an ugly word. I just happen to know, that's all."

Who the hell is this guy? "What business is it of yours?"

"I'm a knowledgeable fellow." He smiled. "I like to know things."

"If you must know, my friend Stella dragged me there. I

decided to work up a feature story on Magda, and well, one thing led to another, and—"

"Yes?"

Lacey hoped to make him uncomfortable, put him on edge. "It takes a few fittings to get a corset to fit exactly the way you want. It's tricky."

A glimmer of interest lit his eyes. "Demure little Lacey Smithsonian? You? In a corset?"

She lifted her coffee cup, along with one eyebrow. "Like I said, it takes awhile. There are all sorts of intimate details to work out."

"Any details you'd like to share?"

"Wouldn't you like to know."

"I would. As a matter of fact, I'm picturing it now." He lifted his latte in a salute.

"Well, stop it before you go blind. Now tell me about this alleged treasure."

"You found her and she was draped in jewels. According to your story."

"Stage jewels. But that was all in the paper."

"And DeadFed," Griffin reminded her. "Do you think they were some sort of message?"

"Enough footsie. Who are you, Griffin, and what exactly do you do?"

"As I said, Nigel Griffin by name, and I am, for lack of a better term, a professional jewel retriever by trade—or in this case, a finder of lost treasure."

"Really? Who do you work for?" She leaned forward. "How did you get into this line of work? Is there health insurance?"

"Ah. Afraid I don't know you well enough to spill all my secrets, Lacey. But give me some time. If we were working together, we might share all sorts of intimacies."

I don't think so. "What sort of lost treasure?" Her heart was beating faster.

"That's the problem," he said, leaning forward in his chair. He scanned two people who just walked into the coffee shop. They looked anonymous. He returned his gaze to Lacey. "I'm not quite sure, but it's Russian, something dating from the Revolution or before, I know that much. It could even be—" His voice dropped to a whisper. "A Fabergé egg. And that would be unbelievable. In my field, it could make a man's reputation."

He struck her, Lacey decided, as a man who already had a reputation. *A bad one.*

"Could one little Fabergé egg be that valuable?"

"My dear Smithsonian, please tell me you are not that naive. Every one of the fifty original imperial Fabergé eggs is worth millions. Eight are unaccounted for." He leaned in close, his eyes gleaming dangerously. "You could use a million or so, couldn't you? Tax-free? And can you imagine solving that mystery? An adventure of, well, if not a lifetime, then at least this year."

"But you said it might not be a Fabergé egg." She toyed with her cheesecake. Griffin arched an eyebrow at her and gazed away into some other world, where Fabergé eggs danced before his eyes.

"So Madame Rousseau never said anything to you?"

"I'd remember the part about a Fabergé egg. I'm pretty sure of it."

Griffin sighed in exasperation. "I am a retriever of jewels, I am not a psychic divining rod for them. Come on, Smithsonian, what did she tell you? Worth your while, I promise you."

"Magda talked about fabric, not Fabergé. Did she look like someone who had a Fabergé egg hidden in her sewing kit? Living in that little cubbyhole over her shop? So tell me, how did you fall into this line of work? And why aren't you better at it?"

"Long story, luv. You'll have to get to know me better." Lacey arched an eyebrow at him in turn. "A partnership, Smithsonian, not a love affair. Sorry to disappoint." He stretched back in his chair. "You're not exactly my type. Too refined. Too demure."

"You are just too charming, you know that, Nigel Griffin?"

"Just telling it like it is. I'm a one-night-stand kind of guy. I'm cheap. Despite my dashing good looks." He pulled out a pack of cigarettes and fished through his pockets for matches. Lacey riveted him with a glare. He sighed and put them away.

"No smoking in here, right? You Yanks have gone so puritan these days."

"Is this babbling going anywhere? I have a job, you know, I am not a freelance Fabergé egg finder on some fat expense account, unlike some people."

"I'm very good at what I do." He straightened up and stared at her. "You're quite good at stabbing bad guys, so I understand."

"Only two! I only stabbed two of them." *Must everyone always bring that up?*

"Alas, your mother and sister helped you out of that jam before you could stab the third one. I was counting on it. Three stabbings would look so much more impressive on your résumé as a semiprofessional assistant jewel retriever."

"Not funny. And why would I need to stab anyone anyway?"

"This project could get difficult. We should be working together, not against each other. There's another chap interested in the egg or whatever it is as well, a hard case, a hit man, ex-KGB—"

"KGB!" she yelped. Several people stared.

"Shall I get you a microphone? The chap in the back corner didn't hear you."

Lacey lowered her voice. "How do you know that?"

"Word gets around in the jewel-retrieving biz. He's a nasty bit of work, I hear."

"And you think I'm loony enough to get involved with you and this—? What's this spy's name?"

"He goes by the name Gregor Kepelov. One of his names, at any rate. You may have seen it on DeadFed." He drummed his fingers on the table.

"Here's a news flash, Nigel Griffin. Take DeadFed with a grain. Two grains. Of anything you like."

He shrugged. "Kepelov surfaced a couple of months ago in the U.S. Why? Well, when he's not killing people, he hunts for Fabergé eggs, or anything Romanov, for private Russian collectors, who pay well. Very well. Kepelov is not above— Well, he's not above anything, or so I'm told."

"Oh, my God! Are you telling me this is why Magda was killed? Some idiot was looking for a nonexistent Fabergé egg?" *Magda, you fool!* She had said she always thought her grandfather had stolen a Fabergé egg, until she inherited his diary and discovered it was the corset. *Who knows how many people heard her say the words "Fabergé egg"?*

"I didn't say he killed her, but if he did— Well, the thrill of danger, eh?" He swigged the last of his latte. "You and I need each other."

"You don't seem all that concerned."

"Me? I'm a pro. Nerves of steel and all that." He yawned. "Besides, Kepelov doesn't know me, I haven't run into Kepelov, and I don't have the egg. Yet."

Either he really doesn't know it's a corset or he's stringing me along. Lacey stood up and wiped her hands. "Well, neither do I. Nor do I want a Fabergé egg. So long, Nigel Griffin."

"Remember, my partnership offer is still open. You probably know things you don't even suspect you know. All those late nights, just you and Magda and her little stories? I'll be in touch."

"I won't be home." She walked out the door. "Mythological beast indeed."

chapter 11

"We may have trouble," Lacey told Brooke that evening. "So you can back out now if you want." She was standing on Brooke's front porch under a yellow light after paying her cabdriver. She had changed taxis twice to make sure she wasn't followed.

"Back out? What kind of friend do you take me for?" Brooke answered the door barefoot in a T-shirt and jeans. Her blond hair had escaped its braid. "I'm packing now. You can help."

"I have to go home soon and pack myself. But I want you to consider the option of staying home instead of going to France with me."

Brooke waved her inside. "What's going on?"

Lacey's friend lived in a redbrick town house in Arlington, situated in a little box canyon of town houses for the young and upwardly mobile. Most of Brooke's rooms were sparsely furnished, as the young barrister had little time to decorate and spent much of her free time at either Lacey's place or Damon's. She told Lacey, tongue in cheek, that her nondecorating style gave the place "an airy Zen minimalist kind of look." Lacey thought it simply looked as if no one lived there. A leather sofa and chair huddled forlornly in the big empty living room. The dining room table showed signs of life, covered with briefs and books, facing a giant wall-mounted flat-screen TV set nearly always tuned to CNN, like so many homes of Washington, D.C., news junkies.

The place was roomy and expensive, but it left Lacey cold. Upstairs in the master bedroom it was better. Lacey envied Brooke's not one but two big walk-in closets with built-in cabinets and shoe racks and padded hangers for her expensive and beautifully tailored—though Lacey thought mostly bland—work wardrobe. The sumptuous bathroom, with its separate shower stall and tub with built-in Jacuzzi, called to her. It said, "You're the one who chose journalism, you chump." Lacey knew her career would never let her afford a place like Brooke Barton's. Not unless there were a lost—and found—treasure in her future.

The bedroom was in an uproar, with clothes covering most horizontal surfaces, but something seemed different. "You've changed things," Lacey commented. Brooke's utilitarian beige ripcord bedspread had been replaced by a sumptuous pale moss-green brocade comforter and cushy extra pillows. A new chaise lounge in a creamy gold velvet looked positively decadent by Brooke's standards. And the walls were no longer white but a soft sage color, the woodwork painted bright white.

"Do you like it?" Brooke asked, throwing herself on the chaise.

"It's gorgeous," Lacey said. "A complete mantrap."

"Just what I was aiming for. Speaking of men, are you sure we can't take Damon along?"

"Not a good idea. Really." Lacey felt herself go pale. "We've gone over this."

Brooke sighed and rose from the chaise. "Spoilsport. Okay, you're the fashion reporter. Tell me what to wear. Paris in November? That's when it drizzles, right? How does that song go?"

"You're not focusing, Brooke. I said we have trouble. Usually news of a charming mysterious stranger and a dangerous former KGB agent would have you delirious with conspiratorial glee."

Brooke focused in a hurry. "Did you say KGB?"

Lacey gave her the thumbnail version of her coffee shop encounter with Nigel Griffin. "So he gave me some mumbo jumbo about being a jewel retriever, a freelance soldier of fortune type of thing. But I think he's a jewel thief."

"Is he handsome?" Brooke asked, obviously tapping into the Hollywood fantasy that jewel thieves are urbane and sophisticated.

"He's not Cary Grant, but he's okay for a Brit. Not my type. Smooth but shallow."

"A handsome British jewel thief? Intriguing. And you say shallow like it's a bad thing. Something Griffin, you said?"

"Nigel Griffin. He wants to get his hands on the corset. He wants me to help."

"He knows about the corset?"

"No, actually he thinks it might be a Fabergé egg or something."

"Fabergé egg? Interesting. Do you think this character is dangerous?" She held up a red sweater for Lacey to approve for Paris.

"Everyone is dangerous, and just how much do you intend to

pack?" Lacey nixed the sweater—it was the wrong red for Brooke's coloration. "We'll only be there a week."

"You're right. Tell me about the KGB spy."

"He's an out-of-work hit man. Dangerous, according to Griffin, who's probably a liar."

"Do you have a name?"

"Gregor Kepelov. That's all I know. Ring any bells?"

"No bells. And what kind of reporter are you?" Brooke held up a gray sweater for approval. "Haven't you Googled him yet? Or checked DeadFed?"

"No, you're the Google queen here. After a day at work, I am sick of Googling. That's all Griffin told me, and you don't look your best in gray." Lacey figured if the name Gregor Kepelov was known on the Web, Brooke would have picked up on it from her obsessive reading of the DeadFed Web site. "Griffin was just playing with me, a fishing expedition to see what I know. For all I know, he's the ex-KGB guy himself."

"Kepelov." Brooke flew to her laptop, which was under a stack of jeans, turned it on and logged onto DeadFed dot com's allegedly secure subscriber server. Brooke had full privileges. She typed for awhile, while Lacey took her ease on the chaise and admired Brooke's new decor.

"There's nothing on a Gregor Kepelov, as a name or a code name or a cover name. No known KGB guys with a name like it. There are several Gregors, but I think it's a pretty common Russian name. Nothing on any Nigel Griffin, either. Maybe a phony name?"

"Maybe Kepelov is really good," Lacey suggested. "Or maybe it's all just a lie by Mr. Griffin calculated to, I don't know, scare me into telling him everything I know."

"We've got to send this Griffin character off in the wrong direction. It'll be fun!"

"If I contact him now with some phony clue, it'll be obvious that I'm trying to play him."

Brooke turned from her computer. "I guess so. But if he can't trust you, wouldn't he have to go check it out anyway?"

"Trust me. It's better to play dumb. And he may be smarter than he looks. Or acts."

"Maybe you're right. But he is a man. Men can be fooled. Therefore Griffin can be fooled. A syllogism."

"We'll be on the plane tomorrow. All we really have to do is get on without him. He can wander around town here looking for me.

We'll have a head start in France." Lacey looked at what Brooke was packing and realized she would have to take her friend's wardrobe choices into her own hands. She began a colorful "Pack" pile and a colorless "Leave" pile. "Please add some color, Brooke, we're talking Paris here, not Washington! Remember: Woman does not impress by Burberry alone. And Brooke, it really could be dangerous. The trip, not your clothes."

"Don't worry, I'll bring lots of money. If nothing else, we'll buy our way out of trouble. And we can buy new wardrobes too. In Paris."

Lacey grinned at her. "Funny, why didn't I think of that?"

"And Daddy knows the U.S. ambassador there. He's already in my cell phone. Now, what did you say I should pack? Subtle, right? Subdued and inconspicuous? Like a spy?"

"Well, Brooke, you may dress to disappear into the drizzle if you like. But not me. I plan to dress to make Paris sizzle."

Lacey planned on dressing for an adventure. And dressing like an adventuress. *When handsome jewel thieves follow you around and beg to buy you coffee and a Danish,* she thought, *it's too late for anonymity. Might as well knock their eyes out.*

Lacey Smithsonian's

FASHION BITES

Bored With Dress for Success? Try for Adventuress Instead

You dressed for success, but where has it gotten you? Your own cubicle next to someone dressed just like you in a cubicle just like yours? You've got the same safe suit, the same knock-off bag, the same pair of pumps you both snagged at Filene's Basement at the same sale. You call that success?

The working world is not exactly the fantasy we dreamed of in college, is it? Once upon a time we thought life would be an adventure, exciting, stimulating, fulfilling. Don't forget fulfilling. Possibly even fun. Well, it can be, if you approach it the right way. As an adventure.

But perhaps you feel invisible. Your clothes are fading away and taking you with them. No one can see you, you're so well hidden in your dress-for-success camouflage. Your shoes match the carpet, your skirt blends into the chair, your blouse copies the curtains. Where's the real you concealed behind the corporate camo? Unless your secret ambition is to star in a remake of *The Invisible Woman*, you and your wardrobe need a shot of pure adrenaline.

Need a little adventure? My advice: Dress like an adventuress. An adventuress knows that the right clothes can change your attitude faster than your attitude can change your clothes. To find the adventure in life, sometimes all you need to do is dress for adventure and let it find you. Let's look at three basics in every adventuress's rolling suitcase.

- A trench coat, of course. Well-worn and rakishly scruffy or brand-new, it should fit perfectly, whether you're built like Ingrid Bergman or Sydney Greenstreet. These days it even comes in daring postmodern pinks and blues and greens, not just the traditional World War I khaki. Long or short, the trench coat is dashing, versatile, and ready for a trip to the office or around the world. Even to Casablanca. ("For the waters," of course.)

- Sunglasses. Every adventure calls for a sleek pair of sunglasses. They protect your eyes and keep your secrets. No secrets to keep? They'll even keep that secret, too. Slip on your shades and *voilà!* A woman of mystery. Think *Thelma and Louise* or Kathleen Turner on the beach in *Body Heat.* Just try to stay out of trouble this time.
- A scarf. A sophisticated adventuress needs a bright and colorful scarf, and she actually knows how to tie it cleverly. (Or she fakes it.) Not only does it liven up that same old suit, it blows in the wind as you speed away in your convertible up the hills of Monte Carlo like Grace Kelly with that handsome jewel thief Cary Grant at your side. Don't have a Cary Grant type handy? Let your beautiful scarf fly; he may find you.

Adventure is, of course, whatever you want it to be. Living your life on your own terms and with your own style can be the biggest adventure of all. Just imagine looking the way you've always dreamed you'd look when you open the door to that big moment and say, "Come on in, I'm ready." And imagine a confident, self-possessed woman striding down the street to meet that big moment, so intriguing that heads turn as she passes by. Who is that adventurous woman? *It's you!*

chapter 12

"Brooke, stop looking for spies! You look too much like a spy yourself."

Lest they be followed to Europe by the mysterious Griffin or Kepelov or suspicious persons unknown, Lacey and Brooke had taken great care not to be tailed to the airport at Dulles. Lacey was now carefully assessing the other passengers as they stood in line to go through security. She had seen no one she knew aside from Brooke, whose excitement at joining this adventure was palpable. Nevertheless, Lacey was half afraid Damon Newhouse or one of his DeadFed operatives would appear out of nowhere. Brooke was still under attorney-client privilege as per Lacey's stipulation. She swore she hadn't told Damon a word about their real plan, but she warned Lacey that Damon might suspect there was more to this trip than just a Paris pleasure jaunt to heal Lacey's heartbreak.

"I can't be responsible for what he might actually think," Brooke said. "This was rather a sudden decision, you know, you running off to Paris just to get over a man. It's a stretch."

"I still can't believe you told Damon that I was heartbroken over Vic."

"Oh, he does believe that part. I had to make it good enough to convince him."

"But I'm not heartbroken. Exactly. I'm feeling more— liberated. That's it. Liberated."

"Whatever. Do you think there's any chance we're being followed?" Brooke looked furtively around over her dark glasses.

"Knock it off, spy girl. I want to get through security without a strip search." Brooke was unloading her laptop and related electronics to pile them on the conveyor belt. Lacey had her ticket and passport ready and she removed her boots to have them irradiated by the X-ray machine, while the surly TSA screeners were no doubt being irradiated in the process. She hated this part of airline travel. She consoled herself that beyond this point their fellow travelers were unlikely to be armed with so much as a sharp pair of tweezers, though she was less confident the TSA could keep something like a rocket launcher off the plane.

Brooke and Lacey both wore black slacks and sweaters. Brooke, because black made her feel like a secret agent, and Lacey, because they were flattering and comfortable. At least half of their fellow passengers were dressed similarly, or else in the bland beige and gray D.C. uniform. Brooke carried her Burberry trench coat and tote bag with all her electronic toys. Lacey carried a smaller tote bag and a dark red leather jacket, purchased under duress on a recent shopping trip with Stella. Its sleek lines emphasized her small waist and the buttery smooth leather was pure luxury. The jacket was beautiful, but way too expensive. Lacey had decided she should never go shopping with Stella again. She had no idea how many times she'd promised herself that in the last few months following the baby-blue custom-made corset episode.

Ahead of Lacey in the security line, a large man stood out in the crowd, wearing a straw cowboy hat jammed down on his head and a turquoise-and-pink Hawaiian shirt, his fleece-lined jean jacket folded atop his briefcase, which bore a DON'T MESS WITH TEXAS bumper sticker. Lacey mentally dubbed him "Tex." With his well-muscled rodeo cowboy body and his handlebar mustache, Tex looked like he broke broncos. Except for the shirt; the shirt didn't go with the rest of the picture. She'd never seen a cowboy in a Hawaiian shirt. *Maybe a cowboy on vacation?* Lacey decided Tex, with his showy handlebar mustache, was just too flashy and obvious. He didn't even try to blend in; bad form for a spy or a jewel thief. *Probably a Washington lobbyist for Texas cattlemen*, Lacey concluded, *off on a taxpayer-supported spree in Paris.*

Retrieving her bag and boots from the conveyor belt, Lacey grabbed Brooke and they finally made it to their gate. Brooke confided that Dulles was positively the most irritating airport on earth. They took their seats at the gate with a view of the ugly Dulles tarmac and waited.

A large blond woman sat down next to them. Brooke eyed her warily. The woman's florid complexion clashed with her brassy hair in a puffy suburban mom style. Lacey named her "Madge." She was dressed in jeans and white sneakers and a blue-and-white striped top, eschewing the conventional wisdom about weight and horizontal stripes not being a good mix. She pulled out a *National Enquirer* and started reading. *Definitely not a spy,* Lacey thought.

Several groggy barely-twenty-somethings with greasy black hair cut into outdated shags with a punky edge stood around complaining. They looked too young to be flying to Europe on their own. Lacey called them "Winken, Blinken, and Nod." But they swore with real bravado, creating their own foul-mouthed protective shield. Other travelers kept their distance. Probably not spies; probably never even heard of Fabergé eggs, Lacey mused. *They'd think it was the breakfast special: You want those eggs scrambled, fried, or Fabergé?* Lacey told herself to stop this nonsense. Simply sharing Brooke's airspace, she decided, could really ratchet up the paranoia.

As they boarded, her attention was caught by a group of interchangeable middle-aged businessmen sauntering on to first class. These forgettable guys in their gray suits and white shirts were by far the most likely candidates to be secret agents, she thought, but they seemed to be together and they didn't even toss a glance her way. *But then, would a real spy wink and wave at his target?* She sighed. Rounding off the group of passengers were several older women and men who looked like ordinary, everyday grade-A American tourists with their eye-popping neon Day-Glo running suits and gaudy tote bags. They were complaining loudly about the exchange rate of the euro. *If these people are spies,* Lacey thought, *my mother is a spy.*

Brooke darted suspicious glances at her fellow passengers, then she opened her laptop and settled down to a flurry of e-mailing until takeoff. Lacey reassured herself that Nigel Griffin wasn't on the plane. And although she had no idea what Kepelov might look like, she didn't have a good candidate for an ex-KGB agent on board.

Once the flight got underway, they each settled in for the seven-hour-plus journey across the Atlantic. Brooke devoured an autobiography by a former master of disguise for the CIA. Lacey listened to her French language instructional CDs until she fell asleep during the lesson on how to order a meal in a French brasserie. She dreamed she was in the Hall of Mirrors at Versailles and she was ordering the Fabergé eggs for breakfast, pleased that this would solve the whole mystery. They arrived at her table looking like hard-boiled eggs wearing little jeweled corsets, and then the orchestra began to play and the eggs all danced in a chorus line. When she woke up her back was stiff from the cramped airplane seat, and they were still hours away from Paris.

* * *

The green-and-white-shuttered Hotel Mouton Vert was located in a quiet neighborhood in Montparnasse in the fourteenth arrondissement of Paris. It was a quaint little two-star hotel. Lacey thought it was adorable. Brooke sniffed. Two-star accommodations were beneath her status as a Washington lawyer, but she was willing to camp out there and rough it for the sake of the mission. She and Lacey had rooms across the hall from each other on the fifth floor, accessed by a narrow winding staircase or a minuscule elevator that barely held two people and their suitcases.

It was already early evening in Paris. They planned to settle into the hotel for the first night and sleep through their jet lag and stiff muscles before picking up the rental car the next day. Although Lacey was willing to take the bus to Mont-Saint-Michel, as Magda had planned to do, Brooke insisted on the car. She pointed out that the farmhouse they were looking for was unlikely to have a bus stop nearby. Lacey gave mass transit one last push as they rode up in the dark, creaky elevator.

"Wouldn't the bus be easier? And safer? Driving here is suicidal." They were to pick up the car at the rental office near the Arc de Triomphe, and Lacey had seen pictures of the traffic there. It looked completely insane.

"Do you know how many hours the bus takes to get to Mont-Saint-Michel? We'd be sitting ducks. And Paris traffic is really no worse than Washington. I've driven here before."

"But won't we be sitting ducks in a car?"

"Ha! Not the way I drive. I drive like a Frenchman. I take no prisoners. Off with their heads!"

"I'm keeping my eyes closed."

"You'll see. We'll leave spies and jewel thieves and government agents in our dust."

"You love making this stuff up, don't you, Brooke? Helps the day go by in your gray-flannel offices, is that it? Thinking you're at the mercy of some mad conspiracy? Not me. I like to think that I'm safe. That I live in a benevolent universe." She leaned against the elevator wall.

"But we're not safe. We don't know how many people are involved in Magda Rousseau's murder. We don't know if they know what we know. Or more. They could be all around us."

"Magda was not a foreign agent. She was a seamstress. Last month you were convinced a supermodel was killed by the 'Government Repossessors.' Logo the Grim Reaper, code name GR, government assassins on the prowl to repossess rogue agents and bionic women gone bad."

"Just because Damon hasn't proven it yet, doesn't mean it isn't so."

"You know not every single word on DeadFed is true," Lacey insisted. "Don't you?"

Slamming Damon's pet Conspiracy Clearinghouse came dangerously close to fighting words, but Brooke took it in stride. "We're going after the prize, Lacey. Imagine the headlines when we find the truth. MYSTERY HIDDEN FOR CENTURY UNCOVERED IN BLOODY CORSET OF ROMANOVS."

"I'm imagining the headline in *The Eye Street Observer.* SMITHSONIAN FALLS ON FACE. AGAIN."

The elevator door opened and they got out, bumping their suitcases together. A middle-aged woman burdened with a heavy-looking bag was trudging slowly toward them down the narrow hall. They made room for her and Brooke eyed the woman. As the older woman boarded the elevator and the doors closed behind her, Lacey whispered, "Don't worry, I'm sure spies only stay at three-star hotels or higher. They have a union."

Brooke rolled her eyes. She opened the door to her room and they both peered inside. "Lacey, my closet at home is bigger than this. So you're probably right. No one could hide in here. I think we're safe for now." Brooke opened the closet wide and checked under the bed.

"I'll see you at breakfast, then," Lacey said.

"No, I preordered *petit déjeuner* delivered to my room. What the heck—it's included in the price. Must account for the second star. *Bonne nuit.*" Brooke smiled and shut the door, and Lacey heard the locks click into place.

She opened the door to her own room and clicked on the light. The room, in shades of rose and burgundy, was adorable, though also quite small, with just enough space to walk around the bed. It had two great features, a bathroom with a decent-sized tub and shower, and tall windows with a southern exposure, letting her gaze down on the Montparnasse street scene below or into the quaint apartments across the road. She flung open the windows and leaned out.

"My God, there are no screens!" she said aloud, shocked that the de rigueur American safety features she expected were missing. A small ledge ran outside, but it would never break a fall to the street below. She had visions of French children hurling themselves out of open hotel windows. More alarmingly, she wondered if anyone could crawl in. She calmed those thoughts with a silent command to appreciate her view of Paris. Paris! She had finally made it.

The street was a charming scene from a foreign movie as it curved gently through a neighborhood of five- and six-storied buildings. They were painted white with soft pastel accent colors and featured shallow-pitched roofs and small gardens. Tiny French cars lined the sidewalk, parked bumper to bumper. The air was crisp with a hint of bread baking and garlic permeating the air from a nearby café.

Lacey backed into the room and flopped onto the double bed, which faced a pretty wood armoire, its mirrored doors hiding a television set. She should be exhilarated, she thought, but she felt slightly deflated. Maybe it was the jet lag. Or the anticlimax. "Here it is, Lacey," she said aloud. "Travel, adventure, Paris, romance. Well, maybe not romance."

The curtains fluttered slightly and the bathroom light flicked on and off. It figured she would get a room with electrical problems. But after that endless plane flight, at least she could look forward to sleeping in a bed. *A bed in Paris.*

The next morning Brooke followed the little woman who delivered the coffee and croissants right into Lacey's room, carrying her own breakfast tray. She set it down, helped herself to coffee, and poured a cup for Lacey, who slipped on a robe.

"Morning, sunshine. I forgot to ask. What do I wear today? And pack for tomorrow?"

"Just because I write a fashion column, Brooke, it doesn't mean I am a fashion expert," Lacey said, picking up the coffee and appreciating the rich aroma. "Haven't you learned by now that I make it all up?"

"But you do it so well." Brooke winked.

Lacey groaned. "We're going to be in a coal room—that is, a room in which coal was stored for a furnace or a stove. It may or may not still have coal in it. And we may or may not find this coal room. For that matter, it may or may not still even exist."

"Right. Sounds dirty. What are you wearing?"

"Jeans, black knit top, sneakers." Lacey had also stocked her purse with a reporter's absolute essentials: pen, notebook, flashlight, camera, plus one of Brooke's international cell phones. She hoped that would be enough. "I don't think you'll need the bulletproof Kevlar vest."

Brooke sighed. "Good. I hate wearing Kevlar; hides a girl's figure."

Brooke had promised to drive. And she had happily covered the rental car costs. But Lacey was unprepared for the transformation. Once she was behind the wheel, Brooke turned into a road-enraged Parisian, honking the horn to a musical beat and using rude French finger language like a native. It was true that everyone else on the rain-slick streets around the Arc de Triomphe seemed to be driving exactly the same way, but Lacey was terrified.

"You'll get us both killed," Lacey complained. "Or guillotined."

"*Mais non*, Lacey. Hold on for dear life," Brooke yelled and floored it, nosing their little rented Citroën into a millimeter of space between a tiny Renault and an even smaller Peugeot.

It was better once they were on the autoroute beyond the Périphérique, which circled Paris much as the Beltway circled Washington, D.C. Once Lacey was sure they had survived the trip across Paris and she was safe, as the lovely green countryside of Normandy passed by her window with Brooke at the wheel, she finally relaxed. And she had other things to think about. She wondered if Magda's cousin would actually allow them into the farmhouse. Magda had overruled Lacey's suggestion to call or write ahead. Magda didn't want anyone to have time to prepare for their arrival, perhaps by poking into long-sealed coal rooms. She preferred to come as a surprise.

"My cousin thinks he's an artist," Magda had said with a smile. "He's quite bad, but you must humor him or we will get nowhere."

Lacey had a letter of introduction from Magda in her bag. Magda had insisted that a letter was in order in case anything happened to her. Lacey had laughed at the old woman's caution, but now she was inclined to believe that Magda knew she was already in danger. But would a letter be enough to gain two strangers from America admittance to her cousin's home?

Lacey navigated their course from her map, and Brooke found the right exit from the autoroute and the right little country lane, only a few kilometers short of Mont-Saint-Michel. Soon a gray stone farmhouse with dark green shutters came into view, and a twinge of apprehension twisted in the pit of Lacey's stomach.

chapter 13

The man stood in the open door of the farmhouse with Magda's letter of introduction in his hand. He stared at the letter and at the two women on his doorstep.

"She is dead?"

Jean-Claude Rousseau's accent was thick, but his English was quite good. He was a dark-haired man with a mustache and glasses, who appeared to be in his late forties. His face had a comfortable lived-in look, the look of a man who liked good wine and food. He wore a clean white shirt rolled up on his forearms, jeans that sported multicolored spots of paint, and sandals, though the day was rather cool. He scratched his head.

The news of Magda's death did not seem to affect him greatly. "Dead. A pity. We write letters, Magda and I. A few letters. I have not seen her for many years," he explained with a shrug, which reminded Lacey of Magda's shrug. An elegant shrug. She should master that graceful, dismissive French shrug, Lacey thought. She could use it on Vic, if she ever saw Vic again.

Lacey complimented him on his English. He smiled. "I lived for a time in America. I spend a year there, in university," he announced with pride. "In Chicago. What a city. Lots of pizza."

"I'm sorry to have to tell you this." Lacey felt awkward, but she had to get it out. "Magda didn't die of natural causes. She was murdered, in her shop." He blinked and said nothing. Now Lacey didn't quite know how to go into the rest of the story, the poison, the knife, the jewels. She wondered whether he would invite them in; he hadn't made any move to admit them. Brooke stood by, offering silent encouragement.

"And you are Mademoiselle Lacey Smithsonian?" He looked from the letter to her.

"Yes, and my friend, Brooke Barton."

Brooke handed Jean-Claude Rousseau her card. "I'm an attorney," she said.

"And you are a journalist?" He peered over his glasses at Lacey. "*Mon Dieu.*" Ignoring the subject of Magda, he looked at them with interest. "Two Americans. And so lovely. Would you like to pose for me? Both of you? I have not painted an American woman in awhile. A very long while. And you could—"

"Ah, no, thanks," Lacey said. "We have so little time. And about Magda—"

"Ah. Magda. So. Someone murder her? Not a surprise." He snorted abruptly. "What did the old gargoyle say to you about me?"

"That you live here in Normandy," Lacey said, while Brooke choked back a nervous giggle. "And that you are an artist. A painter."

"Yes. Did she tell you that I am a bad artist?"

"Of course not," Lacey said.

"Because I am not bad. I am merely underappreciated. By people like my crazy cousin."

Lacey said nothing. Brooke looked away.

With a tremendous sigh, Jean-Claude said, "Poor Magda. Old bat. She never change, eh?" He frowned. "If I let you into my house, will you not pose for me? I paint nudes. Beautiful nudes. And some landscapes. With nudes."

Sorry Magda, she thought, *I'm not humoring your cousin that far.* "We just have so many things to do, Monsieur Rousseau. I'll be writing an article about Magda. And about you, of course. And perhaps your art? If you were to let me into the coal room. Just to take a look?"

"Ha! The coal room. So that is the story. *Ma cousine* Magda and her stupid obsession? I tell you, the woman, she was a crazy, a lunatic! *Fou!*" He clicked his tongue against his teeth. "We, her family, were afraid Magda would come to a bad end." He shrugged elegantly, folded the letter neatly, and put it in his shirt pocket. "After all, she went to America."

"But you said you lived in America," Lacey said.

"Ah. There is a difference," he grunted. "I come home to France."

Lacey took a deep breath. "Magda believed the Romanov corset that your grandfather allegedly took during the Russian Revolution is, or was, hidden in the coal room of this very house."

"Corset! Ha! Now she says a corset. *Fantastique.* Once she tell us all there is a carton of Fabergé eggs. And in my house?" He shook his head as if that were the most idiotic thought of all. Jean-Claude Rousseau rolled his eyes heavenward. "A fantasy. The coal room, it is nailed shut for thirty, forty years. When I am a little boy I play in there." He sighed dramatically and heaved his shoulders forward. "But I suppose there will be no posing and painting today. No American nudes for Jean-Claude. And you will not leave me alone until you get your way. Like all Americans. Americans must always get their way. Why? Because they are Americans!"

Lacey decided to simply stand there like an American who was about to get her way. And Brooke stood beside her as a united front. Brooke was used to getting her way. "It was Magda's dying wish that we at least explore the possibility," Lacey said. "With your permission, of course."

"Dying wish!" he sputtered. "Dying wish. *Mon Dieu.*" He looked just like a frustrated Frenchman in the movies, the exasperated gendarme lecturing the foolish Americans. "Now you bring the ghost of a crazy woman into this matter." Jean-Claude gestured extravagantly, which Lacey assumed meant something eloquent in French. He stopped, rolled his eyes, breathed deeply and sighed dramatically, his hand over his heart. "But who am I to deny a Frenchwoman's dying wish?"

Jean-Claude Rousseau was, Lacey thought, pretty good theatre. As good as Magda.

He swept them aside with an imperious gesture and marched down the front path ahead of them. He indicated that they were to follow him to the side of the farmhouse. They trotted dutifully behind him to a slanting side door that led down into a cellar. Jean-Claude went down the steps first, careful not to hit his head on the low beam. Lacey and Brooke followed, ducking on their way down out of the pale Normandy November sunlight. Lacey clicked on her flashlight.

At the bottom of the stairs, Jean-Claude reached up and pulled a chain. A dim lightbulb swung from the ceiling, barely illuminating the room. He led them to the back of the cellar and knocked on a wooden door scarred by several deep gouges. He bowed deeply to the women.

"May I present to you, my famous coal room full of buried treasures?" He smiled, showing his teeth for the first time.

Lacey drew closer with her light. The coal room door was nailed tightly shut on three sides, from the ceiling to the floor on the latch side, and across the top and bottom. Dried-out seam tape partially covered the twenty or thirty nails that secured it. Monsieur Rousseau handed her a rusty hammer and a pry bar from a nearby toolbox. Her heart sank. *Hard labor.*

"What is the Chicago expression? Ah, yes. Knock yourself out, Mademoiselle Smithsonian."

She took the tools. They were heavy. "Just what I wanted to do on a beautiful fall day in France."

"The door? Very old. So many nails. And probably the door, it is, how you say it, warped? Jammed?" he said. "I doubt if you can open it. A lot of work." Another eloquent shrug.

If he thinks hard work will stop me, he's sadly mistaken, Lacey thought. She hoped it would be easy to pry the nails from the old wood. *I'll get it open if it takes all day.*

"No sweat, Lacey," Brooke said uncertainly. "I'm sure we can handle it." Brooke sneezed several times.

"Why is it nailed shut?" Lacey had the uncomfortable feeling a body was buried behind Door Number One.

"Ha! It is nailed shut because it is a filthy hole that no one with any sense would enter!" Jean-Claude's lips curled into a small sneer. "When this house, long ago, it is wired for the electric, we have no more use for the coal. And the coal dust. So much black dirt. *Incroyable.* And the other door, where the coal you shovel in? From the coal wagon? All covered. My studio now is up there." He turned and walked up the stairs. "Adieu. Your little treasure hunt will end this foolish Magda nonsense once and for all. My cellar is not a rest stop for American tourists. And crazy dead women."

"Wait, Monsieur Rousseau. Where are you going?" Brooke asked.

"To the market. And then to paint. A landscape, not a nude. A pity." At the top of the stairs he turned and looked down at Lacey. "By the way, Mademoiselle Lacey Smithsonian, if there is anything of value, do you not think we would have found it long ago?" Jean-Claude laughed and went out the door.

"I don't know, Jean-Claude," she called after him. "Who nailed the door shut?" But he was gone. Brooke sneezed again behind her. "Are you okay?" Lacey asked her.

"Uh, sure. I think so." She sneezed again. "Damn. Must be a century of dust down here."

"Why don't you go outside, hang out in the car? I don't want your asthma acting up."

"I couldn't leave you here," Brooke said. She sneezed several more times. "But if you're sure you'll be okay?" she asked sheepishly. "I mean, it's pretty scary down here."

"Oh, you mean here in the scary dark cellar in the isolated farmhouse where the monster lurks?" Lacey laughed, but she was suddenly seized by visions of the Man in the Iron Mask lunging out from behind the coal room door.

"Yeah, that's the one. You know, the lunatic skulking behind the furnace."

"Thanks so much, Brooke. I hadn't even considered the furnace." Lacey looked around. "Anyway, I'm sure the lunatic is dead of asthma by now. So it's probably just his corpse. We're the only live lunatics down here."

She aimed her flashlight into the dark spaces in the cellar. There were dim shadows on the wall, a collection of broken chairs in one corner, and behind her an ancient wringer washing machine. Lines of sagging rope were strung from one side of the room to the other to dry laundry, holding a few stiff towels. Brooke sneezed again.

"Okay, this is what I'm going to do," Lacey said. "I'm going to make sure there are no madmen hiding in corners, dead or alive. Then you can go upstairs and watch the door from the car—the locked car—to make sure no maniacs come in or out. If you see anything, honk the horn. Or call my cell; it's in my purse. Okay?"

"I've got your back," Brooke assured her with a sneeze.

A tiny engine roared to life outside. They listened to the sound of Jean-Claude's motor scooter departing.

"We're all alone now." Brooke looked worried.

"That's good. We don't want company. Now go. You're on outside guard duty."

Brooke nodded, but she didn't move. "Guard duty. Don't worry. I'm on it." She paused. "Uh, Lacey? Will you walk me to the car?"

"Chicken." Lacey tried to sound brave, but she couldn't deny the air of creepiness that filled the cellar. "See what happens when you get us both paranoid? Next you'll be telling me about the French version of Bigfoot. *Le Gros Pied*, right? Hang on a minute."

Lacey paced the small cellar, stabbing her light into all the dark corners. She explored the deepest shadow, behind the furnace. There was nothing there but boxes of old dishes. "See, Brooke? No bogeymen." Brooke sneezed. Lacey marched her friend up the stairs into the sunlight, made sure the motor scooter was really gone and Jean-Claude wasn't hanging around with an ax. She saw Brooke safely into the Citroën, gave her a handkerchief, and turned back to face the dim and sinister cellar all alone.

The sharp smell of old dirt and mildew hit her even stronger as she descended the stairs. She marched with determination to the coal room door. Lacey swung the hammer and hefted the pry bar, testing their usefulness as weapons. Satisfied, she placed them by the door and started tearing the brittle tape from the side, the top, and the bottom.

Why would anyone nail the door shut? Why not simply close it? A glimmer of hope rose in Lacey. With such precautions, maybe there *was* something of value concealed behind the nailed door. According to Magda's instructions, the corset was supposed to be hidden behind loose stones in the wall opposite the door, about five feet above the floor. If the door had really been nailed shut for decades, maybe it was still there, no matter what Jean-Claude said about his crazy cousin.

Lacey set the flashlight on a box of dishes and pointed its beam at the door. She took off her jacket and hung it and her purse from the nearest clothesline. She rolled up her sleeves and pulled her hair back into a bun. Then she picked up the hammer, slid the claw under a nail head that stood a little above the wood on the top of the door, and leaned on the handle. The nail gave a little squeak and popped right out. This is easy, she thought, and she pulled the first few nails. She had a tougher time with the next few, but the top row of nails was soon done. Then halfway down the door, near the doorknob, she got stuck. These nails were pounded down flat.

Perspiration was beading on her forehead and running down her back. Magda had promised it would be a piece of cake. *Yeah,* Lacey thought, *just like Marie Antoinette's little problem was a piece of cake.* She turned the knob and rattled the door. At least it wasn't locked too. The top squeaked and gave a little, but the rest was stuck fast. She took a deep breath, grabbed the hammer again, and attacked more nails, adding more ugly gouges to the wood. Lacey hoped *The Eye Street Observer* wouldn't have to buy Jean-Claude a new door. But he had handed her the hammer. "Knock yourself out," he said. And there was no way she could ruin the ambience of this charming dungeon. Lacey wiped her brow, streaking her sleeve with sweat, and checked her watch.

Half an hour had passed and the damn door was still shut. She renewed her attack, digging out around the nail heads with the pry bar, and finally popping out a few more nails. She pulled hard on the door. It almost opened all along the latch side. She grabbed the pry bar again, shoving it between the door and the jamb and leaning on it with all her weight. "Open, damn you!" It didn't, but the nails were looser. The heads were pulled up a little.

She worked hard at the remaining holdouts. Triumphantly, she pulled the last nail and her hand slipped off the hammer and slid across the door, scraping her knuckles on the scarred wood. "Oww!" She observed her torn skin and broken fingernail with disgust. She sucked on her injured finger. "This better be good, Magda," Lacey said aloud, panting.

She pulled on the doorknob again. It groaned, opened a foot, and then stopped. The door was warped, jammed against the cellar floor. Lacey slid the pry bar under the edge of the door and lifted it as hard as she could until she heard the wood give. She grabbed the edge of the door with both hands and gave it one last vicious pull. The door finally gave an awful creak and opened, sending her reeling backward. Lacey realized she wasn't prepared for what she saw inside.

Nothing. The small, dark room seemed to be empty of everything but shadows. She could see nothing but cobwebs, long ropes of cobwebs hanging down three or four feet. She grabbed her camera from her purse and pointed the flashlight into the coal room. A curtain of cobwebs hung from the ceiling and a crack of light in the far wall revealed that long ago there was an opening to the outside through which coal was shoveled, before electricity came to this remote farmhouse.

Lacey ordered her heart to slow down. She shone the light about the dark space, smudged black by ancient coal dust. She stepped into the room, batting cobwebs out of her hair. The room was about six feet by nine feet, with a hard dirt floor. Rough stones formed the walls that met a wooden plank ceiling, through which scores of long nails poked. They looked like an inverted bed of nails, but Lacey realized they simply secured the flooring to the subfloor above her head. A few small chunks of coal still lay on ledges of stone and scattered on the floor. Lacey wiped sweat from her forehead and pulled off a stray spider's web. *Spiders. I hate spiders.*

She threw light along the floor and into the corners. In one corner she saw a small desiccated bundle of fur and bones, and she sucked in her breath. It looked like the remains of a small dog; she saw dog-like canines and a tiny skeletal paw. Blood throbbing in her temples, she backed away from it into the wall. A sharp pain shot through her back. Lacey yelped. She'd connected with a sharp rod lodged between the stones. She stood up and rubbed her back, wondering when she last had a tetanus shot and yelling curses at the room.

"Damn, damn, damn this fool's errand of yours, Magda!"

She heard a step on the creaky cellar stairs. "Brooke, I'm in here! You've got great timing, princess, I did all the work! I'm in the coal room. Come see."

Lacey pointed the flashlight at the back wall. She counted the stones and found that two were loose at the spot where the corset was said to be hidden. She dislodged the stones, letting them drop to the floor. Inside a hollowed-out space lay a metal box. It was rusted shut but not locked. She propped the flashlight in the hole in the wall and pried open the dented and dirty thing.

It was empty save for a torn piece of paper with tiny faded handwriting on it. She couldn't read the words in this light, so she folded the paper and shoved it into her pocket. She shook the box, disgusted that it was empty and that she was covered in spiderwebs and coal dust and sweat. There was no corset, not an errant jewel, not even a thread. She slid the box back into its hiding place and wondered what to do next. She still had to write a story about this debacle. Lacey took a series of photographs, trying to capture the feel of the empty room, the cobwebs, the rusted metal box, as if they could convey the dismay and disappointment she felt.

Another step creaked.

"So help me, Brooke, if you yell 'Boo,' I'll clobber you," Lacey shouted. "What are you waiting for, an escort?"

A cobweb tickled the back of Lacey's neck, and she pointed the light again at the pile of dog bones. It was small. Lacey wondered how big it had been when it was alive, what kind of dog it had been, what its name might have been. She had an urge to flee the coal room, but she was afraid she might be missing something. Other loose stones? Other boxes? Her stomach lurched at the thought of being walled up like a dog in the small black room. Another creak split the silence.

"Stop playing games, Brooke," Lacey yelled. "Don't be such a wuss, there's no conspiracy, there's nothing down here but us. Just spiders, nothing but damned spiders. And a dead dog. Hell."

Lacey stepped out of the coal room into the cellar, her heart beating wildly, the pry bar held at the ready. The dim naked lightbulb was swinging at the bottom of the stairs, as if someone tall had bumped into it. The hair on the back of Lacey's neck rose. She smelled something acrid, something chemical, but she couldn't place it. Did Jean-Claude store paint in the cellar?

"Brooke! I'm really pissed at you," she yelled again. "Where the hell are you?"

From behind the coal room door, one large hand reached out and knocked the pry bar from her hand. She struggled with her unseen assailant for a moment before another large hand pressed a cloth to her face and the chemical smell filled her head. Everything faded to black.

chapter 14

Lacey felt herself slowly emerge from a dark void. She tried to open her eyes; it seemed to take an hour. Her eyelids protested. They felt impossibly heavy. A drunken cancan line was high-kicking behind her eyes and around her temples and doing somersaults on the top of her head. There was a terrible taste in her mouth.

Lacey woke to the sight of Brooke leaning over her. She was laying in the dirt in the pale sunshine outside Jean-Claude Rousseau's farmhouse. "Two-star accommodations suck, Brooke. Next time three stars." She was conscious of the cold ground under her back and the sound of leaves crunching as she moved. She realized it hurt to move her head.

"Lacey, are you all right?" Brooke looked frightened.

"Where's my jacket?" Lacey struggled to sit up, holding her head. Brooke had covered her with her jacket, and she helped her slip into it. Shivering, Lacey buttoned it up and rubbed her arms. "How did I get here?" she asked.

"He carried you," Brooke said, pointing to the man behind her. "After some strange guy ran out of the cellar."

"Which is it, Smithsonian, alive or dead?" A voice spoke with a familiar English accent. "And what on earth were you doing down there? Digging ditches?"

She was covered in coal dust and spiderwebs. She felt disgusting. "That sounds like Nigel Griffin." Lacey peered up at a male form in a leather jacket, silhouetted by the afternoon sun. "Mythological beast."

"That's me," he said, "myth or legend, at your service. Though I must say it was rude of you to skip out on me like that back in Washington."

"And I thought you were hunting a mythical egg, not me." She struggled to her feet, with Griffin and Brooke's help. "What the hell are you doing here? Stalking me again?"

"Keeping an eye on you, of course."

"So you just watched someone attack me? What happened?"

"That's what I was asking you," Brooke said.

"Last thing I remember is someone grabbing me and putting a cloth over my face. It had a strange smell."

"Did you see him?" Griffin asked. "Did you see anything?"

She flashed back to the coal room and gagged at the memory. "A monogrammed cloth, I think. Like a handkerchief."

"Monogrammed? With initials?"

Lacey tried to focus. "I have no idea."

"That big guy must have done it," Brooke said. "The man I saw running from the cellar."

"Kepelov," Griffin said smugly. "I told you he was on this trail."

"Kepelov?" Lacey shook her head to clear it.

"Gregor Kepelov. The Russian I warned you about. Do you have amnesia? Ruthless bugger. Of course, why he didn't just kill you I have no idea."

This was too much information, and the dance troupe was still at work in her cranium from whatever had knocked her out. "Hey, medic," she said to Brooke. "How about some Advil and water?" Brooke brought a bottle of Perrier and some capsules. Lacey swallowed, then closed her eyes and rubbed her head. "And where's my bag and my camera?"

Griffin produced them, as well as the rusted metal box, which seemed to have a few new dents in it. "Found these in the cellar. Dumped on the floor. Anything missing?"

Lacey rummaged through her bag: Nothing was missing, and the camera seemed to be fine. She took a few pictures of the farmhouse, and she led them back down to the cellar to take more shots of the coal room while they looked for evidence of her assailant or a monogrammed handkerchief. They found no more loose stones or metal boxes. Brooke wanted to take photographs of Lacey in the cellar with the empty box, but Lacey insisted on combing her hair and refreshing her makeup first. Brooke laughed.

"Lipstick? Thank God, Lacey, now I know you're going to live."

Lacey was beginning to feel better, but her head was still throbbing. "I wonder what he used to knock me out. He's Russian, right?"

Griffin nodded casually. "Ex-KGB. Bloody cold bastards they are, too."

"Chloroform!" Brooke's voice quivered with excitement. "The KGB used to love that stuff. But if he is, or was, KGB, he may have access to some new knockout potions too, some diabolical Russian chemical cocktail." That old conspiracy-hunter glint was in her eye. "Lacey, you remember when the Russians pumped a secret knockout gas into that theatre during that hostage siege and killed all those people? Hundreds, wasn't it?"

"Yes, but you don't have to sound so happy about it."

"This could be the same stuff, a new chemical weapon with a potential to—"

"Whose side is she on, Smithsonian?" Griffin said with a smirk.

"I'm just saying that this KGB guy could be connected to some secret—"

"Shut up," Lacey said. "Both of you." She trudged back up the stairs. Her head was killing her, and there was no trace of her assailant. Or the corset. Or a clue as to what to do next.

"You knew something was here all along. Magda Rousseau told you." Griffin pounded angrily up the steps behind her. "I offered you a partnership, and you wouldn't tell me."

"Tell you? I thought you were another reporter. Or a lunatic. Or a thief."

He snorted in disgust. "Oh, please. Don't insult me. A reporter?!"

"Now who's insulting who?"

"Whom. And you started it."

"And you think you're going to get anywhere by insulting me?"

Brooke trailed behind them, squinting as they emerged from the dark cellar. "Hey, you guys, don't leave me down here."

"And what happened to you, Sancho Panza?" Lacey turned to Brooke. "Weren't you supposed to watch my back?"

"Lacey, I'm so sorry." Brooke was on the verge of tears. "I took a pill for my allergies. I fell asleep in the car."

Lacey sighed. "So where did this Russian go, if it was the elusive Kepelov who grabbed me and knocked me out?" Her voice was rising in anger. "Why didn't you follow him?"

"I woke up when I heard the cellar door slam. I just saw a big guy running away. I ran down to the cellar and found you unconscious."

"And I was watching Blondie here. I saw her go down and I followed," Griffin said. "After a minute. When I heard her scream."

"You're no mythological beast," Lacey snapped at him. "You're a coward. I could have been killed."

"Well, there was no sense in both of us getting killed. At any rate, I did go down. And there you were, Smithsonian. Filthy." Griffin gestured at her clothes, though it really wasn't necessary. "Nevertheless, I did pick you up. No need to thank me."

"But what did you find?" Brooke asked. "In the coal room? Was there anything?"

Lacey shot her a warning glance to cut her off. "You were just down there with me, you saw everything I saw. And what about the Beast here?" She jerked her thumb at Griffin. "When did you show up? While I was being drugged and mugged?"

"I followed Kepelov here. From a safe distance, of course," Griffin said. "I saw him slip in through that door while Goldilocks here was snoring in the Citroën."

"Wait a minute," Lacey asked. "Where did you follow him, to France, or here to Mont-Saint-Michel? Were you following him or us?"

"I wasn't snoring," Brooke began. "I do not snore and I never—"

He ignored Lacey's questions. "I waited behind the shed there. For developments."

"So you were hiding? Like a coward."

"I had an excellent vantage point. Don't look at me to be some burly he-man hero, Smithsonian. I'm no cowboy. I leave that to you American girls." He flicked an imaginary piece of dust off his jacket, pulled out his cigarettes, and fumbled one from the pack.

Men! Lacey thought she could use a cowboy about now, instead of an effete whiny Brit. "I know some cowgirls who could whip your ass. And if you light that thing we will."

"Bloody hell, Smithsonian, we're in the great outdoors! Can't a man light a—"

"Not in my outdoors."

Griffin reluctantly put the cigarette back in the pack. "You should be more worried about Kepelov than about my vices, you know. Gregor Kepelov is a dangerous guy. Gives us respectable jewel retrievers a bad name."

Brooke looked at Griffin and Lacey. Recognition dawned. "This is the jewel thief?"

"I am not a jewel thief," Griffin said icily. "I am a jewel retriever."

"Yeah, well, you skulk around in the bushes like a thief," Lacey said.

"I don't take stupid risks, unlike some people," Griffin replied, straightening his shirt sleeves under his leather jacket. "Besides, I carried your butt up the stairs."

"And I helped," Brooke pleaded.

Judging from her aching muscles and sore back, Lacey figured they dragged her all the way.

"I suppose you had a good look around for this nonexistent treasure before you gallantly decided to rescue me?"

"It's what I came for, isn't it? Anyway, it didn't take long to see it was just a wretched hole. Nothing valuable there. You were on the floor, half in and half out of that back room. You've looked better, Smithsonian."

"You banged my head on the steps, didn't you?" Lacey felt the back of her head gingerly and pulled cobwebs out of her hair.

"Of course not!" Brooke looked hurt. "Well, I didn't mean to."

"Nothing in the cellar but an empty box. So there is no Fabergé egg?" Griffin glared at her.

"Who knows? I never said there was, you idiot. Why don't you ask your pal Kepelov," Lacey growled at him. "You jewel thieves all seem to know each other."

The snarl of an approaching motor scooter made them all turn. Jean-Claude Rousseau came into view from around a bend in the narrow road. He roared past them and lurched to a stop at his farmhouse door. It was suddenly quiet. They watched Jean-Claude set his motorbike against the wall of the house and turn to them with a scowl on his face and a sack of groceries in his hands.

"What is all this? What has happened here? You took a coal bath in my cellar?"

"New French beauty treatment." Lacey tried to wipe off her clothes.

"What did you find?" he asked. "And who is this, another American?"

"He's English. I found nothing," Lacey said. She was longing to sit down. She settled for leaning against the wall of the farmhouse. "Just a dirty empty room, and an empty box. And a dead dog."

"Dead dog?" Brooke said. "I didn't see a dead dog."

"Very dead. Been down there a long time," Lacey said.

Jean-Claude set the groceries down. "Dog? What dog?" He seemed about to shake Lacey, but he looked at her filthy clothes and reconsidered. "What kind of dog?"

"I don't know. It's mostly bones, but I think it was a dog."

Surely he must have known, she thought. She had assumed he must have put the dog's body down there himself, in lieu of a burial.

Jean-Claude charged through the open cellar door and down the steps. Lacey followed him at a discreet distance, only to hear an anguished cry. The Frenchman had fallen to his knees in the coal dust.

"Pepe! *Mon petit chien!*" Jean-Claude clutched the pile of bones and sobbed. "Pepe, Pepe, Pepe." Until that moment, Lacey wouldn't have imagined that Jean-Claude Rousseau had any deep emotions. She realized she was wrong. She tiptoed back up the stairs. Brooke was waiting alone, shifting her weight from one foot to another. Lacey looked around for Griffin.

"Your big brave jewel thief heard the scream and took off." Brooke pointed to a car disappearing down the road. "What about the bones?"

"It's his dog. Pepe. Walled up down there for years, I guess." Feeling weak, Lacey sat down on a small bench by the door. "Maybe I could have been a little more subtle about the dead dog."

"How could you know it was his dog? Don't beat yourself up."

Lacey felt irrationally sad about the dog. She didn't want to think about the possibility of it starving to death in that filthy black little room. She and Brooke sat in silence. Lacey felt a little foolish, waiting for this rude, unfriendly man to finish mourning for his long-dead dog.

After some time, Jean-Claude reappeared at the cellar door. He cradled a small bundle wrapped in a towel. From his hand dangled the remains of a tattered leather dog collar with a metal tag. "Pepe," he said. He had been weeping. "You see, I never know what happen to him. He disappear when I was about fifteen. I think he must run away, you know, but no, he never ran away, not Pepe. It is funny, eh? Funny how much you miss a little dog like that. *Mon* Pepe. *Pauvre petit chien.*"

"How long ago was that?" Lacey asked.

He sighed. "Oh, a long time. More than thirty years. In the summer, when the strawberries were fresh. Whoever nailed the door shut, my grandfather maybe, the deaf old fool, I think he left *mon* Pepe inside. Maybe he was hiding. Playing hide and seek with me."

"You never heard him barking?" Lacey asked him gently.

"He had a very soft bark," Jean-Claude said. His eyes teared up again. His hand closed over the dog tag. "Such a good little dog. *Pardonnez-moi.* We will talk later. I am sorry, mademoiselle, but I have to go now and bury my dog."

Chapter 15

Who or what the hell was "Drosmis Berzins"*?*

Lacey studied the torn slip of paper she had crammed into her jeans, which now lay in a heap on the floor of the hotel where they were staying a few miles from Jean-Claude Rousseau's farmhouse, near the causeway to Mont-Saint-Michel.

At least she thought the signature said "Drosmis Berzins." The note wasn't in English or French. But it was the only thing of interest she had found in the coal room—other than Jean-Claude's little dog—so she was holding on to it. After eradicating the cobwebs and coal dust, all she really wanted to do was to crawl into bed with the covers pulled up over her head, but duty called. She had made dinner plans with Brooke and Jean-Claude. He was still distraught over the discovery of Pepe's bones, but not so upset that he would pass up dinner at one of Mont-Saint-Michel's chic restaurants at the expense of *The Eye Street Observer.* She stuck the note in her passport case and took it with her into the bathroom, which she locked while she took a shower.

November and the disappointing day called for a somber palette, one with autumnal overtones. Lacey had brought a deceptively plain burgundy wool knit dress that slipped over her curves in a crimson wave with a skirt that flirted slightly below her knees. Simple elegant sleeves ended in cuffs that buttoned. Facing herself in the mirror, she had to admit she looked good. The dress was made from one of Aunt Mimi's patterns dating from the late 1930s and it made her feel sophisticated. The color made her skin glow. She complemented it with the diamond earrings that Vic had given her. She wrapped a heavy black shawl embroidered with red and pink flowers around her shoulders and hoped it would be warm enough for the walk across the causeway to the Mont. In the hotel lobby she met Brooke, who was bundled up in her Burberry trench coat.

"Do you think Griffin will be back?" Brooke asked.

"I don't know, but I hope we've seen the last of him. If he really believes it's a Fabergé egg and not a corset, and it's obvious we don't have it, maybe we'll be rid of him."

"Lacey, what if it isn't a corset?" Brooke opened the front door, and they stepped into the beautiful soft twilight.

"I don't know. Let's look at it this way, I'm in this for a corset. If it doesn't exist, I may have to go buy a damn corset in Paris. And wear it to flirt with some Parisian men."

They came around a curve in the road. The sudden breathtaking sight of the Abbey on the rock rising out of the sea in the misty dusk mesmerized them and they fell silent. Mont-Saint-Michel rose up before them beyond the sandy bay. They walked across the causeway to the little village on the rock, listening to the wind sigh and the gulls cry. Beyond the causeway and the town gates and the clumps of slow-moving tourists taking pictures, they found the restaurant Jean-Claude had recommended, tucked into a corner off the winding *Rue Principale.*

Inside, the whole restaurant was suffused with a golden glow from candles, supplementing the lamplight, which created a comfortable and timeless ambience, as if they were dining in the previous century. They found Jean-Claude Rousseau waiting for them with a glass of wine already in his hand.

"The wine is excellent. I put it on *l'addition,*" he announced as he greeted them both with a kiss on each cheek. Lacey caught Jean-Claude's appreciative glance. "A beautiful dress, Mademoiselle Smithsonian. *Très belle.* Did you wear it just for me?" He turned approvingly toward Brooke, sleek in her austere black suit beneath her trench coat. "Ah, *oui,* the *très chic avocat. Très elegant,* Mademoiselle Barton."

Lacey gazed around the dining room, holding her breath. She saw neither the omnipresent Griffin nor anyone who might be the mysterious Kepelov. She exhaled in relief. She did catch several men looking at her in frank appraisal, a dead giveaway that this wasn't Washington, D.C. Everywhere people were doing the French double-cheek kiss, another clue. The maître d' led them to their table, which looked out across the sands of the bay toward the causeway they had just crossed over. Lacey was briefly riveted by the view, then the maître d' pulled out her chair for her and then Brooke's, as Jean-Claude shambled into his chair between them.

"I'm so sorry about your dog," Lacey said to Jean-Claude.

He grunted and made a dismissive gesture, clearly trying to be stoic and unemotional. "This is the last time I let Americans go into my cellar," he said with a little smile.

"Very wise." *Afraid of what else you might find buried there?* Lacey wondered. An efficient waiter wearing a black vest and a long white apron appeared and inquired in good English about their wine choices.

"Do you make a habit of letting Americans into your cellar?" Brooke asked. She ordered a Chardonnay that made the waiter frown. Lacey asked the waiter to make a suggestion, which prompted a much happier response.

"No, no, never, but that is beside of the point," Jean-Claude said to Brooke. He had no hesitation in ordering an expensive vintage for himself. He obviously thought all Americans had money to burn. Fortunately, Lacey thought, in Brooke's case this was true, but it was *The Eye* that would pick up this dinner tab.

While they looked over the menu, heavy on *poisson* and *fruits de mer* and large numbers next to euro symbols, Brooke and Lacey debated reporting the attack on her to the local police. Lacey opposed it and Jean-Claude agreed with her vigorously. This wasn't Paris, he said, with its sophisticated police department, and even there, Lacey would be a foreigner, a headache from outside. Lacey pointed out that she wasn't popular with the cops in D.C., and some of them even spoke English. She very much doubted she would find her popularity improved with their French counterparts.

"Then what about alerting the American Embassy?" Brooke had friends there.

"And turn it into an international incident?"

"It already is an international incident," Brooke protested. "Two Americans looking for a Romanov artifact, a Russian spy, a British jewel thief, and a violent incident on French soil. And a dead dog with a Spanish name," she added under her breath.

"It sounds even worse when you put it that way," Lacey said. Besides, if Brooke brought in the police or the embassy, it would get back to the newspaper and her editor Mac, Mac with his "I told you so's" and his spiking blood pressure, which he blamed on her. Not to mention the specter of headlines on that accursed DeadFed dot com, which would put the entire World Wide Web on notice that a hunt for a legendary Romanov corset was underway, inviting all kinds of murderous nuts to seek out Lacey Smithsonian for details.

"No more talk of police," Jean-Claude said. "I am trying to

have a civilized dinner and you mademoiselles are ruining it. The gendarmes are the enemy of fine cuisine." He picked up his menu and studied it intently.

"There's always Damon's SWAT team," Brooke suggested, taking a piece of bread.

"Don't even begin to go there," Lacey whispered. The waiter arrived with their bottle and she gratefully accepted a glass of wine.

"May we stop mentioning the police, *s'il vous plaît*?" Jean-Claude set his menu down and used his wineglass for punctuation. "It affects my digestion." The waiter inquired about their choice of appetizers and Jean-Claude ordered for them all with great gusto.

"See?" Lacey said. "It affects Jean-Claude's digestion."

Brooke tossed her braid. "We'll talk later."

After their excellent dinner, Lacey waited until the dining room had emptied a little. Once she was sure no other patrons were watching them suspiciously, she extracted the small torn piece of paper from her passport case and handed it to Jean-Claude. "This was in the box in the coal room. Can you read it for me?"

He set his wineglass down and took the scrap of paper. "It is torn."

"That's the way I found it. It's all I found in the cellar. Except for— Well, you know."

He pulled a pair of reading glasses out of the pocket of his well-tailored but rather worn navy blazer and perched them on his nose. He studied the paper for a moment.

"But this is not in French. This is written in Latvian."

"Can you read it?" Brooke asked. "Your grandparents were Latvian, weren't they?"

"*Oui,* they make us all learn *le Letton,* the Latvian, but it is a very long time. My crazy old cousin Magda, she loved it, she wanted always to speak the Latvian with me. It was very annoying." He waved a hand. "Give me a moment." He cleared his throat, then read haltingly. "'Old friend, old enemy, you think you could hide this from me? Your turn. Seek, Juris, and you shall find. Genesis 3:19, Drosmis Berzins.' There is also an address on the Rue Dauphine," Jean-Claude said. "Paris, you know, the Rive Gauche. A line under the word 'Rue.' As for the Genesis—" He shrugged.

"Genesis. In the Bible," Lacey said. "I don't know that verse offhand."

"Ah. This explains why I do not know it," he laughed, lifting his wineglass in salute.

"Is that all?" Lacey pulled her little Moleskine notebook out of her purse and wrote down his translation and the address. "Torn in half. I wonder if the rest of it said anything."

"Who knows?" Jean-Claude said, pointing out the obvious. "We do not have the rest."

Lacey read it back to him. "That's it exactly? Any words you're uncertain about?"

"No, no, it is that exactly. I learn Latvian well as a child; you never forget it. My grandmother," he said, shaking his head. "Hard old woman. Sometimes it slips away in the memory. But then it comes back." He sipped his wine thoughtfully. "You know, mademoiselles, if you find this thing, this Fabergé egg, this Romanov corset, this whatever it is, it belongs to me. My family. I am the last of my family. You understand?"

Oh, yes, Lacey thought. Jean-Claude Rousseau reminded her a lot of Magda Rousseau.

"Whatever it is," Lacey said, "it's not where Magda thought it was. Who knows what it really is or was, or if it will ever be found?" Lacey smiled. She had no idea who the rightful owner would be. Jean-Claude Rousseau, because his grandfather had stolen it? The remaining Romanov descendants? The Russian government? The French government? Or whoever had the biggest stick and the best lawyers and the corset in hand? But none of that mattered to her at that moment. Lacey felt ill-used by Magda, who had obviously left out some salient details, like who else might be on the trail of a legendary Fabergé egg. And she felt assaulted and abused by a faceless stranger in the coal room.

Jean-Claude sniffed. "The farmhouse is mine, it was inherited to me, I should have been told of this maybe very valuable thing, this whatever, in my own cellar. Why was I not told?" Lacey refrained from pointing out that Magda had apparently been telling him for years that a Fabergé egg was buried in his cellar, and he had dismissed her as a crazy old woman. But clearly something had been there; someone had been in the coal room and left this cryptic torn note in the box. To top it all off, someone withdrew the item without his knowledge.

"Who is Drosmis Berzins?" Lacey asked. "Is that a Latvian name?"

Jean-Claude stared at the paper, then poured another glass of Merlot. "Drosmis Berzins. The other Latvian soldier who was with my grandfather in Ekaterinburg with the Romanovs."

"You knew about him?" Brooke asked. "Did you ever meet him?"

Jean-Claude shrugged again. "When I was a child. I know what my grandfather, Juris Akmentins, said to his grandchildren: Two Latvians refused to shoot the Romanov children. Juris and Drosmis. 'Be proud to be Latvians,' he said, 'Latvians do not murder children.' He did not tuck us into bed at night and say, 'By the way, boys and girls, we stole a corset full of jewels from a dead girl and hid it in the cellar.' "

"So Drosmis Berzins apparently wrote this note to your grandfather. What do you think the message means?" Lacey asked.

"Why ask me? I am not the nosy American newspaper reporter who goes looking for things that do not belong to her in other people's cellars." He sounded brusque, but he seemed to be enjoying himself. He had certainly enjoyed the dinner. The waiter returned with their desserts.

If Drosmis Berzins had helped steal the corset in Ekaterinburg, or had been trying to steal it from Juris, this had somehow gotten lost in Magda's version of the story. Did she not know about him? And why would others, like Griffin and Kepelov, be looking for something at the Rousseau farmhouse if this Drosmis had already taken it long ago? Were they simply following Lacey and Brooke, who were themselves following Magda's only lead, her grandfather's diary? Juris Akmentins had not mentioned a Drosmis Berzins by name in his diary—at least not in the pages Magda had translated into English. Were there pages missing from the Latvian original, she wondered, or had Magda simply not considered Drosmis worthy of mention? Who might Drosmis have told about all this, and if he had the corset, what had he done with it? Among all these questions, one thing struck her with some urgency.

"If those men were to come back to your house, Jean-Claude, you could be in danger."

"Ha! Danger. I sneer at danger." He swirled the wine in his glass before sipping it, rolling it around in his mouth, and then swallowing with satisfaction. "You, Mademoiselle Smithsonian and Mademoiselle Barton, may dance cheek to cheek with danger. *Moi?* I am leaving town."

Brooke nearly snorted her wine. "At least they don't know about the note," she said, recovering her composure. "So as far as they know, we found nothing."

"As far as I know, you found nothing but my Pepe, and for that—" Jean-Claude looked away as his eyes grew moist—"for that, I am very grateful. Tomorrow I will leave."

"How can you be sure you won't be followed?" Brooke interjected. "Or attacked tonight?" Lacey kicked her under the table.

Jean-Claude gestured philosophically with his wineglass. "How can you be sure of the same, mademoiselle? How can any of us?"

"Where are you going?" Lacey inquired.

"I will go to Spain. Until the heat blows off, how they say in the movies? Besides, the women of Spain are beautiful this time of year. I will paint them." The wine was mellowing him. "But will you not pose for me, Lacey Smithsonian? Tonight?" A wicked smile lifted his lips. "To soothe our anxiety from this traumatic attack of yours in my coal room? To create art from this powerful emotion is such a very great, how you say, release?"

"Sorry, Jean-Claude." Lacey was immune to his Gallic charms, whatever they might be.

He turned his attention to Brooke. "Or perhaps you, Mademoiselle Barton, you of the beautiful blond tresses? Such a beautiful color. I have just the pigment for you."

She sneezed and he gallantly produced his handkerchief. "I'm allergic to paint," Brooke said. "Gee, it's a pity."

He turned back to Lacey. "Mademoiselle Lacey, perhaps you could wear something, you need not be in the nude *en total.* Americans, such prudes, you know? A little something. A corset perhaps," he smiled. "I will fill in your so lovely nudity with an artist's imagination." Lacey rolled her eyes. "So many women are even more beautiful in the mind than in the nudity."

"In your mind is where my nudity will have to stay, Jean-Claude."

Jean-Claude sighed. He coolly retrieved his handkerchief from Brooke. "So. An empty cellar. An excellent meal. Good wine. But no posing, eh? I will paint in Spain. And you, mademoiselles, you will pursue the great chase, the lost corset?"

Lacey shook her head. "See the sights," she said. "Go back home. Write my story."

He frowned. "You will hunt no more for the corset, the last unknown object of the Romanovs?" He gestured grandly. "But it will be worth millions, more than a Fabergé egg! It of course belongs to me, if it still exists, but there would be perhaps a reward for someone who returns it to its rightful owner, the last of the Rousseaus."

"There isn't much to go on," Lacey replied. "An address where Drosmis Berzins may have lived decades ago? A verse from the

Bible?" She had every intention of finding that address in Paris, but he didn't need to know that. The fewer people who knew their plans now, she thought, the better.

"Where is your American frontier spirit, Lacey Smithsonian, the spirit of the cowboy?"

"I'm afraid I left it in your cellar, Jean-Claude."

chapter 16

The moon winked at them from behind a bank of clouds. The stars were glittering diamonds against the black velvet sky. And Mont-Saint-Michel was a jewel box ablaze with lights behind them as they walked briskly back across the causeway to their hotel in the cold crystal air.

"You weren't serious when you said you were giving up, were you?" Brooke's breath came out in small puffs of fog.

"Perhaps I exaggerated a little."

"Good. I don't see what's wrong with calling in Damon and a few of his buddies to help."

"First of all," Lacey sighed, "there would be a huge cost."

"Don't worry about that." Brooke grinned. "DeadFed has a contingency fund for emergencies, recently set up by its loyal supporters."

This was news to Lacey. "No doubt supplied by Barton, Barton & Barton?" The night air was causing her eyes to tear up, not the idea that Brooke's law firm was subsidizing Damon's fringe adventures in Web journalism.

"Daddy loves Conspiracy Clearinghouse almost as much as I do. But we are not the only donors who believe in Damon's mission of truth-seeking."

"Nevertheless, bringing in Damon and his sweet band of loonies is not a good idea, Brooke. And remember, nobody really wants to find out what the inside of a French jail is like, and Damon is the most likely person to receive that honor if he gets involved."

"That might be true, but you were almost killed today, Lacey. Just think what could have happened if you'd gotten a bigger dose of whatever chemicals were on that rag. Toxicity by inhalation can be lethal. You want to stop at the hotel bar for a nightcap?"

"Thanks, but I'd rather not, if you don't mind." Lacey's head was feeling a little woozy, and she wondered if it was more than just the wine with dinner. Maybe she shouldn't have had anything to drink after being knocked out by a suspicious chemical.

"We'll leave first thing in the morning," Brooke said.

"No way," Lacey protested. "We just got here."

"But we need to check on that address in Paris."

"I'm sure the Rue Dauphine will still be there whenever we arrive, and no one has the address but us and Jean-Claude. Besides, I'm taking a tour of the Abbey tomorrow, then I thought we'd take a drive to the D-Day beaches in Normandy. Omaha Beach, Brooke."

"But we have things to do, people to see! Corsets to chase!"

"And places I've wanted to see my whole life. You go ahead, I can take the bus." Brooke started to protest, but Lacey said, "Maybe if you'd been flat on your back in that cellar, you'd feel like taking a breather, too."

"Of course. My God, you're exhausted after what you've been through. And I let you down. I'm sorry, Lacey. Maybe we should find a doctor to check you out."

"Not necessary." She wrapped her shawl a little tighter against the breeze coming off the Bay of Mont-Saint-Michel.

"Are you sure? There might be other side effects of that secret Russian knockout gas. You know, brain tumors. Amnesia. Split personality."

"I'm taking your comic books away from you, Brooke. And I'm unplugging that Web site of Damon's that feeds your lurid imagination." Lacey turned to take one last look for the evening at the towering Abbey that was called Saint Michael in Peril of the Sea. It seemed magical to her. "I have to come back here again someday."

"Right. Quite a sight." Brooke was a little less enthralled by the scenery. "What was that Bible verse? Genesis? You suppose there are French Gideons who put Bibles in French hotels?" she asked. "Never mind, I'll find the Bible on the Internet."

"Yes, but will you find God on the Web?"

Brooke ignored her. "So we think this Drosmis Berzins character took the corset years ago. But he couldn't have fenced it, could he? It's never surfaced."

"Not that we know of," Lacey said. "He could have sold the gems off one by one. Or sold the whole thing to a private collector, one of those strange characters you read about who have chambers full of priceless stuff and never show it to anyone."

"Some rich Russian Mafia guy? Maybe that's who this Gregor Kepelov character is? Or who he's working for? Some collector who doesn't know that the corset or the egg or whatever they think it is has already been collected?"

"Russian Mafia? And ex-KGB? Possibly." Lacey picked up her pace and readjusted her shawl around her as a sharp breeze kicked up, carrying a rich aroma from the sea.

"I didn't find an ex-KGB Kepelov on the Internet."

"You wouldn't expect him to have a Web site."

Brooke's skin looked a little blue in the night and her teeth began to chatter. "And what about this Griffin character? No trace of him either." She stopped and slapped herself on the forehead. "What's wrong with me!"

"Are you all right? You look pretty cold," Lacey said. "It's not much farther."

"It must be the jet lag! They're using false names, these guys, whoever they are. Maybe he's not KGB. Maybe he's MI5. Or CIA. Or—"

"Well, of course they're false names, Brooke. But the CIA doesn't look for buried stolen treasure." *I don't think.* "Do they?" Lacey realized she actually knew no more about the CIA than what she read in her own newspaper, *The Eye Street Observer*—not exactly an unbiased viewpoint.

"Rogue CIA." Brooke always had an answer.

"There's a redundancy for you." Lacey picked up the pace. "Tell me again, what did my mysterious assailant look like?"

"I just saw a bald head, from the back, running away. Big. Tall. Bald."

"Bald?" Lacey stopped short. That didn't fit with Lacey's preconceived notion of a dashing ex-spy. "You're telling me our bogeyman is bald?"

Brooke laughed. "Looked bald to me."

"I am so disappointed," Lacey said, joining her in laughter. "I'm expecting a Russian James Bond and I get a big bald guy." They picked up their heels and raced to the hotel.

"Bad news, Lacey," Brooke said, staring intently at her laptop computer screen. "Drosmis Berzins is dead." She turned the laptop so Lacey could read the obituary.

"He would be dead, wouldn't he," Lacey pointed out, "if he was a young man in Ekaterinburg in 1917? Or else he'd be a hundred and some years old."

Brooke had insisted on Googling Berzins' name directly upon their return to the hotel. She eventually found the old news about

Berzins' demise posted on a largely defunct Latvian genealogy Web site, along with his obituary from a Mississippi newspaper in 1988. It didn't say much, only that Drosmis Berzins was born in 1896, he emigrated to the U.S. from Latvia, and he was a quiet, modest man who ran a small tailoring shop and was well respected in his community. Berzins left two sons and several grandchildren and great-grandchildren. Brooke clicked on the links to the rest of the Web site, but they were as dead as he was.

"That would make him about ninety-two when he died," Lacey said. So Berzins had gone to America, but there the trail went cold. She suggested they search on the Bible verse, and Brooke's fingers flew over the keyboard.

"As the man said, 'Seek and ye shall find,'" Brooke said, pulling up an online Bible database. "Ah, here it is, Genesis chapter 3, verse 19, in the King James Version: 'In the sweat of thy face shalt thou eat bread till thou return under the ground; for out of it wast thou taken.' Oh, here's the famous part, Lacey: 'For dust thou art, and unto dust shalt thou return.' Hmmm."

"I don't like the way that sounds," Lacey said.

"So it's all about death. Great. Nothing but dead ends." Brooke sneezed and stared at the screen moodily. Lacey said good night and returned to her own room. Maybe the verse was meant to be Drosmis Berzins' little joke on his old friend Juris Akmentins, saying, in effect, "I went under the ground in your cellar, Juris, and out of it I took what you had hidden, nyah, nyah, nyah." As usual, she thought drowsily, you could read anything you wanted to into a verse from the Bible. All she really had left to go on was an address on the Rue Dauphine.

Life and death are a puzzle, but what better place to contemplate the vagaries of fate, Lacey thought, than the amazing Abbey of Mont-Saint-Michel? The next morning, Lacey hoped St. Michael of the Dangerous Seas would at least give her a sense of peace and some quiet to contemplate the information she had so far, which wasn't much. It may have been an illusion, she thought, but she felt perfectly safe there, on a tiny walled island in the sea with danger far away.

Shafts of golden light illuminated the Scriptorium, the room where the monks copied and illuminated the ancient manuscripts. It would have been the best job available for an educated monk; the room had to be kept warm and dry to facilitate the work. Lacey imagined their centuries-old warm and dry ghosts must be laughing at her foolish quest to find a bloodstained corset, a relic of a horrible execution amid a bloody revolution, its survival (if it did survive) a testament to the optimism of human greed and the desire to fend off death with the indestructibility of gems. She wandered languidly through the vast, cool spaces of the Abbey with a headset and a tape player with a self-guided tour in English, appreciating the stonework and the graceful arches that made each room a delight. At the moment, she had no idea where Brooke was. Her friend had gamely taken a headset of her own and marched off with a purpose.

A trip through the Cloister, the serene Gothic garden ringed by a covered walkway near the top of the Abbey, lacked only the atmospheric accompaniment of a Gregorian chant. Tourists could no doubt buy a CD, Lacey reflected, in the store on the lower level. She realized that here in the Abbey, among the majestic columns and the collected blood, sweat, toil, and prayers of centuries, treasure was a relative term. Peace could be a treasure too.

Lacey thought of the pilgrims over the centuries who had tried to reach the Abbey, only to be swept away by the raging currents of the sea or caught by the treacherous quicksand that separated the island from the mainland at low tide. The thought brought her back to her present predicament. She didn't know what dangerous currents might sweep her into deep trouble, or where the quicksand might lay in wait, but she felt very peaceful there. She wondered about buying a CD in the little store, maybe Gregorian chant sung by the monks of the Abbey.

"Lacey, have you had quite enough flying buttresses?" Brooke swept in on her meditation and grabbed her elbow. "Thank God I found you. Come on, you can buy the book and look at the pictures. We've got to lose that phony jewel retriever of yours and his KGB buddy."

"You've seen them?"

"I went to turn in my headset. I saw them picking theirs up and I turned right around. They're together. And they're following us."

"Together? You're sure they're not just taking the tour?"

"Very amusing. Not a chance, these headsets would be a great cover to wander around and look for us. But they didn't see me. I think." Brooke looked way too excited about this development. She pulled Lacey into a run to drop off their headsets at the entrance to the Abbey. They raced outside the thick Abbey walls, down the hundreds of stone steps to the village gates, and across the causeway back to their hotel.

"Let's hit the road for Paris," Brooke said as they threw their hastily packed bags into the rental car. "We'll see how many tiny French horses our little blue Citroën has under its hood."

Chapter 17

Brooke brought them back to Paris alive, after a harrowing high-speed drive through the green Normandy countryside. Brooke apparently thought she was qualifying for the legendary twenty-four-hour endurance race at Le Mans. Lacey was enormously grateful when the keys of the little blue Citroën were turned over to the rental agency near the Arc de Triomphe and they were back on the terra firma of the sidewalks of Paris.

They took an expensive taxi ride, on the newspaper's tab, back to the Hotel Mouton Vert and dropped their luggage in their rooms before taking a stroll. After the nonstop three-hour-plus drive from the Atlantic coast, Lacey needed to stretch her stiff legs, and Brooke agreed. And if Brooke was correct that she hadn't been seen in the Abbey, they were free, for the moment, from the duplicitous duo of Griffin and Kepelov.

An hour later they were accosted by Nigel Griffin in the Montparnasse Cemetery, near the grave of the American actress Jean Seberg. Lacey and Brooke hadn't planned to wind up there—they simply started walking at the hotel and soon found themselves in the graveyard, passing beneath the statue of an angel with spreading wings and a sculpture of praying hands. A jaunty British accent said, "Hello, girls. Back so soon? Lovely drive, what?"

Lacey spun on his words. "Oh, no, not you again. Go away."

"My dear Smithsonian, is that any way to talk to a dear old friend?"

"With a friend like you, I need an armed guard," Lacey said.

"And Nigel Griffin isn't your real name, you bastard," Brooke growled.

He stopped and stared at her in amazement. "It is so. Who says it's not?"

"Why isn't it on the Web?" she said.

"Because I'm careful, of course. It's a stealthy line of work, mine is. I don't exactly have a Web site. 'Missing jewels? I'm your man! E-mail Nigel at Griffin dot com!' "

"That's Griffin dot *con*, if you ask me. And you should be more careful about who you try to con," Lacey said, fed up at the very sight of him. "Why don't you go away and leave us in peace? We don't know any more about your silly Fabergé egg than you do."

"But you owe me one. I carried your bum up the stairs from the cellar."

"Don't forget I helped," Brooke pointed out.

"I am black and blue from your tender loving care!" Lacey raised her voice and then lowered it; bystanders were enjoying their little scene. They exited the cemetery with Griffin hard on their heels.

"Ladies, I'm crushed by your distrust," he pleaded. "Come on, I want you to meet Kepelov. My treat."

"Kepelov?" Brooke exclaimed, her eyes blazing. "The spy? So you two *are* working together. A conspiracy!"

"Kepelov? Where?" Lacey looked up and down the street for a hulking, bald ex-KGB killer in an idling car, waiting to chloroform her and torture her last secret from her. She hefted her heavy leather purse, ready to use it as a weapon.

"Why so jumpy, Smithsonian? Is this the valiant seeker of truth I read about on Conspiracy Clearinghouse?"

"Take a pill, Griffin. I don't plan on being chloroformed again."

"Oh, I doubt if he actually used chloroform. It's dangerous stuff, you know. Not his style."

"Aha, you are in league with him!" Brooke cried. "You said you'd only heard of him, this KGB loose cannon, that he was a deadly menace."

"We're more like casual acquaintances, actually." He grinned. "He's not such a bad sort."

"Right. He attacked me," Lacey snarled. "What did he use to knock me out?"

"Ask him yourself," he dared her. "At the café just down on the corner of Avenue Maine. He's waiting for us."

"I don't think so. We have nothing to talk about with either of you."

"But Lacey," Brooke pleaded, her eyes wide. "A spy? Maybe a real ex-KGB spy? A real conspiracy."

"More like real BS." Lacey relented with a glare at Brooke; it might be useful to get a good look at her attacker, she reflected, nd possibly throw a drink at him. *And surely,* she thought, *we'll e safe in a public place in broad daylight; won't we?* Griffin led hem a few blocks to a nearly empty corner café with green narble-topped tables. A man sat alone at one of them, his back to he wall, the front section of *Le Monde* hiding his face.

"Kepelov?" Lacey asked.

"Gregor Nikolai Kepelov." Griffin nodded. "Gregor, old man, neet my friends."

"Is he bald?" Brooke whispered. The newspaper inched down, eaving Lacey face-to-face with a man she remembered. Big and ald, with a handlebar mustache, like a cowboy. But this time Tex vasn't wearing the Stetson and the Hawaiian shirt.

Lacey looked at him closely. He was not actually quite bald, but is thin, blond hair was cropped very close to his scalp. At first lance, Kepelov was good-looking and muscular, but the closer ou looked, Lacey decided, the more you noticed that his face was ust a quarter turn off normal. His head was round but his face was aunt, with sharp cheekbones that stretched the skin, angular feaures, and a thin, pointed nose above the handlebar mustache. Keelov's pink skin was puckered by an old scar, a thin white line long his jawline, and his round, pale blue eyes seemed empty of motion. The big mustache called for merry, twinkling eyes; these vere nothing of the kind. His eyes made Lacey think of elecroshock therapy for some reason. He gave her the creeps.

"Hello, Tex," she said. He nodded.

"Wait a minute, you know this man?" Brooke said accusingly.

"No, but I saw him boarding our plane at Dulles. 'Tex' was just ny shorthand for his wacky style. Cowboy hat, Hawaiian shirt."

"Yes, you saw me," Gregor Kepelov said. His voice had a trace f a Russian accent. "And I saw you."

"I don't remember him," Brooke said.

"How could you miss him?" Lacey rolled her eyes.

"Really, mate," Griffin said with a smile, "aren't you spies supposed to be more subtle? No wonder the Soviet Union went out of usiness." He hailed the waiter for a black-and-tan and leaned caually against a table.

"Shut up, Nigel," Kepelov said, crumpling the newspaper with orce. "You bore me."

Kepelov's mood didn't dampen Griffin's spirits. "He's just ranky. A little tiff with the long and leggy girlfriend *du jour.* Course he likes them short and chubby too, don't you, Kepelov? Sit down, Smithsonian, you two make me nervous." Lacey and

Brooke stood their ground. Griffin pulled out a cigarette and a lighter.

"Griffin, you're not lighting that," Lacey said, "or we're out o here. Right now."

"Give me a break, Smithsonian, this is Paris!"

"Fine. See ya." Lacey nudged Brooke and they headed for th door.

"Put the cigarette away, Nigel," Kepelov ordered. "For th ladies."

"Oh, come on, Gregor, you can't be bloody serious—"

Kepelov pierced him with a cold blue glare. Griffin sighed an put the cigarette away. Kepelov turned to Lacey. "Ladies. Nice o you to come. Where is the egg?"

"I don't have any idea." Lacey held up her hand. "Scout's honor."

"We didn't even know it was an egg," Brooke said and was me with the frigid glare.

"Shut up," Kepelov commanded. "You go chasing to Franc after the old woman dies, and you don't know it's a Fabergé eg you're hunting for? You must do better than that."

"I am a reporter. I'm writing a feature story on a seamstress and her craft. How did you hear this fantastic tale anyway?" He wa silent, so Lacey changed direction. "And what's the big idea at-tacking me? You could have killed me, you big oaf."

"If I wanted to kill you, Miss Smithsonian, you would be dea by now." He indicated that she and Brooke should sit down. "Yo were looking for something in that farmhouse. What?"

Lacey took a seat warily and Brooke followed suit. "I was jus following Magda's instructions. I didn't know what I'd find. Sh was supposed to be with me. It was supposed to be a surprise." That sounded lame even to her. "But I guess you were the surprise right? A big, ugly surprise. And I suppose you killed her."

Kepelov looked at her for a moment before speaking. "I wish you were a spy. You would talk less and say more."

"Just a reporter on a story. I guess we're done here." Lacey stood up to leave, but Griffin blocked her way and she sat down again.

"Don't you think we can come to an agreement, between com-rades?" Kepelov showed his teeth. It was supposed to be a smile but it had the opposite effect, that of a lion going in for the kill. "If we all cooperate to find this egg by Fabergé, there will be plenty of profit to go around. Among comrades there is no conflict."

Lacey sighed. Brooke nervously tapped one foot, but she said nothing.

"That's right, we're all mates, all in this together." Griffin took his beer from the approaching waiter, who set down several shots of something clear in front of Kepelov. The waiter looked at the women for their order. Lacey ordered a Coke and Brooke followed her example.

"So now we're all friends?" Lacey said, lifting one eyebrow. "How do you suggest we go about being friends?"

"We share information," Kepelov said. "Like friends do."

Lacey glared at him. "You knocked me out. You must have searched the cellar. How do I know you didn't find something there?"

To her surprise, Kepelov started to laugh. "Because, foolish one, if I had found something, I wouldn't be here now with you, to share information. Like friends." He downed a shot of what Lacey supposed was vodka. "So, comrade. Now is the time to share."

"How long were you down there? After you dropped me on the floor?" Lacey asked calmly, privately aghast that she was sitting decorously at a table with the very pig who had manhandled her in Jean-Claude's cellar. She knew that men had a capacity for chumming it up even after they beat the hell out of each other, but she wasn't like that. She had a long line of vengeful Irish blood running in her veins, along with a bit of French and a few other nationalities with long memories, and she wasn't one to forget so quickly. Kepelov shrugged, not that elegant French shrug she had admired, but a deadly cold shrug. Perhaps he was honoring some sort of male code of civility among enemies, she thought, enemies whom he would just as soon kill as have a drink with.

"Maybe ten minutes, then I left. I was done there." His brow wrinkled.

"You left me laying there in the dirt and the spiders?"

"You are looking at this the wrong way. I was looking for a Fabergé egg. But I found nothing. A waste of my time."

"So what do you want from us?" Brooke said.

"He's getting to it, Goldilocks," Griffin said nastily. "Don't get your knickers in a twist."

"Maybe you read or heard something, something small, something that didn't even make sense, but it caught in your mind. Something the old woman said, something her idiot cousin said. Something you saw. And now that we are all friends?"

"I saw a dead dog."

"Yes, I saw that too. A pity. I like dogs. Dogs never lie."

Kepelov downed another vodka, while Lacey and Brooke sat with their hands on their Cokes. "You are not drinking. You think I might drug you? Put something in your drinks?"

"Someone who uses chloroform might use anything," Lacey said.

"Chloroform? You are sure it was chloroform?" He chuckled. The vodka was doing him good. "Why would I want you unconscious again, Lacey Smithsonian? Now that we are friends and we are sharing all this wonderful information," he said with a heavy dose of irony. Kepelov licked vodka from his handlebar mustache. He reminded her a little of Yosemite Sam with a Russian accent. She attempted a smile and hoped it didn't look too much like a sneer.

"Since you feel that way, why not give me the handkerchief you used? As a sentimental gesture." Lacey wanted to know what the monogram was. "Now that we're such good friends."

Kepelov smiled with everything but his eyes. "You are funny, you know that?" He laughed and Griffin joined in, but he made no move to produce a handkerchief. Kepelov stopped laughing and looked at his watch. He downed another vodka and gestured at the women dismissively. She and Brooke looked at each other and stood up to leave.

"This is such fun," Griffin said cheerfully. "Old pals in Paris. Let's keep in touch."

"Let's not," Lacey spat. The jewel thief and the spy sat drinking as the women left the café.

"God, I'm starved," Brooke said on the sidewalk, the tension finally getting the better of her nerves. "Aren't you starved? Obviously, we didn't dare eat or drink anything those thugs could have slipped something into. Let's get out of here. My hands are shaking. Aren't your hands shaking? Where do you want to go?"

Lacey was too angry to speak. She let Brooke chatter her nerves away and swaggered down the sidewalk of the Avenue Maine with a sense of bravado, determined to reclaim the afternoon and put this experience behind her. She was caught by the window of a lingerie shop. It was calling her. Frenchwomen were said to set great store by their lingerie, Lacey had heard. Bras and panties had to be sexy, they had to match, they had to be exquisite and expensive. And here they were. This obviously called for some serious firsthand research. She eyed the gaudily corseted mannequins in the window.

Brooke sneezed. Across the street there was a *tabac*, that odd French combination of a tobacco shop and a drugstore, where she told Lacey she would try to find more allergy medicine. "I'll meet you in the lingerie shop in fifteen minutes. I want to check out some garter belts too."

"I'll do reconnaissance. Don't be long, Brooke, then we'll find a restaurant." Lacey strolled into the store. After a few mandatory pleasantries in French with the saleswoman, she was left alone to browse. All about her were lovely and delicate garments in sherbet shades of peach, lime, and blueberry. Her hands immediately reached toward a blue lace bra and panties set. She picked it up, admiring the workmanship and the beautiful re-embroidered lace.

"So, Lacey Smithsonian." A soft voice came from behind her. "Are we not friends now? You seemed so upset, I wanted to remind you: I did not kill you. And I did not kill the old woman."

Kepelov had materialized behind her in the store. She whirled around, angry that she had let him sneak up on her again. "And I'm supposed to thank you for small favors?" *Sociopath!* She looked for Griffin; she didn't see him. "And if you didn't kill Magda, who did?"

He shrugged nonchalantly. "That is very pretty, the blue lace. Would be very sexy on you."

Lacey dropped the underwear as if it were on fire. Her hands itched to slap him. *What the hell is he doing in this shop anyway? This is female territory!* "You left me on the ground unconscious, covered in dirt and bugs!"

"Only spiders. How was I to know you do not like spiders?" Kepelov's expression was bemused. Even his blank blue eyes seemed to hold a hint of amusement.

"Are you crazy, or do you know women who actually like sleeping with spiders?"

Kepelov gave her a weird grin that made her think maybe he did. "The world is full of all different kinds of women."

"Why are you following me? I have nothing for you. That coal room in Normandy was the end of the trail for me."

"Then why are you here in Paris?"

"Because it's Paris, you bonehead! I've never been to Paris! I've wanted to see it my entire life."

"Ah. You should see Moscow." He moved closer and she backed away. "We could work together, you and I. Find this treasure. A Fabergé egg would make us both very rich, even after bribing all the people we would need to bribe. Do you have any idea how rich?" Lacey ducked between racks of garter belts. Kepelov handled them appreciatively, but his gaze never left her.

"What about your pal, Griffin?" *And where the hell is Brooke?*

He snorted. "Nigel is sometimes useful, but we are acquaintances only. He's a fool."

"And why should I throw my lot in with you?"

"Because I am resourceful, and not a fool. I would rather not discuss my particular talents, but you have seen the Spy Museum in Washington, D.C.? Some of my lesser work is on display there. Under other names, of course."

"You should really be having this conversation with my friend Brooke. She loves this stuff. So tell me, are you really KGB?"

"Ah. KGB is no more. Perhaps you heard? Disbanded in 1991. Turned into something else. Never the same again. No more USSR either, eh? I am currently between engagements."

"Don't look at me to fill your time." *What the hell does he want with me?* She turned her back on him to pick up some pretty cream-colored nightgowns. Maybe ignoring him would make him go away. She was wrong. The saleswoman was carefully giving them space, as if they were just another squabbling couple selecting some naughty nightie for a romantic tryst.

"I have a dream, Lacey Smithsonian," he said. She wondered why he kept using both of her names: *Maybe it's a Russian thing,* she thought. "It is the American dream, my dream, to buy a big ranch and settle down. In Texas."

"You're playing with me, aren't you?"

"No, no, it's true. I like big sky country."

"That's Montana, not Texas."

"Ah, it's all big sky country in the West. Like Siberia. Only hot. Someday, I will invite you there for Texas barbecue. We will laugh about all this."

"Oh, I'm already laughing," she said grimly. "Good luck finding that egg, Tex." Lacey fled to another aisle. Kepelov shrugged and picked up a sheer black nightgown to admire it. He gestured for the saleswoman, handed it to her, and followed her to the desk to purchase it. He smiled at Lacey. *He'd better not think he's buying that for me,* she swore under her breath, *or I'll make him choke on it.*

"So you do have a girlfriend," Lacey commented acidly. "Is this for 'Long and Leggy' or 'Short and Chubby'? What's the lucky lady's name?"

"I am a very popular fellow, but I never kiss and tell. Do you think she will like this?"

The tag said it was more than two hundred euros. *Is this for the woman who sleeps with spiders? He must like her a lot.* "Very naughty, Tex."

"Excellent." Kepelov smiled again. "Good to have advice from a fashion expert." The saleswoman began wrapping his purchase. Lacey caught a glimpse through the shop window of Brooke approaching, and she ran out the door to meet her. She had lost all interest in this particular lingerie shop, and she didn't even want to visualize Kepelov with his naughty Spiderwoman.

chapter 18

When Lacey and Brooke returned to the Hotel Mouton Vert that evening, Lacey detected a lingering scent of perfume in her hotel room, a woodsy rose scent with a hint of musk. It wasn't her own scent, nor did she think it belonged to the maid who had cleaned her room. It was vaguely familiar and it made her feel ill at ease. There was a memory connected to it somehow, but she couldn't place it. Someone wearing a rose scent had been in her room while they were out.

The signs that someone had gone through her things were subtle too, but they were there. Whoever searched the room was careful; it was apparent Lacey wasn't supposed to know. Her clothes in the drawers and in her suitcase were only slightly out of order, left slightly askew, as were her toiletries in the bathroom. The clothes she had hung up were spaced just a little too evenly on the rod. But her camera, her notebook, the diary, her cell phone, and her passport case with the torn note were all in her purse. They had been with her all along.

There was a knock at the door. "Lacey, it's me, Brooke. Are you in there?"

She opened the door. Brooke silently motioned for Lacey to follow her into the elevator. Grabbing her bag, Lacey locked the room and followed Brooke. She pushed the first-floor button. "I gather from these precautions that someone's been in your room too? Besides the maid?"

"I wasn't sure at first, but the Scotch tape I put on my drawers was broken."

"You put tape on your drawers?" Lacey was tempted to comment on Brooke's usual paranoia, but she held her tongue. Paranoia didn't seem quite so inappropriate now.

Brooke nodded. "Of course. Don't you? How did you know there was an intruder?"

"A scent of perfume. A woodsy rose, I think. And my things were disturbed. Not much, but I don't think housekeepers have time to rummage carefully through guests' suitcases."

"Perfume. Good catch, I didn't notice that. My allergies are still acting up."

"It's November, how can you have allergies?"

"Leaf mold. It happens every fall." Brooke paused, then opened her hand to reveal a tiny round disc with a broken wire trailing from it. "Best of all, Lacey, I found a bug."

Lacey felt her eyes open wide. "Are you sure?"

Brooke proudly pulled what looked like a fountain pen from her purse. "Of course I'm sure. I brought a mini radio frequency scanner with me." She waved it like a magic wand.

"Where did you get that thing?"

"A friend." Obviously, finding the bug justified all the trouble Brooke had taken in bringing her toys to France. "Damon will be so pleased."

"Pleased that our rooms were searched?"

"No, silly, pleased that we're on to them, that the scanner worked." She examined the thing in her hand, waving her scanner pen as if she were Tinker Bell. "This is the only one I found and it's a bit out of date—might be obsolete KGB stuff—but there could be more."

"Where did you find it?"

"Under the lamp next to the bed. It's obviously a quick and dirty job. They didn't go to any special lengths to plant it." She looked disgusted. "I mean, what do they take us for, a couple of airhead debutantes?"

By the time the tiny creaking elevator made its way downstairs, Lacey had decided to request new rooms. But as they reached the first floor, Brooke hit the button to return to their floor. "This was just a diversion. We have to go back and see if there's a bug in your room." Lacey sighed. "Turn on the radio loud while I do the scan," Brooke said, "so they won't hear anything."

Back on their floor, Lacey put the key in her lock and opened the door again. Brooke went to work with her mini scanner and soon nailed the bug, in the same location. Whoever had placed the bugs was predictable. Brooke shook her head at their buggers' naïveté. Lacey wasn't entirely convinced that the small round discs were bugging devices. Sure, they *looked* like some of the displays at the Spy Museum in Washington and at the Spy Store, Brooke's favorite electronic toy store. But perhaps Brooke was simply disabling the Hotel Mouton Vert's security system or something? Brooke rolled her eyes.

"Okay, we'll settle this. I want to smell your room," Lacey said.

Sure enough, the faint scent of woodsy rose wafted gently on the air in Brooke's room. It was definitely the same scent, the same person. "Can you smell that?" Lacey asked.

"Smell what?"

"The scent. It's the same as in my room."

"I can't smell a thing. Decongestant hasn't kicked in yet."

Back downstairs, Lacey told one Monsieur Henri Colbert, the hotel concierge, that she had taken a nap and had a terrible dream that her room was haunted, and she simply couldn't stay in there. It was the best pretext she could come up with on short notice. And Brooke assured him that she too would feel better on a different floor, near her friend. Monsieur Henri was unperturbed.

"But of course: Marie. It was no dream, mademoiselle. It was our ghost, the resident spirit of the Hotel Mouton Vert. I am so sorry, but really she is entirely harmless." He straightened his vest and smiled a little sadly beneath his trim mustache. Lacey and Brooke shared a stunned look. "Her name is Marie, a very tragic story. A tragic love affair. She becomes lonely. She means no harm. She is drawn to ladies who are in love, so they say. Perhaps she is longing to be near a happy love story, a happy ending. She is a romantic ghost. *Très triste.*"

No wonder I haven't actually met her, Lacey thought. *No happy endings in my romantic life.* Perhaps Monsieur Colbert was himself in love with Marie, she wondered, or at least with her legend.

"I can give you other rooms, mademoiselle, but I cannot guarantee Marie will not visit you again. If she has formed an attachment to you—" He shrugged.

"All the same, two other rooms please," Lacey said. "I'd rather not bump into Marie." He nodded agreeably, as if he heard these requests every day.

"Does Marie show up in a lot of your rooms?" Brooke asked with interest.

"Most often the floor you are on, where she died. Of a broken heart," he hastened to reassure them. "No violence. But she has been known to visit any room in the hotel. She was a chambermaid here, many years ago." Henri assured them they need only move their bags to their new rooms on the third floor and turn in the old keys. If they needed assistance, he would be happy to arrange it. They declined his offer.

"Does Marie wear perfume?" Lacey asked, feeling a little foolish. "Has anyone noticed any particular aroma when she's around? Or after she's left?"

Henri frowned. He couldn't recall any reports of a ghostly perfume. "But if you hear a woman crying and there is no one there, ah! It is poor, poor Marie." He sighed as he handed her the new room keys.

"I can't believe he's trying to make me feel guilty over hurting a ghost's feelings," she whispered to Brooke as they headed for the elevator once again.

Lacey didn't want anyone, living or dead, rummaging through her things. A new hotel room would help ease the feeling of intrusion, she thought, even though it was almost identical to the one she had just left, decorated in shades of blue instead of rose. Brooke's was done in yellow and gold instead of green. And she was satisfied that whoever had searched their old rooms hadn't found what he or she was looking for. Certainly not a Fabergé egg or a bloody corset.

Brooke scanned their new rooms efficiently and declared them bug-free. The air was also pleasantly scent-free. While Brooke was freshening up in her own room, Lacey felt compelled to take a moment to apologize to the alleged ghost, who she realized probably didn't even speak English.

"Marie, I'm sorry," she said aloud to the empty room. "I used you as an excuse, but I needed to get out of that room. *Je suis désolée.* No hard feelings, Marie. Let's be friends, *d'accord*?" Lacey felt utterly ridiculous, but suddenly the room lights flickered off and then back on, as if in acknowledgment. The hair on the back of Lacey's neck stood straight up. "Oh. Okay then. *Merci. Bonne nuit,* Marie."

Before leaving for dinner, Brooke carefully taped all their drawers and room doors with snippets of Scotch tape, and this time Lacey didn't even utter the word "paranoia." She and Brooke went in search of a restaurant at random, strolling around the neighborhood and through a small park. Lacey decided she didn't need to mention her possible encounter with Marie, not just yet. There was plenty to talk about concerning their earthly intruders, and she filled Brooke in more fully on her puzzling encounter with the softer side of Kepelov in the lingerie shop.

"Sorry I missed that, Lacey," Brooke said, amazed. "Imagine that goon buying lingerie."

"You think maybe it was Kepelov's girlfriend who searched our rooms?" Lacey asked. "A girlfriend who wears woodsy rose perfume? 'Long and Leggy,' the one Griffin mentioned?"

"Why not? There's always a woman behind every big dumb lug. She's probably the smart one. Maybe the black nightie was a thank-you for the search-and-bug operation. Only I vote for 'Short and Chubby.' "

"He does seem more like a thug than a spy."

"Maybe he's just the muscle," Brooke mused, "and Miss Eau de Rosewood is the brains. Let's try that little brasserie on the corner, it looks cute."

All through a dinner just as delicious as the one on Mont-Saint-Michel but at a third the price, Lacey's mind kept returning to the note, the torn note she had found in Jean-Claude's cellar. Did Juris Akmentins discover the corset was gone and then see the note left in its place in the metal box? Did he tear the note in half? If so, why, and why leave half in the box? Or did his old comrade Drosmis Berzins for some odd reason deliberately leave only half the note? She inspected it again by candlelight, pretending to examine the wine list while Brooke watched out for Kepelov and Griffin. The tear didn't appear to pass through any of the handwriting, though it was so dirty it was hard to tell; perhaps Drosmis simply wrote the note on an already torn slip of paper, so the note she had was all there ever was. Or perhaps it was torn between lines of writing.

Two questions remained: What did the other half say, if anything? And if it did say something, who had the other half now? With a sigh, Lacey added a third question: Why would someone wall up a poor little dog?

chapter 19

"Rue Dauphine is on the Left Bank, in the Latin Quarter, right in the heart of the city," Lacey announced the next morning, consulting her Michelin map book of Paris. "It's not far from the Ile de la Cité and the Cathedral of Notre Dame, so if we come up empty-handed, we can always tour the cathedral." The sun shone brilliantly and it promised to be a beautiful day. She showed the map book to Brooke over the table in a little bistro near the hotel over breakfast. They had agreed not to discuss anything related to Magda or the corset in the hotel for fear of undiscovered bugs.

"How do you propose we check the address?" Brooke yawned and poured herself coffee.

"We just walk down the street like we own the place, like everyone else in Paris, not drawing attention to ourselves," Lacey said. "Not like tourists."

"No, no, we *should* look like tourists! I know it isn't chic, Lacey, but really, if it's painfully obvious that we're harmless tourists no one will pay the slightest attention to us."

"And your path to being blissfully ignored?" Lacey smeared cherry jam on a croissant.

"Deception and illusion, of course." Brooke grinned like a little girl with a new Halloween costume. "On the plane I read the most fascinating book on disguise by this ex-CIA guy."

"I'm going to regret this, aren't I?"

"He says people see what they want to see, the big picture. Whether your hair is up or down, glasses on or off, those little things don't matter. Make a big change. Think of it as a reverse makeover. It doesn't make you look better or worse, just different. Not like ourselves."

"Aha. You want us to look like hideously clueless tourists, don't you?" Lacey's heart sank. This wasn't part of her looking-like-a-fabulous-Parisian-in-Paris plan. The bug scanner was just the tip of the iceberg of Brooke's bag of tricks. "Where do you suggest we find ugly touristy stuff? Is there a Chez Ugly Tourist boutique on the Champs Elysées?"

"There probably is, but I came prepared to make us over." Lacey thought Brooke could no longer surprise her, but the young lawyer produced a plain black tote stuffed with disguise goodies. Lacey was impressed. One might suppose that Brooke Barton, Esquire, was a frustrated actress, but one would be wrong. She really was a frustrated spy.

"Espionage has always intrigued me," Brooke said. "Did you know?"

"Never had a clue."

Brooke gave a modest little shrug of her shoulder. It was almost French. "It's really like a private investigator's traveling disguise kit, just the basics."

"I don't want to look ugly." Lacey took another bite of croissant. "I'm not allowed to look ugly in Paris, it's in my contract as a Lost Corset Raider. Underline 'Lost.'"

"You're not getting into the spirit of this," Brooke said, downing the last of her coffee.

"Do your basics include false noses? 'Cause I like my nose the way it is."

"I didn't bring noses. They're too much work. But I have a dental bridge. According to the spy disguise book, you don't really need that much to fool everybody. Just something big enough to catch their eye and stick in their memory and obscure the *real* you, the you that we now don't have to bother to cover up." She grabbed her bag and pulled Lacey from her seat. "It's a theory, anyway. Let's hit the ladies' room. We'll walk out of here two completely different people."

"We won't match our passports." Lacey paid the bill and followed her friend, still grumbling, feeling a little like Eeyore, the constantly complaining donkey in *Winnie the Pooh. Go ahead, make me look like an ugly tourist. Pin my tail on crooked. Just kick me.*

By the time Brooke was finished with her, Lacey was just glad she wasn't wearing an eye patch and a stuffed parrot on her shoulder. Instead, a dark brown bob curved around her cheeks like the famous Washington Helmet Head hairstyle that she loathed, and her eyes were peering through a pair of little black square-framed glasses, like an earnest new intern on Capitol Hill. And the ugly pale gray sweater and oversized navy blazer nailed the look. She could pass as one of the prematurely serious Washington, D.C., wonklings whom she tried so hard to imbue with the elements of style in her columns, "Crimes of Fashion" and "Fashion Bites." It was depressing.

"You look like an intellectual," Brooke said. "Or pseudo-intellectual. Not like you at all."

"I look like my date for Saturday night is a bowl of popcorn and my sexy back issues of *Congressional Quarterly.*" She gazed in horror at the reflection in the mirror. "Come to think of it, I look like I'll never get a date again as long as I live. Yuck."

"So now you're a crime of fashion. Have some sympathy for your victims. The last thing you look like is that stylish fashion reporter Lacey Smithsonian. Now, what do you think of me?" Brooke posed with her curly red wig, topped by a Yankees baseball cap, round red-framed glasses, and a pink I LOVE PARIS hooded sweatshirt.

"You look like a circus clown. Why can't we dress like femmes fatales?"

"Because we *are* femmes fatales. This no-flirting-zone look is what I was going for. I totally don't want anyone flirting with us."

"You're totally safe. However, some flirting here in Paris would really lift my spirits."

"I think," Brooke said, "finding the Romanov corset will lift your spirits."

"Don't you mean lift and separate?" Lacey said with a smile. "Besides, I don't have a clue about the corset."

"You're wrong, we do have a clue, the address on the Rue Dauphine. And if we look clueless, no one will follow us."

"No," Lacey admitted. "They'll be averting their eyes. But we can't stop them from laughing at us."

"A small price to pay for our freedom." Brooke smiled at herself in the mirror before hefting her heavy bag. "Well, my work is done. Almost. Let's drop this off at the hotel."

Brooke informed Monsieur Henri, the efficient concierge, that the bag was for Mademoiselle Barton, who would pick it up later. Henri, who had flirted with her single-mindedly for ten minutes earlier that morning, took her bag without a flicker of recognition.

"Did you see that, Lacey?" she whispered. "He didn't recognize me. What do you think?"

"I'm wondering if I've ever done anything quite this goofy before."

They navigated Paris with relative ease, Lacey realized, because they were used to Washington, D.C., a city designed in part by the French architect Pierre L'Enfant when George Washington himself was laying out the city. L'Enfant drew broad avenues radiating from circles like the spokes of a wheel on a horse-drawn cart, the vehicle for which the city was built. Later a rectangular grid of narrow streets was superimposed over the original hub-and-spoke avenues. The resulting layout may have been good for horses, but it was dreadful for things like cars. Hopelessly snarled traffic was a fact of modern life in Washington, just as in Paris. But Lacey and Brooke's mental map of Washington helped them make sense of the chaotic streets of Paris.

They took the subway to the Odéon Métro station and emerged on the Boulevard Saint-Germain with their tourist maps in hand and their Clueless Tourist looks firmly in place. A short walk the length of the Rue de l'Ancienne Comédie brought them to the Rue Dauphine, a narrow and bustling street of restaurants, shops, and hotels. It was just a few blocks long, ending at the Pont Neuf, the oldest bridge across the Seine. They walked the length of the street, up one side and down the other, checking every address, even a little alley marked Passage Dauphine. The street addresses were all two-digit numbers. But the address in Drosmis Berzins' note was 1101 Rue Dauphine. Puzzled, Lacey stopped in front of the Hotel Le Régent at number 61, near the end of the street where they began, and checked the map again.

She wondered if Paris streets, like those in the District of Columbia, might stop only to start again blocks away. But the Michelin book listed no other Rue Dauphine in the city. There were other places named Dauphine: a park, a circle, a gate, the passage off Rue Dauphine they had inspected along the way. None of them was a Rue, and the note had the word "Rue" underlined.

"Are you sure there's not more to it?" Brooke asked. "Show me the map again."

A Frenchman stopped and offered his help. He looked like a professor, not a spy, wearing a tweed jacket and dark brown sweater and slacks. Lacey explained that she and her friend didn't speak French very well and were lost. It was one of the first phrases on her French lesson CD, and it seemed to work. Lacey wrote an address on a piece of notebook paper, carefully making it 1103 instead of 1101. *If we find one*, she thought, *we can find the other.* He looked at the address and frowned.

"I am so sorry, mademoiselle. There is no such address on Rue

Dauphine. The street, it is short, as you can see, from here to the Seine. This number is too big. Perhaps a wrong address?"

"*Merci* anyway, monsieur." Drosmis Berzins, wherever he might be, was laughing at her.

"Ah, mademoiselle, I see you are unhappy. A pity, such a lovely lady, and on such a lovely day. Perhaps you would allow me to take you to lunch?" Brooke coughed loudly behind him. "And your charming friend, of course," he said, without looking at Brooke.

How can he flirt with me in this awful wig? Maybe just to keep up his skills. Maybe it's a French law. It seemed to Lacey that things were suddenly looking up. She felt her waning spirits revive with this masculine stranger's misplaced attentions, but Brooke grabbed her arm.

"We're meeting our mothers for lunch." Brooke showed her watch. "We're already late."

He bowed slightly, not at all offended. "Perhaps another time. *Au revoir.*" He turned to go.

"Pardon me again, monsieur, but is there more than one Rue Dauphine?"

"Ah, *mais non,* here is the only Rue Dauphine in Paris. *Désolé.*"

"Have the street numbers ever changed?" she pressed. "Could an address this high have been here once, years ago? Say, thirty or forty years ago?"

The Frenchman laughed. "Oh, no, Rue Dauphine is a very old street. Why change the numbers? We all would get lost, not only the pretty American tourists." He checked his own watch. "*Au revoir,* mademoiselles."

"Come on, this is no time for romance." Brooke pulled her away down a little side street. "It's not here. You heard the man: no such address."

"If it isn't here, it isn't in Paris," Lacey said. "It can't be."

"We have to debrief. Regroup. Make a new plan."

"Regroup? Brooke. Reality check. This is it. There is no other Rue Dauphine. And no such number on this Rue Dauphine. It's too high. End of debriefing."

"Maybe it's written in invisible ink. Or some kind of code."

"Right. A code. Let's call the CIA." Leave it to Brooke to look for a secret code. "This is what we know." Lacey counted out on her fingers. "Rue Dauphine, but a bad address. Seek and ye shall find. Genesis 3:19. 'Dust thou art,' et cetera. It's more like a nasty joke on old Juris, Magda's grandfather, than a code. Maybe it's a joke on us too: 'Seek and ye shall find nothing but dust on the Rue Dauphine.' "

"Let's try word association," Brooke suggested. "Let's see the original note."

"It's in Latvian! What kind of word associations do *you* have in Latvian?"

"I don't know; you're the writer. The wizard with words."

"The wizard is fresh out of words." Lacey looked at the map book again. "Here's my new plan. I'm walking *that* way." She marched purposefully up the Rue de St. Andres des Arts.

Brooke perked up and fell into step beside her. "Okay, where?"

"The Cathedral of Notre Dame de Paris. We look like tourists, let's act like tourists."

"So what are we going to find there?"

"Peace. The peace that passeth understanding."

"Wait, you don't have a clue?" Brooke's face fell. "Really?"

"That's right. We're out of clues, out of luck, and out of ideas." Lacey shrugged as if releasing a burden from her shoulders. *I'm getting the hang of this shrugging thing.*

"But what about the story, the corset?" Brooke shook her curly red wig. "There's got to be something more we can do."

"There is," Lacey said. "Light a candle and pray, you heathen Protestant you. I'll show you how."

"Candles? If it's dark in there I'll fall asleep. Can we get some coffee first?" She yawned.

"Sure, why not? May I present the Ile de la Cité?" Lacey led Brooke across the bridge, the Pont Saint-Michel, and took a detour past the Conciergerie, where Marie Antoinette was imprisoned before she was beheaded by the guillotine. The imposing building had been part of the royal palace until the late fourteenth century, she read to Brooke from the guidebook. So many French edifices seemed to have the same life cycle, Lacey mused. They began as monasteries or palaces, then became prisons, and finally museums.

"Come on, Lacey. I can't keep my eyes open much longer."

They stopped for refreshments at the Café Quasimodo, near the Cathedral of Notre Dame. *Obviously somebody had a sense of humor,* Lacey thought. Inside, the throng of tourists made her feel more at ease, less like she stuck out in the crowd like a sore thumb. There was more than one sore thumb in this crowd. The harried waiter took little notice of them, bringing their coffee and an eclair for Brooke and slapping *l'addition* down at the same time. Lacey thought she must be nearly invisible in the glasses and dark hair, as if she might move among these tourists unseen and leave no footprints. But she realized she didn't want to feel like a ghost for long. She too often felt like a ghost back in D.C.

They drained their cups and left the crowded café, dodging an American family of six with a crying baby and a busload of retired couples wearing loud matching sweaters. As they approached the Cathedral of Notre Dame, Lacey tried to imagine the hunchback Quasimodo tolling the bells and demanding sanctuary for the gypsy Esmeralda, the love he could never have, and Abelard and Heloise writing their passionate love letters. Another tragic love affair. A sudden image of Vic Donovan's smoldering green eyes flickered before her, but she pushed it aside. *I brought you here for some peace, damn it,* she told herself crossly, *now don't ruin it!*

Entering the Cathedral, Lacey made the sign of the cross. Brooke peered around like an interested visitor from another planet, scanning the crowd for Griffin or Kepelov. Lacey inhaled the warm aroma of burning candles and basked in the colored light filtering through the stained glass of the glorious rose windows high above. She dropped money in the box, lit the candles, and contemplated the cool serenity of the vast sacred space of the Cathedral. They found room in a pew near the back and sat down, Brooke yawning by her side. Lacey tapped her on the shoulder.

"How can you be sleepy?" Lacey asked. "This the land of lovers, the Three Musketeers, the Revolution, the Arc de Triomphe. The City of Light. Land of wine and cheese. The guillotine. Perk up."

"Yeah, it's inspiring." Brooke yawned again and wiped her eyes. "I didn't sleep much last night. I was afraid I might talk in my sleep."

Lacey felt her mouth drop open. "What on earth do you think you'll spill? Who really killed JFK? Vince Foster's assassins? Names of the dead aliens in Area 51?"

"You laugh." Brooke sniffed. "What if I said something about the Romanov corset?"

"I can't believe you lay awake worrying about these things," Lacey said. "You did the sweep in our new rooms. No bugs. Who would hear you mumbling about the corset?"

Brooke stifled another yawn. "And mostly I couldn't sleep because, well, I miss Damon."

"Oh. Of course you do." Lacey felt a sudden pang of guilt. Not only was she half of a couple in full breakup mode, she was keeping other couples apart. She was a carrier of the breakup bug. And in her clownish tourist disguise, Brooke wasn't even getting to enjoy the famous French flirtation. "Maybe it was the ghost who kept you awake," she said, hoping to cheer her friend up, and herself too. "What do you think, should we try to contact the spirit of Marie?"

Brooke's spirits rose at once. "Maybe she saw who searched our rooms! Maybe we could communicate with her!"

Lacey thought about the lights that flickered off and on at the Hotel Mouton Vert. "We'll invite our ghost-loving concierge, Monsieur Henri. You do believe in ghosts, don't you, Brooke?"

"Of course I believe in ghosts. I came to church with you, didn't I? And I believe in you, Lacey. I don't want to spoil this day for you," Brooke said. "I know you'll think of something brilliant. Something about the corset. Something we've missed." She yawned deeply.

Lacey suddenly felt empty and defeated. She stood up and shouldered her bag, and she gave her sleepy friend a hand up. "What we've missed is that we really are clueless. And if you think I can solve every mystery that comes my way, you have been reading too much DeadFed dot com."

Brooke smiled at the very mention of her boyfriend's Web site. "You're right. We're both clueless. Maybe I'll be smarter after I get some sleep. Call us a cab, mademoiselle."

Lacey's wig was beginning to make her scalp itch, and her tiny glasses were hurting her nose. She couldn't wait to shuck off her tourist disguise, and a plan was forming in her mind for a solitary stroll through the streets of Paris in search of inspiration while Brooke napped. She smiled. *At least it's a plan.* She lit two more candles, one for each of them, before heading back to the hotel. Lacey looked up toward Heaven, somewhere in the direction of the stained-glass windows high above them in the immensity of the Cathedral. She said one more fervent prayer.

I feel like a complete fool here. You got any bright ideas?

chapter 20

They caught a cab and were back at the hotel by one. Brooke went straight to dreamland in her room, after another scan for bugs. And after promising she would wake her up if she had any random brilliant thoughts, Lacey exited to her own room across the hall. It seemed very peaceful. There was no hint of a woodsy rose perfume, no bugs, and no ghosts.

She stripped off her depressing tourist costume, feeling happy to be free of the dowdy garb, and quickly changed into black slacks and a fitted black-and-red sweater that showed off her curves. She freshened up what her Aunt Mimi would call her "war paint," making her eyes smoky and sexy and her lips a deep red. Her highlighted hair, freed from Brooke's itchy wig, flowed down to her shoulders. Lacey saluted herself in the mirror, promising herself a wonderful solo outing on the streets of Paris. She felt much more like herself again. Brooke was a dear, but her obsessions and paranoia were cramping Lacey's style. Believing that at least half of looking good is attitude, Lacey felt she could now go toe-to-toe with any French femme fatale.

Grabbing her red leather jacket, her purse, and her map, she checked with the concierge for directions and headed for the Métro. Her first target: the Eiffel Tower. Lacey knew if Brooke was making up for a sleepless night she would have at least a couple of hours on her own. And if any Frenchmen wanted to flirt with her, bring 'em on, *chérie. Mais oui!*

One nagging thought intruded on Lacey's good mood. She would have to give up on Magda's dream of a lost Romanov corset, if it was a corset, as truly lost. *Once something is really gone,* she told herself, *accepting its loss should bring a measure of peace.* She had done her best to make Magda's last wish come true. She had traveled all the way to France, she had followed up on

Magda's only lead, and she had even found a brand-new clue, or half a clue. It had led her nowhere. But she had tried.

By the time the Métro train rushed to a stop, Lacey had mentally absolved herself of blame. She was free! If life were a musical, she mused, this would be a moment to break into song. A tap-dancing-up-the-stairs number, à la *An American in Paris.* Alas, she had never taken those dance lessons, but she was dancing in her heart.

Feeling lighter than she had since she arrived in France, Lacey emerged from the subway at Ecole Militaire, practically skipped down the Parc du Champ de Mars, and was rewarded by the riveting sight of the symbol of Paris familiar from all the photographs, the Eiffel Tower, a monument to structural steel, the sweat of untold workers, and the eccentric vision of Gustave Eiffel. It stood massive and proud with its multiple latticed layers, looking both monumental and as airy as lace. She breathed a sigh of relief; she felt almost giddy. Standing still for a moment, she savored the sight. Like any tourist on vacation, she pulled out her camera and took photos. *Ah, Paris.* If only she could ask someone to take her picture here. *That's me at the Eiffel Tower, Mom, it's the tall thing behind me.* But of course that was the whole point of this outing, to see a little bit of Paris entirely on her own.

"Smithsonian! There you are! Wait up!" Griffin's oh-so-English accent came from somewhere close behind her and it scraped her nerves like a cheese grater. This was not the way she intended to see the city, with a British barnacle on her butt.

Her moment of solitary elation suddenly deflated, Lacey whirled around to see his lanky figure running to catch up with her. He was thin, but he sure wasn't fit. He was wheezing as if he'd run a mile. She snapped his photograph with his mouth open and eyes shut.

"Why do you have to walk so fast?" He was out of breath. *Out of shape. A smoker.*

"What the hell do you want?" She wasn't feeling very friendly toward Griffin. She tucked the camera back into her leather bag and resumed walking briskly toward the Tower.

He tried to match her steps as they quickened. "Thought we could talk. Quietly. Without. That. Bugger. Kepelov," he gasped. "Good Lord, slow down, would you?"

"Oh, you mean your *buddy*, Kepelov?" She stopped short and turned on him. "Why? To give you another chance to search my room? Wasn't it enough the first time?"

"What the devil are you talking about?"

"Your little plan yesterday, you and Kepelov. Waylaying us? All that blather about working together? Just to keep us busy long enough to send your accomplice into the hotel, search our rooms? What's the matter? Didn't find anything?"

"Look, Smithsonian, I had no part in anything like that, you have to believe me." She snorted and resumed charging ahead. "Hold on! Someone actually tossed your rooms? I had no idea. Must have been Gregor's little scheme." Griffin sounded genuinely distressed. "He's a bloody bastard. Really."

"What's the matter, didn't he tell you? He doesn't trust you either?"

"Don't blame me." He advanced on her and she started walking.

"So who is she?" Lacey tossed the question over her shoulder.

"Who?"

She stopped and faced him. "The woman who searched our rooms. Who is she?"

"I have no bloody idea!" Griffin leaned over and coughed, trying to catch his breath, his hands on his knees. "None at all. How do you even know it's a woman?"

"The scent of a strange perfume was wafting through the room when I returned. It's a woman. Or you." Lacey didn't tell him the aroma was just on the edge of a memory that she couldn't quite recall. "I'd say it must be her signature scent."

"I don't know any woman who'd do that."

"Who's Kepelov's girlfriend? 'Long and Leggy,' you called her. Or 'Short and Chubby'?"

"I don't know. I swear."

"Tell me her name."

"Sorry. It's always a different one. I haven't met the new one. I don't even know how he pulls them, either. It's not his charm and beauty." He coughed again and shook his head. He reached into the pocket of his trench coat for a crumpled pack of cigarettes. "Got a light?"

"Don't you dare light that here," she growled. "That's the Eiffel Tower!"

He looked at the cigarettes, considered a moment, then put the pack away. He sighed. "You're a little cranky today."

"Maybe I just get that way when I'm attacked and people search my rooms and invade my privacy. Did you ever think about that? And maybe I get cranky when I'm followed by lying thugs and jackasses. Like you." Her one moment of freedom in Paris had been taken away by this jerk. And she vowed she would see that he suffered for it.

"This no-smoking business," he wheezed, "is this a Yank thing?"

"No, it's a don't-mess-with-Lacey-Smithsonian thing. You're not very smart, are you?"

"Don't get personal, please. It's not very nice."

"Her name, Griffin. I want her name." Lacey advanced on him and he backed up.

"He didn't tell me. Besides, I've never seen this one. I've only heard tales."

"What kind of tales?"

"The usual, kinky sex, that kind of thing. You know, boy stuff. But as far as anything else goes, believe me, Smithsonian, Kepelov's cut me right out of the loop."

"Bull. First you say you don't even know him, you've only heard of him, you're *fwightened* of the big bad Kepelov. Then suddenly you're buddies, partners, chums. Now you whine that your pal doesn't *tell* you anything. Every time I see you, you have a new story. Just pick one, Griffin. And tell it to someone else." She turned and stormed on ahead, determined to get to the top of the biggest tourist trap in town alone. If Griffin persisted in following her to the Eiffel tower, she could call security. Perhaps he'd fall off; it could happen. Perhaps she would take the stairs. *That would kill him for sure.*

He caught up with her again, breathing hard. "Wait! Please!"

"Leave me alone."

Griffin grabbed her arm. She tried to shake him off. "Get your big fat hands off me!"

"You don't understand," he pleaded, gasping for breath.

Griffin ought to be in better shape, Lacey thought. He wasn't that old, maybe mid-thirties. He was puffing like a steam engine, but he was hanging on for dear life, she couldn't shake off his grip. Suddenly, the air was charged with something she couldn't quite define and she was aware of another presence looming over them. Griffin was suddenly wrenched away from her and Lacey found herself briefly thrown off balance.

"She said leave her alone," a familiar deep voice said.

Oh yes. Testosterone. That's what Lacey had been missing. She didn't trust her ears and she was almost afraid to look at the speaker for fear she had only imagined he was there. Her eyes glanced at the shadow of him, long and tall, with a stance that was instantly familiar. He was wearing cowboy boots and lean faded jeans, a beat-up black leather jacket, and a black turtleneck. Then she looked at his face and her heart caught in her throat.

They shared a long look that was solace to her soul, right before he hauled off and punched Griffin in his soft gut, sending the Brit sprawling on the ground beneath the Eiffel Tower.

Lacey took out her camera again and shot a handful of photographs of Griffin rolling on the pavement, clutching his guts and gasping for air. She allowed herself to savor the moment.

Then she turned to face the man in the cowboy boots.

chapter 21

Lacey drank in the sight of Victor Donovan. From his curly dark brown hair to his well-worn boots, Donovan looked as broodingly handsome as any French movie star, but he was one-hundred-percent American. And he looked good to Lacey. Maybe too good. She didn't know what to say. Finally she breathed his name.

"Vic? What are you doing here?"

"Taking out the trash." He gestured toward Griffin without taking his eyes off Lacey. The Brit was now sitting on the ground, holding his midsection. "And I do mean trash."

"Very efficiently too." She glanced briefly at Griffin. "Thank you." How on earth was it possible that Vic was standing here right in front of her?

"Donovan? Bloody hell." Griffin looked nauseous. "What the devil are you doing in Paris?"

"You never learn, Nigel," Vic said. "You have to block that punch. Or roll with it. You can't do either one. And you can't run worth a damn either. You're hopeless."

Lacey's eyes went wide in amazement. "You know this guy?" she asked Vic.

Donovan just rolled his eyes, so Griffin filled the silence. "Prep school, wasn't it, Donovan? Dear old St. Albans, back in the District. Back in the day." Griffin seemed slightly recovered as he staggered to his feet. "You look well, old man. I've felt better actually."

"Put a sock in it," Donovan said without turning around.

"Vic! You went to prep school? With this twit?" Lacey asked. *Prep school, bastion of rich boys everywhere? And Vic?* This wasn't possible.

"A proud wearer of the jacket and tie," Griffin interjected. "Both of us. I have the photographs to prove it. Somewhere. No need to show the lady the secret handshake, old man, I'll vouch for you."

Lacey was absorbing too much information at once. "Military school, Vic, I could believe that. But prep school? I thought you went to high school in Alexandria. A normal high school."

Vic Donovan, the man she knew as a country boy from Northern Virginia, a military brat, a University of Colorado graduate, a former chief of police of both Sagebrush and Steamboat Springs, Colorado, and now running his father's security consulting firm, was right at home in a trout stream, a tent, a cabin, a Jeep, a police cruiser, or on a stakeout. A regular guy, with the soul of a cop. Lacey couldn't picture him as a teenage preppie, wearing Top-Siders without socks, with friends named Muffy, Buffy, and Biff, not to mention Nigel Griffin. But then judging from the way Vic greeted him, they were possibly not the best of old friends. Vic wasn't answering the prep school question. And Lacey had more pressing questions.

"How did you get here?"

"I had a ticket to Paris, Lacey. Be a shame to waste it."

"But you didn't want to come to Paris." He smiled and shrugged. "A wasted ticket? That can't be the whole reason, can it?"

"No, that isn't all, sweetheart." He put his hands on his hips.

When is he ever going to put them around me, she wondered.

"You said you hated Paris! You said everybody smokes in restaurants here! You said they let dogs smoke in restaurants here!"

"It's true, you know," Griffin cut in. "I believe they do. I bummed a ciggie off Fifi the poodle just yesterday at the Café les Deux Magots." He fished his pack of smokes out of his pocket again. "Anybody got a light?"

"Put those away or I'll hit you myself this time," Lacey said.

"Sit, Nigel," Vic commanded. Griffin sighed. He moved out of range of Donovan's fists and sat down on the ground. They ignored him.

Lacey looked at Vic. "You have to tell me why. Right here. Right now."

He took a deep breath and faced her, his green eyes alight with something she couldn't put a name to. "You're going to make this hard, aren't you?"

Lacey stood her ground. This was a moment of decision and it had better be good, because her heart was in danger of breaking. She couldn't speak for fear she would burst into tears.

"It's like this." He paused, then he rushed on. "I love you, Lacey Smithsonian."

"You do? You love me? Say that again, cowboy. Please."

"I love you, Lacey. Because of you I came to the last place on earth I ever wanted to see again. Paris."

"Paris is lovely," she said, feeling a little tongue-tied. "And I—I would love to—to see Paris. With you. Now that you're here—" *He said he loves me. Then why wouldn't he come to Paris with me?* "Wait a minute, you've been here before?"

"Long time ago. Not a fond memory. And you know they let just anybody in? Like him." Vic gestured at Griffin, slumped miserably on the ground.

"Watch the insults, mate." Griffin struggled to his feet and poked his head in between them. "I have to say I didn't expect to see you either, Donovan. Didn't exactly make my day."

Lacey shoved him and he toppled back to the ground. "Will you stop interrupting people!" She focused her attention on Vic. Her nerves were on edge, her stomach in a jumble, her heart pumping furiously. She remembered a day in the spring when Vic arrived at her apartment before dawn just so he could take her to see the cherry blossoms at sunrise at the Tidal Basin. *What happened in Paris? Did a woman break his heart in Paris?* "And you, I thought we broke up. Didn't we?"

"I didn't break up with you. I said I needed to step back and take a breath." Vic sighed heavily. "That's all. You're the one who got all carried away about breaking up."

"Carried away?" Her cheeks started to burn. "I did not!" Vic stepped in, held her in his arms and kissed her, leaving her dizzy.

"You take my breath away, Lacey," he murmured. "You always have. To tell you the truth, you scare the hell out of me."

"Oh, you're not supposed to tell her that, Donovan!" Griffin interjected. "You're giving away the bloody game, mate, the Holy Grail. Women have already got the upper hand—don't give away the whole bloody store. Men afraid of women?" Griffin smacked himself in the forehead. "Of *course* men are afraid of women! Some little vixen's got the great Kepelov wrapped around her finger, and now *you*, you turncoat."

"Shut up, Nigel." Vic glared at him.

"We were mates once," Griffin protested. "Well, sort of mates, anyway." Donovan held up his hand and Griffin shut up.

"You said you loved me?" Lacey said wonderingly.

"That's right. I love you." He said it with a trace of resignation in his voice, as if he'd been fighting it, but now he was resolved and not too unhappy about it. He smiled that slow, lazy smile that made his green eyes crinkle. She stood, momentarily mute. "And I came all the way to Paris to tell you that. I just have one problem. I need a place to stay. Got any ideas?" She couldn't find any words for a moment. "That's okay, maybe a park bench. They're nice in Paris, three stars. There's one."

He started to walk toward it. Lacey stopped him with a blush and took his hand. She shook her head, and Vic smiled. His smile could melt an ice cap, she thought, even the one that had chilled her heart. She almost forgot to breathe and she was trying hard to erase the irritating presence of Nigel Griffin. Here they were, she and Vic and her shadow, in the most romantic city on earth, at the foot of the Eiffel Tower. It was a scene she had never imagined, and yet now she imagined it could be even more perfect. A moment they would remember forever. A moment without Nigel Griffin.

"Vic, would you mind telling me that thing about love again at the top of the Eiffel Tower? Just the two of us?"

"Oh, good God, Donovan," Griffin moaned, "are you going to let her lead you around by your nose like that? The great Vic Donovan? Cock of the walk, captain of the guard, and all that rot. Get to the good stuff, will you? This sentimental prologue is making me sick. If you're talking sex, then let's talk sex."

"He babbles like this," Vic said. "Always has. Shall I run him off? Or punch him again? That shuts him up for awhile." He looked like a cat seeking permission to pounce on the rat.

She glanced at Griffin, then back to Vic. She raised an eyebrow. "You'd do that for me?"

"Hell, yeah, darlin'," he said. "It would be my pleasure."

Griffin retreated a few steps out of punching distance, as if he'd had years of practice at it. He dusted off his trench coat. "No more punching, mate, I can take a hint. See, I'm shutting up." The cigarette pack came out again and he shook it and took one.

"Good, I was beginning to think you were just in this for the beatings," Vic said.

"He's always had a twisted sense of humor," Griffin confided, leaning in toward Lacey. "Someday I'll tell you all about this rogue. But for now, Smithsonian, I'm leaving the option open for our partnership. And what I wanted to tell you was—"

"Don't hold your breath, I'd have an idiot for a partner," she said. Vic laughed.

"Sticks and stones," Griffin said.

"What about your buddy Gregor Kepelov?" Lacey asked.

"Oh, we were never serious about each other. Just exploring our options." He fished a lighter out of another pocket, but it was empty. "Damn, out of fluid. It's over between me and Kepelov, and that's why—"

"You must have other people to bother," Lacey said.

"No, not really. You're my favorite this week."

She leaned against Vic. "Can you make him stop? Without hitting him again?" Vic shook his head sadly.

"Go away, Nigel," he said. "I'll find you and beat you up properly later. Promise."

Griffin perked up at having permission to flee. "Later, you say? Well, my little news can wait. Wrong time, wrong place, it seems. And you two probably deserve each other anyway. This isn't the last of me, you know." He took a step back. "Donovan, old man, we'll have to catch up, old times and all that. Call on me anytime, I'm never in." They ignored him. "Right. Later, then."

Vic took a step toward him with his fist raised, and Griffin sprinted away. "I'll be in touch, Smithsonian," he shouted from a safe distance. "I'll tell her everything, Donovan!"

Vic laughed as Griffin retreated in the distance. "Thank God he left. I thought I'd have to keep punching him." He put his arms around Lacey, kissed her gently, and then harder. "This Paris trip is not just another fashion story, is it? Are you in some kind of trouble again?"

She looked at him, trying to think what on earth to say. "And it was such a nice day, Vic."

"It's one of those up-to-your-neck-in-alligators stories, isn't it? And he's one of the gators, right?"

"It's complicated," she said, remembering this was the point where Vic usually got upset.

"But not boring, I bet." Resignation crossed his face, but a smile came with it. "While you're at it, tell me which sewer Nigel Griffin crawled out of. And how in the name of sweet justice is he connected to you?"

"First tell me how he's connected to *you.* What prep school did you two go to? St. Albans? The one by the National Cathedral?" She was wondering what the tuition must have been. Donovan's family had to be stinking rich. "I'm sure Griffin would be happy to tell me all about your golden schooldays together."

He put up his hands in surrender and laughed. "I give up. We'll save the double cross-examination for later. Just tell me one thing," Vic asked. "You're not in mortal danger, are you?"

"Don't be silly," Lacey said, linking her arm with his. "At least not anymore."

Donovan peered up at the Eiffel Tower. "I suppose you were on your way to see this monumental tourist trap? And you want to trap me on it too? It's not such a great view, you know. All you can see is Paris."

"Paris'll do. And you. I was about to buy a ticket when my shadow arrived. And then you." They approached the ticket window. "How did you know I was here? You did come looking for me, right? How'd you round me up out here on the open range, cowboy?" She wondered if it would be too romantic to imagine they had some kind of instinctual bond, that he could find her anywhere just by tuning into her wavelength, like a homing beacon. *Nah.*

"I believe his name was Henri, at your hotel. Helpful, for a French concierge. Said you asked which Métro stop and how long to get here." He thumped his head. "Being the brilliant sort of guy I am, I put *deux* and *deux* together and got *duh.* By the way, I left my bags with him at the hotel, but I can still sleep on that park bench."

Lacey flashed her eyes at him to *shut up* about sleeping on park benches. She realized the chatty concierge Henri had probably put Griffin on her trail as well. She bought two tickets for the Eiffel Tower and handed Vic one. "You've been here before?"

"A short visit, a long time ago. And I occasionally have to go to London. I like England, except for having to duck Nigel."

"I've always longed to see Paris. Did I ever tell you?"

"Only a thousand times or so. So tell me, Lacey, Lacey, Lacey." He held her hands and repeated the question she had been dodging. "What the hell kind of mess are you—*we*—in now?"

"Who says I'm in a mess?" They joined a line behind a group of Japanese tourists wearing beige topcoats and carrying video cameras. "And did you say 'we' or '*oui*'?"

"I said 'we.' And you didn't have to. There's our mutual friend Nigel Griffin, for one thing. He's prima facie evidence of a mess of some kind. I know his history, which we will discuss later. For another thing, there's Damon Newhouse, a lovesick puppy convinced that you and your barrister Brooke Barton, the love of his life, are in mortal danger. Of course, he also thinks the alien invasion of Earth is just weeks away."

"Damon?! What does that cyberpunk would-be journalist have to do with anything?" She paused. "What will Brooke tell him when we get back? She told Damon she was just coming along to comfort me over our, you know, our breakup. Vic, are you sure we didn't break up?"

"Positive. And whatever Brooke's telling Damon, she's telling him right now. If they get around to talking."

"No! He's here?!" Lacey grabbed his arm as they entered the elevator to the upper levels of the tower. "Vic, do *not* tell me Damon Newhouse is here in Paris!"

"You got it, honey. I won't tell you." They moved to the back to let more tourists on.

"Tell me! Tell me!"

"I dropped Damon off at your hotel along with my bags. And his bags."

"No! You guys didn't travel together?!" A trans-Atlantic flight with Damon Newhouse and his crackpot conspiracy theories would drive anyone crazy. *Poor Vic.*

"What can I tell you? He was half convinced we'd find the two of you floating dead in the Seine. For so many different reasons."

"Yeah, I bet he was the Scheherazade of Air France, with a thousand and one wild tales."

Vic put his arm around her, smiling. "He's in love. It can be pretty hard on a guy."

"Tell me about it. Is it hard on you?"

"You have no idea." He held her tight and kissed her forehead.

"I'd love to explore that line of questioning, Vic, honey, but first tell me, what has Brooke been telling Damon?" Brooke was still under attorney-client privilege, but Lacey was afraid something might have slipped out. She had visions of lurid headlines burning up the Web, courtesy of Dead Fed dot com: RADIOACTIVE SPIDERS ATTACK SMITHSONIAN! SUBTERRANEAN CHAMBER OF DOOM! MASS GRAVE OF SMALL FRENCH DOGS!

The elevator door opened and the tourists flooded out onto the platform to enjoy the spectacular bird's-eye view of Paris. Lacey grabbed Vic's hand and drew him toward her as she elbowed for a position overlooking the Seine.

"Brooke has been telling him you swore her to secrecy," he said, "which of course set off all the worst kinds of alarms for Damon."

"Subtlety was never her strong suit." Lacey closed her eyes and leaned against the railing.

"Apparently Newhouse found your gag order very suspicious. And there has been none of the usual banter about conspiracies filling her e-mails to him, no evil empires, gunrunning rogue federal agents, no chat of intergalactic chicanery, just innocent chatter about cafés and cheese and the weather. Also very suspicious. Then he pointed out—"

"What?" Lacey opened her eyes. Her worries that people might overhear them seemed to be unfounded. All around them, tourists were chattering, taking photographs, and stealing kisses.

"That the two of you together are double trouble and no doubt in need of help. Damon admires your spirit, he says, but you are, quote, 'a lightning rod for catastrophe.'"

"I am no such thing."

"He pointed out," Vic continued with a smile, "that you have certain natural self-defense instincts, you're dangerous with knives and other sharp implements, and you could probably go bear hunting with a buggy whip. But he thinks Brooke is a delicate little creature."

"'Bear hunting with a buggy whip'! If I get my hands on him, he's a dead bear," she growled, much to Vic's amusement. "And Brooke's no delicate flower. She's bigger than I am."

"But perhaps without quite as much heart. You don't even need a buggy whip, and besides, darling, your hands are going to be full. Now that I'm here."

She felt herself blush, all thoughts of Damon and Brooke and the hunt for the lost corset momentarily vanquished. She looked out over the Seine at the Basilica of Sacre-Coeur shining in the distance, and she made a mental note to see it up close. With Vic. Maybe it was a good thing that Damon was here to keep Brooke busy and safe. That would give her time alone with Vic. She took a moment to savor the spectacle of Paris spread before her at her feet in the November afternoon sun. She closed her eyes and breathed it in deeply. Vic Donovan's arms were around her and she was inhaling the warm scent of him, intensely male with a hint of cloves and spice. The afternoon was beautiful, Paris was lovely, the air seemed light and full of promise. It felt like Heaven.

"Vic, would you please say that thing you said before? Now that we're at the top of the Eiffel Tower? This would be a good time for it. I promise."

Vic smiled and held her a little tighter in his arms and whispered in her ear.

Oh, yeah, this is Heaven.

chapter 22

"So tell me about this story you're on," Vic said later, holding her tight as they admired the view of Paris. "Does it has some wacky fashion angle? And where does the danger angle come in?"

"You never want to know about the wacky fashion angle." Lacey didn't want to lose that heavenly feeling under his interrogation. "All that girly stuff. Do you really want to know?"

"Of course I want to know. I love girl stuff. Besides, your fashion stories have a habit of winding up with you trying to bean some killer with a frying pan."

"I have never used a frying pan!" She recalled using whatever was at hand in self-defense: a sword cane, scissors, hair spray, the power of the press. But a frying pan was not in her repertoire. So far. "And it hasn't been that often."

"The frying pan was a metaphor." He kissed her hair. "All I'm saying, Lacey, is maybe we shouldn't keep our secret lives as crime-fighters quite so secret. Not from each other." He took her hand. "Why don't you try trusting me?"

"Does that mean you're going to tell me all about your own private investigations?"

"They aren't nearly as interesting as your fashion stories. Some of them are still classified. And we were talking about you and how trouble seems to follow you. I should buy you a baseball bat to ward off the bad guys."

"A baseball bat?"

"Your mother seems to like golf clubs as a weapon, but knowing how independent you are, I doubt you'd want to compete in the same sport."

"She's even more lethal in the kitchen." Rose Smithsonian had a disturbing tendency at holidays to pour marshmallows on too many dishes: the Jell-O salad, the sweet potatoes, the Rice

Krispies Treats, the meatloaf. "You'd love her killer cranberry marshmallow Jell-O Mold Surprise."

"I'm already crazy about you, why wouldn't I love your mother's— What's that again?"

"You are crazy, cowboy. So what's on your mind?" Lacey pulled Vic by the hand to circumnavigate the top platform of the Eiffel Tower. She wanted to see the city from every angle.

"The same thing that's been on my mind since I first laid eyes on that cub reporter from the *Sagebrush Daily Press* who stomped into my office at the Sagebrush P.D., demanding to see the police log and all my case files. All big eyes, long hair, killer body, and righteous indignation." Tingles crawled up and down her spine. Funny how he still had that power all these years later, she thought. "But seeing as how we're in a public place and I can't act on those impulses, you'd probably better tell me about your current dance with danger."

"What did Damon tell you?" She braced herself for the worst.

"Way too much. I had to stop listening. He'd half-convinced me you'd been kidnapped by some foreign government that brainwashes journalists into spies. Maybe they were aliens, I forget."

"Aliens brainwash fashion reporters?"

"Not just any fashion reporter. There was talk of U.S. 'government repossessors.' Damon says most of these brainwashed reporters have been eliminated. I think he mentioned Area 51."

Lacey laughed. "I'm sticking with Damon's story. Beats my story, which is a wild-goose chase to a dead end."

"Come on, Lacey. I need to know what I'm up against." Lacey noticed a man a few feet away eyeing her in a flirtatious French way, not a 'government repossessor' way. He gave her a little wave, but Vic frowned and the man retreated. "And you're too damned cute. That's another reason I had to come to Paris. You are too tempting. These guys here are French, you know."

"That's so sweet," Lacey said, and he rolled his eyes. "This interrogation may call for wine, Vic. A glass of wine and I'll tell you everything I know. And then some."

"Deal. I'll ply you with wine. There's a café here in the Tower somewhere. Let's go see."

But the little open-air café on the upper level was packed full of tourists, and the formal restaurant on the second level, the Jules Verne, had a wait of days, if not weeks, for a table.

"The Champs Elysées, Vic? Please." She'd only glimpsed it in passing, picking up and dropping off the rental Citroën, and she was dying to see the entire avenue. She wondered if she might be able to string the story out long enough to tour the whole city. A bit over wine here, a bit more over dinner there? A bon mot or two at the Cluny Museum, where she could see the famous unicorn tapestries? Above all, she wanted both to see Paris and keep Vic from going off the deep end over her corset caper. In bite-size morsels the lost corset tale might seem a little less crazy. And she could keep him totally focused on her, just as he was right now. "Besides," she said, "I need to get a feel for French street fashion. I've been too busy to pay attention to what the stylish natives are wearing."

"Good idea," he said, as he hailed a cab for the trip across the Seine to the eighth arrondissement. "Fill me in on the fashion clues when a woman is murdered and, I quote, 'covered in a blanket of twinkling jewels.' Quite a picture."

"Aha. You read my story in *The Eye*."

"I'm a dedicated follower of fashion." He took her hand to help her from the cab and led the way to the Champs Elysées.

Lacey's plan to parcel the story out a little at a time evaporated under the influence of a second glass of Bordeaux and Vic's penetrating green eyes at a small corner café on the famous avenue. With Vic at her side, Lacey could finally relax enough to observe the street scene. Their corner was a prime spot for Parisian people-watching, which seemed to be the main spectator sport in the city. Men and women paraded past them with a haughty air of self-satisfaction seldom seen in the harried and beaten denizens of Washington, D.C. The variety of street fashion was stunning, from breathtaking elegance to pure grunge. Lacey was charmed by the sidewalk stands offering not the hot dogs and pretzels of Washington, but delicious fresh crepes with a variety of fillings. Vic, however, remained focused on her, as she had hoped.

Lacey was also charmed by the French custom of turning all the sidewalk café chairs toward the street to observe the passing scene, as if every day were a parade day. It was a lovely afternoon, warm enough to sit outside with their backs to the glass windows of the café. The French, it seemed, loved to look, if not to take part in the little dramas occurring on the street. Well-dressed gentlemen frequented a small newspaper and magazine stand nearby. The French version of the ladies who lunch provided a collage of color and elegant afternoon fashion. Lacey regretted not taking actual written notes for her story, but Vic's presence was very distracting.

She found that she wanted to tell him everything. Perhaps the wine was helping, but the thought suddenly struck her that she trusted him. Lacey trusted few people, probably a side effect of being a journalist, even a lowly fashion reporter. The code of cynicism was deeply ingrained in her instincts.

But this new version of Vic proved not to be judgmental about Lacey's role in the story of Magda and the supposed Romanov corset and the duplicitous Griffin and Kepelov, though he occasionally raised a dark eyebrow in disbelief.

"Let me get this straight." He set his wineglass down. "You were mugged in a dark cellar in a farmhouse in Normandy? By a Russian thug looking for a Fabergé egg? And this thug is in league with that nitwit Nigel? And all you found is a dead dog and a torn note in Latvian? I don't know who's crazier in this story."

"Probably me. But it's not a Fabergé egg. At least, Magda was looking for a corset. She only said she used to *think* it was a Fabergé egg, before she inherited the diary."

"So you said. But a phantom corset full of Romanov jewels? Wow. Even for you, Lacey, this is a wild and woolly tale." He shook his head and downed his wine. "And darling, you have a peculiar habit of making dangerous promises to dead people."

"Technically, they're usually still alive when I make the promise. This is the last time, Vic, I promise. Really."

"Promises, promises. I should have been there with you in that cellar."

"You want to beat up the big bad Russian for me? I'm flattered, but I'd like a chance at him first."

"You never wait for me," Vic complained. "You're always in the front line with bayonets fixed."

"There are no appointments for self-defense, Vic. It happens when it happens."

"Fair enough." He cocked an eyebrow again and smiled. "I don't think there's a snowball's chance in hell this corset thing still exists. If it ever did."

"But just imagine if it did." Lacey gazed at the sidewalk scene. A blond woman in tight blue jeans decorated with rhinestones running up the seams teetered precariously on impossibly high heels with pointed toes. Fake jewels were everywhere. The woman staggered on, loaded down with designer shopping bags and a little dog in her purse. "A front page story around the world. History in the raw."

"Or a hoax on the hoof. How did Griffin get involved?"

She wrinkled her forehead in concentration. "He showed up at Magda's memorial service, demanding information. Wanted me to collaborate with him."

"What did you tell him?"

"Nothing! I thought he was a phony, maybe another reporter. And I have enough trouble with Damon Newhouse poaching my stories and turning them into science fiction."

"Nice to see you reporters trust your own kind."

"Not one whit." That sounded sharp, so she amended it. "Maybe on a case-by-case basis. I occasionally trust Trujillo, but not always even him." Lacey pulled her notebook out of her jacket pocket and flipped through it. "Griffin says he's a 'jewel retriever.' What can you tell me?"

"His name pops up once in awhile in certain circles where I travel."

Vic rarely talked about his world, those circles rife with private investigators, Pentagon contracts, and classified intrigue. Lacey leaned in to him. "You two go back a long way together."

"Unfortunately. About twenty years."

"You met when you were sixteen?"

"About that." Vic rubbed his face. He looked sleepy. "This information is off the record."

"Off the record! I can't believe you would say that to me!" But then she remembered how often she used the "off the record" phrase when talking with Trujillo and Mac at *The Eye*. "Okay, so tell me. Off the record. For now." She poised her pen to write.

"Nigel Griffin was a British embassy brat at St. Albans. And a thief. Couldn't keep his hands off other people's stuff. I learned pretty quickly you had to lock up everything with him around. Young Master Griffin was a delinquent in training. Always in trouble, but with the family connections to get out of it. Officially. Although he used to get beaten up a lot. Unofficially."

"So you were in prep school together. I thought you went to a regular high school, in Alexandria."

"I thought we covered that. I transferred to St. Albans from T. C. Williams."

"And why? We covered why Griffin was there, not why you were there. But we'll pick up on it later."

"I may have to plead the Fifth. May I continue?" She nodded. "Nigel developed quite a reputation at school. His room was known as Griffin's Lift-a-Gift, Nigel's Five-Finger-Discount Store. You could usually recover most of your stuff if you threatened to put his lights out. He didn't mess with me much." Vic sipped his wine, pausing to watch the sidewalk crowd. "His repertoire included forgery and car theft. I heard he furthered his criminal education at Oxford before they kicked him out. Never went to class, stole valuable pearls from a girlfriend and hocked them. Eventually he stole something from a professor's wife, which was too much."

"Wait a minute, he went to St. Albans? And Oxford? He doesn't sound that bright."

"Actually, Nigel's always been smart, too smart for his own good. He can be very clever. But he has a bad habit of tripping himself up. A clever fool."

"Maybe he has some kind of mental problem. Like kleptomania."

"My heart bleeds. The guy's a liar and a thief, and I don't want some sort of mumbo jumbo about a bad childhood excusing him." Vic leaned back in his chair and stretched. He yawned deeply. Lacey felt sorry for him. *He must be as jet-lagged as I was on my first day in Paris.* "Nigel didn't learn his lesson, though, till he came back to the U.S. and tried to fence the goods from a big jewelry heist. Over a million in diamonds and watches. Only a complicated plea bargain let him stay out of prison."

"So what does he actually do now?"

"As part of the deal, he works for the insurance company that busted him. As a fraud investigator."

"What? Griffin's a good guy? They figured it takes a thief to catch a thief?"

"Something like that. And the jury is still out on Nigel being a good guy."

"They really pay him to do this?"

"Yep. On top of his salary, he gets a percentage of what he recovers."

"Hence the 'jewel retriever' tag. So that part is true?"

"According to his boss, a friend of mine, he likes figuring out how other thieves do it almost as much as he liked being a thief himself. But I imagine he's probably working both sides. A little for the boss, a little for Nigel. That's much more his style."

"Why jewels?" Lacey glanced down at the small emerald ring on her right hand that Aunt Mimi had given her when she graduated from college.

"They're the perfect thing to steal. Small, valuable, portable, easy to sell. He started stealing jewels from his mom when he was a kid and pawing through purses at his folks' parties."

"What a little creep. How do you know all this?"

"It's the kind of thing you talk about in prep school. Very educational environment. And his folks are rich. He didn't even have to steal. Just a natural-born thief."

"So, speaking of rich kids, Vic, are your folks rich?"

He shook his head. "We're comfortable."

"Oh, my God. You *are* rich. That's what rich people always say. 'Comfortable,' huh? You're picking up the check, rich kid."

Vic smiled. He pulled money from an inside pocket of his black leather jacket and tossed it on the table. "Can we get out of here? I need some sleep. I'm jet-lagged beyond belief."

Lacey couldn't contain a sigh. *And I thought tonight was the night.*

chapter 23

Vic pleaded jet lag to escape the café, but he seemed to catch a second wind in the cab ride down the sunny Champs Elysées and across the Seine. At the hotel he stowed his bags in her room. There had been no discussion of his getting a second room, even though they had just established that as a rich kid, he could probably afford it. Lacey had carefully avoided the subject, half afraid he might do just that. He threw himself down on her bed and made room for her next to him.

"Why don't you join me? Just a little shut-eye, then maybe we'll get up and go out on the town. It's not even prime time yet by Paris standards."

Lacey had wanted this man for so long, and now here he was, in her hotel room in the City of Light. She could hardly believe it. Her reactions seemed to be splintered: She felt alternately too shy and too bold. She sat primly on the edge of the bed, unsure what to do next.

He kicked off his boots and pulled off his black turtleneck, revealing his tautly muscled body, still tan from the summer he had spent in Colorado.

Oh, my God, you're gorgeous, Vic Donovan. She filled her eyes with the sight of him. Lacey had longed to see Vic just like this. His chest had dark curly hair, which she had often imagined but seldom glimpsed. She slid over next to him, fingered his curls, and admired the rest of him. His shoulders were broad and his hips were narrow. She could imagine him as a Greek statue come to life. "I've thought about this moment for a long time, Vic." *Ever since Sagebrush.*

"And you kept it to yourself? You could have said something, sweetheart." He sat up and hugged her. "I would have been right there if you so much as snapped your fingers. From that first day you walked into my life. How many times did I ask you out, and you kept saying no? You didn't have to go to Paris to get my attention." He reached out for her, caressing her back with his warm, strong hands and peeling her sweater off. "This is very nice, very pretty, very alluring," Vic said, nuzzling her hair.

She laughed. She could feel herself blush. She was glad she was wearing her sexiest black lace underwear. Paris—and Vic—deserved her very best. They embraced, kissing, hugging, laughing. "Let me look at you," he said. "What a small waist you have. You don't need any Romanov corset, do you?" He put his arms around her waist and massaged her lower back, moving his fingers slowly upward. "You feel delicious."

Lacey turned and kissed him hard as they sank down on the bed. She found it difficult to believe this moment was actually happening. Maybe it wasn't. Maybe she was dreaming. She didn't care. She didn't want to think, analyze, doubt, shy away from him. She was tired of saying no to her feelings and tired of saying no to Vic Donovan.

"Please, Lacey, say yes. Tell me the answer is yes this time."

This time she said yes.

"Oh, Lacey," he sighed into her hair. "Say it again." She whispered yes yes yes. He kissed her lips, her eyes, her lips again.

"You have a great bottom," she said.

"You're stealing my lines. Come here, beautiful, let me see it." He fondled her while he kissed her again. "No, you have the great bottom. It's so cute."

She loved the scent of him, so male it made her mouth water. She traced her fingers up his arms and down his chest. He did likewise, and it sent shivers all over her skin.

The rest of their clothes came off in a heartbeat and suddenly they were a tangle of bare arms and legs and skin as he lifted her onto the bed. They were rolling on the fresh sheets. They made love for the first time, and she decided she wasn't dreaming; this was too substantial to be a dream. They rested in each other's arms while she gazed at his beautiful naked body. If this was a sin, Lacey thought, there were worse sins than loving someone.

He slept a little and she nestled up to him, wrapping her arms around him. She wanted always to remember the sight of the late-afternoon light and the shadows dancing on the walls while she lay there, feeling so lovely and naked with him. Vic awoke, and soon they were again making love, tasting love, feeling love. And then he held her quietly and they didn't need to speak for awhile.

"Thank you for coming to Paris for me," she whispered to him when she thought he was sleeping.

"You're welcome." He reached out and held her tight.

"Vic, did something bad happen in Paris? To you, I mean. Forgive me for asking."

"All forgotten. Doesn't matter anymore," he said, nuzzling her ear. "By the way, is there anything you haven't told me about this crazy escapade we're on together?" He was kissing the nape of her neck now. She gasped as a tingle went down her spine.

"Is this a new interrogation method?"

"No, it's an old one. Is it working?"

"A little to the left," she giggled, and watched the curtains billow in and out, as if they were taking sweet breaths of the Paris twilight. "Keep interrogating me, I'll let you know in a few hours."

Vic kissed her silently for awhile and she luxuriated in his arms. "You know, Lacey, I've been thinking about what you told me today, believe it or not. Your dead end on the Rue Dauphine? There's a Rue Dauphine in New Orleans. Mostly they call it Dauphine Street, but the street signs also say Rue Dauphine. Did you know that?"

"You're kidding. New Orleans, Louisiana? You think the address is in America?"

"Just throwing it out for consideration." She propped herself up on her elbow and gazed at him. "And you have a funny look on your face," Vic said. "That look spells trouble."

"You do think it exists! The lost corset. You don't think I'm crazy. Or not completely crazy."

"Oh, no, you are crazy. But I love you anyway. And I just thought you should know there is another Rue Dauphine a little closer to home. For all I know, there's a Rue Dauphine in every third village in France, but I've walked down the one in New Orleans."

"Is it a long street?" she asked, remembering the address on the note was too high for the street she and Brooke had walked down in Paris that morning.

"All the way from the French Quarter into the Faubourg Marigny."

"What's that?"

"The next neighborhood over."

"You seem to know it pretty well. Got a girl there, cowboy?"

"I'm a Southern boy, honey. New Orleans at Mardi Gras time is practically a required course. And I will have a girl there. If you and I go there together." He propped himself up to look at her. He brushed the hair from her face.

"Drosmis Berzins died in Mississippi. Just up the river." She kissed him. "I've never been to New Orleans."

"It's a great place to visit. Long as you're not alone."

"Better than Paris?" She raised an eyebrow at him.

"Paris has proven to be far better than I ever could have hoped." He lay back and drew her down for another kiss. She lay on top of him and looked into his deep green eyes.

"Vic, will you take me to New Orleans?"

"Thought you'd never ask." He kissed her behind her ear and followed it with kisses down her neck and a little farther. It made it hard for her to concentrate on travel plans.

"Next week, after we get back home?"

"Wild-goose chase? With you? Wouldn't miss it." He stroked her neck.

"You do think there's something there."

"No, I think you need to get the legend of the lost corset out of your system."

"Think so? You got anything you need to get out of your system?" He laughed and kissed her. She returned his kisses and raised him, double or nothing.

Eventually, they slept a little. When Lacey woke up, the curtains were still, the last of the daylight was fading, and the sky was a deep azure. Vic had showered and dressed.

"Hey, sleepyhead." He sat down on the bed and gently smoothed her face. "We have reservations for dinner. You getting up?"

"Who made reservations? Is it morning yet?" She stretched luxuriously.

"I did, for the four of us. And it's dinner time. Well, dinner time in Paris."

"The four—You mean Brooke and Damon too?" Lacey pulled the covers up and snuggled under them. "Call room service. I want to stay here forever."

"There is no room service. You'll get bored without me." He pulled the covers down to reveal her face. "And hungry. You don't want to miss the dynamic duo, do you?" He grinned his leprechaun smile. "Damon wants the whole story. Come on, open your eyes, Sleeping Beauty. The restaurant should amuse you."

"Amuse me?"

He nodded. "It's close by, and, rumor has it, was a haunt of Hemingway and Fitzgerald."

"Oh, darling! So it's a moveable feast?"

"If you get up and start moving, it is. By the way, dinner's on me."

"That could be very dangerous, Vic. I could get used to that I think."

"That's the idea." He kissed her. "I want you to get used to me."

Not such a bad idea. She slowly rose to her knees on the bed and dropped the covers. She held out her arms to him and smiled. "But I don't know what to wear."

"I think you look great just the way you are, sweetheart, but you'll get cold. And everyone will be able to tell your temperature." He kissed her again and let his fingers trail down her back, giving her fresh chills. He checked his watch. "We're meeting them at the restaurant in thirty minutes."

"Thirty minutes!" She jumped out of bed. "Are you crazy? I have to shower and dress!" She looked in the mirror. "And put on makeup. And do something with my hair." Lacey ran into the bathroom and turned on the shower.

Vic laughed and followed her. "Shall I wash your back?" He looked dangerously handsome, dressed or undressed, and more than half ready to jump back in the shower with her.

"Go away! Shut the door!" He backed out of the bathroom laughing and let her shower by herself. It was her quickest shower on record. She returned to the room with a fluffy white bath towel wrapped around her.

"I like it. Let's go! You'll stop traffic on the boulevard in that outfit." He turned back to the mirror and started putting a knot in his tie. The crisp white shirt and patterned blue tie made him look elegantly sexy, and she briefly wondered why she rarely paid attention to what most men wore. Probably because most men didn't look like Vic.

She would have loved to stop and simply stare at him, at the wonder of having him there in her room. But she didn't have time. She dashed to the tiny closet. "How fancy is this place we're going to?"

"Not too fancy. It's a place to see and be seen. You'll think of something. After all, you're the queen of the style page."

She selected the burgundy dress that she'd worn in Mont-Saint-Michel. "I'm not the queen here in Paris, darling, but maybe this will do." She was glad she had brought it with her.

He stopped tying his tie and turned to look at her. "That's the first time you've ever said that to me."

"Said what? 'This will do'?"

He put his arms around her. "'Darling.' I like the sound of it."

She kissed him quickly and smiled up at him as she put on her diamond earrings, the ones he had given her, only a couple of months and a lifetime ago. She tried to concentrate on getting dressed. With Vic's eyes on her it would be far too easy to get undressed and end up back in bed. But then they'd starve.

"'Darling.' Isn't that a French word?" she said. "I've been taking lessons, *chéri.*"

chapter 24

Dinner was lovely, until the shooting. But of course that didn't happen until after dessert.

The restaurant that Vic had chosen, La Something or Other on the Boulevard du Montparnasse—Lacey missed the name in the excitement—was very ooh la la in that dazzling French art deco way, from the huge glass dome over the dining room to its tall painted pillars, their murals painted by artists like Chagall in the Twenties, Vic said, in exchange for drinks. Mosaic tiles covered the floor in intricate patterns. The aroma of fresh bread filled the air. After that amazing afternoon with Vic and a nap in his arms, it seemed to her like a dream, as if they had walked into a French movie set where Cary Grant was about to romance Audrey Hepburn over an elegant dinner.

Vic and Lacey arrived first and were ushered to their table by a very severe maître d' who pulled out Lacey's brown velvet chair with mathematical precision. He handed them menus and disappeared with a curt nod of his head. In an instant the busy man was back with their dining companions. "Isn't this nice," Brooke gushed as she was seated. "I read Josephine Baker used to hold court here." She looked flushed and happy. Damon was glowing. Lacey didn't have to ask how her friend had spent the afternoon, and she hoped Brooke would show the same restraint, despite her glow. *Come to think of it,* Lacey thought, *Vic and I are probably glowing too.*

For dinner, Brooke had chosen a snug black sweater and skirt, and in honor of Damon's arrival, she wore her thick blond hair down and tousled, a seductive right-out-of-the-bedroom look. Damon matched her black-on-black look in his formal cyberpunk journalist mode, jet-black suit and charcoal silk turtleneck sweater, and his trademark tiny black-framed glasses tried vainly to add a mature air to his boyishly handsome face with its trim little black goatee. But to Lacey he still resembled a baby beatnik looking for the Lost Generation. The thin and pale Damon Newhouse was cute and au courant, but he was no match for Vic Donovan. Lacey found it very hard to stop staring at Vic. His midnight-blue bespoke suit fit him like a glove and made her want to reach out and touch him. She bit her lip and kept her hands to herself.

Her own burgundy dress with its snugly fitted curves and flowing skirt netted admiring glances from men in the room, and Vic reached over and touched the diamond earrings. "Very pretty. I'm glad you still like them."

"I like them even better now that you're here to see them," Lacey smiled back.

"Lacey," Damon said, "so good to see you in one piece." He cocked an eyebrow at her.

One glance at Damon and she knew that Brooke had spilled the entire story. Lacey gave her friend a look. *Maybe she didn't tell him about the corset,* Lacey hoped. *The corset is the best part.*

"How did it feel to be chloroformed and dumped on a dirt floor in a cellar full of spiders?" Damon continued. Vic looked on with bemused interest.

She hated those journalistic "how did it feel" questions. "How do you think it felt, Damon? If you want a firsthand example, I'm sure it could be arranged."

"If I were you, Damon, I'd take her word for it," Vic counseled.

"Lacey, chill! Please, just a question," Damon said. "No need to go all radical on me."

"Sounds like everyone's hungry," Vic said. "Why don't we order before we bite each other's heads off?" Everyone dutifully picked up their menus.

"I had to tell him, Lacey. About the *egg,* you know?" Brooke said, giving Lacey a look.

"Ah, yes, the Fabergé egg," Damon said. "Do you happen to know which one of the missing imperial eggs it's supposed to be? It doesn't really matter—in the long run, any one of them would be worth millions. But it would help my story. Authenticating detail."

"To help *your* story, Damon, I would never tell you. But off the record, I have no idea which egg it might be." Lacey had seen pictures of the Fabergé eggs that had been auctioned off several years before. They were gorgeous and absurd objects, preposterously delicate yet intricately bejeweled. "Brooke told you we didn't find it, right? We hit a dead end?"

"Yes," he said soberly. "Of course. I was just asking. I thought perhaps you would have been curious enough to ask Magda Rousseau what she was sending you chasing after."

Brooke touched Damon's hand. "To be fair, Damon, it's been a nerve-racking couple of days. I'm just glad we remember our own names."

He looked at her fondly. "I'm just glad it wasn't you in that cellar."

While Brooke, Damon, and Lacey bantered, Vic consulted with the smartly dressed waiter, whose air of superiority went well with his starched white shirt, many-pocketed black vest, and long white apron. During a pause, Vic broke into the conversation. "I took the liberty of ordering appetizers and wine. Escargot and pâté. Is that all right?"

Lacey shot him a grateful look and squeezed his hand. "I have to freshen up. Brooke, are you coming?"

Damon looked over at her. "You look fine." But Lacey was up already and Brooke was following. "It's a girl thing, isn't it?"

"Yes it is," Lacey stage-whispered in his ear. "The secret world of women behind the pink doors of the ladies' room. Don't you wish you knew what it was all about, Damon? The clandestine rituals? The secret ceremonies? It's a conspiracy."

"We'll be right back," Brooke announced brightly. She kissed Damon on the head and whispered, "Don't worry."

Vic patted Damon on the back. "It's a girl thing. Have some hot bread, Newhouse."

As she and Brooke passed through the doors, Lacey thought, *Thank heavens for ladies' rooms and their secrets.* Entire dark conspiracies of deep global import were conducted in ladies' rooms every day.

"Can you believe our guys came all the way to Paris just to see us?" Brooke said, staring at herself dreamily in the mirror. She fingered her hair and sighed happily. "And how did *you* spend your afternoon, Lacey?" She winked.

"We'd both better plead the Fifth. And did you tell Damon the whole story?"

Brooke snapped to attention. "Lacey, I wouldn't! I couldn't. Attorney–client privilege. But I could tell him what's been happening here, because I didn't say I wouldn't, and besides, those other creepy characters were all talking about Fabergé eggs. You notice Damon didn't say 'Romanov corset,' did he? And for all we know, it might really *be* a Fabergé egg. I figured I could tell him anything *they* said. And who knows what blabbermouths they might be?"

Lacey had to admit Brooke was right. What other people said was fair game. At the moment she didn't care if the Fabergé egg story got out. In fact, it might take the heat off the corset story, at least until she had a chance to check out the Rue Dauphine in New Orleans. Assuming Mac would let her go. But she decided not to tell Brooke about the Louisiana connection yet. The French Quarter might be another dead end, and Damon with his keen ears and the fastest keyboard on the Internet was always listening in and getting the story wrong. He was sure to expand on the facts, blow them all out of proportion, and add equal parts nonsense. And Brooke looked so happy it seemed cruel to dangle another likely disappointment in front of her.

"You're not mad, are you, Lacey? Damon is my soul mate."

"But he's so not your type: He's not a gray-flannel trust-fund attorney."

"That's why I love him."

Lacey drew a comb through her hair. "I understand how you feel, so I guess as long as nothing about the corset slips out, it's okay. But for heaven's sake, don't make me sound so pathetic! Knocked out cold in the coal room? Spiders and dirt? Yuck." Lacey washed her hands again to wipe away the feel of the cobwebs.

"You told Vic, didn't you?" Brooke sniffed.

"Vic can keep his mouth shut. But Damon and you and I are going to have to come to an understanding about whose story this really is."

"No problem. He adores you. You're his hero!"

"Now that's scary." Lacey rolled her eyes and opened the ladies' room door.

The pâté and escargot arrived just as they returned to the table. Between bites, Lacey gazed around the room. Her attention was caught by a woman wearing a houndstooth suit that made Lacey's eyes hurt. The suit had a peplum set off by a shocking-pink ribbon and a ruffled skirt. Apparently not content with this outrageous abuse of houndstooth, the woman wore a pair of matching houndstooth stilettos. Even Brooke and Vic looked over with amusement.

Lacey forced her attention back to the table as the remains of the appetizers were whisked off and replaced by salads and later by their entrées. Vic had the curried lamb, while she had the beef in a wine sauce. Brooke and Damon indulged in the salmon with some sort of cream sauce.

Finally Damon and Lacey hammered out an agreement. She

would write her story about Magda and the spies who loved her, or at least coveted her alleged treasure, whatever it was. Newhouse would link Conspiracy Clearinghouse to her story and provide his own crackpot commentary, claiming freedom of the press. But he swore he wouldn't step on her story or write anything on it at all until he returned to D.C.

"I promise," Damon said. "I mean, how could I, Smithsonian? I didn't know the dead woman or her intimate thoughts, her dying declaration. You have all the cards here."

"And most of them are blank. But remember, it's my story, not DeadFed dot com's story." But this meant Lacey would need to write most of the story before she got back to Washington.

"Actually, I'm very relieved nothing more happened to you, Lacey. The damn thing is probably cursed anyway," Damon said with a straight face.

"He's right," Brooke jumped in. "We could have been killed."

"But we weren't," Lacey pointed out.

"So what are we doing tomorrow?" Vic asked.

"Damon and I are going to visit the major spy sites in Paris!" Brooke lit up like a Christmas tree. "You know, like the Spy Tour in D.C.? Places where famous spies defected, documents changed hands, traitors got executed, all that stuff."

"You'll join us?" Damon said. "Maybe we'll run into this Russian. Might be interesting."

"We wouldn't want to cramp your style," Vic said, much to Lacey's relief.

"Right. We have plans," Lacey said. *Boy, do we have plans.*

"There's a big movement to restore all the Romanov artifacts to Russia," Damon said. "Just the kind of recovery project to appeal to an ex-KGB spy. Maybe that's why they're on this case."

Maybe Damon's ravings are right, Lacey thought suddenly. *I see Kepelov now!* He had materialized somehow while they weren't looking. She watched him out of the corner of her eye, slamming down shots of vodka at the bar as if he were in a saloon somewhere in Siberia. There was no sign of Griffin. Her flesh crawled at the thought of Kepelov tailing them. He looked oddly pathetic in a rumpled brown ill-fitting suit and, oddest of all, dark red leather cowboy boots. *At least Tex isn't wearing his Hawaiian shirt.* He kept checking the door as if he expected someone.

Brooke, who was sitting opposite her, didn't see him, and Lacey didn't want to create a scene. Vic would simply throttle him, Damon would try to interfere, and they would all wind up in a

French jail. And who knew if Brooke's friends at the American Embassy could save them?

Lacey's first instinct was to locate a weapon; she wondered which piece of the elegant silverware would be the deadliest. She ordered herself to calm down and wait to see if he made a move. She would show no fear, she decided, so much easier with Vic by her side, and rejoined the conversation.

Kepelov, however, must have given up his surveillance, because the next time she glanced his way, while deciding between the chocolate mousse and the crème brûlée for dessert, he was gone. Lacey reached over for Vic's hand. He squeezed hers back and she felt a rush of relief. Maybe she wouldn't have to decide which piece of cutlery would be appropriate for self-defense. She imagined her mortification to be caught stabbing someone in a fancy restaurant in Paris using *the wrong knife.* It wasn't an etiquette challenge for which she was prepared. She ordered the crème brûlée.

After the fattening dessert course, Brooke and Damon finally said good night, still glowing. Lacey and Vic lingered lazily over digestifs for half an hour. Even their very correct waiter had warmed up to them ever so slightly, going so far as to offer the happy couple a fleeting smile. Vic leaned in for a kiss. Lacey closed her eyes, awaiting a kiss sweeter than all the desserts in Paris.

Then the shooting began, a volley of sharp popping sounds outside the front windows of the restaurant. Vic immediately pulled Lacey down to the floor, keeping the table between them and the windows. Lacey could tell by his face and the fact she was on the floor that the sounds were gunshots. She realized they sounded just like the shots she had heard in Dupont Circle last month when a woman had been gunned down before her eyes. Vic put his arms around her and pulled her close. She felt her heart plummet. This must have something to do with Kepelov being there. But was it Kepelov doing the shooting? And whom was he shooting at?

"Just because we heard shots, it doesn't mean you're involved," Vic whispered into her ear. "They have street crime in Paris too."

"I need to tell you something, Vic." He lifted an eyebrow at her. "I saw Kepelov in the restaurant, earlier, but then he was gone."

"Good to know. First, don't jump to conclusions. Second, let's get out of here, calmly and quietly, without attracting attention. We're just two fools in love sitting on the floor in a restaurant in Paris. Perfectly ordinary behavior."

"That part is certainly true." Lacey realized that Vic was getting much better at discussing certain subjects with her, like crime and danger and trouble, and why she was always in it or around it. He hadn't yelled at her at all. She was charmed by his cool, capable demeanor. *Paris is good for him,* she decided. *For both of us.*

Most of the other diners were paying no attention, either to the two Americans sitting on the floor or to whatever had happened on the street, although a few walked to the windows to peer out. Vic paid the bill just as the police sirens wailed and an ambulance sped down the street and slammed on the brakes. He helped Lacey up and draped her shawl around her shoulders.

As they approached the front door, a distinctive woodsy rose and musk scent hung in the air, the same perfume she had smelled in her room after it had been searched. The scent that tickled the back of her mind with a half-hidden memory. She closed her eyes and breathed it in. The scent was stronger here, and the memory was closer. She was almost there, just another deep breath and she would—Yes, there it was, she had it. She finally remembered who it was that wore that perfume.

It was Magda. And Magda was dead.

chapter 25

"Lacey?" She opened her eyes. Vic was holding the front door of the restaurant open for her.

Outside, the crisp air was a slap in the face. It shocked her fully awake and stung her eyes, which were full of tears for Magda. People were moving swiftly around them, and more official cars were arriving. Lacey held Vic's arm as they walked past the police perimeter. She stopped only long enough to see a crowd of emergency workers around a figure lying on the ground. She couldn't see the man's face, but she saw his red cowboy boots and she knew.

Squeezing Vic's arm, she whispered, "It's Kepelov."

"How could you possibly know that?" He sounded a little testy. "You couldn't."

"The boots, Vic. He was wearing those red cowboy boots. I saw them earlier."

He turned and looked at the boots just as the man on the ground was surrounded. "Well, those are damned silly," he said and started walking again. "A Russian spy in red cowboy boots."

"We should do something," she said, feeling helpless. "We can identify him."

"Are you sure? You don't even know that's his real name. Lacey, there is nothing to do except get out of the way and let the gendarmes do their work." She protested, and he pulled her along gently. "You didn't shoot him. You didn't see who shot him, and you don't know why he was shot. And don't tell me it was because of the red boots."

"Maybe the French are even tougher fashion critics than I thought. But I also smelled the perfume, just now, the same perfume I smelled in my room."

"Lacey, this is the world capital of perfume."

"I'm just saying there's a woman, a girlfriend of his, and maybe she—"

"You don't even know who this alleged girlfriend is, her name, what she looks like. *If* there is a girlfriend. Frankly, Lacey, this Kepelov sounds more like a lowlife thug than KGB. Thugs shoot other thugs. Fact of life."

At the corner Lacey stopped to wrap her shawl tighter. "He was stalking us."

"Or someone else. He was drinking. Maybe he picked the restaurant at random. He takes one look at you and bolts."

"That's flattering."

"Only because you sow terror in the hearts of men."

"That better be a compliment, honey."

He held her tight and kept them walking away from the scene, past the taxicabs parked at the corner. "For all we know, your thug was depressed. He failed to score this Romanov treasure, be it egg or corset, hit the vodka too hard, and decided good-bye cruel world."

"That's so dumb, it could be true." They strolled along the street. Even though it was nearly midnight, the streets were full of people strolling, and some restaurants were still serving dinner. Lacey agreed it would be awkward to go to the police. "I still feel weird leaving the scene."

"Yeah, it'd be great to have your friend Broadway Lamont here to interrogate you."

"Very funny."

"By the way, sweetheart, about Thanksgiving." Vic stopped. "Do you have any plans?"

"Thanksgiving? How can you bring up Thanksgiving at a time like this? I'm speechless."

"That'll be the day. So do you have plans?" He drew her close to him and said softly, "We'll talk about Red Boots later, when we're sure we're alone."

"Vic, are we being followed?" she whispered. He shrugged and eyed the pedestrians walking past them.

"I don't think so. Just checking. About Thanksgiving."

"I turned my mother down. So no, I have no plans." He didn't need to know that Rose Smithsonian had invited him too. Throwing parents into the mix right now was too unpredictable. She drew her shawl tighter and snuggled next to him.

"You're invited to my folks' house, then. Lots of food, lots of room, lots of people."

"Your parents?" She had a sudden pang of panic. She hadn't met his parents. She'd been wondering whether she ever would.

And now she knew they were "comfortable." *Vic's rich parents. What on earth will they think of me?* "I don't know."

"Don't worry. They'll love you. I have orders to bring a guest. I want it to be you."

"But you said your parents *loved* your ex-wife, Montana." Vic had sworn she was out of the picture, but Lacey suspected Montana might still have other ideas.

"Maybe not *loved,* exactly. They, um, felt sorry for her."

"I don't know, Vic, suddenly meeting your parents is just plain scary. And throwing in the holiday is loading the dice. If they don't like me I'll have ruined their Thanksgiving, not just some random evening. They'll hate me."

"They'll like you! They don't bite. And you couldn't ruin one of my mom's dinner parties with an atom bomb."

"Famous last words." She realized she was tired, they both were. This was not the evening to start a silly fight over being *included* in his family's holiday plans, of all things. "Ask me again tomorrow, Vic. Please?" The little hotel beckoned, safe and warm and ghost-free, and Lacey and Vic picked up the pace for the next few blocks until they were back at the Hotel Mouton Vert.

Upstairs in their room, she sat down on the bed and kicked off her heels. Vic sat on the floor beside her and lay his head on her lap. Lacey hugged him close.

"I just hate not knowing what happened," she lamented. "Is he alive? Is he dead? Who shot him? Why? I should tell Brooke." She reached for her phone, but Vic put his hand on hers.

"You'll just get her all wound up, both of them. They'll be up all night surfing the Web for news. In French," Vic said. "Save it for tomorrow."

Lacey let him unzip her dress and she peeled it off, revealing her flashiest red underwear.

"Just relax, Lacey. Let me rub your shoulders." He kneaded her tight muscles with his strong hands. She willed herself to let go of her worries. *Oh, this is helping.*

"I'm thinking you have a lot of useful skills," she said, as he unhooked her bra.

"You'd be surprised." He started kissing her and didn't stop.

A knock on the door the next morning woke Lacey up. She threw on her black silk robe and staggered out of bed. "Who is it?" she asked through the closed door.

"It's Brooke."

Lacey opened the door a crack and peered out. "What time is it?" Brooke was entirely too awake and cheerful. Her hair was braided. She was wearing jeans, running shoes, and a gray hooded sweatshirt that said YALE in letters at least a foot high.

"Why don't you just wear a sign that says JE SUIS AMÉRICAINE?"

"I am American. Who needs a sign?" Brooke leaned on the door, pushing it open a bit more. She peered in at a sleeping Donovan. "Oh, you guys aren't up yet?" She grinned.

"No, and I'm going back to bed right now." Lacey started to shut the door.

"Hey, did you know there was a shooting last night outside the restaurant? Right after Damon and I left. Did you guys hear anything?"

Lacey opened the door a bit wider. "We heard gunshots. What do you know about it?"

"Not much," Brooke said. "That was all Monsieur Henri could tell me."

Lacey slipped into the hall and shut the door gently so they wouldn't disturb Vic. *If I tell her it was Kepelov, I'll get sucked into the deadly vortex of DeadFed dot com.* "So what are you going to do today?"

"This morning we're going to visit locations on the Champs Elysées and the Palais Royale from the movie *Charade.* You remember, Cary Grant, Audrey Hepburn, murder, intrigue, romance. It's one of your favorites too, I know. You guys should come along."

Lacey eyed Brooke's outfit du jour. "Sans Audrey's fabulous wardrobe by Givenchy." Lacey momentarily thought about those beautiful suits Audrey Hepburn wore in *Charade*, all those three-quarter-length sleeves designed to be worn with long gloves. *Très elegante.*

"Well, I'm dressed for speed. I have to be able to move to play hide and seek," Brooke insisted. "Spy versus spy. Us versus Kepelov."

"I have a feeling he won't bother you today." Lacey had no idea if Kepelov were still alive. Part of her hoped he was, the silly man with his silly mustache and his absurd American dream. She also reminded herself that he had stalked her, attacked her, and knocked her out. And he was just plain weird, if not a complete lying sociopath.

"Damon and I can still play." Brooke caught Lacey's smile. "I'm sure you and Vic have your little games to play too."

"We've been playing a game for the past six years."

"So now it's game, set, match? Or is it love all?" Brooke zipped up the hooded sweatshirt and bent down to tie one of her shoelaces. "Gotta run. We have so much ground to cover before we go see Jim Morrison's alleged grave in Père-Lachaise cemetery."

Lacey slumped against the wall and hugged her robe tight around her. "Wait. Not Jim Morrison of the Doors? Heroin overdose? You said 'alleged.' You don't believe those rumors, do you? Oh, of course you do. What was I thinking."

Brooke smiled at her naive friend. "Heroin overdose is the official story, but no one ever saw the body, except for his girlfriend who reported the death and a doctor no one ever heard from again." Brooke stretched her quads and then her back.

"Oh, Brooke. You think the Lizard King is still alive, right?"

"He told people he was going to fake his death just a couple weeks before he, quote, 'died,' unquote. Coincidence?"

"Nobody ever just plain dies in your universe, do they? The cemetery is on my list too, but not to visit Morrison." Lacey put her hand on the doorknob and yawned. "I can't believe you're so into dead people."

"Only some dead people," Brooke corrected her. "And missing persons who *pretend* to be dead. Damon is writing a case study on how to disappear and why Paris is such a good place to do it. So why don't you two meet us there at—" She checked her watch. "Say two thirty at the, quote, 'tomb,' unquote, of Jim Morrison."

"But I don't even like the Doors! 'Light My Fire' just makes me want to—"

"It'll be fun. We'll see you there. Damon's waiting for me. Au revoir, *chérie.*"

Lacey watched Brooke sail down the stairs in her jogging shoes, her blond braid flying. She opened the door to find Vic up and getting ready to shower.

"But I thought we could— You know. Go back to bed?"

"You don't want to miss anything, do you? Especially if we have to meet those two at two thirty at Père-Lachaise."

"You heard all that?"

He grinned. "Darling, you expect me to just let you slip off into a dim hallway where ghosts, spies, jewel thieves, killers, or your lunatic friends could spirit you away from me?"

"Ah, you haven't met the ghost yet," Lacey said. Over Vic's shoulder, Lacey watched as the lamp beside the bed flickered on and then off again. Vic saw her eyes go wide and he turned around, but it was over.

"Don't worry, darling," Vic smiled. "The day is young."

chapter 26

Consistency is the key to a woman's signature look, Lacey decided.

Lacey had always strived for a consistently pulled-together look, but especially since becoming the fashion reporter at *The Eye Street Observer.* Everyone she knew suddenly expected her to look well-dressed all the time. *Quel drag.* The other reporters simply took her word for it; they assumed whatever she wore was in style because she was wearing it, the way readers assume that the sports reporter understands football. But this was Paris. Parisians, she assumed, would be highly critical connoisseurs of style.

This morning her reflection in the mirror satisfied her, and she hoped it would even satisfy hypercritical Parisians. The plain black skirt, tights, and boots went with anything, and the emerald sweater made her blue-green eyes sparkle. A matching emerald jacket with a belted waist, copied from a vintage Forties jacket in Aunt Mimi's trunk, completed the look. She added gold hoop earrings and a cuff bracelet. But maybe looking good had more to do with being in love, she thought. Whatever it was, it was working.

"You're gorgeous," Vic said. "Let's go."

"You just interrupted my work. I was making up a new theory about fashion."

"Time's a-wasting. It'll come back to you."

Before they left for the day, Lacey wanted a chat with the helpful concierge. With Vic waiting outside on the sidewalk, Lacey turned the charm of her carefully chosen outfit on Monsieur Henri. The fastidious little man was wearing a starched white shirt and a green wool vest with brown slacks. He greeted her, his perfectly trimmed mustache conveying utmost seriousness.

"*Bonjour*, Monsieur Colbert."

"*Bonjour*, mademoiselle." He gave a curt nod and a lightning appraisal of her outfit. She must have merited his approval. His face relaxed and his mustache flirted with the hint of a smile.

Lacey thanked him for his excellent service and asked if he knew the hospital where last night's shooting victim was taken. He did. Would he be so good as to make a call and ask about the condition of the victim, a man named, she thought, Gregor Kepelov?

"For you, mademoiselle, but of course." He picked up the phone. While he was engaged, she picked up brochures featuring Parisian attractions. Henri was taking what seemed like a long time to the final au revoir. She looked up.

"Ah, Mademoiselle Smithsonian. I regret to inform you they say there is no Gregor Kepelov at the hospital," Henri said. "And so, thinking there was perhaps a mistake with the name, I inquired, was a man who was shot outside this restaurant last night admitted? I was informed she could not say, which means, of course, he was. But it must be a different man. I am so sorry."

Henri looked perturbed that his special charm had not wormed more information out of the hospital. Lacey assured him he was brilliant and thanked him profusely.

Kepelov, no doubt, had many aliases. Whatever his real name was and wherever he was, if he was still alive, there was nothing she could think of to do to learn more about him. She briefly pondered whether Griffin might have shot him, but Griffin didn't seem the murderous type, and he could barely open a pack of cigarettes. And who was the mystery woman wearing Magda's scent? Lacey determined she would not dwell on Kepelov or Griffin today. Or phantoms.

Lacey and Vic were on the Métro on their way to the famous Cluny Museum of the Middle Ages when she suddenly realized she needed to jot down notes for a "Fashion Bite," her irregular column of humorous fashion advice and commentary. Her editor, Mac, professed not to understand a word of them, which gave her the freedom to write nearly anything she pleased.

She had begun to wonder if she were hanging out in all the wrong places in Paris to catch a glimpse of the elusive glamorous Frenchwoman of fashion legend. In the fashion world the mystique of the effortlessly stylish Frenchwoman with her legendary scarf-tying abilities would never die. Lacey thought most of the women she saw on the streets here looked perfectly normal, some slightly better dressed than others, some worse. Where were those dazzling and elegant trendsetters she had been conditioned to expect?

In the real world of Paris fashion in the street, Lacey was not seeing anything like a parade of haute couture knockouts, but she was noticing some trends. There was a certain consistency of style among Frenchwomen that could be counted on, and it was in the details where their genius lay. And the genius was sheer confidence, an attitude that said, "Of course what I am wearing is in style, because I am wearing it!"

"Laundry list?" Vic asked, peering at her notes.

"Fashion clues." She kept writing as he nibbled on her ear. "I like Paris, it brings out the romantic in you."

"I'm a natural-born romantic, didn't you know? Are you writing about the alleged corset?"

"No, I'm working on a column. A 'Fashion Bite.' "

"I'll bite. What's the key clue?"

"Attitude, *mon cher,* attitude." Lacey wrote a few more notes on her theme that the Frenchwoman had the style war won over the American woman in only one key attribute: attitude. They believe they look great, and this gives them the confidence to look their best, so everyone else believes it too. She closed her notebook, thinking that perhaps if she could don a little of that nonchalantly fearless attitude, perhaps others would see the same courage in her. Perhaps even she would begin to feel it herself.

Lacey sat on a bench in the darkened circular hall of the Cluny Museum. She was reveling in the exquisite artistry of the brilliant unknown weavers who had created these six vibrant tapestries: *The Lady and the Unicorn.*

Every mystery requires a key to unlock it, she was thinking, as she drank in the sight of the famous tapestries. Lacey marveled at the skill it must have taken and wondered about the La Viste family who had commissioned the tapestries, though no one quite knew why. What did the images signify, beyond what the glossy guidebook told her? What was the key?

She learned that the tapestries were woven in the late 1400s. Five panels of *The Lady and the Unicorn* depicted the five senses: *Sight*, *Hearing*, *Taste*, *Touch*, and *Smell.* The focus of each panel was a soigné blond Lady and a playful white unicorn. Each featured a scene symbolic of that sense, enacted on a sapphire-blue rug or island set against a blazing crimson background, dense with birds and flowers and small animals. A sixth panel, *A Mon Seul Désir*, "To My Sole Desire," seemingly depicted the Lady putting away her rich necklace, renouncing her worldly passions, or so the book said. Lacey peered closely at the necklace in her hands, poised above a chest of similar jewels offered by her maidservant. The image seemed ambiguous. *What if the Lady were picking up the jewels,* she wondered, *not putting them away?* Perhaps the Lady in the tapestry was trying to tell her something, offering her a key to her own mystery. Should she put away all thought of finding the elusive corset and their legendary jewels? Or should she try to take the mystery in hand and pick up the thread of the search?

The Lady was inscrutable, and her unicorn smiled enigmatically. Lacey was pleased the two of them were taking such an interest in her dilemma. She wished Magda could have been here to see this sight again. Magda had seen them years ago and had never forgotten them. The old corsetiere had told Lacey that if she loved stories told by fabric and style, she must see the tapestries at the Cluny.

They were a revelation. For Lacey, the Middle Ages had always seemed a dismal, dirty, dark era, cold and muddy, a place where no one bathed. The sumptuous French tapestries revealed a different world altogether, with their luxurious bold colors and serenely mysterious tableaus. Untold numbers of stitches from unknown numbers of weavers had created them for an unknown purpose, to tell an ambiguous story. It seemed to Lacey that so much of France's history was told in stitches. It was told in tapestries and in the elite world of haute couture. It was told even by the women who knitted at the guillotine and dropped a stitch every time a head rolled, making a count of the bloody victims of the Revolution.

Vic had been discreetly casing the hall of the tapestries to make sure that they hadn't been followed by Griffin or a mystery woman perfumed with a woodsy rose scent. He returned to her side, resting his arm over her shoulder and putting his lips to her temple. She smiled at his touch and felt a little sorry for the Lady in the tapestries, attended by her pretty unicorn, her servants, and her jewels, but with no man in the picture.

"I take it we're safe?" She was enjoying this new side of Vic. He had demonstrated his protective side before, but she hadn't seen such tenderness.

"So far."

"You know, I'm not followed by bad guys all the time."

"Yeah," he said. "I bet you can go for weeks sometimes. Seen enough?"

"A little while longer, please. You could go to the shop or the garden and wait there for me." She smiled at him and turned back to the sixth panel. "I want to absorb it."

She thought how nice it would be if someone would hand her a glossy book with a key to the whereabouts of the missing Romanov corset. Maybe with a sidebar on who came up with the idea of stitching jewels into the corsets, and who sewed them into their hiding place, and who had taken them from Jean-Claude's cellar. And a neat final chapter on where they were now.

Perhaps this book would give her a metaphor to work with for her story for *The Eye.* But instead of the five senses, it would no doubt be the Three Stooges: Magda and Lacey and Brooke. The blond Lady of the tapestries wasn't telling any secrets. She wore a bemused and knowing look. Her riches were secure, whether she was picking them up to wear or putting them away, and she and her pet unicorn would be adored forever in the round room of the Cluny Museum.

The room was becoming crowded. Lacey gave the Lady one last look and went to find Vic in the gift shop. She bought a couple of small tapestries, and she suggested a book for Vic's dad and a pretty scarf in a brilliantly colorful *Lady and the Unicorn* print for his mother.

"You have nothing to worry about, Lacey darling, they're going to love you."

Not if they love his ex-wife too, she thought. Lacey liked to think that she and his ex, Montana, were as different as silk and polyester. The scarf was silk. Lacey hoped Vic's mom would like it. A lot.

"Do you'll think they'll be here?" Vic asked. "In this rain?"

The air was cool, but after the slow-moving crowds in the Cluny, it felt delicious to be walking in the immense Père-Lachaise cemetery in the light November drizzle. Lacey adjusted her shawl over her jacket and put her arm around Vic. The cemetery seemed washed clean in the rain and the scene was lovely, impressionistic. Burnished leaves clung to the cobblestone paths. Lacey wished she could keep the memory of this moment forever. With a little help from Vic, she thought, she might.

"I don't think a monsoon would keep Brooke away from the 'Lizard King.' "

Vic shook his head. "Does she actually like Jim Morrison's music?"

"The Doors? She's more of a Broadway show tunes girl. It's the mystery that moves her."

"Right. We're not expecting to see Morrison too, are we?" Vic turned up his collar against the rain and lifted the multicolored umbrella they'd bought at the Metro station.

"I hope not, there's nothing attractive about an old dead heroin addict. Or even an old live heroin addict. Brooke says Jim Morrison is their case study in faking your own death and disappearing. They're working on some story. My money is on the dead man telling no tales."

They opened the map of the cemetery Lacey purchased at a stand outside the gates and charted a circuitous course around the winding pathways of Père-Lachaise, past its grand mausoleums and extravagant monuments to the dead, including such luminaries as Isadora Duncan, Maria Callas, and Oscar Wilde, his tomb and its winged figure covered with a thousand tender lipstick kisses. With their map they were a magnet for mapless tourists, including a scruffy American in a Doors T-shirt who demanded, "Dude, where's Jim Morrison?!"

"Dude, he's dead!" Vic informed him, and the man wandered away, mumbling. "It's a Lizard King fan club meeting," Vic said to Lacey, "and we didn't wear our fan club T-shirts. Let's get out of here."

But Lacey took Vic's arm and the map and led him past the graves of Molière and Chopin to a tomb in the far corner of the cemetery, a double tomb beneath an elaborate gothic canopy. The recumbent statues of a man and a woman lay side by side, Abelard and Heloise, the tragic twelfth-century lovers whose letters left a heartbreaking romantic legacy. A bouquet of fresh red roses rested on the statue of Heloise, the woman who had spent the rest of her life in a convent but never forgot Peter Abelard, the man she loved. *Even though he didn't deserve her*, Lacey thought. Rose petals covered the ground before the tomb, and yellow and brown autumn leaves, slick with rain. Vic put his arms around Lacey and whispered in her ear. "Not every love story is a tragedy."

She looked up at him, not knowing what to say, hoping for a kiss, when she heard a familiar voice.

"Hey! Here they are!" Brooke's voice echoed cheerfully through the tombs. She was umbrella-less and soaked.

"You guys are in the wrong place." Damon appeared from behind a stone angel, looking just as sodden as his girlfriend. He wore a grin and wiped the rain from his face.

"No, we're not," Lacey said. "We're right where we want to be."

"Ever hear of umbrellas?" Vic added.

"Left it on the Métro." Losing an umbrella wasn't going to

dampen Damon's spirits. He and Brooke led the way, and Vic and Lacey trudged dutifully to the nearby grave of Jim Morrison, the legendary bad-boy front man for the Doors of "Light My Fire" fame, dead in 1971 of a drug overdose. Or not dead? Damon and Brooke were clearly in the "not" camp.

Two young Asian couples in dripping Doors T-shirts stood in reverential silence before a low, nondescript tomb strewn with bedraggled long-stem carnations. The bronze marker read JAMES DOUGLAS MORRISON 1943–1971.

Damon took a stream of digital photos. "Lacey, get in the shot," he pleaded.

"No way, Newhouse." She made a face. "You're not putting me on your Web site with this story. SMITHSONIAN RIPS LID OFF LIZARD KING MYSTERY."

"Spoilsport."

"Spot any undead rock stars on the Métro?" Vic asked. "Morrison, Elvis, the Big Bopper?"

"Not today, but we didn't expect any," Damon said nonchalantly. "We're just here to explore a successful disappearance. That's becoming harder and harder to do in this society."

"True," Brooke said, sniffling in the rain. "Jim Morrison faked his death before DNA testing. So much easier back then to stage your own death and disappear. You could easily get your hands on a birth certificate for someone who died as a child, then apply for new Social Security documents and bank accounts and credit cards in that name and voilà! Start a new life."

"Of course," Lacey agreed. "Who wouldn't want to stop being a rich, famous rock star and go work in a record store somewhere?"

The two other couples standing at the grave said nothing. They merely stood in the rain holding their black umbrellas over their heads, perhaps waiting, Lacey thought, for an apparition or a revelation. Or for the long-vanished Jim Morrison to appear in disguise among them and ask, "Dude, where's Jim Morrison?!"

Damon took more photographs from different angles. Lacey was half afraid he would lie down on top of the grave for a corpse-eye view of the cemetery. She wasn't about to suggest it. So far as she was concerned, the very real remains of Jim Morrison lay beneath that marker.

"You guys better get out of this rain before you catch pneumonia," she warned. Lacey snuggled closer to Vic and felt perfectly warm.

"We're fine," Brooke protested, sneezing violently.

"Let's warm up and get a glass of wine," Vic said. "There's sure to be a café nearby."

"It's medicinal." Lacey was about to herd them back down the path when a familiar figure in a sodden trench coat emerged from the foggy drizzle, clutching a broken black umbrella. He looked cold and soaked and miserable, as if he'd crawled from a soggy crack in the earth.

"What is wrong with you bloody people?" he shouted. Griffin's accent was unmistakable.

"Nigel." Vic sighed. "Never one to miss a drink, are you?"

"Are you at all aware that it's a dog's mess out here today?" Griffin didn't seem happy to see them. "And what are we doing out here in this bloody boneyard?"

"Isn't this your native weather?" Lacey asked. Griffin snorted. "Rain is good, it keeps the crowds away. But unfortunately not you."

"Why are you following us again?" Brooke demanded. The silent mourners at Morrison's grave moved closer.

"Put a lid on it, would you, Blondie," Griffin said. "You're lucky it's me. You better hope the rain keeps the shooter away."

"What did you say?" Damon was instantly alert. "What shooter?"

"I came all the way out here in this god-awful bloody weather to warn you that Rasputin's been shot," Griffin complained. "And all you can do is give me grief. At least buy me a drink."

" 'Rasputin'?" Brooke asked. "You mean, Kepelov, your partner?"

"How did you know where to find us?" Lacey asked.

"Your little pet concierge in your hotel told me. Of course I had to drop a few euros to get him to open up. Pompous little bugger."

Lacey was pleased Monsieur Henri had forced a bribe from this irritating Brit. Henri was easy, but he wasn't cheap. "If I buy you a new umbrella, Griffin, will you go away?"

"I came out of the goodness of my heart to warn you there's an assassin about."

"So Kepelov is dead?" Lacey asked, a little ill at ease. She had feared he was dead.

Griffin looked at the broken spine of his umbrella, decided it wasn't that bad, and held it up again. It didn't help. "Don't know, actually. Shot, though. Not his fault if he's not dead. And here you are barking at me. Shoot the messenger, Smithsonian, why don't you."

"The goodness of your heart, Nigel?" Vic scoffed. "Where did you steal a heart, the Paris sewer?"

Griffin barely had time to look offended before Brooke jumped in. "Wait a minute, back to the shooting. Kepelov was shot? Where was he shot? When?"

"Outside your bloody restaurant. Last night."

"Oh, my God," Brooke said, putting it all together. "The shooting just after we left the restaurant?" She looked at Lacey. "Did you know?"

Lacey shrugged. "Maybe a little."

"You knew and you didn't tell me?" Brooke fumed. "I have to learn it from this twit?"

"I didn't want to spoil your plans, what with the ghost of Jim Morrison and all. What can *we* do about someone shooting Kepelov? Besides, that's all I know." *Except the perfume*, she thought. But this was France. As Vic said, everyone wore perfume. It was everywhere.

"But Lacey, you're supposed to tell me *everything*." Brooke whirled on Griffin. "So why are you telling us? Or did you just come to upset everyone?"

Jim Morrison's silent Asian mourners found this whole scene very entertaining. They whispered among themselves. Griffin threw down his useless umbrella in exasperation.

"I'm telling you because someone could be trying to kill all of us, you stupid cow!"

Brooke stood openmouthed. Vic stepped forward to correct Griffin's manners, but Damon was closer. The short but wiry Newhouse packed a surprisingly powerful punch. He landed a right to Griffin's chin and followed it with a quick left to his gut.

Griffin doubled over, shook his head, and fell to the ground, pretty much as he had when Vic had punched him the day before. Griffin seemed to have a gift for annoying people, and Lacey wondered whether he got himself punched in the guts every day.

"Don't you talk that way to a lady, you coward," Damon spat. "Now get up and fight."

Griffin sat rubbing his chin thoughtfully. He made no move to get up. "No. I don't think I will. You two chaps start without me."

Chapter 27

Brooke gave Lacey a thumbs-up. "The old one-two. Oh, Damon, I'm so proud of you."

"Very impressive, Newhouse," Lacey admitted. Damon nodded, his nostrils flaring. He was kind of a nutcase, Lacey thought, but he backed his convictions with action.

Brooke aimed her digital camera at the downed Brit and waved Damon into the frame. "Smile, Damon!" He stood over Griffin and grinned like a hunter who had bagged a trophy game animal. She clicked and clicked. "I can't wait to upload these to the Web."

"What is it with you bloody Yanks? You're a bunch of barbarians," Griffin complained from his seat on the ground.

"Not really, Nigel," Vic said. "We're sensitive guys. We're just sensitive to overbearing foulmouthed cowardly bullies like you."

"Foulmouthed? Me? What did I bloody say? Try to be helpful, this is your thanks."

"You're not going anywhere until you apologize to the ladies. And to all Yanks everywhere," Vic said. He turned to the ladies. "Anything else he should apologize for?"

"I have a list, but that will do for now," Lacey said.

Griffin rolled his eyes heavenward and then grudgingly apologized. Damon extended a hand to pull him up, and the Brit hesitated, then took it. The two couples of Jim Morrison's Asian fan club applauded, apparently pleased with the show. Lacey wondered what they had made of all that. *Probably thought we were feuding over what was the all-time greatest Doors song.* They smiled and bowed and then marched off, their umbrellas retreating in the mist.

Ten minutes later the five of them, Vic, Lacey, Damon, Brooke, and a chastened Griffin, found themselves sharing a bottle of Cabernet Sauvignon and a basket of hot bread in a small pink café.

A waiter was hanging up their wet coats. Brooke's teeth had stopped chattering and her braid was drying. Vic was questioning Griffin, Lacey was taking an occasional note by hand with her fountain pen, and Damon was tapping away on a BlackBerry like a madman. He was no doubt planning to file a story and try to scoop Lacey. *That's all I need. How could I explain that to Mac?* She realized she had to find a way to file a story immediately with *The Eye. Damon throws one punch and now he thinks he's got a scoop? No way, this is my story!*

"What's the status of Kepelov?" Vic asked.

"I have no frigging idea, mate. Dead for all I know. I didn't send flowers." Nigel looked for his cigarettes. "Mind if I smoke?"

"Yes, we all mind," Brooke said. "And it's my turn to punch you this time."

"It's Paris, for pity's sake! You're practically required by law to smoke here! Bloody hell. Bunch of clean-air fascists." He groaned and put the pack away.

"So who shot Kepelov?" Vic asked again. Griffin shrugged and reached for the wine.

"And why did you feel compelled to tell us?" Lacey asked. "Why not just run for it?"

"Thought you might know something. Obviously wrong," Griffin sniffed. "I'm interested in saving my own skin, thank you very much, even if you lot could care less about yours."

"Tell us what you know." Vic leaned back and crossed his arms. "Make it good."

"Or what? You'll let the girls have a go at me?" Griffin whined. "Cruel and inhuman, that would be."

"You better hope we don't have a go at you," Brooke said.

"I told you, Nigel, we have nothing on an imperial Fabergé egg," Lacey said. "The coal room was it, the big clue. That's all Magda told me about. She said nothing about a Fabergé egg."

Griffin drained his wineglass and filled it again. Everyone else was still on their first glass.

Vic put his elbows on the table and leaned in to Griffin. "So if Kepelov didn't have the Fabergé egg, why kill him? And if he knows something, why not just follow him to it?"

"I don't know. He was a lazy bastard sometimes. Maybe someone thought he wasn't being bloody efficient," Griffin suggested. "Whoever he worked for. Russians and you Americans are simply obsessed with efficiency. Take an afternoon off and they send in the bleeding assassins. Not like we English: One thing you can say about us, mate, we don't bloody care. 'Have another pint, mate, there's always tomorrow.'" He tore off a piece of bread. "I assumed he was working for some Russian collector. You know the type. Wants to repatriate all the eggs back to Mother Russia. Revive the Empire, bring back the Czar, all that rot."

Damon was nodding his head. "Absolutely. There's a huge movement out there, just beneath the surface, Russians yearning to restore the monarchy. They want to find all the Romanov relics, symbols of their power. Maybe Kepelov was no good, slacking off, so they cut their losses."

"What if more than one unknown Russian collector had hired more than one spy to steal back the egg?" Brooke asked, touching Damon's arm. "There might be more than one team racing after this thing."

"You're right," Damon said. "Kepelov might have been too good, getting too close, so the competition took him out."

"Do you ever listen to yourself, Damon? You just said Kepelov was shot because he was no good, and shot because he was too good." Lacey laughed. "So how close was he or wasn't he to this nonexistent egg?" she asked Griffin.

Griffin was fidgeting like a man who needed a smoke. "No idea, but he did have something else. Wanted me to look at a piece of possible Romanov jewelry he was coming into."

"What was it?'

"I never saw it. He said it was platinum, full of gemstones. He wanted me to evaluate it. Last night. At that restaurant. That place is so overrated, you know, why the bloody hell does everyone in Paris have to go there, just because Hemingway used to get sloshed there with—"

"So he was waiting for you?" Brooke asked. "He wasn't following us?"

"Or he was keeping an eye on all of us. Not a trusting chap, Kepelov." He winked at her and swallowed some wine. "I was a little late. Not my fault. I see Kepelov on the ground, too much blood, too many police. I realized I had urgent business elsewhere, as they say."

"Suppose we believe you," Vic said. "Kepelov had something Romanov. Maybe he's close to finding more. So the competition kills him—we're assuming he's dead—to take it? To keep him from getting to some bigger Romanov treasure trove first? And to eliminate anyone who even suspects it exists?"

"Would that include us?" Lacey said.

"Bingo, bright girl." Nigel lifted his glass to her. "No one ever listens to me."

"That can mean only one thing," Brooke said. She and Damon exchanged a look.

Damon lowered his voice. "The Romanov Revengers. That's what my CIA contacts call them, anyway. A Russian equivalent of the U.S. Government Repossessors, a highly clandestine shadow government group. Since the collapse of the Soviet Union, the Revengers operate with various partners. The Romanov monarchists. Rogue ex-KGB elements. Maybe even the Russian Mafia. Who knows?"

Griffin looked bleary-eyed. "Good lord. What are you blathering on about?"

Damon looked at Griffin with pity. "Nearly every major industrialized nation has a quasi-governmental group to do its secret dirty work, protect national interests, eliminate threats that can't be addressed in a court of law, that kind of thing," Damon explained patiently. "The U.S. group is known as the G.R. Code name 'Grim Reaper.' "

"It's common knowledge," Brooke said, quite as if it were.

"Bloody hell. You're saying that our Rasputin was blasted by these Romanov radicals?"

"It's just one of any number of possibilities," Brooke suggested. "For all we know, Griffin, you're the next one on the hit list." She smiled sweetly. "Pass the wine, please."

"I have never seen a conversation spin so out of control," Vic said later. "I think they're very useful."

"Who?" Lacey asked.

"Brooke and Damon, of course, the most gifted obfuscators I've ever seen. She even had Nigel baffled into believing her. Or at least not disbelieving her. She must be awesome in court."

"She has a gift." Lacey nodded. "And yet she believes all that stuff herself. I think."

Lacey and Vic finally found themselves alone on the street. Brooke was feeling feverish, so Damon hailed a taxi to take them back to the hotel for a nap and some aspirin and tender loving care. Griffin was interested only in more wine. Lacey and Vic left him at the café, with the wine tab. It was the least he could do, they all agreed. Everyone but Griffin, that is.

A nap sounded divine to Lacey, but unfortunately, she had work to do. They were walking purposefully. "Where's that Internet café you found for us?"

Vic checked the map. "Close. Around the corner, down the block."

The little café had several vacant computers and a high-speed connection. Lacey picked the one in a semisecluded corner, next to a purple velvet wing chair where Vic could keep her company. She regretted she was not out on the streets of Paris. She had reread part of *A Moveable Feast* on the airplane to France, and it was haunting her imagination. She thought about Hemingway writing *The Sun Also Rises* while sitting on the terrace at La Closerie des Lilas, the famous café in Montparnasse. Hemingway wrote with a fountain pen, Lacey's favorite instrument, or else a clattering manual typewriter. What would he have thought of the Internet? Would he have written a blog? *The Blog Also Rises dot com*? She sighed. The fun of the Parisian café was watching real Parisians, not staring at a soulless computer screen. But at least she was staring at a soulless computer in a café in Paris, she thought.

Vic agreed she should file a story for *The Eye Street Observer* from the nearest Internet connection. She had her notes with her, and in her head, and at least she'd have a chance of filing something before Damon could concoct some wild tale. Once some of the information about Magda's supposed treasure was out in the open, everyone would be safer, they both believed. It would be too late to stop the story by killing anyone, Lacey included.

Lacey began by calling the newsroom at *The Eye* on the sleek international cell phone Brooke had loaned her. The six-hour time difference made it just before noon in Washington, and she caught Trujillo on the way to lunch. She cut short his barrage of questions about Paris and learned that the D.C. cops were definitely calling Magda's death a murder, and the cause of death an unknown poison, but they had no leads and no suspects. The toxicology screen for the poison was still pending, the dagger and crime scene yielded no prints, and Trujillo said Mac had been telling Broadway Lamont that Lacey had gone home early for Thanksgiving. "So what's the well-dressed fashion reporter wearing on the Champs Elysées this season?" Trujillo asked.

"Wouldn't you like to know?" She told Trujillo to alert Mac to an incoming story, promised to CC it to him as well, and clicked off. Then she began to type.

She summarized Magda's family history, her grandfather's diary, the dead end in the coal room in Normandy, the attack in the cellar, and the shooting in Paris of the alleged ex-KGB agent Kepelov. There were certain facts she withheld for safety's sake. She did not mention that Magda's "treasure" was said to be a Romanov corset. Nor did she mention the phantom address on the Rue Dauphine or identify Jean-Claude Rousseau or the location of his farmhouse, sparing the Frenchman from having strangers excavate his cellar, or perhaps doing it himself at gunpoint. She would supply an epilogue, she decided, after she and Vic went to New Orleans.

TREASURE SEARCH ENDS IN COBWEBS AND GUNSHOTS

By Lacey Smithsonian

PARIS—Magda Rousseau created treasures of the seamstress's art, crafting beautiful costumes for the theatres of the Nation's Capital, elegant gowns and corsets that were the stuff of many a Washington woman's dreams. However, it was a very different treasure Magda dreamed of. She lived her life with the dream of returning to her native France to find a treasure she believed was hidden there long ago by her grandfather. Some people believe the treasure she spoke of was an imperial Fabergé egg, one of a handful that remain missing, its potential value untold millions. A murderer cut short Magda's dream. With her dying breath, she asked me to carry on her search for it.

Her directions led me to a farmhouse in the green countryside of Normandy, where I wound up flat on my back, covered in cobwebs. There was no treasure there. But there were others looking for a legendary Fabergé egg, and perhaps willing to kill for it. . . .

Three mocha lattes and one caffeine buzz later, Lacey looked up from the computer and realized there was no fashion angle. "That's bound to cause trouble in paradise. I better call Mac," she said to Vic, dialing the cell phone again. Using Brooke's expensive minutes, she finally reached Mac, back from lunch and chewing antacid tablets in his office.

"Nice of you to call, Smithsonian, while you're wasting the paper's money in France."

"If it makes you feel any better, Mac, I was chloroformed in the cellar of the farmhouse by a Russian ex-KGB agent who later went lingerie shopping with me and ended up being shot on a Paris street."

He paused for a moment. Lacey heard him chewing. "You writing fiction now?"

"No, it's the truth."

"I take it you're not injured?" He sounded mildly curious.

"I'm fine." She felt grumpy and her muscles were stiff. She stretched.

"Who shot this spy?"

"I don't know. But I didn't do it. He'd been stalking us."

"Are you in danger now?"

Actually, she felt pretty safe with Vic there. "I don't think so. I'm okay."

"Answer me one question, Lacey. Can you even walk down the street anywhere in the world without causing trouble?"

She could imagine Mac's brown face glowering, his bushy eyebrows knit together, his free hand reaching for his blue and white bottle of Maalox. "Aren't you glad I'm okay?" She could hear a sigh.

"Of course I'm glad you're all right, damn it. There. I said it. But I gather you're not calling just to make my ulcer bleed. What's up?"

"I'm e-mailing the story in a few minutes."

"Wait a minute, Smithsonian." This was a major change in plans. They had agreed she would finish the story in Washington. "That's not because you're going to be in a French prison tomorrow, is it?"

She made a face at the phone, and Vic lifted an eyebrow at her. She shook her head at him and said to Mac, "You are *so* not amusing. No, Damon Newhouse is here in Paris and I know he's going to have some garbled half-fictionalized version of this story on Conspiracy Clearinghouse."

"How soon?"

"No telling, could be tomorrow. He's following me around. Thinks he has a scoop."

"Maybe I should hire the guy. He's persistent."

"Except you don't publish fiction. And if you hired Newhouse, he'd have to work the fashion beat too, 'cause I'd quit."

"Kidding, Smithsonian, only kidding!" he grumbled. "What's the fashion angle?"

Lacey closed her eyes. "Well, there's not exactly a fashion angle."

"Smithsonian, your beat is fashion. There's got to be a fashion angle. What about the corset?"

"What about international intrigue?" she said. "Shady characters, dark conspiracies?"

"The corset, Smithsonian."

"We can't mention the corset, Mac."

"Why the hell not? You're over there because of the damn corset!"

"It's complicated." She heard his growl from across the Atlantic. "And dangerous. I haven't found the corset. If there is a corset. But the people looking for it think it's a Fabergé egg."

"What?" He sounded ready to explode. "Are you crazy? Are *they* crazy?"

"No. Really, some people think the treasure is a Fabergé egg. Look, I'll just mention her career as a corsetiere and seamstress. How's that?"

"Make it work. And this better be good. Don't cause an international incident."

She hung up and slumped in her chair. Then she returned to her story and added a sidebar on Magda and the elegant art of the corsetiere. As a peace offering, she also sent Mac her "Fashion Bite" on Parisian women and their relentlessly self-confident fashion attitude. Vic checked his watch and started massaging her shoulders.

"I've read every magazine in the café. Twice. Even the ones in French. How's it going?"

"He wants the fashion angle."

"Tell him where he can put his fashion angle," Vic said soothingly. "Let me buy you dinner." He smiled and held her jacket for her.

"We only have one more day in France." Lacey felt sorry for herself. She paid for her Internet time and pocketed the bill for her expense account. He held the door for her, and they strolled into the glorious late afternoon. The rain had stopped. There would be a beautiful sunset.

"Let's make it count, then," Vic said. His smile was all she needed. "What do you want?

"Romance and Paris and you and all the sights we can see."

He rolled his eyes. "Are you always this demanding?"

"Vic, honey. You don't *know* demanding."

Lacey Smithsonian's

FASHION BITES

French Fashion Superiority? It's All in the Attitude, *Chérie*

Oh, that fabulous, fabled, fashionable French female! So chic, so superior, so legendary. Her allure makes strong men weak, and weak men turn to crime. They are the stuff of sultry film noir. Her legend is so potent, it's enough to make you wonder if she's real or simply a myth with a superb press agent. Or is it just the accent? *Ah, men, zey are fools for ze accent, chérie. N'est-ce pas?*

We know the type. We've seen her in the movies, in the incarnations of Bardot, Deneuve, Moreau, and the rest, and we've read about her in books and in *Cosmopolitan*. The Frenchwoman is a style icon, so effortlessly stylish, so cool, so *ooh la la*. She drinks coffee and guzzles wine and smokes cigarettes all day so she can eat a nine-course meal at night and stay thin as a supermodel. Her fabled scarf-tying skills are the stuff that fashion myths are made of. She is soigné. All she needs is a black dress, a cleverly wrapped silk scarf, a smudge of smoky eye makeup, a smear of red lipstick, and a healthy serving of elegant disdain. And a light.

There's a French saying: If a woman is not beautiful at twenty, it is Nature's fault. If she is not beautiful at forty, it is her own fault. Tough graders, those French, but you be the judge. Exhibit A: Catherine Deneuve at sixty-something.

Here are a few observations from Paris, the City of Light. Not every Frenchwoman is Catherine Deneuve, but she does have a few tricks that any woman can use, beginning with attitude. The French have attitude by the wine barrel. The Frenchwoman believes she is chic because she is French, and because she thinks so, everyone else thinks so too. I know, this seems too simple to be true, and yet it is. These lessons are passed down from French mother to daughter. (Remember, get the attitude down, *chérie*, and everything else follows. You can fake *ze accent*.)

- Frenchwomen are consistent. They don't dress up one day and dress down the next. Their style signature is something you can count on. If they wear makeup, they wear it every day. If they like a piece of jewelry, they wear it a lot. If scarves are their keynote, they have a drawer full. If they wear high heels, they wear them everywhere. She's memorable, and she makes it a pleasure to remember her.
- They love lingerie, how it looks, how it hugs the body, how it lays the foundation for the rest of their clothes. They are very particular about their bras and panties, and love them to match. They spend *beaucoup* euros on this necessity. It's worth it.
- They are not afraid to pamper themselves. That too is a necessity. If that means buying the best and most expensive face cream, then that's what it means. Ditto: manicures, pedicures, and facials. They think they're worth it. Aren't you?
- Frenchwomen wear clothes that fit, and fit perfectly, which is the first essential for looking chic and put together. They know that simple classic pieces will last for years, maybe decades, therefore they spend money on them. Or they get the *monsieur* to spend it on them.
- They do not waste their euros on bargains they will never wear. What American woman can say that as she tucks that ghastly purple polyester bargain into her shopping bag, or that chartreuse velvet jacket that goes with nothing and makes her skin turn green, just because it was on sale and it was "too good" to pass up?

Feel free to borrow or steal these style clues, but don't let the mystique of the arcane art of French scarf-tying tie you up in knots. With just a soupçon of French style and attitude, you'll be flaunting your own sense of style, your sense of self, and your savoir faire with the best of them. And remember, you don't have to smoke like a Frenchwoman to be *smokin'*.

chapter 28

A delicate white orchid was delivered to the room with their coffee and croissants the next morning. The card had no name, but she knew who it was from. She had seen Vic in close conversation with the concierge last night after their early evening trip down the Seine on a Bateau-Mouche, the romantic Parisian tour boat where Cary Grant and Audrey Hepburn bantered romantically in *Charade.* Their view of Paris from the river was breathtaking as the Bateau-Mouche carried them slowly beneath the bridges of the Ile de la Cité and the Ile Saint-Louis, just as the lights of the City of Light winked on all around them.

Lacey cherished the orchid. It was almost too beautiful to touch.

"So they do teach you to be smooth in prep school. Why didn't you ever show me this side of you before?" She wondered how she could enjoy the blossom and keep it with her all day.

"Because I knew you'd be a smart-ass about it."

She kissed him. "I'll wear it in my hair." She wouldn't worry about what people would think. That was one lesson she had learned about style in France. She tucked the blossom behind her ear, securing it with a bobby pin. She glanced in the mirror, pleased. She had picked out a clever high Empire-waisted blue-green sweater with a sweetheart neckline that brought out her eyes and emphasized her curves. She wore it over her black skirt and tights. "How do I look?"

He returned the kiss. "It's what any self-respecting femme fatale would wear."

"Who's the smart-ass now?" Lacey wanted to linger over coffee, but Vic was eager to get out.

"Time's a-wasting, honey," he said in his best Colorado police chief manner. It was their last day in Paris, and Montmartre was calling. "If we want to have any time to ourselves before meeting our friends the spy-chasers and entering another dimension."

"Don't blame me, Vic, you brought Damon to Paris."

Lacey had seen the famous black-and-white photos of Paris artistically shrouded in fog. But the landscape of Montmartre, the district of artists and bohemians, came alive in Technicolor under a clear azure sky. Yesterday's rain had given way to brilliant sunshine. The air was cool though comfortable, and the crowds returned in droves to the streets, wandering among painters and fruit sellers and flower stands, bistros and shops. She and Vic wound their way up and down the streets shopping and taking pictures.

Before they met Brooke and Damon, Lacey had to meet an old friend of Magda's. She called ahead to a lingerie shop in Montmartre to meet with a Madame Suzanne Noir, who had been an apprentice with Magda years before in an exclusive lingerie shop. They had learned to fit corsets and other foundation garments together, and Magda had remembered her well. Vic left her at this temple of lingerie and went in search, he said, of more manly pursuits.

Lacey had expected to meet a twin of the old corsetiere she had known in Washington, but Madame Suzanne Noir reminded her not of Magda, but of a pale corpse, a tall, thin corpse about to ride the last Metro out of this world. Her dyed black hair did nothing to ease the walking-dead effect, though it was worn in flirtatious ringlets from a center part. Two round patches of rouge on the cheeks had obviously been applied by a woman whose eyesight was fading. The tired gray eyes were circled in heavy eyeliner, and face powder had settled into the wrinkles. Madame Noir wore a severe black dress with a lace collar, a cross at her throat and a gold wedding ring her only jewelry.

She was gracious when Lacey introduced herself and conveyed the sad news that Magda had died shortly before the trip. Lacey decided to save the footnote that Magda had been murdered. It might put a damper on this social call. *It was the sort of information,* she thought, *that you could always get around to later, but you could never take back.*

"How curious life is, no? Magda's heart gives out mere days before our grand reunion. I tell you I was so very surprised when she wrote to me. It had been so many years, you see."

"I know she looked forward to seeing you again," Lacey said. "Can you tell me what she was like when she was young?"

Madame Noir was quiet for awhile before finally speaking.

"When we were girls, I was the serious student. Magda was more—playful, perhaps. It was very strict working in the shop in the old days. Magda liked to say that corsets hide secrets. I would say, of course, they hide the waist that is thick, the hips that are lumpy, the breasts that sag. Magda Rousseau would laugh and say, '*Mais oui*, all that and more.' "

"That sounds like Magda."

"Oh, yes. For me, it was my work, but for her—" The old woman threw up her hands. "It was something more." She seemed at a loss for words. Or perhaps she didn't want to say more.

"Do you mind if I look around your beautiful shop?" Lacey was dazzled by the lovely lingerie, pools of silk fabrics in every color. She was glad she wasn't being harassed this time by a rogue Russian ex-spy with an odd American dream.

"Please do. I'm sure you will find something to amuse your young man," Madame said with a sly smile. Lacey smiled too.

"Well, *amuse* isn't exactly what I'm going for. Perhaps *entice* is a better word."

Madame Noir floated lightly around the shop, pointing out some lovely underwear sets. Lacey picked up a delicate set in sky-blue silk with lavender lace. "Perhaps you would tell me, Mademoiselle Smithsonian. A delicate question. What was it that Magda wanted of me?" Lacey glanced up at her in surprise.

"She just told me that she wanted to visit her old friend." Lacey didn't know what else to say, so she focused on the lingerie. This set, one of the least expensive ones, was well over a hundred euros. She peered into a case where even pricier underwear nestled securely behind glass. A little shocked, Lacey resolved not to faint in front of this cadaverous Frenchwoman whose clientele apparently thought nothing of buying three-hundred-dollar bras.

Madame Noir smiled, revealing yellow teeth behind dry, cracked lips. "We were friends once, it is true, but we parted badly. May I tell you the secret? I married the man Magda loved, you see. I took him away from her. Why would she want to see me, except for revenge?"

"So there was once a man in Magda's life?" Madame Noir nodded. Lacey was surprised by this revelation, but happy to learn that Magda had at least known love once. *I thought she must be a widow*, Lacey mused. *This must be the man I'd sensed in her past.* "And Monsieur Noir?"

"My husband died some time ago." The woman rubbed her plain gold wedding ring as if to reassure herself. "I am alone now."

"Maybe she didn't want revenge at all," Lacey suggested. "Perhaps she just wanted to tell you she had forgiven you."

"How very kind of you to say that," Madame Noir said. Lacey had the distinct feeling that by "kind" she meant "stupid."

Lacey tried to frame a sensitive question about their love triangle, the who, why, and when of that long-ago love affair. "May I ask you a rather—" But Madame had her own questions.

"What did she tell you about me? Why did Magda want to see me now?" Her eyes narrowed like a cat's, and Lacey was afraid she was about to pounce. "What did she want?"

"I'm sorry, Madame Noir, I don't know. I was just going to accompany her to France. She wanted to see you again. That's all." Was it possible that Magda wanted to reconcile with her old friend? Or did she just want to flaunt her hoped-for treasure in this bitter woman's face? For revenge for an old wound? And why was Madame Noir, the winner in their love triangle, so bitter toward Magda, the loser? She had no idea, and now she wanted to leave. Lacey picked up two bra-and-panty sets, one in white lace and the one in sky-blue silk. "I'll take these."

"You do not want to try them on?" Madame seemed shocked at this American breach of fashion protocol, but there was no way Lacey was going to take off her clothes in a dressing room with this malevolent old crow hovering over her.

"I think they'll fit." Lacey fumbled in her purse for her credit card.

Madame Noir stared at the lingerie and then at Lacey with a trained eye. "These will most likely fit you very well, but I must recommend a fitting." She grabbed a measuring tape. "I must measure you!"

"I have to meet my friends," Lacey said firmly. "I'll take them."

The old woman shrugged curtly. "*D'accord!* I cannot be held responsible if you are not happy." Madame Noir seized the merchandise and carried it to the register along with Lacey's credit card. "A very nice choice, mademoiselle. My compliments."

Lacey smiled stiffly. Madame Noir offered her card back and then suddenly grabbed Lacey's wrist when she reached for it, pulling Lacey's face close to hers. "Magda Rousseau was a crazy woman! She had crazy ideas! She said her grandfather stole a treasure, a long time ago, in the Russian Revolution. She said the old man talked in his sleep." Madame Noir stared into Lacey's face as if looking right through her. Lacey turned her wrist, but the old woman held her fast. "Magda swore she would find it one day. She hated me because I took her lover. She swore revenge on me. I am very poor, mademoiselle. I have no pension. No husband. I can give her nothing. You must tell me: Did Magda find her treasure? Let her have it, and leave me in peace!"

"I'm sorry, Madame Noir. There is no treasure. I only came because I thought you were her friend, you would want to know she had died." Lacey spoke very calmly. "Now let me go."

"But of course." The woman released her wrist. "*Désolée.* I forget myself. *Pardon,* mademoiselle." She curled her mouth into a cold smile. She finished wrapping the lingerie sets in floral tissue paper and slipped them into a small black bag with embossed gold lettering. "Will that be all, mademoiselle?"

Lacey calmed herself, trying not to be furious with this embittered old woman. She noticed that several bottles of perfume for sale at the register had been disarrayed in their brief struggle. Madame Noir was quietly straightening the display.

"No. One more question, Madame. Magda wore a certain perfume, it was very distinct. I don't know the name. Perhaps she wore it when you were friends. Do you remember?" Lacey felt herself flush. "But never mind, after all these years she couldn't have still worn the same—"

Madame Noir pulled a stopper from a delicate amber bottle and offered it to Lacey. "Is this it?"

The familiar woodsy rose scent was overwhelming. Lacey felt her stomach rise. She wanted to run from the store, but she resolved not to lose her self-control. "Yes, thank you. That's the scent."

"Shall I wrap it up for you? Will that be a charge to the same card?"

"No, thank you, Madame. But the name of the scent, please?"

"It is a very old-fashioned scent. *Forêt de Rose.*" She put the stopper back in the bottle. "She always wore it, a long time ago. It was her favorite."

"*Merci,* Madame, I'm so sorry that Magda couldn't be here to see you herself." *Magda would have known what to say. She would have put the old woman in her place.*

Madame Suzanne Noir pulled herself up very erect and pale. She was once again the consummate saleswoman. "It is of no importance, Mademoiselle Smithsonian. We all die. Some sooner than others. Au revoir."

Lacey bolted from the lingerie shop, her heart beating wildly. Vic was just emerging from the elegant menswear shop next door with a sack. She slipped her arm into his. He turned to her with his brilliant smile. "Hi, everything okay?

"Of course." She snuggled into his arms. "Never better."

He frowned. "Are you sure?"

"I was just frightened by a scary underwear saleswoman." Lacey couldn't believe she'd spent so much money with that old harridan. She hoped desperately her new underwear would fit. She must have been mesmerized into buying it. How could she ever return them if they didn't fit?

"Yeah, I hate it when that happens. How scary?"

"Several hundred dollars' worth." She showed off the chic little bag she carried and his eyes grew wide.

"Whoa. Now I'm scared too." He peeked in the bag and smiled. "That must be about a hundred dollars an ounce, honey. Can I see about two ounces of that later?" Lacey blushed happily. Vic tucked both of their packages into his black leather backpack.

They were meeting Brooke and Damon at the Basilica of Sacre-Coeur, the crowning glory of Montmartre. Passing by a block of pretty houses across from the Lapin Agile, said to be Picasso's favorite cabaret, they saw scrawled across the side of one house in huge painted letters the lovesick declaration of some unknown French swain: AGATHE JE T'AIME. *Lucky Agathe,* Lacey thought.

They were breathing a little harder by the time they approached the top of the many steps of Sacre-Coeur. The Basilica atop the hill, with its striking domes of white stone, reminded Lacey of a whitewashed castle looming against the sky. Tourists, students, and worshipers milled around the church, admiring one of the finest views of Paris. Lacey spied Brooke and Damon at the top of the steps and stopped to take a picture of them silhouetted against the Basilica.

"You're late," Brooke said, rushing down the steps to meet them with Damon close behind.

"Ten minutes," Lacey replied. "I have a good excuse."

"Thirteen minutes," Brooke corrected, pointing at her watch. "I was half afraid you'd been shot and killed by Kepelov's phantom assassin." Several people who must have spoken English turned to stare. She lowered her voice. "So what's your excuse?"

"A run-in with a scary old friend of Magda's," Lacey said, catching her breath. "'Friend' may not be the right word. And I bought several hundred dollars' worth of sexy French lingerie."

"Cool! Can we see it?" Damon said. Brooke smacked his arm. "Hey, babe, it's research."

"Do your own research, buddy," Vic suggested with a grin.

"Grow up everyone! It *is* research for me," Lacey said. "Fashion research. Have you been inside the Basilica yet?"

"Not without you," Brooke said. "We were keeping watch."

"No sign of Nigel Griffin," Damon said, "no word on Kelepov, and no telling who else in this city, or even in this crowd, might be a foreign operative."

"No telling," Vic agreed. "Maybe even us. Shall we go in?" They started up the last few steps together. A sudden breeze caressed Lacey's cheek and brought with it a rich wave of *Forêt de Rose*, Magda's perfume. She felt dizzy, and a little tickle of fear went up her spine. *Does everyone in Paris wear that damned scent?!* She stumbled on a step and grabbed Vic's hand.

Above them there seemed to be some kind of commotion. She looked up to see a white-haired man lose his balance and slip off the very top step. "Hey! Stop—!" he shouted in English. The expression on his face was sheer shock as he tumbled head over heels down the stone steps straight at her. Lacey blinked. She seemed to be reacting far too slowly.

A pair of strong arms lifted her off her feet and swung her out of the way just as the man careened past her down the steps, taking several other people with him as he fell. "Oh, my God, Vic." She was shaking in Vic's arms. "He came straight at me."

Vic made sure she was all right and left her with Brooke before he and Damon pounded down the steps to the crumpled heap of victims writhing below. Several people were unconscious and bleeding, but the white-haired man was conscious and shouting for help. The others had broken his fall. Lacey heard Vic tell him to lie still, help was on the way. He was protesting loudly in English that he hadn't lost his balance at all.

"Pushed! I was pushed! Some bastard pushed me!" The man's leg was twisted beneath him at an unnatural angle. He told Vic he felt hands on his back and a swift vicious shove. "Some son of a bitch did this on purpose!" Unfortunately he hadn't seen who had pushed him down the stairs, nor did he have a clue who it might be or why. He was still swearing from pain and anger when the paramedics and the gendarmes arrived and Vic and Damon stepped away. The white-haired man and several others were carried away to the ambulances.

Vic and Lacey made very brief statements to a gendarme hastily canvassing the crowd for witnesses. Neither they nor Brooke or Damon had seen anything but the man's fall. No one in the crowd stepped forward to point to a culprit or to claim responsibility. Tourists shrugged and resumed their business of enjoying the spectacular view, but for Lacey, the charm had gone out of her last day in Paris. Paris was still lovely, she thought, but her first trip abroad had so far included a mugging by chloroform, a dead dog, relentless stalking, room searches, electronic bugs, the ghost of a lonely chambermaid, a shooting, the unsettling Madame Noir, and now an innocent bystander launched in her direction like a missile.

"Are you okay, sweetheart?" Vic seemed quite willing to hold her securely in his arms until she stopped shaking.

"It's time to go home now," she said.

They were on the plane back to America before Lacey felt safe enough to relax. The couples had swapped seats so Brooke and Damon, both feeling feverish from their wet afternoon in the rainy cemetery, could sit together, and Lacey and Vic sat together several rows behind them.

Just before she could doze off on Vic's shoulder, Lacey remembered his Thanksgiving dinner invitation, which she had tentatively accepted. She felt her anxiety rising about Vic's invitation to his parents' house. *Great. Something else to worry about. I escape Paris with my life only to end it all at Thanksgiving.* Indicative of her basic shallowness, she thought glumly, the first thing she worried about was what to wear. This meeting was so important. She wanted them to like her. She sighed. *This may be a bigger problem than just a wardrobe decision.*

Vic's folks lived in McLean, Virginia, a very well-to-do suburb full of wealthy politicians and lobbyists and CIA bureaucrats. She assumed the "comfortable" senior Donovans were wealthy, sophisticated people; she hoped they had high standards for holidays. Lacey believed that if you drag out the good china, you dress up. *You don't wear blue jeans with the good china.* A sophisticated soirée in McLean might have its charms. It might play to her strengths, she realized.

"What's the dress code for Thanksgiving dinner?" she asked.

"My mother likes people to dress, but it's not way formal. More semiformal."

"What are you wearing?"

"Um, slacks, sweater, blazer, that sort of thing. I mean, if you want to go really casual, Mom won't throw you out or anything—"

"Casual? You must be kidding. What will your mother be wearing?"

He shrugged. Clearly this was a question he didn't address very often. "You know, a dress or something. I don't know. Maybe slacks. Is this a big problem?"

"I don't know what to wear," she whispered.

"The fashion icon of *The Eye Street Observer* is worrying about what to wear? Say it ain't so!" Vic laughed. Lacey glared at him, but she couldn't help smiling. "How about some wine for Madame Fashion Reporter's nerves?" He opened a small bottle of Air France's finest screw-top Cabernet for her and poured it into two glasses.

Lacey took a sip of wine. "Let's proceed to question number two. What should I bring?" Lacey imagined Vic saying, "Not to worry, just bring some flowers or something."

"I said we'd bring dessert."

"Dessert? Are you crazy? You said *we* would bring dessert?" *Homemade dessert! For a big family Thanksgiving!* She just stared at him.

"Sure. Why? My mother doesn't make desserts. Not like your mom. But she loves sweets."

Lacey was appalled. "A dessert like *my* mom makes? Surely you aren't suggesting I whip up a big bowl of Rice Krispies and chocolate and marshmallows and graham crackers and maraschino cherries and gummy bears and—"

"Whatever. Anything you like. Sweeten her up. She'll love you, darling." Lacey sank down in her seat and covered her face with her hands. "It's okay if you can't cook, you know, we'll just pick up a—"

"I can cook," she snapped. "I just don't do it very often, that's all. I can ride a horse, too, but I try not to do it every day." In fact, once in a while she even indulged in baking. But she didn't want the secret to get out. It was bad enough being the fashion reporter: If her editor found out she could cook too, he'd expect her to go brownie-to-brownie and tart-to-tart with the evil Felicity.

"We'll pick up a pumpkin pie at a bakery. No problem," Vic assured her. "She'll never know the difference."

Lacey rolled her eyes. "Men! Of course she will, how could she possibly not know?"

"That's what I do. She always says, 'Yum, great pie.'"

"Because *you* brought it! Vic, dearest, store-bought pies come in those little aluminum tins. Everyone knows that!" Vic looked unconvinced. "I can't believe you want me to start off by lying to your mother with a store-bought pie. I can't believe you would suggest that. Do you want this woman to *hate* me?" Even if Vic didn't have a clue what this was all about, Lacey did. This was an audition: She would be trying out for the role of Vic's girlfriend, with his mother as the show's producer. She could just see Vic's mother smiling that cool producer's smile, saying, "So nice of you to read for us, dear. Don't call us, we'll call you. Next!"

"Don't worry. She'll like you." Vic nuzzled her cheek warmly. "How could she not?"

Lacey drank her wine. "Okay, Vic. This is what we will do. *We*, you and I, will bring a homemade dessert, like you promised, because you and I are going to bake something together."

"Is that right?" He stroked her face with the back of his hand.

"If it turns out great, we will share the praise, and if it turns out *badly*—"

Vic kissed her forehead. "We'll just pick up that crummy dried-out store-bought pie in the cheap tin. And a big old can of Cool Whip." He grinned at her. Lacey groaned, a groan that turned into a giggle as he nuzzled her ear. This little test would either cement their relationship, she thought, or kill it deader than a day-old doughnut.

Chapter 29

"New Orleans? Smithsonian, are you out of your mind?" Douglas MacArthur Jones's eyebrows arched dangerously into his forehead. Lacey wondered if that hurt. "Wasn't being chloroformed by some deranged Russian enough for you?"

On the morning after their flight back from Paris, still reeling from jet lag, Lacey sat as usual in Mac's overstuffed office, shoehorned in among stacks of copies of *The Eye* and who-knew-what. Mac was eating a piece of pumpkin pie, Felicity Pickles' autumnal recipe of the day, pausing in his tirade to appreciate the food editor's talents.

"Great pie, Lacey. Homemade. Felicity would save you a piece, I bet."

Lacey ignored that. "I don't know if it was chloroform, Mac." Lacey regretted that Gregor Kepelov hadn't given her that monogrammed handkerchief he'd used. Perhaps a lab could tell her whether she'd been gassed with something safe or Brooke's secret Russian killer knockout cocktail. Kepelov himself wouldn't say. And now, if Griffin was to be believed, Kepelov was dead. Vic had gotten a frantic long-distance call from him that very morning, midafternoon Paris time, and he'd alerted Lacey at the newsroom. "But the story isn't over yet."

"Careful, Smithsonian, you are on thin ice. You were attacked, knocked out, by your own admission. Running off to New Orleans is out of the question. Too dangerous."

Rats. Now I'm going to have to use the personal leave card. "But Mac, you've always told me to take some time off after these, um, little incidents. Some personal time. To deal with the stress?" She tried hard to look pathetic. It wasn't working.

"I can't believe you still want to go looking for this crazy-ass corset that doesn't exist."

"But the story—"

"Damn the story. You've come down with gold fever, Smithsonian. Like one of those miners in the Gold Rush, dead in the bottom of a mine with a bullet hole in them, just for fool's gold."

"They didn't all die, Mac, and I know you're from California, but you really don't want to go toe-to-toe with me here. I'm from Colorado and I know all kinds of stories where miners struck it rich. I was raised on the unsinkable Molly Brown. And Baby Doe Tabor." Lacey left out the part about Baby Doe's bad end at the Matchless Mine, penniless and freezing to death.

He grumbled. "I don't like that look in your eye. Besides, you wrote the story. Finished. Done. Thirty. The end." She knew the story was barely adequate without a satisfactory conclusion to the search. Mac didn't seem to care.

"I'll take time off. Do it on my own time."

"To go to New Orleans?" His eyes narrowed suspiciously.

"I hear it's a good place to unwind, Mac. I really am jet-lagging badly here."

He finished off the last bite of his pie and set the plate on top of the day's issue of the paper. "Let's look at what you got." He licked his fork for the remaining crumbs. "You got an address and half a smart-ass note that you say the jewel thief and the dead Russian spy didn't know about. What makes you think this address is in New Orleans?"

She wasn't sure herself. Except there *was* a Rue Dauphine in New Orleans, though the exact address hadn't shown up in her Internet search. Sometimes it was just a feeling, she thought, and the feeling was getting stronger. "The corset wasn't in Normandy, where Magda thought it was. This Drosmis Berzins character probably took it. Maybe he'd helped Juris steal it, and they had a falling out over it. He emigrated to the U.S., to Mississippi, close to Louisiana. The address wasn't in Paris. Finding a street in America that echoes a street in Paris sounds like a deliberate misdirection to me. So maybe Paris was a red herring, but what if it's a real address? Those two old Latvian guys were old comrades—maybe they were playing games with each other." She realized her face was set in that stubborn look she found so hard to wipe off at will. "It's a theory anyway, Mac, why not check it out?"

"Why do *you* have to check it out?" Mac burped and thumped himself in the chest. Lacey spotted his Maalox half hidden on the desk and handed it to him. "What's the real reason?"

"I made a promise to Magda Rousseau."

"You gotta stop making promises to dead people."

That's what Vic said. "It's on my list of New Year's resolutions."

Mac drank Maalox straight from the bottle. "New Year's is a month and a half away. Plenty of time for you to get into more trouble."

"I resent that."

He rubbed his chin and played with a pencil on his desk, letting her squirm. "I can't stop you from taking vacation time, Smithsonian. Or running around and causing trouble for people in New Orleans whom you haven't even met yet. Wiedemeyer would call them 'poor bastards.' But if you find yourself knee-deep in a real story on this thing, this imaginary artifact, *The Eye* would be interested, particularly if that maniac Newhouse and his Web site are going to be following you around like an addicted gambler tracking a long shot."

"He doesn't know."

"That's what you think." Mac raised his eyebrow. "He's probably put a global positioning tracker in your purse. But we want the factual, readable version of the story. Not the lunatic fringe version."

"And this is leading to what, exactly?"

"If you get the story, *The Eye* will pay for the trip."

"If I don't?"

"Then it's on your tab. One more thing, Smithsonian."

"Yes, Mac." She rose from her chair, sensing the interview was at a close.

"Stay safe."

"I will." She reached for the door handle.

"I mean it, Lacey. I always mean it."

"I know you do." She was halfway out the door. "Thanks."

"When do you leave?"

"Day after tomorrow."

"God help you. God help New Orleans. God help us all. Maybe you should bring that crazy friend of yours with you, the hairstylist."

"Stella? I don't think so; she has to work."

"Too bad. She could bring her camera." Lacey wondered whether Mac would ever let go of certain memories, like the time Stella snapped Lacey Smithsonian with a sword cane in her hands, fending off an attacker at a black-tie ball. Mac had run it on the front page.

"Stella would be so proud to know you care."

"Get out of here, Smithsonian. Call if you need any help."

She smiled and waved bon voyage and backed into the hall, straight into Tony Trujillo. His black lizard-skin cowboy boots screeched to a halt.

"I want your fashion beat, Lacey." He was smiling, but he had a faint air of irritation. "I'm tired of you snagging all the good stuff. I'll wear a little black dress and high heels if I have to."

"Oh, please, Trujillo, has crime in D.C. come to a standstill? How many people have been murdered in the District since Magda? A dozen? Besides, you read my story: I wound up flat on my back looking like a fool."

He grinned. "Interesting picture."

Thank goodness nobody has a picture of that. "I'd love to chat, Tony, but I've got to pack."

"Pack? You just got back from Paris! Now where?"

"Vacation. I need some time off."

"Hold the phone, Lois Lane. I'm calling for rewrite. Let's talk. May I interest you in a cup of sludge?" He indicated the kitchen, where the coffee was burned black and thick and disgusting. "On second thought, let's swing past Felicity's desk and see what's cookin'."

Trujillo steered them to Lacey's corner of the news world in the LifeStyles section. Felicity was absent, but one large slice of pumpkin pie was left undefended, next to a stack of paper plates and plastic forks and a notepad. Felicity always asked the journalists who doubled as her food tasters to give her feedback. They were just happy to get fed. Trujillo grabbed the last piece and asked Lacey politely if she wanted some before taking the first bite.

Normally Lacey would refuse, but with an important Thanksgiving dessert to come up with, she changed her mind. "Just a bite." She stuck a fork into Tony's pie and nibbled on a bite. Had Felicity come up with the magic recipe, a pumpkin pie to melt a mother's heart? She considered for a moment. *Nope, this isn't it.* Lacey tossed her fork in the trash can.

"What's up with that?" Tony asked, pulling his plate away from her. "You never eat Felicity's stuff."

"Sue me. I have to bring a dessert to Vic's folks for Thanksgiving dinner. I need ideas."

"Whoa! Last time we spoke the romance was off. Now it's back on and you're going under the microscope at his folks' house? Quick work, Smithsonian."

"You really ought to write a gossip column, Tony."

"How can I, when you always keep me out of the loop?"

"I'll leave it up to your imagination."

Trujillo laughed and took another bite of pie. "You really don't want to do that. I have a dirty mind." He dug in again as she sat down at her desk and plowed through her inbox. "So where are you going on vacation?"

"Just away for a few days. No place special."

"Why so evasive?" He sat on the edge of her desk and she pushed him off. "This story must be really good. Who's dead now?"

"Leave me alone, Tony."

Trujillo showed no intention of doing so, but Mac emerged from his office and crooked a finger at him.

"Saved by the bell," she laughed as Trujillo took one more bite from his plate and ran to answer their editor's call. Lacey grabbed her purse and headed for the door while the coast was clear.

Chapter 30

As Lacey walked up Connecticut Avenue to Dupont Circle, she realized that the feeling she'd had when she awoke from the attack in Jean-Claude's cellar was still haunting her. She had flashbacks: a monogrammed handkerchief coming at her, a chemical smell she couldn't name. The feeling of spiderwebs across her face and in her hair clutched at her too often, bringing back the dank aroma that surrounded her in the darkness, that awful feeling of helplessness. Sometimes she jerked suddenly as if someone were behind her. Lacey was finding it difficult to rid herself of the feeling.

If she were a man, she thought, she would just slug down a few whiskeys, pick a fight, and beat the hell out of some unsuspecting stand-in for her attacker. The more she dwelled on being knocked out in the cellar, the more it bothered her. She knew she had to stop thinking about it.

She contemplated a trip through Aunt Mimi's trunk later that evening to change her mood. Lacey realized that not all mysteries are meant to be solved in one lifetime. She thought of Aunt Mimi's quest to find out what happened to her friend Gloria Adams, who had disappeared during World War II. Mimi never found out. That puzzle was left for Lacey, more than half a century later. She just hoped the answer to the lost Romanov corset would not be withheld from her.

But first she had something to do. Because she was a woman, and therefore not as self-destructive as a man, rather than a bar fight in a saloon, she had booked an appointment with her stylist, Stella, at Stylettos in Dupont Circle for a trim and a touch-up of her highlights. Looking good was her favorite form of revenge, and she hoped it would dissolve the memory of spiderwebs stuck in her hair. Maybe with a chorus of "I'm Going to Wash That Man Right Out of My Hair" from *South Pacific*.

"About time you showed up, Lace," Stella greeted her at the front desk of Stylettos. "Look at that mop." She grabbed Lacey's hair and shook her head. "Holy cow, you need the works."

"Good to see you too," Lacey said.

"What? You never call, you never write. I don't even get a postcard from Gay Paree!"

"I was pretty busy."

"Ha!" Stella began by shampooing Lacey's soon-to-be-improved hair. "So, I see you got into more trouble over there in France. You needed me, Lace."

"You read the paper! I'm so pleased."

"Very funny. I always read your stuff. It's the rest of the paper I can't stand."

"I came out in one piece." Lacey shut her eyes as Stella sprayed water vigorously.

"I shoulda been there, Lacey, I coulda helped."

"Thanks for the offer. I'm sure you would have helped." Lacey could just imagine Stella punching Griffin herself. But what about Kepelov?

"And I can see you need my help now." She examined Lacey's hair like a forensic scientist. "Take my word for it, you're looking stressed." Stella never was shy about her clients' flaws. "I think your hair's got jet lag. And your skin looks, hmm, I don't know. Distracted, maybe. Or confused. You been conditioning like I taught you?" Lacey's stylist frowned and pointed her rat-tailed comb like an interrogator.

Lacey peered in the mirror. She did look a little stressed, she thought. At least Stella wouldn't see the glow she felt inside and draw any conclusions about whether there was a man in her life in Paris, and whether that man was Vic Donovan.

"Jeez, Lacey, I really wish I'd been there for you. I figure Paris wasn't so good for you, what with being chased by all those bad guys. And your snooty pal Brooke was no help, right?"

"Oh, it wasn't all bad." Lacey closed her eyes and a picture of Vic came into focus. An image of Vic one afternoon in Paris with the shadows dancing on the walls of their room and he was just about to— She opened her eyes to a sharp tap on her shoulder. Stella was staring suspiciously at her in the mirror.

"Hey, what're you smiling about? You look like the cat that ate the canary."

"Nothing."

Stella grinned. "Yeah, right. First, we're gonna get some highlights in your hair. And second, Miss Mona Lisa, you're gonna to tell me what that smirk is all about."

Stella foiled Lacey's hair and painted on the chemicals while she worked Lacey for the facts like a pro. Lacey had to give her credit: If she had any journalistic discretion at all, Stella would make a heck of a reporter. And she had a secret weapon no reporter could match: She gave a fabulous head rub. Clients getting their scalps massaged while leaning back in Stella's shampoo bowl often found themselves unburdening their souls as if under a truth serum, but Lacey knew the secret. She resisted the hypnotic urge of Stella's magic fingers. She insisted to Stella that she just needed a few days off, in New Orleans. She repeated it all the way to the rinse-off and the haircut.

"You got yourself knocked out in that basement. It wouldn't have happened with me there," Stella was saying. "I wouldn't have left you alone. Your pal Brooke says, 'I got you covered, Lace,' and where is she when you need her? She's in la-la land."

"Brooke had an asthma attack or something." Lacey often felt she had to defend her friends to each other, but she knew Stella and Brooke would never see eye to eye.

"Yeah, she's *delicate*," Stella sneered. "Me, I'm tough." Beneath her scrappy little exterior, Stella also had the scrappy heart and soul of a street fighter, Lacey had to give her that. Stella foiled Lacey's roots, let her highlights process, then rinsed her off and dried her hair enough to cut. She moved Lacey back to her station to begin her trim. "So this vacation. You're going to New Orleans just to hang out? You? Ha. You're going to New Orleans on the story, aren't you?

Stella's downright spooky sometimes, Lacey thought. "I'm taking a few days off. I'm going to New Orleans to rest."

Stella laughed. "Tell me another. Nobody goes to New Orleans to rest. Trust me. And I know you ain't caught Magda's killer yet."

"I'm not looking for Magda's killer. You know I'm letting the police handle it."

"That's what you always say. But Conspiracy Clearinghouse says different and so do I."

Lacey hadn't seen the story, but she could imagine what it said, in various shades of purple prose. "I am not as in love with danger as you think I am. I am a very sane person."

"I didn't say you were in love with danger, Lacey, it's in love with you. It follows you around." Stella pursed her bloodred lips. "You know what you need?"

"Oh, for some reason I'm sure you're going to tell me." Lacey closed her eyes and heard Stella's scissors snipping away.

"Protection." Stella turned Lacey's head to check the cut. "I should go with you."

Lacey's eyes opened wide. "What?"

"You need someone to keep you out of trouble." Stella squeezed her shoulder. "I know you don't think I can keep a secret, but I can. Sure, I got a big mouth sometimes, but I'm the soul of discretion. You can trust me, Lacey."

"I know that, Stel." *I know you think you can be trusted.* Lacey was not in a position to dissent too much with Stella's scissors in her hair.

Stella finished her wizardry with a blow-dry. "Look at the facts. I know my way around New Orleans. Bourbon Street, Café du Monde, House of the Rising Sun. And you need backup."

"Backup? You sound just like Brooke."

"I ain't nothing like Brooke!" Stella spun Lacey's chair around and handed her a mirror. "What do you think?"

Lacey looked at her hair. It was brighter, trimmer, more alive. "It looks fabulous."

"Of course," Stella acknowledged her genius. "But I'm talking about the trip." Stella pulled the plastic cape from around Lacey's neck and set it aside. "Your friend Brooke fell asleep in the car while you were being doped and groped in the cellar. Your words, in your story."

"I don't think I used the words 'doped and groped.' "

"Whatever. Anyway, I got your back. Trust me, Miss Wordsmith, it'll be faboo." Stella unbuttoned her Stylettos smock, revealing a pair of red capris and a red bustier with pink and orange trim. And Lacey noticed there seemed to be a healthy amount of blue on her eyelids. With her new sleek jet-black hair, Stella looked positively vampy.

"You've really turned up the color volume on that outfit." Lacey shielded her eyes.

Stella grinned with pleasure. "I been taking your advice."

"My advice?" She wondered what "Crimes of Fashion" advice her stylist had twisted now.

"There's too much black, beige, and gray in this town, according to your column."

"I've never seen you wear gray or beige."

"This is true," Stella agreed. "But you gotta admit, I have a serious thing with black."

"Color is good," Lacey agreed.

"And New Orleans is the kind of place where you can let your colors fly." Stella lifted one seductively arched eyebrow. "If you know what I mean." Stella strutted her bustier to the register.

"Maybe if you're a pirate."

"I am a pirate, Lacey! I wanna go! Come on, I need a vacation too. And I need a man."

"And you expect to find one in New Orleans?"

"Honey, if I can't get a man in New Orleans with this equipment, I must be dead." She rang up the sale. "That city is *so* not like D.C., full of self-involved metrosexuals. New Orleans is full of *retrosexuals,* if you know what I mean. See, a trip to the Crescent City would do us both good. We both need men, and at least one of us knows how to get them. Besides, Turtledove is going down for a gig with his band. How perfect is that? We'll go see him play, and boy is he easy on the eyes." Turtledove was the Conspiracy Clearinghouse code name for a security specialist and blues musician named Forrest Thunderbird, a fine and fiercely beautiful man, and an impressively muscled man with a gentle side. Lacey recalled that Turtledove had once promised her he would come to her aid if ever she needed it, because he thought she was on the side of the truth. He was the one friend of Damon Newhouse that she didn't think was crazy.

"That's great, Stella, he's a good guy," she said. "But, um, Vic will be joining me, after a couple of days."

"What? Get out of here! Vic? *The* Vic? You're back with the gorgeous Vic Donovan and you didn't tell me? Good golly Moses, Lace! Is it for real this time? Between-the-sheets for real?"

Lacey's face flushed red-hot with embarrassment. "Stella! Do you want everyone in the salon to answer that question for you?"

"Oh, my God! It is for real! Jeez, Lace, it's about freakin' time!" Stella's brain was working on the facts before her. "But wait a minute, you're telling me he's gonna meet you after you been there a couple days? He's gonna let you go there alone, knowing the way you get into trouble?"

"Hey, that's not fair. And it's only a day or two, he's got a project he can't get out of."

"Fair, schmair, it's the truth. Deal with it." Stella's face lit up with a big grin. "I'm goin'. And I don't need a passport for this trip. So when do we leave?"

"Stella, I haven't agreed to anything." That's what she always told Stella. It never worked.

* * *

"No way. That harebrained hairstylist of yours can't go with you," Brooke told Lacey on the phone that evening. "She's crazy. She sticks out in a crowd. Hell, she *is* a crowd."

"Ah, but Stella informs me she blends in beautifully in the French Quarter," Lacey said.

"Unfortunately that may be true. On Bourbon Street Stella would just be another loony half-naked chick with a loud voice." Brooke had a fever and a heavy schedule waiting for her after Paris, and there was no way she could go with Lacey to New Orleans. She was stuck in bed surrounded by work that she did not feel like doing. It wasn't so bad, she informed Lacey: The adorable Damon was medicating her with chicken soup and hot toddies with lots of whiskey and honey. "Oh, I wish I could go with you," she wailed. "What if you find it?"

"I'm sorry, Brooke. You know I probably won't, but I have to try. I'll have given it my all. By the way, did you ever find out more about Kepelov?" Lacey knew Brooke would have scoured hundreds of Web sites and exhausted her dubious contacts within the conspiracy community.

Brooke sneezed into the receiver. "First of all, no one is sure who he really was. Second, everyone believes he was terminated, but nobody knows who the shooter was. The hospital won't reveal anything, so no one even knows who claimed the body. Must have been disposed of quietly. Third, I really want you to stay out of trouble."

"That's not what you would say if you were with me," Lacey teased.

"That's because I could bail you out if I were there." Brooke sneezed again. "I thought Vic was going with you."

"He's stuck here on some hush-hush job for his dad, but he'll be joining me. Please just feel better, Brooke. Stay in bed. Tell Damon I said to keep you there." Lacey signed off. She rubbed her eyes and almost wished she had not signed up for phase two of this great adventure. And before she got on the plane to the Crescent City, she had to find a fabulous dessert to make. A dessert to melt a mother's heart.

Chapter 31

"You didn't say I couldn't leave town," Lacey found herself protesting to an angry Detective Broadway Lamont, who materialized at her desk the next day, looming over her like a grizzly bear.

"You might have mentioned you were planning to leave the damn country after witnessing a murder. Anyone ever tell you that looks suspicious?"

"Hey, I came back, Broadway." She was wearing a romantic light ruffled blouse she had picked up on a whim her last morning in Paris. It added a feminine touch to her severe-but-fabulous fitted suit from the Forties in dark purple worsted wool. But even with the fitted waist and pretty ruffles flowing below her sleeves, it wasn't going to divert this detective's attention. "Am I a suspect? You better tell my editor—he'll want to visit me in prison."

"You withheld evidence, Smithsonian." Lamont's voice boomed off the walls. Reporters were beginning to stare. Out of the corner of her eye she could see Harlan Wiedemeyer edging in for a better view.

"No, I distinctly remember telling you there was a diary. I said it was in Latvian. I said it might have important information. I told you to keep an eye out for it. Did you find it?"

"Information that you knew and did not disclose."

She lifted her hands in self-defense. "It's in Latvian! Do you read Latvian?"

"Don't play dumb with me, Smithsonian. You may be a lot of things, but even you know when you're skirting the law."

"Really, Broadway, I told you all about—"

He wasn't in the mood for her explanations. "And no, I did not find no damn diary, Latvian or otherwise! You expect me to believe that these spies and jewel thieves are involved in the murder of this dead corset-maker over some diary, in Latvian, of all things?"

"They are after what she was after." She inched her chair away from him. He followed her.

"A treasure? It's a—what is it again?" He sat down on her desk, still towering over her.

"They were talking about a Fabergé egg. I only report what I'm told. People don't always tell me the truth. Does anyone ever tell *you* the whole truth?"

"Obviously not." He glowered at her.

"I wasn't interfering in a murder investigation. I really have no idea who killed Magda." She realized that was the truth.

"You're playing tag with the Angel of Death, Smithsonian. You're putting your neck in a noose. The way I see it, you're killer bait." Lamont seemed to like the way that sounded. "Yeah, killer bait. I ought to put a tail on you, arrest everyone you come in contact with. Clean up this whole damn city."

Lacey knew what Broadway Lamont was really after. He could have just called on the phone to complain, or he could have gone over her head and complained to Mac. But Lacey knew that if Lamont came to yell at her in person, he might be able to snag whatever Felicity was cooking up for her weekly food section. Unfortunately Felicity wasn't around. It was a rare day when Lacey actually wanted to see the food editor, but now she stood up and peeked around Lamont in search of fresh-baked salvation.

"Hey, I'm talking to you," Lamont bellowed.

"Surely you're overstating my power, detective." She heard him snort, a big bull of a cop pissed off at a mere fashion reporter. "Anyway, none of this spy stuff or greedy jewel thief stuff happened in your jurisdiction."

"Damn lucky for you." He narrowed his eyes and put down his head. For a moment she was afraid he might charge her like a bull. Just then she smelled baked goods approaching down the hall, Felicity Pickles with a tray of something aromatic. Lamont's nostrils flared and he raised his huge head, turning toward the aroma like a compass needle. Felicity came bearing cinnamon apple dumplings with a glazed spice icing.

Felicity offered him a dumpling and a smile, like a queen handing out a knighthood. "It's Detective Broadway Lamont, isn't it? It's *so* nice of you to drop by," she said flirtatiously. He gazed at the dumpling admiringly. "Is Lacey in big trouble again?" Her voice was full of hope.

He nodded and took a big bite. Lacey rolled her eyes. Harlan Wiedemeyer came bustling out from his eavesdropping perch to keep his eye on this huge interloper. They all took a dumpling, even Lacey, who sighed, thinking about the Thanksgiving dessert she had rashly promised to make. Felicity's dumplings were good, she thought, but they were way too much of a hassle to make. But perhaps this generous helping of fat, butter, and sugar would soothe the big detective perched on her desk. He hadn't even heard her latest news yet. *Here goes.*

"So, Broadway, I guess I should tell you that I'm taking a few days off."

"Yeah? You fleeing the country again?"

"No, but I'll be leaving town for a rest."

"Where you gonna rest?" He crossed his massive arms. Lacey thought his jacket would burst.

"New Orleans."

He snorted. "Nobody rests in New Orleans unless they're dead or dead drunk. So I guess what you're really telling me is you're chasing some crazy-ass idea."

"I didn't say that."

"Didn't have to. What you got on this Magda Rousseau murder?"

"Zero. I got nothing." *So far.* "What do you have?"

"I don't have no Fabergé egg, no Russian spy, no Brit jewel hunter. What I do have is a dead woman. And she was right. She was poisoned. And stabbed." Broadway Lamont rubbed his hands and looked ready for another dumpling. Felicity, hanging on every word, jumped up from her desk and presented him with a fresh dumpling as if he were king for a day. He smiled. "Why thank you, Miss Felicity Pickles, you read my mind."

Felicity blushed and helped herself to the last dumpling. Harlan Wiedemeyer began to slink away miserably, but she offered to share hers with him. It wasn't very often that Felicity was the belle of the ball, and she was enjoying every minute of it.

"So which one killed her? What kind of poison was it?"

He shook his head. "Don't know. The tox screen isn't back yet." Lamont had mellowed under the influence of sugar and dumplings, as Lacey had hoped. "You're taking yourself out of my jurisdiction, right?"

"That's right." *And not a moment too soon,* Lacey thought.

"Well, lucky me." He took the last bite of his dumpling. "You coming back?"

"Of course I am, Broadway, I'd miss these little lunches of ours."

"And just when things were looking up." He took a napkin, wiped off his hands, and hefted himself to his feet. "See you around, Smithsonian. Stay healthy."

Lacey waited until Lamont was safely out of view before she stood up, grabbed her purse and an extra copy of the paper with her story about Magda, and headed to Stays and Plays, Magda's costume shop. She caught a cab to the Eastern Market neighborhood. Lacey had no idea what she would learn from Magda's partner, if anything, but she needed some kind of closure.

Climbing the steps to the second-story shop, Lacey opened the door to the sound of the bell chiming. A wave of Magda's perfume, *Forêt de Rose*, washed over her, and even though she knew the old woman was dead, her first instinct was to look for her. Instead, she found Analiza fitting the call girl she knew as Jolene in a scanty dress of body-hugging strips of some gauzy silver material. It laced up the back, but it didn't conceal much.

At the sound of the door chime, Analiza spun around on the blue brocade ottoman where she was sitting. "Oh. It's you," she said to Lacey. She turned back to fitting the statuesque Jolene.

"Oww! You stabbed me," Jolene whined. "That hurt."

"You're done." Analiza paid no attention to the woman's complaint. "Look in the mirror."

Jolene stretched and did as she was told, admiring her provocative reflection.

Lacey was wondering which one of them was wearing the perfume when a fresh wave of it filled the room. Natalija, Magda's neighbor upstairs, entered from the back door. "Oh, hello," she said, looking at Lacey as if for an explanation of her presence in the shop.

Lacey knew she should have said something polite, but all she could think of was, "Is everyone wearing Magda's perfume today?"

"Why shouldn't we?" Analiza asked with a shrug. "Magda isn't here to enjoy it, and she had five new bottles. She was always afraid she would run out. She ordered it by the case. Perfume goes bad, I used to tell her, but she didn't care. Always so careful about the cost of everything else, but her precious perfume—"

"It is unusual, isn't it?" Jolene stretched languidly. "It's like we're in an exclusive little club. The only women in America with Magda's perfume." Lacey nodded.

"Why are you here?" Analiza demanded.

"I brought you a copy of the story I wrote about Magda." She handed it to Analiza, who set it down on the floor beside her without looking at it.

"Yes, we've seen it," Natalija said, standing there with her hands on her hips.

Jolene reached out for the newspaper. "Oh, I haven't seen it, give it to me."

"So you found nothing?" Analiza turned her attention back to Lacey. "No treasure, whatever it was, no money?"

"That's right. I'm sorry."

"So it was all for nothing after all."

"I'm sure Magda told you many things, Analiza," Lacey suggested, hoping the woman might tell her something she didn't know. "Things a partner would share."

"Not like she told you!" Her voice grew louder and more strained. "Did she suggest that I should go on vacation to France with her? Or Latvia, where I would like to go? To see my family? No, I had to stay here in this shop and work for every nickel and dime. Prick my fingers till they bleed." Analiza raised herself slowly from her seat and her knees cracked loudly. She thrust her hands out. "See how they bleed?" They were covered with large veins and scars; they looked much older than her forty-some years.

Bloody thread, knock 'em dead. Magda's words echoed in Lacey's head while Analiza continued. "Magda was always dropping little hints about what she would do someday, when she had money. For years we just got by with this shop, some years better than others. What money, I ask her. You going to win the lottery? Oh no, she was going to inherit family money, she said, big money her grandfather had hidden away. Magda and I had this shop together for fifteen years. She said she would turn her back on it in a second. Turn her back on me."

"At least you finally got to take some time for yourself, Analiza," Jolene said. "She couldn't stop you any longer."

Analiza wrapped up her unruly hair and stabbed some hairpins into it. "That's right, she can't tell me what do anymore. I come and go as I please."

"Did you close the shop?" Lacey asked, suddenly far more interested in what Analiza Zarina had been up to in the past few days. "Take a little vacation?"

"Is it any business of yours?" Analiza asked. The woman with the flyaway strawberry hair was far more bitter than Lacey had suspected. Clearly the new proprietress felt her best years were behind her, but she did seem more assertive, more at home in the shop, than Lacey had ever seen her. In fact, all three of them looked very cozy there, bathed in Magda's perfume.

"She has a life now. And a new man," Jolene smirked. Natalija laughed.

"Did you leave town?" Lacey pressed.

"That's enough," Analiza said to Jolene. The beautiful call girl sniffed and concentrated on Lacey's newspaper article, twirling her fingers through her blond hair as she read.

"Did you believe her, about the money, the treasure?" Lacey persisted, but Analiza was silent. "Do you think there really was a Fabergé egg?"

"Who could believe Magda?" Natalija said, glancing past Lacey at her own reflection in the shop's mirrors. "She was a funny old woman. She liked to talk. And talk and talk and talk."

"She made one hell of a corset," Jolene said without looking up from the newspaper. "No one could sew like she did."

Analiza bristled and threw down her measuring tape. "Take that dress off if you want it finished."

"Sure thing." Jolene tossed the newspaper on the sofa where Magda had died and strutted off to the dressing room. Stella had confided to Lacey that Jolene was thoroughly enhanced, from her plastic fingernails to her extravagant breast implants, not to mention her very blond tresses, courtesy of Stella. But there was something about her that seemed genuine to Lacey.

"Did the police take anything?" she asked Analiza. "From the shop, or her apartment?"

"Just some old books." She looked suspicious. "Why?"

"No reason." Lacey was wondering if Broadway Lamont had kept anything from her.

"They don't know who killed her." Analiza pushed her hair up again and anchored it with more bobby pins. It was no improvement. "No suspects. That's what they told me."

"My money is on some psycho," Jolene said, stepping out of the dressing room in her street clothes, tight jeans and a tighter shirt that showed off major cleavage. She handed the silver dress to Analiza.

"A psycho who uses poison?" Lacey asked.

"Takes all kinds, sweetie." Jolene shrugged and grabbed her purse. "I'm out of here."

"You can pick this up tomorrow," Analiza called after her as the call girl jogged down the stairs to her next appointment.

"What's going to happen to Magda's apartment?" Lacey asked.

"It's my apartment now." Analiza busied herself with Jolene's dress.

"It makes more sense for her," Natalija told Lacey, "because it's right above the shop. Next to mine. So much more convenient. And it's easier for us to work together. I am helping out right now. In the shop. I'm very good with numbers and handling money."

"I don't know what I would do without her." Analiza smiled fondly at Natalija, who gave her a warm hug. Analiza turned back to Lacey and her smile faded. "Is that all you wanted?"

Lacey realized she hadn't even taken off her trench coat. "Yes. I just wanted to let you know how sorry I am about Magda."

"You are not going to look for the killer? Like you did before with those other women?"

"It's out of my hands. The police are handling it."

Analiza nodded and seemed to remember her manners. "Would you like a bottle of the perfume? Magda's perfume? There is an extra one." She made a move as if to retrieve it.

"No, thank you." The very thought of the perfume haunted her. Lacey knew she would never wear it, and she knew she would never forget the way it smelled. Besides, she didn't think Magda would approve of Analiza parceling out her precious scent so cavalierly.

Lacey took one long last look around the shop, at the costumes and the corsets and the elaborate wigs, at the case where the fake jewels were kept, now all neatly tucked away again. She glanced at the sofa in the middle of the shop where Magda had taken her last breath. She wondered if it had been cleaned since then. Apparently it held no bad memories for the women who still worked there.

I'm sorry, Magda. I guess I let you down. Now I have to let you go, Lacey said silently to her friend. Then she turned and walked away. The shop door chimed again softly behind her. She ran down the steps and finally took a deep breath when she was outside on the sidewalk. The crisp autumn air and the smell of a wood fire burning in someone's fireplace made her long for something that she could not name.

Chapter 32

"Lacey, there's cake batter on the ceiling." Vic turned off the electric beater and stared at the mess hanging over his head like edible stalactites. "And the floor. And your nose."

"Really?" She looked up at the ceiling. Sure enough, there was cake batter up there. She gazed at the incriminating beaters in Vic's hands. "Funny, that's not what the recipe calls for."

Lacey was not often seduced by food. However, in her hunt for the perfect Thanksgiving dessert she had been hypnotized by an issue of the magazine *Southern Living*, glossy and brazen and full of promises of holiday culinary glory. This issue featured "Our Best Recipes." The desserts were especially seductive, and diabolically difficult. Every one required skill, discipline, determination, and baking pans Lacey did not possess. She had eyed every photograph, every recipe with mingled admiration and horror. She considered and rejected the Perfect Pumpkin Chess Pie, the Cranberry Apple Cobbler With Cinnamon Biscuits, the Apple Walnut Cake, and the Red Velvet Cake With Whipped Buttermilk Frosting.

Finally, under the influence of the gorgeous glossy cover photograph, she settled on the preposterously named Pecan Pie Cake, a luscious-looking torte with pecan pie filling garnished with nuts and pastry leaves. It was mesmerizingly beautiful. "Our Favorite Fall Dessert," the cover copy proclaimed. And Lacey was determined to make it for the Thanksgiving dinner with Vic's parents, no matter how much batter wound up on the ceiling.

"Sweetheart," Vic pleaded, "my mother does not need you to go to all this trouble."

"Yes she does. Just remember to turn the beaters off before you take them out of the bowl. Don't worry, this is just a test run. We'll make it again fresh the night before Thanksgiving."

Vic's jaw dropped. His look said *Are you insane?* But wisely he did not utter that sentiment. "Listen, I know a great little bakery."

"Stop right there, Victor Donovan. This is going to work, if it kills us." She didn't want to tell him she had bought an expensive set of beautiful new cake pans, as well as an expensive cooling rack. She felt absurdly proud of herself: She had never owned a cooling rack before. She hadn't even tallied up all the money she'd spent on ingredients for this extravagant dessert. She actually didn't know which seemed more ridiculous, trying to find the lost corset of the Romanovs or trying to bake the perfect autumnal dessert from a recipe in *Southern Living*. At the moment it was a very close call.

"You will be careful, won't you?" Vic asked.

"With the cake?"

"In New Orleans."

"Trust me, Vic." She popped the cake pans in the oven and surveyed the disaster, looking for the timer. "If I live through this baking experience, I'll be in New Orleans tomorrow."

"You promise not to go chasing crazy leads? Not till I get there?"

"I promise not to get in trouble." She found the timer and set it.

"It always starts like this."

"Like what, with cake batter on the ceiling? You know, cowboy, a gal could get the impression that nobody trusts her."

"I trust you to go off half-cocked," he said. "What did Broadway Lamont tell you about the murder? Is anyone in custody?" he asked, with a glimmer of hope.

"No, but he did confirm he was pissed off. He also confirmed that Magda had been poisoned, big surprise, but the final tests aren't in yet." Lacey rubbed her lower back. It ached.

Vic lifted her hair and kissed the nape of her neck. "You know what we could be doing while the cake is in the oven?"

"Sorry to disappoint you, but I set the timer for twenty-five minutes." She winked at him. "Want to go for a speed record?"

Vic groaned. He settled for a beer and a rundown on her plans for New Orleans while he admired the picture of the fabled Pecan Pie Cake. "What about the leaves on that cake?"

"I don't think we need to do the leaves. They look, um, labor-intensive."

"But, honey, they're in the picture. They look mighty pretty."

"They're optional. But if you want the pastry leaves, Vic, why don't you do them?"

"You're on." Vic surprised her by doing an excellent job of rolling out the pastry dough she had made just in case. He was pretty good with a cookie cutter too. "Now what?"

Lacey referred to the recipe. "Well, according to the dessert fanatics at *Southern Living*, to get that autumn-leaves-blowing-in-the-wind look, you have to drape every pastry leaf you cut out over its very own crumpled-up ball of aluminum foil. Artistically. Brush them with the egg mixture, sprinkle with sugar, and bake them on a greased cookie sheet. You make the little pecan sandwiches out of the leftover pastry dough and the pecans. Then we glue them all on top of the cake with extra pecan pie filling to create an artistic autumn scene of tasty blowing leaves."

He stared at her. "So this thing takes two ovens, four cooks, and about forty man-hours of labor. If we made one of these to sell, we'd have to charge a hundred dollars a bite."

"It's Southern, Virginia boy. 'Southern' doesn't mean quick and easy, does it?" She crumpled a small piece of foil into a ball and tossed it to him with a grin. "First one's on the house. Is your mother worth it?"

Vic sighed. He took the crumpled ball of foil and draped a pastry leaf over it. Artistically. "More foil, please."

Three hours later every pan in Lacey's apartment had been used, her kitchen was a disaster of unbelievable (though edible) proportions, and their tempers had frayed but never quite snapped. But the cake was beautiful, a work of art, worthy of the cover of *Southern Living*. They admired it for a moment and then cut into it for a taste test.

"You know, darling," Vic said, chewing thoughtfully, "it's kind of bland. Really bland. Did we leave something out?"

"Are you kidding? Everything in my entire kitchen is in this cake. Pie. Pie cake. Whatever they call it. It is not bland, it is a masterpiece. You got that? A masterpiece." Lacey took a deep breath and waggled a mixing spoon at him like a teacher with a slow pupil. "I have one more thing to say here, Vic. I just spent over a hundred dollars on pans and ingredients and untold hours creating this culinary wacky wonder of the world, and my kitchen looks like the night of the living cake-batter zombies. You better reconsider what you just said about my Pecan Pie Cake, if you want to get another bite of anything tonight. Are you with me?"

"Yes, ma'am. At least we have each other." He took another bite. "Mighty fine. Best damn Pecan Pie Cake I ever ate, ma'am." He flashed his devastating smile at her. "Now you try it."

Lacey bit into her slice. "Damn it, it is bland! Okay, no problem. I'll adjust the recipe. I'm thinking maple syrup and cinnamon. Lots of maple syrup. It'll be a Vermont Pecan Pie Cake when we're done with it. We'll get thrown out of *Southern Living*, but who cares? It'll be great."

"We're really going to do this again? How crazy are we?"

"You tell me, cowboy. Are we going to go to your folks for Thanksgiving or not?"

"This is how you approach everything, isn't it?"

"What do you mean?" She took another bite of the cake. "Maple syrup, definitely. We'll whip this thing yet."

"You're relentless. You hit the wall and you just change course and keep going. You didn't find the corset in France, so you just switch directions and go to New Orleans instead. You could just give up, you know. Forget about the corset. Buy a pie for dessert."

"Vic! Give up when we're so close? I wouldn't dream of it. And besides, you were the one who told me there was a Rue Dauphine in the French Quarter."

"Damn. I'd forgotten about that."

"Forget about buying a pie, Vic. This will work, we'll make it work. And as soon as we clean up the kitchen, darling, I have to decide what I'm wearing tomorrow for New Orleans."

Lacey Smithsonian's

FASHION BITES

Welcome to Tonight's Thrilling Episode of *What Will I Wear Tomorrow?*

Beyond *The Twilight Zone*. More gripping than *What Not to Wear*. More frightening than *Fear Factor*. It's every working woman's own nightly reality fashion show, filmed live in her own closet, starring, well, *you*. It's tonight's thrilling episode of *What Will I Wear Tomorrow?* Tonight we present for your viewing pleasure a special exercise in terror, entitled, "I Can't Even Decide What to Wear *Today*, and I Have to Leave in Fifteen Minutes!"

We join our heroine, thwarted in her desperate hunt for the perfect outfit, flinging clothes hither and yon like Scarlett O'Hara ripping down the drapes at Tara. Tonight's episode may be disastrous for your closet, and even more disastrous for your peace of mind. And this show is rated F, for female audiences only. *Bye-bye, honey, go catch your bass-fishing show. Please?*

Never let the man in your life see you try to decide what you're wearing tomorrow. He won't get the story, the passion, the epic drama. The big lug doesn't try on five outfits the night before a big day, does he? Why not? Because he doesn't care. He doesn't obsess about his clothes and what they say about him. His clothes say, "I'm a guy, *duh*. So I'm wearing clothes. Big deal." He doesn't talk to his clothes. They don't talk to him. He doesn't have the sound track from *Doctor Zhivago* or *Gone With the Wind* running through his head while deciding what to wear.

A man seldom perceives the importance of selecting the right clothes before a strategic power meeting or a job interview. A suit's a suit, right? And jeans are jeans. He may offer such brilliant advice as this: "Tomorrow? Just wear what you wore yesterday, honey. Nobody will remember." It makes your head hurt, doesn't it? I thought so.

What Will I Wear Tomorrow? is a true tale of the life-and-death struggle between a woman and her closet, aided possibly by the one female friend whose opinion counts. Consult Old-What's-His-Name only for the most crucial basic information: Is it a poolside picnic or a black-tie dinner? Will the President be attending? Will there be metal detectors? What is his mother wearing?

On *What Will I Wear Tomorrow?* your clothes sometimes seem to have their own story lines. They can turn into your enemies faster than an infestation of alien pod people. Who knows why the same outfit that was perfect on Monday is perfectly horrible on Thursday? How can you look svelte in that cute dress at 9:05 a.m. only to discover that by mid-afternoon you look like a hippo, and it's the darn dress's fault? Maybe your clothes have cannier writers than you do, and they all want to be villains. Every star knows it's more fun to play the villain. What's a fashion-savvy woman who wants to be the star of her own fashion story to do?

- Think about the clothes you love and that always love you back. Analyze what they have in common, why they are so flattering on you, whether it's an Empire waist or a straight skirt or the perfect colors that flatter your skin tones. Memorize these golden outfits. Use them as your touchstones when you're shopping, when you've forgotten momentarily who you are and what you look like. (It happens to all of us.) However, a warning to all of us obsessive-compulsive types: This does not mean you have to chart your successful outfits on a spreadsheet, seal them in Ziploc bags, and hang them in your closet labeled by the days of the week. Although, come to think of it, that's not a bad idea.
- How much of your wardrobe is stuffed into a dark corner where you can't see it? Are you often surprised by what you find there? Do you lose track of something you bought on sale in the spring, only to find it in the

fall? Do you remember buying great clothes that have somehow slunk into that dark corner, never to be seen again? Seize control of your closet!

- We all need fewer clothes that work better and harder. (Or bigger closets.) Always thin the herd of the weaker specimens. Be ruthless. One way to be sure you'll always know what to wear tomorrow is to get rid of the clothes that don't work for you today, especially the sneaky ones that turn on you in the middle of the afternoon.

If you only have clothes that work together and flatter you, then you won't make any wrong choices. It's a theory, right? Of course, that only happens in the movies, where the heroine has the giant walk-in closet with all the bells and whistles, the shoe racks, the skirt rods, the clear glass drawers for everything from sweaters to scarves. It's a Hollywood fantasy.

But you can avoid the trauma of another nerve-shattering episode of *What Will I Wear Tomorrow?* Take control of your own fashion story now, don't wait until showtime. And soon *What Will I Wear Tomorrow?* will be the feels-good, fits-right hit of the season.

Chapter 33

Lacey and Stella hadn't even arrived in the French Quarter and already the taxi driver was dissing her choice of accommodations.

"Dat Beaumont House Hotel? I ain't take nobody dat hotel three years or mo'. Why'n'cha stay at de Royal Sonesta or de Fairmont? Now dat's a *hotel, cher,* you wanna talk hotels—"

Lacey was sick and tired of people bemoaning her choices, but she didn't even have to respond—the taxi driver kept up a solid string of commentary throughout the drive. They should eat at Brennan's, he said, and Emeril's. He was encouraging them to drop a lot of cash in the Big Easy. She wondered if he got a kickback. And nobody says "Da Big Easy" in New Orleans, he informed them, only outsiders, and besides that, *cher,* the city is correctly called "Nawlins."

Stella had a hangover and was feeling queasy, but that wasn't keeping her from flirting. "That's so cute. You're cute too, cutie. You remind me of a nice old grandpa."

"Grandpa!" He chuckled. "Ah'll show you a grandpa, *cher.*"

While Stella flirted with the taxi driver, Lacey was wondering how to lose her friend while discreetly checking out the address on Rue Dauphine. This was such a fool's errand, she told herself. Drosmis Berzins was long dead, and the entire landscape could have changed. Yet time was said to move slowly in the Big Easy. *Nawlins*, she corrected herself. The seasons seemed to move slowly as well. Though Indian summer had lingered in Washington, it brought crisp golden days and chilly nights. But here in New Orleans, the November air was positively balmy and the breeze cuddled the skin rather than chilled it.

The taxi pulled up to their hotel on Decatur Street. "So what's wrong with this place?" Lacey asked, but the driver shrugged. "Nuttin'. 'S aw right. Y'all be fine here." The Beaumont House

Hotel was proudly pink with filigreed white balconies decorated with hanging ferns and baskets of flowers. It looked to Lacey as if it had put on a party dress just for her.

"Y'all take care now, *cher.* Y'all need a cab, ya call me, hear?" He hauled out their bags and handed Lacey his card.

"Thank you! We love the hotel! It's totally girly," Stella told the driver. He grinned and took off to counsel other tourists on how best to spend their money in *Nawlins.*

"Wait till you see what I brought," Stella announced on their way up in the elevator. *Can't wait*, Lacey thought with a smile. No doubt a suitcase-full of tarty Bourbon Street outfits. "This is a wild and crazy party town, Lacey, not like D.C. So I pumped up the color, like you told me."

"That is a startling statement coming from you, Stella."

"Well, there's startling, and then there is *really* startling. I'm unleashing my inner Catwoman here." Stella meowed, but it turned into a yawn. "Oh, Lacey, my head feels like a jackhammer." She fumbled with the room key and unlocked the door, tossing her suitcase inside. "I'm so sorry to wimp out on you, but would you mind if I crash for a few hours? That was really an early flight." The little stylist leaned against the open door into her pink lair and struggled to keep her eyes open. "I mean it's only nine thirty in the morning for pity's sake! And I was up way late celebrating our trip. So wake me up later, okay, we'll go get some spicy Cajun, which I guarantee will knock any hangover right out of your head. What do you say?"

A long nap was tempting. But this unexpected gift of precious time without a bodyguard was too much for Lacey to resist. "Absolutely, Stel. I need a good three hours myself. Then we'll get lunch."

Stella blew her a kiss and stumbled into her room. Lacey was delighted to find that her own room down the rose-carpeted hall, in shades of rose and moss green, had French doors to a balcony with huge baskets of flowers overlooking Decatur Street. Vic would no doubt grumble about the security of such an accessible room. Any monkey, he would tell her, could reach a second-floor balcony, and there were large gaps around the slightly warped French doors. But she tried not to think about that. Kepelov was dead and Griffin had not resurfaced since Paris. He'd told Vic when he called with the news of Kepelov's death that he was "going to ground," as he called it. Lacey hoped that meant he was in a burrow somewhere and he'd given up on trailing her.

She changed from her standard all-black traveling clothes into a light lavender knit top and periwinkle-blue capris and a pair of comfortable sandals. After wearing so many boots and dress shoes in Paris, sandals made her feel like she really was on vacation. The delicate light blue satin corset Magda had made for her peeked out from under her other clothes. She had packed it on a whim, perhaps to remind her of her goal in New Orleans. Or perhaps just to amuse Vic.

As corsets go, Lacey's corset was very modest. It would look chic with the sleek black skirt she packed to wear to a fancy restaurant with Vic, throwing a shawl over it if she felt too bare. She tucked it back into her suitcase, inside the closet. Then she grabbed her shoulder bag and fished out her guidebook and map of the French Quarter. She had a date with the Rue Dauphine.

On foot in the French Quarter, Lacey could see the early Spanish influence in the architecture, with its pretty filigreed wrought-iron balconies and galleries. Buildings were painted in pastels, and plants and flowers bloomed in abundance. She noted the street signs in the Quarter were all bilingual in French and English, in honor of the city's French origins. The hotel was on Decatur Street, also marked as Rue Decatur. Lacey smiled as she read in her guidebook that New Orleans was known as "the Paris of the South." *Okay, Magda,* she thought, *this is our last shot, let's make it good.* Lacey turned up Rue Decatur and headed deeper into the Quarter.

New Orleans felt and looked dramatically different. Washington, D.C., in the fall is crisp and businesslike, with a first-day-of-school feel. The sober citizens of our Nation's Capital put away their summer clothes and break out the tweeds and woolens, even if it still seems too warm. The Crescent City, in contrast, retained a lingering sense of eternal late summer. People strolled along the streets and lazed about in cafés in cutoff jeans and T-shirts. It was a different kind of casual. Whether the attitude was joie de vivre or "I don't give a damn," Lacey wasn't sure. But everyone seemed happy and relaxed. *Washington is never ever like this*, she thought.

A pretty curly-headed brunette about twenty wobbled leisurely past Lacey on an ancient three-speed bicycle, seemingly without a care in the world, and without a bike helmet. She wore a Hawaiian print dress and clear Lucite heels at least four inches tall. So unlike Washington, Lacey thought, where *The Eye Street Observer*'s editorial writer Cassandra Wentworth grimly pedaled her high-tech titanium bicycle to work in an ecologically correct fervor.

Cassandra's bike outfit of black stretch tights, yellow reflective jacket, oversized sunglasses with rearview mirrors, and streamlined neon-yellow helmet made her look like an exotic alien insect. An insect with a deadly serious purpose and no time to waste on merely enjoying the day.

New Orleans was sweet eye candy and an exotic world. Lacey was thrilled she didn't have to learn a new language to enjoy it, although she overheard the locals speaking an exotic variety of English. Her attention was caught by a stocky man with close-cropped hair and a bullet-shaped head, dressed according to some code, tight black T-shirt, black shorts, black running shoes, white socks. But what caught her eye were the twenty pairs of gleaming silver handcuffs clipped to his heavy black belt. Lacey didn't even want to guess what he might do for a living. "S&M club bouncer slash bounty hunter" came to mind.

Lacey's own pace was casual. She glanced in the store windows at the tourist bait, cheap Bourbon Street beads and voodoo kitsch and purple-and-green Mardi Gras masks everywhere, but it was a black cook's apron featuring a white skull that brought her back to her present purpose. DON'T MAKE ME POISON YOUR FOOD, the apron warned.

Lacey checked her map again. She passed Jackson Square and Café du Monde on Decatur Street and took a left turn on Ursulines Street. She walked four blocks, past Bourbon Street, to Dauphine Street. She felt a little tingle of excitement to see the street sign also identified it as Rue Dauphine, just as Vic had said it would. On the corner of Dauphine and Ursulines, at 1101 Rue Dauphine, the address in Drosmis Berzins' note, she found a two-story brick building that housed a pharmacy on the street level. Lacey double-checked the address. It seemed that time hadn't changed this mostly residential part of the French Quarter. The building must have been there for at least two hundred years, she thought.

Lacey hesitated, wondering what to say to whomever she might find inside. She would try the truth, she decided: a reporter looking for information. Her Congressional press pass was in her purse in case anyone needed proof. She opened the door and stepped inside the pharmacy. She felt as if she had stepped into a time capsule. The floor and walls were trimmed in white-and-rust-colored tile and the ceiling was pressed tin. An old-fashioned soda fountain with a marble counter and a row of small round stools filled one wall, but clearly it hadn't been used in awhile. Posters from another era decorated the walls, advertising long-forgotten products.

The pharmacy, however, looked businesslike and well-stocked. *How did this place connect with Drosmis Berzins?*

"May I help you?" A pleasant-looking middle-aged woman behind the pharmacy counter greeted Lacey with a smile. She wore her light brown hair in a flip from the same distant era as the posters. Her name tag said MOLLY.

"I'm not sure." Lacey identified herself as a reporter. She explained that she was looking for anything connected to the man whose name she wrote down for Molly on a sheet of paper. "He was an elderly Latvian immigrant named Drosmis Berzins. I believe he may have lived here, or worked here, or had family or friends here. Perhaps he was a customer here. And he may have left something here, some time ago, for someone to pick up? Perhaps a message, a book, an envelope, a package?" She felt like an idiot. *Someone I never met may have stashed something here that I can't describe. Who knows what, when, or why. Got anything like that?*

The woman stared at her for a moment. She looked away and seemed to remember something. "My goodness. What was that name again?"

"Berzins, Drosmis Berzins. I'm not sure how it's pronounced."

"Just a moment, please." The woman took the paper and slipped into the back room. Lacey wandered around the little drugstore. No one else came in the store, but Lacey assumed it was still early by French Quarter time. Molly left Lacey waiting long enough for her to imagine the woman coming back with a shotgun to run her out of the store. Instead, Lacey heard a couple of voices joined in laughter. Molly emerged alone from the backroom holding an object in her hands.

"I hadn't looked at this thing in so long I wasn't sure about the name. But sure enough, it's the same. It's been up on a shelf in back for years and years and years." Molly chuckled. "Kind of turned into a family legend. A curiosity, you might call it."

The woman handed Lacey a tarnished brass urn, the kind used to store human ashes. "Ashes to ashes" came to her mind in mocking tones. *Ashes? Oh, no! He couldn't have burned the corset!*

"I don't know what to say," Lacey said. *What did that crazy bastard Berzins do with the corset?* She looked at the urn. It was engraved DROSMIS BERZINS. And a fragment of the Bible verse mentioned in the note in Jean-Claude's cellar was engraved in English beneath his name: FOR DUST THOU ART AND TO DUST SHALT THOU RETURN.

"Relative of yours?" the woman asked politely. "Must have been a religious gentleman."

"Must have been," Lacey agreed.

Could the urn possibly contain Berzins' own ashes? Lacey wondered. Brooke had found his obituary on the Web; he died long after Jean-Claude's coal room was sealed up with his torn note in the metal box, the clue Lacey was following in this devious little scavenger hunt. But perhaps he had instructed someone to bring his ashes here after he died? *Please no,* Lacey thought, *no human remains this morning. I haven't even had lunch yet.*

"How long has it been here?" Lacey asked.

"Oh, my. I really couldn't say. My husband's been trying to remember; he's back there filling prescriptions. We've been married twenty-five years—that's when we took this place over, and it was here before that." The woman looked at Lacey for some kind of explanation. She seemed to be willing to wait. *Time does move more slowly here,* Lacey thought.

"It's pretty heavy, Molly." *Is that the brightest thing I can think of to say?*

"Feels about like a ten-pound sack of sugar to me," Molly mused. "I kind of hate to see it go, but my husband says it's time, I guess. Now that you've come for it and all."

"Would you mind if I set this down here?" It felt full. *Of what?* she wondered. It didn't rattle when she shook it, but its contents seemed to shift softly inside. It could have been her imagination. Lacey put the urn down on the marble counter of the soda fountain. She rummaged through her purse for her digital camera.

"Oh, that's a good idea! Do take a picture, and would you mind letting me get in the photograph? I'd love to have a copy too, if y'all wouldn't mind."

Lacey photographed Molly with the urn and then took a seat on a stool at the counter. "When did you stop serving soda fountain customers here?"

"Back in the Seventies, my husband tells me. His folks had the place till they retired." Molly wiped her fingers along the marble counter.

"That's too bad. It's so pretty, so old-fashioned. It's a shame not to use it."

"His folks always said it was such a lot of work and folks would just sit here and gab all day, I hear tell. Couldn't get them out of here. Here, let me get you a sack for that thing, so you can take it with you," she said and reached beneath the counter for some brown paper bags. Molly put the heavy urn inside, double-bagged it so it wouldn't tear through, and set it back on the counter. *Oh, my God,* Lacey realized, *she's simply giving me this thing?*

"So. The urn. Thanks for the sack, Molly. And I can just—um—take it with me?" Lacey didn't know what she was supposed to do with it, but she was beginning to have an idea.

"Oh, yes, ma'am. That's what the letter said."

"Wait a minute. What letter?"

A middle-aged man with a friendly round face poked his head out of the back room behind the pharmacy counter.

"So y'all're the urn lady! Well, well. Been here a mighty long time. Yes, indeed."

"The urn lady. That's me," Lacey said. "Molly mentioned there was a letter with the urn?"

He patted his wife on the shoulder and smiled. "Oh, my, yes, but the letter is long gone. My daddy kept it for a long time, but I don't know what happened to it. He died ten years ago. I do, however, mind what the letter said, at least the gist of it. This thing here has been a family curiosity, you might say." He leaned on the soda fountain counter. "I never thought I'd live to see the day someone would come for it. Name is Tom." He put out a large hand for Lacey to shake. "My daddy ran this store after his daddy died. Family's owned it nearly a century."

"How did the urn come to be here in your store?" Lacey took out her notebook and pen.

"Old man left it here one day. Don't recall if my daddy said he was a regular or a stranger. Paid Pop fifty dollars—lot of money back then—to keep it safe here till someone came for it."

"Did he say who that would be?"

"Nope. Note said whoever came looking for the name on the urn should have it."

Lacey stopped writing and stared at Tom and Molly. "Anyone who came looking for that name? Didn't that strike anyone as a little crazy?"

"This is *Nawlins, cher.*" Tom pronounced it like a native, or so she'd been told. "Crazy things happen every day. Guess it didn't strike my daddy as *too* crazy. He used to run a post office in this place way back, for the neighborhood, took delivery of packages and such. He told me once he figured someone'd come for this thing in a few days, a month maybe. It was safe right here with him, waiting for the right person to claim it. Nobody's gonna just pick that foreign name there out of a hat, now are they? Time went on, it became kind of a conversation piece, you know?"

Lacey gazed at the brass urn in wonder. She took a deep breath. "Well. Thank you for keeping it safe. Do I owe you anything? For storage, all these years?"

"No, ma'am, the story value is as good as anything," Tom said. "My daddy was willing to store it in perpetuity, waiting for someone to come for it. Till now. Must be a story to go with it, wouldn't you say?" He looked at her with the same mild curiosity Molly had displayed.

"About that story," Lacey began, "it's a rather delicate thing. And unfinished." Lacey needed a close inspection of the urn and its contents, no matter what it contained, even human remains. It might lead her anywhere, or nowhere, but the last thing she wanted was for this story to get out prematurely. Just the kind of wacky local feature story an enterprising *New Orleans Times-Picayune* reporter might jump on. She could imagine the headline: FRENCH QUARTER MYSTERY OF LONG-FORGOTTEN URN. And the DeadFed dot com version: SMITHSONIAN TAKES ROMANOV JEWEL HUNT TO BIG EASY! Lacey couldn't risk the Fabergé egg hunters catching her trail before she could get the urn—and herself—to a safe place.

"I don't have the whole story yet," she said, "and if this gets out too soon I may never get it. Could I ask you not to say anything about this for the next few days? To anyone? Let's say until after Thanksgiving?"

Tom and Molly looked at each other. "Yes, ma'am," Tom said. "But why Thanksgiving, particularly?"

"I only need a few days. I hope. But it will be a much better story if I have a chance to tie the loose ends together. And I can guarantee you will have your picture in the newspaper in Washington, D.C., and you'll have a whole new story to tell your customers. That is, if you would *like* to have your picture in the paper."

Tom laughed. "I do love a good story, ma'am, and if my Molly here can keep her mouth shut, you got a deal."

His wife playfully slapped him on the arm. "Y'all don't have to worry none about me, if this old bird can just hold his tongue."

Lacey took several pictures of the two of them with the urn, took a few more notes, and then gave Tom her card with her phone number at *The Eye*. She filled up the top of the bag with drugstore supplies: cough syrup, antacid, aspirin for Stella's hangover. She also purchased a package of diapers and tucked the urn inside to disguise its shape.

"Y'all're being real careful," Molly observed. "I don't think it's all that fragile."

"You know us reporters," Lacey said, not knowing if they did, but it sounded good at the moment. She was thinking of the unpredictable Nigel Griffin. She hoped he'd given up on her, and yet she found herself scanning every room and every crowd for him. "So if anyone comes in and asks what I was looking for and what I found?"

"Why, sugar, I'll just tell those nosy reporters you had one killer of a hangover and needed something strong for it," Molly said.

"Thank you, Molly, Tom. So nice to meet you. We'll keep the story between us for now?"

"Y'all can count on us, Miss Smithsonian." Tom read her business card. "We'll keep a lookout. Y'all come back, y'hear?"

"Thanks again. I'll be in touch." Lacey winked and hefted her bag. She prayed that she and Drosmis Berzins' mysterious urn would make it back to her hotel together.

chapter 34

Crazy and horrible thoughts flashed through Lacey's mind as she strolled casually back to the hotel with her drugstore bag in hand. She forced herself to slow down so as not to draw attention in this slow-moving city. Did Berzins burn the corset? Could the jewels be hidden inside, or did it actually contain human remains? And why? And whose? And what will they look like? The last thought made her queasy. Midday in New Orleans was just as lovely as the morning had been, and just as relaxed, but Lacey's heart was beating as hard as if she were running through a dark forest pursued by wolves.

Lacey had her room key ready in the elevator. She checked the empty hall and ran to her door and unlocked it in one smooth motion. She sniffed the air, relieved to detect no suspicious woodsy rose perfume, only a hint of the housekeeper's cleaning supplies. She double-locked the door behind her and turned the dead bolt, rolled up a towel and jammed it against the bottom of the door, and stuck a Post-it over the peephole.

Don't be so paranoid, she told herself. *Brooke and Damon have really gotten to you.* She flicked on the lights and took the urn to the desk, first spreading out the complimentary copy of *USA Today* to cover the surface. The brass urn was dark with tarnish, so she took a clean washcloth from the bathroom and rubbed it to make sure nothing else was written on it. It was clean. She realized she was also rubbing away decades of fingerprints, but she didn't care; too many curious hands had already held the urn for it to matter.

The urn looked a little like a trophy, she thought, perhaps a golf trophy, missing the little man with the club. Another irony, she thought. Was this Berzins' idea of a prize in his scavenger hunt? She tried to gently pry the lid off and realized that it screwed on. It was too tight to turn, but after carefully running hot water over the lid, she loosened it enough to get it started. One more hard twist and it came off in her hand. She peered inside, waiting with bated breath to see the white of human bones or teeth among soft ashes, or the glint of jewels wrapped in tattered rags from a long-lost corset. But the urn contained none of those things, no jewels, no human remains. It was full of dirt. And what looked like the edge of a piece of paper sticking up out of the middle.

Drosmis Berzins, you son of a bitch!

Lacey paced the room for a minute to stop her hands from shaking, then she tipped the urn out carefully on the newspaper. The dirt was caked hard—only the top inch or so was loose. Not having so much as a sharp nail file to dig with, thanks to airline security, she chipped away at it around the edge of the paper with a ball-point pen from the desk, ruining the tip. Chunks of dirt soon made a pile on the newspaper. She hoped for at least an errant diamond or ruby. *Nothing.*

The paper that poked up through the dirt turned out to be a small envelope. Inside was a folded-up map of the St. Louis Cemetery Number One, a New Orleans landmark just at the edge of the French Quarter, along with a bill of sale and a deed to a single crypt. And on the back of the deed was a surprisingly long handwritten note in what she presumed was Latvian. Lacey sifted through the larger clumps of dirt, breaking them into dust, revealing nothing; no gemstones, no jewelry, not even a scrap of material. She was chagrined. Sweat was pouring off her forehead. She wiped it off and washed her hands before documenting the mess with her camera.

Lacey presumed that if she was following Drosmis Berzins' mad plan correctly, this note, the map, and the deed were the next pieces in the puzzle. Berzins seemed to be damned fond of notes and of leading people around. She funneled the dirt back into the urn from the newspaper, replaced the lid, packed it back inside the package of diapers, and hid it at the back of the top shelf in the closet, behind an extra pillow. She assumed the tiny safe on the wall next to the bathroom would be the first place a burglar would search, and it looked way too easy to break into. Finally she sat down and called Mac in Washington. She heard herself telling him it was urgent for the paper to get immediate permission to open a tomb. *No wonder Mac worries about me,* she thought. *This isn't your mother's fashion beat.*

"Your attraction to dead bodies is taking a turn for the worse, Smithsonian," he said. "Now you want to start digging up crypts?"

"Just one, Mac. Not all of 'em. I'm sure our crack legal team can pry permission from the Catholic Church to pry open a crypt, right? After all, why do we even have lawyers?"

"I hope it's not to bail you out." He sounded cranky, but no more than usual, she thought.

Lacey was glad she didn't have to see the look on his face, which was no doubt stuck in his famous menacing editor mode. He was probably wearing a blue plaid shirt with an orange tie, one of his favorite combinations. "I'm faxing these documents to you," she told him. "I'd also like to know what the note on the back of the deed says. Did I mention it's probably in Latvian?"

"Right. Latvian. Good God. I'll see if I have an intern to torture," Mac muttered. "Latvia's probably got an embassy here, right?"

"That's the spirit." Lacey hung up and trudged down to the hotel's business center to fax the documents to *The Eye.* She refolded the originals and tucked them into her hip pocket.

Loud knocking at the door woke her up. Lacey's eyes felt as if they were glued together, but she pried them open and wrenched herself from the bed and stumbled to the door. She realized she must have collapsed, asleep before her head hit the pillow. The last thing she remembered thinking was how pleasant it would be to close her eyes for just a minute.

"Open up," Stella yelled. "You dead or something, Lacey? You better not be dead, because I am starved! Come on, Lace, time for lunch."

"I'm coming." Lacey opened the door and yawned as Stella strode perkily into the room.

"I feel like a new girl." She turned to Lacey. "What happened to you? You look beat."

"Jet lag," she managed to mumble. "I need to wash my face."

"Yeah, and let's use some concealer on those dark circles." Stella followed her to the bathroom while Lacey pressed a cold washcloth to her face. "Hey, you want me to do your makeup? My treat. Just close your eyes. You won't know yourself when I'm done with you."

That opened Lacey's eyes wide. She gazed at her stylist, who was still channeling her look from some 1920s film star, her shiny black hair slicked back and her eyes rimmed dramatically in black kohl. The bloodred lips added the only color in her face. Stella's clothes, on the other hand, were modern with a touch of vintage Madonna, a purple micro-miniskirt and a tight pink bustier top, spilling even more cleavage than usual. She completed the look with jeweled pink flip-flops and a silver purse shaped like a stuffed bustier.

"That's okay, Stel. I'll do it. I need the practice." She freshened up, grabbed her shoulder bag, and ushered Stella out the door to the elevator.

They stopped at a café just past Jackson Square down Decatur Street, famous for its muffuletta sandwiches, or so it said. Stella ordered the seafood gumbo, "extra spicy," for her fast-fading hangover. Lacey had the jambalaya.

"I know a great place for Hurricanes and hot jazz up on Bourbon." Stella had a weakness for the famous cocktail that was sold all over the Quarter. "You can walk around in the street with a drink here, Lace, did you know? So cool!" Of course Stella would have to go to Bourbon Street, the loudest and craziest street in the Quarter. She needed some beads, she told Lacey with a wink. "And a man. And 'the girls' and I know how to get 'em."

"Later, Stella," Lacey said between succulent bites of the Southern dish. She turned the pages of her guidebook with one hand. "You and your sassy girls there can have all the beads and all the men they can handle after I go back to bed, but first we have to go on a cemetery tour."

"Cemetery?" Stella's black-rimmed eyes looked stunned. "You're kidding, right?"

"The cemeteries in *Nawlins* are fascinating, I hear." Lacey handed Stella a brochure with the tour schedule. "Look, the tour starts at a bar. I bet they'll make you a Hurricane to go."

"But I thought we were going to party. I want *lots* of Hurricanes."

Lacey lowered her voice to a stage whisper. "Remember, we're on a secret mission here!"

Stella's eyes grew even wider. "Lacey! You mean the cemetery is important? Like a clue?" she whispered back.

"Exactly like a clue."

"Wow, Lace, why didn't you tell me? Well, then, let's rock that cemetery! Do we need weapons?"

"I hope not. That's why we're going in broad daylight."

"Maybe switchblades or something? With your record, Lacey, we gotta be prepared. Like Boy Scouts, you know. Make that Girl Scouts. Gee, I'm feeling lots better." Stella leaned back and waved at a couple of businessmen wearing convention badges. They were enjoying the view of her "girls" and their impressively bustiered cleavage. Lacey paid the bill and pulled her away.

On their way to the bar where the tour started, Lacey's attention was diverted by a store window full of fantasy dresses, delicate chiffons and silks with an early-twentieth-century garden party feel. *F. Scott Fitzgerald meets Tennessee Williams,* she thought. The boutique was called Passion Flowers. The dresses were lovely, but Lacey couldn't imagine where she might wear one. Perhaps high tea with the ambassador? Cocktails at the governor's mansion?

She wanted to press on, but Stella's eye was caught by one of the elegant formal dresses. It wasn't the punk stylist's usual style, yet she stood riveted before an ivory dress, a full-fevered Blanche DuBois number right out of *A Streetcar Named Desire.* The dress fell softly to the hips with a dropped waist and full skirt. The three-quarter-length sleeves floated down the arms. "You could wear that to a wedding," Stella said wistfully, reluctantly tearing her eyes away. "If anybody ever went to a wedding." She sighed. "Not us, huh, Lace?" Lacey couldn't remember the last wedding she'd been to. But she agreed the dress would be perfect for a wedding.

Across the street, more New Orleans fantasy apparel was on display, hundreds of elaborate one-of-a-kind hats with colorful straw brims, hats that would never be worn in the real world, Lacey thought, at least not *her* real world. But this was *Nawlins*, not the stiff bureaucratic capital she had just left. She would love to see a party where such sweet excess would be the norm. The store was named Chapeaux de Paris, but Lacey hadn't seen anything like it in Paris.

"I gotta try one of those hats," Stella announced and marched into the store, with Lacey trailing behind.

"I thought you wanted to go to Trashy Diva," Lacey said, a boutique that was much more up Stella's alley, featuring corsets that were nearly the equal of Magda's, bustiers, and retro dresses, sophisticated copies of clothes from the Forties and Fifties.

"That goes without saying, Lacey, it's like my favorite store on earth. But just look at these hats!" Stella swooped up an elaborate black-and-white straw chapeau with an elegantly twisted brim, decorated with feathers and bows. "Wow! How do I look?"

"That's really something," Lacey said, not knowing quite what to make of Stella in that spectacularly un-Stella-like creation. "Where do people wear these hats?" Lacey asked the saleswoman, a young blonde named Annabelle wearing a simple yet elegant chapeau.

"Oh, just anywhere," Annabelle exclaimed in a soft Southern accent. She was fresh-faced, wearing a natural straw chapeau with a brown bow. It went well with her brown-and-white polka-dot vintage shirtwaist dress. "A lady needs hats for all sorts of occasions."

Yes, these were exactly the kind of hats a woman needed in her closet, Lacey thought, just waiting for that special moment in time, that fairy-tale event that will probably never happen, but Annabelle went on. "Oh, and you wouldn't believe how many women buy them to wear at the Kentucky Derby. You know, it's *such* an elegant event and they want to wear something unusual they can't find at home. We ship our hats all over the world."

"I never thought of that." Of course, the Kentucky Derby was a rarefied fashion event as well as a very Southern tradition. Lacey wondered if she could ever convince Mac to let her cover something like that for a fashion story. *Right,* she thought. *After this adventure, I'll never even get to leave the office for lunch again.*

"Oh, my, yes," Annabelle said. "An English lady just ordered six of our hats to take home with her. And of course they're all custom hats. No two alike." She indicated a milliner working on a hat in the open workshop area.

"I think I'm in love," Stella said, gazing at herself in the cherrywood-trimmed cheval.

"With yourself?" Lacey teased.

"Well, of course. But I'm in love with this hat too." Stella removed it reluctantly and turned over the price tag. Her jaw dropped. Her look clearly said it couldn't *possibly* be that expensive. She put it gently back on the hat rack and patted it with a sigh. "I may be back for it later."

"Dare to dream," Lacey remarked with a smile.

Stella stared at her and her eyes went wide. "Lacey, you're right! I *will* be back for it later!"

"I didn't mean you *had* to buy it."

"You only live once," Stella said, and Annabelle nodded in agreement. "I might as well have the hat," she said as Lacey led her out the door. "I'll get married in it. Or buried in it. Whatever." Stella threw a backward longing glance at all the tempting eye candy.

Outside, the scent of flowers from hanging baskets floated down from the second-floor balconies, but the perfume of blossoms was soon forgotten as they passed an antique shop and the open door released the sharp tang of mildew. Lacey picked up the pace and they soon arrived at the bar on Ursulines Street where they would join the tour.

They were greeted by Philipe, their guide, a tall, lanky man wearing a top hat, a blue brocade vest over a white shirt, and black slacks, and carrying a cane, adding a touch of drama. Philipe spoke with a sexy French accent and explained, in response to Stella's flirtatious questions, that he was French, not Cajun or Creole, but he had been guiding these tours for several years and he also moonlighted as a jazz guitarist. And yes, he was single, he added, with a wink at Stella.

In addition to Lacey and Stella, several couples were lining up for the tour, chilling with cold drinks. An overprocessed blonde in a tight turquoise top with silver spangles and tight white capri pants held a cigarette in one hand and a Hurricane in the other. Her chubby husband wore cut-off jeans and a T-shirt, and Lacey wished he hadn't, as a public service to the world. Another couple in their late thirties wore matching blue jeans and white shirts. Nearly everyone had a drink. Lacey wanted to be awake and aware, so she sipped an iced tea. She planned to get Philipe's attention and ask a few questions quietly before the tour.

"Good God, Smithsonian, what is it with you and graveyards?" That increasingly annoying British accent close to her ear made her jump.

"Hell and damnation, Griffin! What are you doing here?" She turned to glare at Nigel Griffin, not wearing his shabby trench coat for once. He looked very out of place among the T-shirted tourists. "I'm here on vacation here, you Brit twit."

"Really? What do you expect to see here? The ghost of Marie bloody Laveau, the bleeding Voodoo Queen?"

"If you don't like it, don't go! And leave me alone!"

"I have to go; I just bought the damn ticket." He showed the ticket stub. "Purely for the pleasure of your company."

"If it's pleasure you're after, you're on the wrong tour," she sneered at him. Lacey tried to hide her alarm that he would actually follow her to New Orleans. She would have Brooke conduct an electronic sweep of her apartment when she returned to town. Maybe get a restraining order against him. Or maybe just let Vic teach him a lesson.

"I'm hurt, Smithsonian. After all, we spend so much time together. These long chats warm my heart."

"Shut up," she growled at him. "How did you find me?"

"I have my ways. I find things, remember?"

"Find your way out of my life, Griffin." Lacey was seething. Stella, on the other hand, seemed to find this new male presence with the British accent enthralling. She didn't even seem to mind his boring-for-Stella khaki slacks and blue oxford shirt rolled up at the sleeves, as Lacey thought she would. She would definitely have to have a ladies' room conference with Stella, as soon as possible.

"I still don't understand this cemetery mania. In Paris you're at Père-Lachaise in the rain waiting for Jim Morrison to rise from the dead. And here you are waiting for the crypt keeper to lead us off to the boneyard. What does it all have to do with the bloody egg?"

Lacey threw Stella a desperate look, pleading with her silently not to reveal anything about their mission in New Orleans. Philipe was rounding up the stragglers and leading the way to Rampart Street and the cemetery.

"Oh, but these *Nawlins* cemeteries are fascinating, you know, full of your better class of zombies," Stella said, placing her hand ever so lightly on Griffin's arm. "Or so Lacey tells me. You have such a cute accent, I bet you're English. I'm right, aren't I?"

Lacey could hardly keep herself from slapping that hand away. *Leave it to Stella to develop an instant crush on Mr. Goofball Menace.*

Griffin regarded Stella's twin peaks with a slow smile. "And who might you be, luv?"

"Stella Lake, pleased to meet ya. I'm Lacey's friend. And her stylist." She grabbed a lock of Lacey's hair. "See? Those are my highlights." Lacey gently removed Stella's hand and backed away from the two of them. "My work is my art," the stylist bragged.

"Nigel Griffin. Call me Nigel. And I can see it is, Stella luv. You're a work of art yourself."

"So, Nigel"—Stella's New Jersey accent nasalized his name—"call me Stella." She beamed at him. "Love your accent, it's totally James Bond. So, are you shaken or stirred?"

"You're a piece of work, Nigel Griffin," Lacey snarled. "What are you hanging around me for? I wrote the story. It ran in *The Eye Street Observer.* There's no egg. Go bother someone else."

"I daresay you could have chosen better adjectives to describe me. 'Romantic,' for example. 'Handsome.' Or 'dashing,'" Nigel said. "I don't think you did me justice."

"You're lucky I didn't use the adjectives I'm thinking of right now. And a few nouns."

"Sticks and stones, Smithsonian." Nigel smiled. The tour arrived at the front gates of St. Louis Cemetery Number One. Philipe turned to command their attention and the group fell silent.

"The City of the Dead awaits you," he began, sweeping his cane grandly over a cemetery unlike any Lacey had ever seen. "As you will see, this city houses the dead above the ground, not below." Lacey gazed at the monuments and tombs, following the group as they listened to Philipe explain the peculiar challenges of disposing of the dead in New Orleans, a city lying mostly below sea level, and how the cemetery was established in the early days of that predominantly Catholic city. He pointed out the tomb of the voodoo queen Marie Laveau, with its offerings of alcohol and coins from her adoring fans. Lacey marveled at its multiplicity of *X*s ceremonially scratched into its whitewashed walls in homage, Philipe said, by her fellow voodoo practitioners, a practice no doubt frowned upon by the Catholic Church. Lacey noticed that many of the tombs were freshly painted and well cared for, while others, revealing the red brick under their white stucco, were neglected and falling into ruin. Several crypts gaped open, empty save for dust and broken bricks.

"The bodies are buried in this way, above the ground," Philipe continued, "because as the water table rises with floodwaters, the coffins would not stay underground in graves dug in the soil. Coffins and rotting corpses, they pop right out of the ground. *C'est vrai.* The crypts, they stand like little whitewashed houses, no? So in the Crescent City we call this the City of the Dead."

Stella was fascinated, and even Griffin seemed to be caught up in Philipe's narrative. He led them to an empty crypt at eye level, not yet sealed up. The interior was just coffin-sized. He tapped it with his cane. "Bodies here, by law, must be housed in the tomb for a year and a day," he said. "The temperature inside the tomb reaches as much as 250 degrees. A year and a day it takes for the flesh to drop from the bones and turn to dust. The tomb acts as a slow crematorium," Philipe said. "All that is left is ashes, dust, and bones." Once the tomb has done its work, he said, the bones are removed to the bottom of the crypt or to a family mausoleum with other predeceased relatives.

Lacey scanned the cemetery, trying to memorize the layout. Where was the crypt Drosmis Berzins had purchased? According to her memory of the map in the urn, now safely in her hip pocket, it must be two or three rows from the back wall, well off Philipe's tour route of crypts of the famous and infamous. She itched to slip away and find the crypt, but she would have to wait for Vic. And could *The Eye* really get permission to open it? It all seemed so unlikely now.

She certainly wasn't going to lead Griffin straight to it, no matter what was in it. Griffin was a determined rascal, she had to give him that much. What if the trail petered out and she never found the corset? The thought horrified her. Would Griffin hang around her neck like an albatross forever, convinced she was on the trail of a lost Fabergé egg?

Chapter 35

The air had changed in the City of the Dead. The sun had gone behind a cloud and the atmosphere felt heavier, as if the barometric pressure had dropped suddenly. A sadness descended on Lacey. She wondered if a crazy old man was capable of hiding the Romanov corset in a tomb here in New Orleans just to play a cruel joke on his old comrade from the Revolution. Had Drosmis Berzins hoped it would be incinerated to dust and the jewels walled up and lost forever? Or was it just a way of tormenting his old pal over a stolen treasure that had proven too valuable and too notorious for either of them to ever profit from? She was lost in her thoughts and barely realized that the tour had ended. Philipe was bowing to applause from the little band of tourists.

"Come on, Lacey." Stella grabbed her arm. "Great tour, you were so right. Let's go! Bourbon Street. Hurricanes. I want to catch some Mardi Gras beads." She did a little dance, a seductive shimmy obviously meant for Griffin's benefit.

"It's not Mardi Gras," Lacey protested.

"That doesn't stop the boys from tossing beads if you show 'em something worth tossing 'em for." Stella winked and led the way, a bemused Griffin and a reluctant Lacey in tow.

Stella's destination, Maison Bourbon on Bourbon Street, had a wailing old-time jazz band and a full house of tourists sucking down Hurricane cocktails in huge glasses. Before Stella could dive into one, Lacey detoured her friend to the ladies' room for a little chat about the facts of life and Nigel Griffin. She reapplied her lipstick while Stella smoothed her hair.

"But don't ya love his cute accent, Lacey?" Stella said. "I think he's kinda dreamy."

"Yeah, dreamy like a nightmare. Stella, he is one of the bad guys."

"No way." Stella took her eyeliner out of her silver bustier purse. Before Stella, Lacey hadn't been able to imagine who would carry a purse like that, but now she knew.

"Yes, way. I don't know exactly how bad he is, but trust me, he is up to no good. We can't let him find out why we're really here." Stella practiced a seductive look in the mirror. "We may need to keep him distracted," Lacey went on, "so he doesn't catch on."

"No problem, Lacey! My girls have got him plenty distracted already," Stella said, admiring her cleavage in the mirror. "Do you think I should sleep with him?"

"With Nigel Griffin?" Lacey dropped her lipstick in the sink. "Stella! Of course not!"

"But what if I want to? You know, I could seduce him and spy on him. Like Mata Hari."

"Stella, they shot Mata Hari!"

"But he's a doll and he's got that cute accent, and maybe I'll be more like Belle Starr, one of those glamorous female spies who didn't get shot?"

"You have to be subtle." Lacey took Stella by her shoulders. "Repeat after me."

"Subtle! I got it, Lacey." She winked. "I wrote the book on subtle."

Stella, her silver bustier purse, and her "girls" bulging out of their pink lace sashayed out the door. Lacey shuddered. *Stella's book would be called* How Not to Be So Damn Subtle*!* Lacey's cell phone rang, so she stayed behind in the ladies' room for privacy.

"Hey, sweetheart, I'm so sorry this job thing came up." His voice was like hot buttered rum, soothing and stimulating at the same time. "How's it going?"

"It's going."

"Are you all right?" Vic's voice sounded alert.

"We may have a little trouble."

"What kind of trouble?"

"Trouble with an English accent."

There was a pause, then an exasperated sputter. "What the hell is Griffin doing there?"

"Stalking me, I guess," Lacey said. "Although he is currently being very thoroughly distracted by Stella. I'm afraid she'll let it slip that we're here to find Magda's killer."

"Say that again. Because I really hope I didn't hear what you just said."

"That's what she thinks we're doing, and nothing I say can convince her otherwise." Lacey peeked out the ladies' room door to keep her eye on Stella, who was letting Griffin light her cigarette. Lacey groaned. *She promised me she quit!*

"What about the corset?"

"She doesn't exactly know about the corset. Now she wants to play Mata Hari, with Griffin as her conquest." Lacey pawed through her purse for aspirin.

"Where did she come up with that?"

"I blame the Spy Museum."

"Lacey, I'll be there tomorrow. Can you keep her out of trouble till then?"

"Hey, I'm not a magician. You're really coming tomorrow?"

"Yes, you *are* a magician! Hold on till I get there." Vic hung up, and Lacey realized this relationship was moving forward. Vic apparently thought she could keep Stella out of trouble, and herself too. At least for one day. This was real progress, she concluded. She headed for the bar to rescue Stella and their mission from the insidious clutches of Nigel Griffin.

"Did it ever once cross your mind, Lacey, that this urn might contain human remains?" Vic's green eyes were boring a hole into her soul. "Remains that require a little respect?"

"Yes! No. Maybe. I wasn't exactly sure. It didn't, did it?"

They were working their way through an order of fresh hot beignets and chicory coffee at the Café du Monde. A greedy-eyed brown-speckled pigeon waited by their table for crumbs.

"But you opened it anyway." Vic's eyes scanned the patrons in the café. He ignored the pigeon. Vic had caught an early flight down from D.C., and it was ten in the morning, still the crack of dawn by New Orleans time. "I suppose you couldn't resist. Reporter."

"Drosmis Berzins was some kind of nutcase, and I had a suspicion that he planted something in there. Maybe even the jewels, but no. He was orchestrating this whole weird game."

"It might have held somebody's grandmother, you know. And pardon me for saying this, but the crazy old dead Latvian isn't the only one in this whole weird game who's nuts."

Lacey rolled her eyes and reached for another beignet. She was so happy to see Vic that his traditional lecture on her cavalier disregard for the safety of her own hide didn't even bother her. She felt utterly safe and secure in his company beneath the green and white awning of the open-air café. Fans overhead circulated the drowsy air and hungry birds waited to swoop in for the crumbs. The speckled pigeon flew in closer. Apparently the entire tribe of French Quarter pigeons had a jones for the powdered sugar crumbs that fell from the tables at the Café du Monde. Outside on the sidewalk a burly musician wearing a baseball cap and sunglasses made love to his saxophone.

"Did you hear what I just said?" Vic asked.

"Sorry, I was admiring the line of your jaw."

"Lacey—"

"And the way your eyes crinkle when you look at me."

"This is serious," he said, but a smile was beginning to make its way to his handsome face.

"It must be, or you wouldn't have asked me to your parents' house for the holidays," she said. Vic gave up and kissed her. The street musician eyed them and obliged the moment with a sweet rendition of "As Time Goes By," also known as "A kiss is still a kiss. . . ."

"You drive a man to distraction," Vic whispered in her ear.

"As long as it's this man." Lacey gave him a seductive smile. "Have you noticed there's something different in the air here?"

"It's the alligator pheromones. They float downstream from the swamps in a big toxic cloud. Careful not to succumb to their allure, I'll eat you up like a gator, lady."

It was nice to know that all kinds of pheromones flowed in New Orleans, she thought, just like the liquor on Bourbon Street. But Vic was right, she needed to be careful. Lacey told herself not to become so intoxicated with his presence that she forgot why she was there.

"So," he said, dusting crumbs from his hands, "where are the unlikely lovebirds?"

Lacey harrumphed. Stella had disappeared with Griffin without so much as a wave good-bye during Lacey's call from Vic in the ladies' room. She didn't answer Lacey's calls to her cell phone until late that evening, and then she had bristled at Lacey's suggestion that Griffin could be a killer and a jewel thief.

"You got him all wrong, Lace, he is a *reformed* jewel thief," Stella had whispered. "Just like Cary Grant in that old movie, you know? But I don't know anything about this Fabergé egg thing. I know what you wrote about it, but Magda never said anything like that to me and I was her *hairstylist*, Lace! I think I would *know*, you know?"

"Please be careful, Stella. And please come back to the hotel, I'll send a cab—"

"Lacey, I'm a big girl! I'm busy pumping him for information, if you know what I mean." Stella had clicked off her phone and she didn't pick up when Lacey called back.

"The lovebirds? Good question," Lacey said to Vic, but she was interrupted by her cell phone. The display showed her editor's number in Washington.

"Smithsonian! How's the reckless tomb raider today?"

"Hi, Mac, I'm fine, so far." She mouthed "It's Mac" to Vic. "I think."

"Good. You're supposed to be at St. Louis Cemetery Number One today in exactly one hour. I just want you to know the newspaper had to pull all kinds of strings to do this."

"One hour? Really?" She was impressed. Their publisher, Claudia, must have known which strings to pull. Lacey had hoped it might be possible to open the tomb, but she had expected days of delays and red tape, if it would be allowed at all. "Thanks, Mac. I'll be there."

"What is it, Lacey?" Vic interrupted, but she raised a finger for him to wait.

"You get one chance, Smithsonian. They open it up. You see if the corset or whatever is in there. If by some bizarre miracle this thing is there, you bring it back to *The Eye Street Observer* and you have one hell of a scoop. If not, you'll be on the bag-and-shoes beat till kingdom come."

Lacey started writing notes. "So you managed to get the note translated from the Latvian?"

"Yes, indeed," he purred with satisfaction. "Latvia loves America, did you know that? It's not long, but it is interesting. If the translation is correct, it seems to corroborate this story that Magda Rousseau told you." Mac paused for effect, and Lacey could hear him take a bite of something, no doubt whatever Felicity Pickles was pushing that day.

"Go ahead, Mac, just keep me in suspense. Take another bite."

"Here it is. Berzins gives a very brief and bloody eyewitness account of the execution of the Romanovs. He says he helped steal a corset from one of the dead princesses, and the remorse will haunt him forever." She heard Mac smack his lips. "He says taking part in the murders and stealing the corset have shamed him and his friend Juris Akmentins, and he swears no one will ever profit from the bloody corset. And that goes for anyone who discovers where he hid it."

"Ah, say that word 'corset' again, Mac. You believe me now?"

"It's insane, but it's pretty good stuff. I mean, he hides it out of shame, but then he leaves clues to find it? A wacko. Talk about ambivalent. But it means *The Eye Street Observer* has new information from an eyewitness to the assassination of the Romanovs. You might call it a late-breaking scoop from the Russian Revolution. When you get here with the documents, we'll have them authenticated. The Latvian embassy will help. And the paper will reprint this note to go along with your front-page story. Now today—" He paused for another bite of the mystery dessert.

"Go on, I'm listening," she said.

"There'll be one workman waiting for you at the cemetery gate. Name of Dante. Not a big delegation from the archdiocese; everyone involved wants this done very quietly. As I understand it, all he has to do is take some nameplate off the front of the tomb where they shove in the deceased, then break through the bricks with a sledgehammer. I'm told it shouldn't take long."

"Oh, dear." Lacey thought of one more thing.

"What now?" Mac demanded.

"What if there someone's bones in there?" she asked. Vic was at full attention now.

"Not my problem, Smithsonian. This is your tea party." Mac paused for a moment. "Take a camera. Don't let me down. Or you can see if the *Times-Picayune* there needs a new fashion reporter." He hung up, and Lacey looked at the expectant Donovan.

"This is actually kind of hard to explain," she began, and realized she hadn't really expected to get permission to open the tomb. Her explanation to Vic had only gotten as far as the incident with the urn and the envelope from Drosmis Berzins and its contents.

"Let me guess," he said, "*The Eye Street Observer* pulled some strings, perhaps made a sizable contribution to the upkeep of the historical St. Louis Cemetery Number One, and all so that Lacey Smithsonian, ace fashion reporter, can look inside a tomb."

"Wow, it's so much easier when I don't have to explain anything." Lacey laughed. "You must be psychic or something."

He took a last swallow of chicory coffee. "Or something. Probably crazy."

"You'll watch my back, won't you, Vic?"

"Your back, your front, and everything in between."

The clouds gave way to a brief rain, darkening and cooling the interior of the café. The street musician collected his earnings and headed for shelter. Lacey thought she had a chance that this day would go all right, if only she could keep Nigel Griffin away from her. She dialed a number on her cell phone and let it ring. It rang for quite awhile before someone picked up.

"What!" Stella yelled into the phone, her voice heavy with sleep.

"Hi, Stel. Gosh, did I wake you?"

"Duh! What are you, a farmer or something? What the hell time is it?"

"It's just after ten o'clock in the morning."

"Like I said." Stella yawned and whispered something to someone sharing her pillow. "So go milk the cows, why don't ya. Plant some corn."

"I'm sorry to wake you, but look, Stella, Vic is in town, he just flew in, and we really wanted—" She looked at Vic, who winked in response. "We need some time alone. You know?"

"You woke me up for this? Gee-whiz, Lacey! You go, girl, knock yourselves out."

"Thanks, Stel. You go back to sleep. We'll meet this afternoon for a drink, okay?"

"Fine by me."

"I'll call you. Later," Lacey said. "I'll be turning off my phone while we, you know—"

"Whatever." Stella clicked off.

Lacey smiled and tossed a crumb to the hungry birds attending their table. She leaned over the table and kissed Vic.

"The coast is clear, darling, I just fed the lovebirds a big fat fake crumb."

Chapter 36

The rain had stopped, but the air was still moist and thick, and their breath came out in wisps of steam. Lacey and Vic met the man named Dante at the front gate of St. Louis Cemetery Number One. Dante was a short, wiry-looking young man with muscular arms. He didn't talk much. Lacey showed her press pass for identification. He nodded. She produced the cemetery map she had pulled from the urn, along with the deed with the number of the crypt.

"Old map," he said. "Ah'll find it for ya. All ah need's the number. Right this way, ma'am, sir." He tilted his head toward the cemetery, and they followed him inside the white-walled City of the Dead. They passed a large white tomb with the name ROUSSEAU carved in block letters. It gave Lacey a sudden chill, as if Magda were there overseeing the project. Magda's last words, *Find the corset*, kept echoing in her head. She sniffed the air for the old woman's familiar perfume, *Forêt de Rose*, but she smelled only the damp soil and decaying leaves. They passed a tomb with a large opening through the red bricks and she peered in. Inside she saw a pile of vandalized statuary, including a plaster statue of a headless angel praying. The thought struck her that maybe it wasn't such a good idea to hunt for good news in a graveyard.

Dante stopped in front of a clustered tomb of crumbling red brick with twelve crypts for coffins. It looked as if it had been abandoned years before. The whitewashed stucco had fallen from three sides, exposing the bricks to the New Orleans sun and rain. The crypts were stacked four across and three high. Only a couple of them had nameplates still attached.

Their guide pointed to one in the middle and waited for Lacey to confirm the number. She read a fading inscription on the nameplate: BERZINS. HERE IT ENDS. She had a small moment of panic. Did she really want to find out what lay behind it? Was she disturbing the peace of the dead? But the dead were only echoes of the past, Lacey told herself, and she had come too far to stop now. Drosmis Berzins had practically dared her to follow him here.

Lacey looked at Vic. He smiled and put his arms around her. "Go on, dragon-slayer," he whispered in her ear.

"Yes, this is it," she told Dante. Vic took her hand. It was cold and trembling, and he rubbed it to warm her up. They stepped back to make room for the man to work.

Dante unscrewed the nameplate from the front of the crypt and set it on the ground. The mortar between the bricks was loose and crumbling, and it took only a couple of blows with his hammer to break through. He enlarged the opening, then he stood back to let Lacey peer into the crypt. There was something in there. She nodded to Dante, who reached in and withdrew a dusty and battered metal lockbox, larger than the one she had seen in the coal room in France.

"No bones?" she asked. She wasn't sure she was disappointed. The man shrugged.

"Ah ain't surprise by nothin' this here graveyard. No, ma'am, bones or no bones." Lacey reached out to take the box from Dante's hands.

"Not so fast, Smithsonian."

She turned at the sound of Nigel Griffin's voice. He was hefting a long, rusty iron bar as if it were a club. It looked like a piece of the railing that surrounded some of the tombs. "Ha. I knew you were holding out on me! I offer a partnership, being the nice chap that I am, but *no,* you want it all for yourself. No sharing with good old Nigel. All for Little Miss Priss here. Well, I don't bloody well think so!"

"Put that bar down," Vic said quietly, "you look like an idiot. Never pick up a weapon you don't want rammed down your throat." Griffin swallowed and took a step back. He looked wild-eyed and out of control, swishing his rod at them like a broadsword. Vic seemed very calm, but Lacey could see he was alert and watchful, waiting for the right moment.

"I'll hurt you, Nigel," he said. "I mean it. But I'm not going to hurt you unless I have to. Now drop that thing."

Dante took this advice to heart and dropped the box and his tools on the ground between Vic and Griffin, vaulted a low railing, and disappeared over the cemetery wall. Nigel laughed at his good fortune and reached down to pick up the box. Vic took one step, drop-kicked him in the jaw, and pulled the iron rod from his hands.

He rolled Griffin over, slammed him to the ground facedown between two tombs, pulled one arm up behind his back, and planted one knee in Griffin's back. Griffin sprayed invective into the gravel.

"Blasted bugger! Damn you, Donovan, you bloody—"

"It's not like I didn't warn you, Nigel." Vic shook his head, took a pair of handcuffs from his belt, and swiftly cuffed the cursing Brit. "When are you going to learn? You're no good at this stuff. You should stick to stealing from Mummy's purse."

Lacey looked at Vic. "Where did those handcuffs come from?"

"Just part of the tool kit," he said. "They come in handy more often than you'd think."

"Oh, my God, Lacey, did you have to kill him?" Stella wailed, running up the pathway in her faux-leopard high heels. She stopped short at the sight of Griffin on the ground complaining with his hands cuffed behind his back. "Oh. You didn't kill him. Never mind then. I know he's a rat, but I kind of like him, and I swear to you, Lacey, I really tried to keep him busy."

"Fine job you did too, Stella luv," Griffin leered from the ground. Donovan lifted his knee from the Brit's back and Stella helped him sit up. His mouth was bleeding a little. "I say, let's do last night again soon, shall we, doll?"

"Will you just shut up, Nigel?" Vic said.

"Not bloody likely. Free country, you know. You'd have to kill me. Anyone got a smoke?"

Lacey picked up the box and blew the dust from the top. She tried the lid, but it was rusted shut. She was about to take a deep breath and pry it open with Dante's screwdriver when a gunshot rang out. It echoed through the whitewashed tombs. The entire City of the Dead seemed to freeze for a long moment, then Vic grabbed Lacey and pulled her roughly down to the ground behind the tomb. Lacey in turn grabbed Stella, who reached for the handcuffed Griffin, but she missed him. Vic, Lacey, and Stella crouched behind the crumbling brick wall of the tomb, leaving Griffin lying on the path in front. "We gotta go back for Nigel," Stella whispered, but Vic hushed her.

"Smithsonian!" A voice boomed out with a faint but familiar Russian accent. "Come out. We must talk. No use running. Difficult to talk while running."

"It's Kepelov," Lacey whispered to Vic. He looked disgusted. "Keep him talking," Vic whispered to her, pulling out his cell phone. Stella's eyes were as wide as saucers.

"Kepelov, is that you?" she shouted. "I thought you were supposed to be dead?"

Kepelov laughed. "Not everyone you meet in a cemetery is dead, Smithsonian. Come out."

"Somebody shot you. In Paris. Griffin said you were dead," Lacey yelled. Vic nodded encouragement and put his finger to his lips to silence Stella.

"Griffin. Such a liar. It takes more than bullets to kill Gregor Kepelov. Come out, come out, Smithsonian!" His voice was getting closer. "You have something I want. The box. I have something you want. Your freedom."

"Who shot you?" Lacey demanded. "Your girlfriend? The woman with the perfume?"

"Ha! Who cares? The bitch is not important." His voice came from right on the other side of the tomb now. "Ah, my friend, the liar Nigel Griffin." Lacey heard a sound like a boot kicking a body, followed by a grunt. "Poor Nigel. Handcuffed again. Tell me again what it is you are good for?"

"Gregor, old man, lend us your handcuff key?" Griffin whined. "Come on, get me out of this, mate, we'll work it together, I'll sell the stuff for you, the two of us can—"

"No, no, sit, Nigel, I like you just the way you are. Hey! Smithsonian!" he shouted. "I have a burning curiosity to know what is in that box you are holding."

"It's not a Fabergé egg!" Lacey hugged the box tightly and grabbed Stella's hand. "Stay right here! Don't move!" Vic whispered to Lacey and slipped away around the corner of the tomb.

"We shall see. Give it to me," Kepelov demanded. "Then we will all find out together."

"Why did Griffin say you're dead? You two are still partners?" Lacey asked. *Where did Vic go? What the hell is he up to?*

"So many questions! I have a question. Who will shoot poor Nigel Griffin if you do not come out and give me the box? One guess. Say bye-bye to the nice lady, Nigel."

"My God, Lacey," Stella squealed, "he's gonna shoot poor Nigel!"

"Kepelov! Good God, man, we're partners! Partners don't just go around—"

"No one cares for you, poor Nigel," Kepelov said. "And one less bite out of the Fabergé egg, eh? What do you say, Smithsonian, do I shoot poor Nigel? Up to you!"

"Go ahead and shoot him, Kepelov!" Lacey shouted. "I can't

stand him either!" *Please God,* Lacey prayed silently, *let this be a bluff, not a death warrant.* Stella's jaw dropped.

"Lacey! What're you doing?! Oh, my God—" Stella pulled loose from Lacey's hands. She scrambled out from behind the tomb and snarled at Kepelov like a bull terrier.

"You big bald Commie bully! Who said you could go around shooting people? An unarmed man? Look at him! He's handcuffed for pity's sake! Who the hell do you think you are?!"

Kepelov was laughing. "Smithsonian! You are doing this all backwards! You are sending me *more* hostages! You want me to shoot both of them? For one little box?"

Lacey looked at the box in her hands and considered it for a moment. *It's not worth it, whatever it is. Sorry, Magda.* "Nobody's shooting anybody, Kepelov, I'm coming out." She stood up and walked around the edge of the tomb, the box hugged tight to her chest. "Put down the gun."

"Ah! There she is, the girl reporter, the little solver of mysteries." Kepelov smiled and leveled his gun at her, a black pistol that almost seemed lost in his big fist. Stella was crouching over Griffin, fuming. Vic was nowhere to be seen. "Much better. I do not want to kill you, Lacey Smithsonian," he said. "You have spirit. You amuse me. And now the box, please."

"I amuse you?"

Kepelov gestured expansively. "You amuse me. You try so hard. You and your little game. All over now. I win. Give me the box!"

You amuse me. Somehow that offended Lacey even more than the attack in the coal room, or being robbed at gunpoint. Kepelov took a step toward her. Lacey held the box in both hands and took a deep breath. Kepelov reached for it, keeping the gun pointed at her.

Lacey hurled the metal box as hard as she could right in Kepelov's face. He had no time to react. The box struck him hard across the forehead with a crack. He stumbled back and waved his gun hand wildly for balance, wiping at a stream of blood from his face with the other hand. Vic stepped out from behind a tomb and swung Griffin's iron rod down on Kepelov's gun arm like an ax. The gun went flying over the tomb, Kepelov grunted, and Vic put one fist in the big Russian's belly, then another. He folded in the middle and went down. Vic landed on him and levered one arm up behind his back until the Russian bellowed in pain.

"Damn it, I'm out of handcuffs!" Vic growled. "So if you even twitch, I'm gonna rip your arm off and beat you with it. You got that, Kepelov?" Kepelov groaned and tried to nod, his mustache jammed hard against the dirt. Lacey snatched up the box, her heart beating wildly.

"Oh, well played, partner," Griffin said to the downed Russian. "Insult the lady and get your head handed to you. Very smooth. You're the old master at this spy stuff, aren't you?" He leaned his head back against the crumbling tomb. Stella dabbed at his cut lip with her handkerchief, making "poor baby" noises.

"So you *are* partners, you lying skunk," Lacey said. "Was he actually going to shoot you?"

"We make lousy partners, more's the pity," Nigel said. "And I wouldn't put it past him."

"Shut up, you idiot," Kepelov gasped, his face contorted in pain. Lacey wondered how many bullets he'd taken in Paris, and yet he'd followed her all the way here. It must have taken superhuman will. But he looked completely subdued now with Vic sitting on him and twisting his arm.

"That wasn't exactly my plan, sweetheart," Vic said, his jaw set. "Didn't I tell you to stay put and don't move?"

"Well, yeah, but I couldn't. Stella could have been shot. What was your plan?"

"Look behind you." Lacey turned around to see the smiling face of a man she knew as Turtledove, his code name among Damon Newhouse's Conspiracy Clearinghouse crew. He winked at her. Turtledove had family in the bayou country, and Stella had mentioned he was in town to play a gig at the Spotted Cat, the little jazz club in the Faubourg Marigny near the French Quarter. When he wasn't playing his trumpet, he was in private security. Lacey knew she could trust him with her life, just as she would Vic. He was flanked by two equally large and impressive men who looked quite a lot like Turtledove, as if they might share his family's diverse ethnic stew. Turtledove whipped out handcuffs of his own, and they took over babysitting Kepelov.

"*That* was my plan." Vic stood up. Lacey clung to him and kissed him with all her might.

"Good plan," Lacey said when she caught her breath. "Turtledove, good to see you. *Really* good to see you."

"My pleasure. Sorry we missed the excitement." Turtledove hugged the ladies and shook hands with Vic. "Meet my cousins." They nodded silently and shook hands. Stella eyed the cousins invitingly. She seemed to be contemplating switching sides. Turtledove manhandled Kepelov to his feet with one hand while the cousins managed the skinny, out-of-shape Griffin. The two of them looked like tree trunks next to a droopy twig.

"Gently, please. Force is not necessary, gentlemen, as you can see." Griffin indicated the handcuffs. "I am already subdued. Quite subdued. Perfectly bloody calm."

"Shut up, imbecile," Kepelov growled.

"What do you want to do with them?" Turtledove asked, holding Kepelov at arm's length. His biceps barely strained. "Police? FBI? Toxic waste disposal? Or just feed 'em to the gators?"

"I like number four, but let me make a call first," Vic said, pulling out his phone again.

Before he could punch in a number, the sound of boots crunching on the gravel pathways of the cemetery broke the silence. Everyone turned to stare at the new arrival.

Chapter 37

Tony Trujillo, the cop-beat reporter for *The Eye Street Observer*, rested one black lizard-skin boot on the top step of a whitewashed tomb, looking relaxed and curious.

"Mac said I should keep an eye on you, Lacey. Keep you out of trouble. And here you are, taking the cemetery tour. Hey, Vic! Long time no see, man. Stella, howdy! And it's Forrest Thunderbird, right?" Trujillo knew Turtledove by the name on his business card. He shook hands all around, except with those too handcuffed to shake hands. He eyed Griffin and Kepelov curiously.

" 'Keep an eye on me'? Are you kidding?" There was danger in Lacey's voice. "Mac didn't tell me you were going to show up."

"He thought it would be a nice surprise. You know how Mac loves surprises."

"Nice surprise, my aunt Mimi! He doesn't trust me."

"Who wouldn't trust a fashion reporter? But you know how it is, Lois Lane. Even Superman says, 'Trust but verify.' " He smiled his lazy Southwestern smile. "He doesn't want you to come back in a box."

"You're just here to steal my story."

"To *share* the story, Smithsonian. Double byline. Mac got all cranked up about it. Thinks he's been neglecting your occupational safety and health." Trujillo glanced from Griffin and Kepelov to Turtledove and his cousins, and back to Vic and Lacey and Stella. "Did I miss anything? Fill me in."

"No way! This is my story! It's great that Mac finally believes there's a big story here," Lacey said. "But you are not poaching on my territory." She held the box close to her chest.

"Whatever. Your story is a feature. A personal journey. 'I was there, in the cellar and on the battlements,' et cetera. That's cool,"

Trujillo said, "but I can bring some objectivity to the story, the kind *The Eye Street Observer* is known for."

"Ha! *The Eye* has never been known for objectivity," Lacey fumed. She caught a glimpse of Vic. His mouth seemed to be fighting a smile, and losing.

"Always a first time," Tony said. "Besides, I'm here, I got my orders too, so let's deal."

Lacey knew when to yield to her editor, but she'd be damned if she'd let Trujillo muscle in on her story without working for it. "Fine. Follow along, Tony. Try to keep up." She carefully documented the scene and the principal characters with her digital camera, and she was surprised to see Trujillo had brought one too. They both took photos of the unopened box from the crypt from every angle. Lacey wondered why Mac hadn't also sent her Hansen, the long-legged staff photographer, who was usually up for anything and took direction much better than Trujillo.

Vic and Turtledove decided Kepelov and Griffin would be kept amused by the cousins for the rest of the afternoon, until some decisions could be made. Turtledove would start a tab for their entertainment expenses, and either Vic's security company or *The Eye* would cover the costs. "No problem," Turtledove assured him with a wink. "They'll dig my cousins' bayou tour. Tourists love an up-close look at the gators." Kepelov kept a stoic silence and a grim look on his face.

"All right, Donovan, this little joke has gone far enough," Griffin protested as one of the cousins took his arm. "I've had a bellyful of your Yank barbarity."

Vic grinned at him. "Don't let the gators get a belly full of you, Nigel." Lacey shot Vic a questioning look. "Don't worry, sweetheart, it would be animal cruelty to make an alligator eat these two rotten apples."

"You hear that, mate," Griffin said to Kepelov, "you'd gag a gator." Kepelov grunted.

Turtledove's cousins took the two prisoners in hand to march them out of the cemetery. Stella's loyalties seemed to be divided for all of a minute, then she pecked Griffin good-bye. "You're going to be totally okay, Nigel. Maybe we'll party later. The handcuffs are so *you*."

Vic and Trujillo found the screwdriver and hammer Dante had left behind and Lacey prepared to open the metal box.

"At least let us see what's in the bloody box!" Griffin shouted as he was being led away.

"Up to Lacey," Vic said. "Maybe you should say 'pretty please.' "

Griffin glared back. "Bloody hell. All right! Pretty bloody please, Smithsonian, please open the bloody box. Please."

"Only because your plea has moved me," Lacey said, with a smile at Vic.

Vic set the box on the concrete apron of a tomb and tapped the screwdriver gently into the gap under the lid with the hammer. One twist of the screwdriver and the lid gave, but he left it shut and handed the box to Lacey. Lacey lifted the lid. The box contained only a handwritten letter on one sheet of unlined writing paper, lying flat in the box. Lacey lifted out the note with Trujillo's Swiss Army knife tweezers and demonstrated that the box was otherwise empty for Griffin and Kepelov's benefit, and for Trujillo's camera. She showed the note to Vic and laid it carefully back in the box.

"So what is it? What's on the bloody paper?" Griffin whined, quivering with curiosity.

"Maybe it's a *clue*," Lacey said. "Maybe you'll have to read about it in the paper. In *my* story," she said, arching an eyebrow at Trujillo, who just grinned at her. She waved good-bye to Turtledove and his cousins. Turtledove winked at her and the three men turned and marched their two captives away, Griffin still fuming and complaining, Kepelov as silent as the tomb.

The note was brown and brittle, and Lacey was afraid it might crumble, but it was readable, and, *thank God*, Lacey thought, it was in English. She read the note aloud as Vic and Trujillo and Stella peered over her shoulder:

To Whom It May Concern,

If you're reading this note, you must be the person Drosmis said would come looking for the thing he asked me to hide for him.

Although I promised him I would hide the corset in this tomb, I knew it would be damaged or destroyed before too long. I cannot think that is what he intended. Therefore I have stored it in a safe place.

Come see me at my shop, Passion Flowers on Royal Street, and I will turn it over to you. If you have come all this way from France to find it, you deserve to have it.

Sincerely, Madeline Demaine.

* * *

Royal Street ran through the French Quarter just on the other side of Bourbon Street from Rue Dauphine. It was close enough to walk, the metal box with the note and Berzins' crypt nameplate tucked safely into Lacey's tote bag, her hand in Vic's. She should be feeling lighter than air, she thought, to have survived that confrontation in the cemetery, but she wasn't. A feeling of dread descended on her as they turned up Royal with Trujillo and Stella close behind and walked silently the last few blocks to the boutique called Passion Flowers. Lacey realized it was the shop she had peeked into the day before, the one with the extravagant and slightly absurd 1920s dresses, across the street from the exclusive custom hat store. Today the elegantly garbed mannequins were still stationed in the windows, eternally greeting passers-by in blank-eyed silence.

They entered the store, an oasis of cool, calm, and quiet. The walls were a deep pink, and the floor was covered with an antique floral carpet, red roses on a deep blue background. The ceiling was covered in rose-colored grosgrain ribbon. The effect, Lacey thought, was charming and old-fashioned, and as feminine as a century-old copy of *Godey's Lady's Book.*

"Lacey, how long will this take?" Tony cracked. "It's so frilly and froufrou in here I can feel my testosterone level crashing."

"Be a man, Tony." Vic smirked. "I got extra if you need it."

"Feel free to wait outside while I get the story," Lacey invited him. "Breathe in some gator pheromones." Trujillo looked puzzled, but he leaned on the counter while she strolled around the shop, admiring the vintage evening gowns guarded by a velvet rope and a pair of green velvet Victorian armchairs. A ledge along the wall displayed a collection of antique hats and hatboxes, an old-fashioned padded dressmaker's dummy, and beaded and brocaded evening purses.

Lacey was about to lift the rope and sneak into the gown area when a pretty blonde in a 1930s vintage navy dress with a white satin collar emerged from the back room. The woman could have taken her place next to the mannequins in the window. "May I help you?"

"I hope so." Lacey pulled out the metal box and showed her the note she had found in the City of the Dead.

As the woman peered into the box and read the note, a look of dismay crossed her face. She turned to Lacey. "I'm so sorry! Madeline Demaine is my mother. I'm Nicole Demaine. I own the shop now." She offered Lacey her hand.

"Lacey Smithsonian. I'm a reporter from Washington, D.C. May I speak with your mother, please? It's very important."

"Oh, that would be impossible," Nicole said. "You see, she has Alzheimer's. Where on earth did you find this note?"

"That's such a long story, but I'm very interested in finding the corset she mentions," Lacey pressed. "Do you have any idea where this 'safe place' of hers might be?"

The woman ran her hand through her hair. "Mama barely recognizes me—she doesn't even know I'm her daughter anymore. Sometimes she thinks I'm her sister who died fifty years ago. Most days, I have no idea what she's babbling about. And I don't know where she might have hidden a corset for someone. Why hide a corset anyway?"

Nicole perched behind the front counter on a tall stool and moved aside a display of fancy vintage linen handkerchiefs. Lacey set the box on the counter. Vic and Trujillo stood silently. Stella had become deeply involved with the racks of frilly vintage frocks.

"Did you ever know someone named Drosmis Berzins?"

"Oh my, yes!" Nicole beamed. "He was a friend of my mother's. He gave her the money to start Passion Flowers. She was always grateful to him. He was such a nice man. Cutest accent. I used to call him Uncle Bertie."

"What was their relationship?"

Nicole smiled. "If you're suggesting an intimate relationship, I have no idea. I was pretty little when he died." Nicole Demaine peered at the note again. "If I knew what Mother was talking about, I would of course turn it over to you, like she says. It's obviously Mother's handwriting."

"Would you happen to have any vintage corsets here?" Lacey asked.

"We only carry dresses and accessories, I'm afraid. But I could give you the name of a good corsetiere. Corsets are getting awfully popular again, have you heard?"

"It would be quite old, an antique, from about 1917."

"I would be happy to honor any debt of my mother's, but I have no idea where it could be." Nicole spread her hands. "I know the entire inventory by heart. There is nothing like that here. And there is no safe or secret closet or attic or anyplace she might have hidden something. I'm afraid I haven't helped you very much, have I?"

"Thank you anyway," Lacey said. *The corset is gone,* she thought. *Vanished into the recesses of an old woman's shattered mind.* "Perhaps he didn't really want it to be found," Lacey said, amending silently, *the bastard.* Nicole Demaine went to help a customer. Lacey turned away from the counter.

"Are you okay, sweetheart?" Vic said.

"I guess I never realized how much I wanted it to be true. I wanted to see it. For Magda. For myself."

Vic put his arms around her. "It's still a hell of a story. Let's get out of here. Let me cheer you up over dinner."

"No corset. Bummer, man," Tony chimed in. "Mac's gonna have an attack."

"When he has to pay your trip expenses," she retorted.

"I'm thinking it'll be an okay story even without the corset," Trujillo said. "If we manage to bring back the Rousseau killer. Is it Kepelov or Griffin, you think? Or someone else?"

"Okay, stop it. Now." Lacey raised one eyebrow. "I don't know who killed Magda."

"You did everything you could," Vic consoled her. "Let's go. We need to do something about those two creeps. Where's Stella?" Lacey had lost track of her stylist as she hunted through the racks of ruffles and rows of frilly party dresses. "Stella!" Vic called out. "Hey, Stella!" He sounded just like Stanley Kowalski. *Oh, that was a priceless New Orleans moment*, Lacey thought wryly. *I guess that was the only treasure I'll find here at Passion Flowers.*

"Just a minute," Stella hollered from a dressing room. "I'm coming!" She emerged in a rose-colored version of the 1920s fantasy dress on the mannequin in the window, dropped waist, full skirt, floating three-quarter-length sleeves, the dress Stella had imagined wearing to a fantasy wedding in *Great Gatsby* Land. She admired herself in an enormous gilt-framed mirror and blew herself a kiss. Her vampy makeup complemented the dress.

Nicole laughed and clapped her hands. "Oh, it's you! See how it brings out your eyes?"

It was wildly different from anything Lacey had ever seen Stella wear. But somehow it had clutched the strings of her punkette stylist's heart and played the tune "I Feel Pretty."

"Stella—?" Lacey began. "Who are you, and what have you done with my friend Stella?"

"I'll take it," Stella said. "Charge it!"

"I need a drink," Lacey said.

Lacey felt as if she'd been blown hither and yon by a hurricane, and she needed a cocktail. It seemed to be easy for everyone else to be philosophical, but she was disheartened. Not only had she failed to find the corset, she doubted that Magda's killer would ever be brought to justice.

Her blue mood somehow induced her to wear the blue satin corset Magda had made for her. Lacey felt wearing it tonight would be a kind of tribute to her. To the corsetiere's credit, Lacey's corset did not look like one of Stella's racy bustiers or one of the blond call girl Jolene's fetish fantasies. Instead it served as a beautiful and dressy top, and its firm stays seemed to give Lacey a little extra backbone, something she felt she needed tonight. She wore it with a fitted black skirt and a black embroidered shawl of Aunt Mimi's to ward off the faint chill in the New Orleans November night air.

Lacey pirouetted for Vic. He whistled at the sight of her curvy figure snugly laced up in blue satin. "You could scorch the chrome off a bumper, lady."

"Is that considered sweet talk where you come from, cowboy?" He kissed her shoulder and lifted her hair, and proceeded to shower kisses up the back of her bare neck.

"You look gorgeous, Lacey. Let me show you some real sweet talk."

"First show me some dinner, pardner, and maybe you'll get lucky," she teased. "You know, I've been wondering, Vic, why you never told me your folks had money."

"You mean why I never told you I was 'comfortable'?" His kiss sent shivers up her spine.

"Yeah, 'comfortable.' There's that rich kid's secret code again for having money."

He leveled his green eyes at her. "Maybe because I could tell just by looking at you that you could never be bought."

It was Lacey's turn to whistle. "You're very clever with words when you want to be."

He gave her another kiss behind the ear. "Maybe I just wanted you to love me for me. Instead of my vast untold wealth." He smirked at her, and she pushed him back on the bed and climbed on top of him.

"You're a real smart-ass, you know that?" She bit his ear.

"Darling, you say the sweetest things."

"Why don't you sweet-talk me more over that dinner you promised me?"

Dinner at the Praline Connection in the Faubourg Marigny near the Quarter was glorious, black-derby-wearing waiters and huge plates of soul-food-style shrimp jambalaya. Very down-home. Vic turned out to have wonderful taste in restaurants, whether it was a chili place in Old Town Alexandria back home, or something chic and amusing in Paris, or daring her to eat fried Cajun "alligator bites" in New Orleans. Her estimation of his Good Boyfriend potential was growing.

After dinner they wandered up Frenchmen Street to the Spotted Cat to hear Turtledove wail on his trumpet, sitting in with his cousins' band. Vic had promised Lacey "the Marigny" was the neighborhood where the "real people" in New Orleans hung out to hear live music, unlike the tourist-filled jazz joints in the Quarter. They arrived during one of the band's breaks, and the small bar was overflowing and spilling out on the street.

Stella rushed up to them from the massive arm of one of Turtledove's sexy cousins. She was wearing a revealing black and faux-leopard print bustier, her kohl eye makeup was pure Catwoman, her black hair was slicked back, and she carried a huge drink in one hand. All that was missing to complete her fetish tiger-trainer look, Lacey thought, was a whip.

"Oh, my God! Lacey, I'm so proud of you," Stella raved. "You are fabulous!"

"Me? What for?" As far as Lacey was concerned she was a failure. She'd come up empty-handed, not only in Mont-Saint-Michel and in Paris, but here and now in New Orleans.

"For wearing your corset! Magda would be so proud of you too! Let me look. Oooh!"

You're so wrong, Stella, Lacey thought. Magda would be so disappointed in her. In fact, the memory of the dead woman was like another guest at the party that night, she had intruded so often on Lacey's thoughts; a silent and reproachful guest. She realized Stella was poking at her and tugging at her laces. "Stop that."

"Whoa, Lacey, you are pure boy bait in that thing! I'm sure your boyfriend likes it too." She winked at Vic. "Hi, boyfriend!"

"He does like it," Vic agreed with a grin.

"I can't tell you two how happy I am you finally, you know, got it together," Stella said with a dramatic roll of her kohl-lined eyes. "I mean, I really thought you two were riding the 'stubby yellow school bus' of relationships, if you know what I mean. My favorite 'special needs' couple?" She took a sip of her drink. "Like 'retarded,' you know?"

"Yeah, we get it, Stel," Lacey said, feeling her cheeks burn. Vic howled with laughter.

"Don't worry, Stella, we're on the express bus now. No stops."

Stella grabbed Lacey's arm to guide them through the crush of jazz-loving locals. "Come on, you crazy kids, they're holding a table for us. Your cute Tony Trujillo is here too somewhere."

The Spotted Cat was small, and they were in constant danger of being jabbed by elbows, spilled on by waitresses weighed down by trays of drinks, and jostled by more people squeezing into the bar. It was way past capacity. Nobody seemed to care. Turtledove's trumpet was the star of the show tonight. He transported the crowd to a blue late-night world with new takes on cool-jazz standards like "Flamenco Sketches" and "So What." During the next break, Turtledove plowed through the crowd to their tiny table and sat down, mopping his brow. He hugged Lacey hello.

"What happened to Kepelov and Griffin?" Lacey asked.

"Oh, we entertained 'em all afternoon with a rehearsal and a jam session. For free," he said in his husky baritone. "Pretty lucky guys if you ask me. Catch and release, just like bass fishing, and they were very subdued when we let 'em swim away. And Lacey, no humans were harmed in the making of this evening's entertainment."

Turtledove always made her smile. "But what about the poor alligators?"

"Gators spat 'em back out," he laughed. "That English guy's too bitter to stomach. And the Russian, he's no jazz fan, lemme tell ya."

"Why not just turn them over to the police?" she asked Vic after Turtledove returned to his trumpet. "Now they're back on the loose."

"All we've really got on them is disturbing the peace, discharging a firearm, menacing a reporter. Louisiana is different. Probably no jail time for them, sweetheart, and too much time and trouble for you." Vic flagged down the waiter to order a Guinness stout. "If you ever hear from either one of them again, I'll take care of him."

"What if they were responsible for Magda's death?"

"Then we need to make a case on a murder rap, not disturbing the peace. And as far as I know, darling, we don't have any evidence that they did it, right? I know Griffin wouldn't dirty his own hands with something like that. He's too slick. And a coward."

The music resumed and Lacey leaned back in Vic's arms. Stella danced out on the sidewalk with one of Turtledove's cousins, the jazz turned sweeter and bluer, Lacey floated away in Vic's embrace, and all should have been well. But something Lacey remembered was starting to bother her.

Was it possible Magda had left Lacey a message, hidden somewhere? The thought of a lost message from Magda began as a whisper. It tickled her brain all evening until it was a roar. Magda loved the idea of secrets, secrets hidden by your clothes, secrets hidden *in* your clothes, secrets sewn into fabric. She even had her own theory about how the Romanov jewels might have been stitched into their corsets; she had demonstrated to Lacey one evening just how it might be done.

This whole wild goose chase, Laccy reflected, was full of old people leaving cryptic little notes for someone to find years later. *Such a quaint twentieth-century idea,* she thought ruefully, *in this era of just zapping an ephemeral e-mail around the globe and feeling cranky if it takes a whole minute to arrive.* Juris Akmentins and Drosmis Berzins and Madeline Demaine, three people Lacey had never met, had been busy penning little notes that ended up before Lacey's eyes. Two of them were dead. Madeline Demaine was lost in a world of her own. Magda was dead now, too.

So where was the little note to her from Magda?

Don't be ridiculous, she told herself, and tried to concentrate on the evening and the music and her good friends and Vic. But the thought came back again and again. Was there a hidden message somewhere from Magda? And if there was, where was it?

There was only one place to look.

Chapter 38

Lacey finally removed the blue satin corset after their evening of dining and dancing and drinking. She had never worn it for more than a few minutes at a time before, and she drew a deep breath and scratched her ribs where the boning had held them in. She pulled on a soft pink knit shirt and turned to the task at hand.

"I love the way you look in that silly thing," Vic said. He kissed her and slid his hands up her back beneath her shirt, tickling her spine. "Although this is definitely a more user-friendly garment." She smiled and tried to remember she had an idea to investigate. Vic went to find the hotel ice machine.

Why had Magda been so insistent that Lacey must have a corset? She hadn't made much money from it. Was it just for the story's sake? To impress Lacey with her art? She fingered the pretty blue material. The garment was beautifully made of the finest-grade satin with delicate topstitching. MADE EXCLUSIVELY FOR LACEY SMITHSONIAN BY MAGDA ROUSSEAU was embroidered in gold thread on a white silk label that miraculously did not irritate the skin. It was a lovely final touch that marked the corset as a custom-made, one-of-a-kind creation. Lacey examined every square inch of the garment, returning again and again to the label, which was attached along an inside seam.

Lacey admired again the tiny hidden pocket Magda had sewn in for her between two stays. It was just big enough to hide away a folded-up bill, or a love letter. And of course it was empty. She smoothed every perfectly straight seam with her fingers. Perhaps it was just her imagination, but the fabric felt slightly thicker in one of the back panels along the seam near the label. Lacey convinced herself it was. She dug out her small manicure scissors, the pointed ones stashed in her check-through luggage for the plane trip.

"Lacey, what are you doing?" Vic asked, back with a bucket of ice and a couple of Cokes.

"Checking something out. Just a hunch." She took care to open the seam at the label so she wouldn't rip the material. She would have the seam re-stitched later.

"What hunch?" Lacey threw him a look. He cocked an eyebrow. "Fashion clue?"

"Maybe." Where the fabric seemed thicker, she wriggled one finger inside, then two, and found a piece of fabric that was not attached to the garment. She pulled it out carefully. It was a small slip of white silk with a message in tiny handwriting in blue ink. "Oh, my God."

"What is it?

"A note from Magda."

"You're kidding. Stitched inside the—? That's ridiculous. Let me see." He reached for it, but she backed away, laughing.

"Hey, this is *my* clue, Vic." She held it out of his reach, behind her back. "It's a secret message." Her heart was beating fast. What was this mania for hidden messages? Was it a mindset of people who had gone to war? Lacey knew from reading newspaper clippings in her Aunt Mimi's trunk that spies during World War II used maps printed on silk and stitched into their jackets, hidden behind the lining. Magda obviously knew this trick too.

"Okay, okay! Hide your secret message from me," he chuckled. "You'll be sorry when you need me to translate it from Latvian for you."

Lacey brought the slip of silk to the light and read it aloud.

> *Clever girl! Those of us who work with needles and thread are fond of secrets between the stitches. So for you, my dear Lacey, I leave a drop of good fortune. Bloody thread, knock 'em dead!*
>
> *Your friend Magda.*

"She hid this inside your corset?" Vic asked. "What for?"

"Just for good luck, I think. Look—" Lacey held the silk out to him. "See the little drop of blood? There." He peered at a brown blot on the white silk. "She told me, 'Bloody thread, knock 'em dead' was a theatre costumer's saying, that it was good luck for her to prick her finger while sewing, it meant she was putting her heart and soul into the garment."

"So it *is* a fashion clue. What's it mean?"

"I don't have a clue in the world, Vic. 'Between the stitches.' Damn! I am fresh out of hunches." She collapsed back on the bed. "Maybe I'll think of something tomorrow."

Vic set the silk aside. He leaned over her and smiled. "Is that a promise or a threat, Lacey?"

"Both."

"Move over." He kissed her and joined her on the bed. "I gotta hand it to you. Hidden messages inside your clothes? That's a real live fashion clue. Of course I've been reading hidden messages inside your clothes for years, sweetheart."

"Oh, you are a sweet-talker, aren't you?"

The next day dawned better and brighter. Lacey draped a light sweater over her sleeveless coral cotton dress. Today, she was determined to do something fun, something with nothing to do with the lost corset, and she roused Vic early so they might elude late-sleepers, like Stella, and interlopers, like Trujillo. They strolled away from the hotel down the Mississippi River waterfront and watched a flock of geese paddling up the river like a miniature flotilla. Lacey pointed at them.

"There we are, Vic. It's a wild-goose chase," Lacey said. "And I'm the lead goose."

"You're a pretty goose. And you threatened to come up with more ideas today," he said cautiously.

"I did, didn't I?" She shook her head. "Idle threat."

This was going to be one of those mysteries featured on public television, Lacey figured glumly, like what really happened to Amelia Earhart; what happened in the summer of 1917 to the fabled bejeweled corsets of the Romanov imperial princesses. This corset had vanished from a locked coal room to a walled-up crypt and into the impenetrable mind of a woman with Alzheimer's.

"If I take you for a cruise on the Steamship Natchez, will it cheer you up?" Vic asked. They found themselves standing in the ticket line for the short cruise up the muddy Mississippi River and back, one of the quintessential New Orleans tourist attractions.

"Absolutely. Why let this trip go to waste? Let's be tourists." They joined the line of tourists and families, toddlers, grandparents, and conventioneers, some still wearing name tags. Then she grimaced at Trujillo, who had sprinted from the hotel and had just caught up with them.

"But I don't understand why you're here, Tony," Lacey said. "Riverboat fan?"

He shrugged. "My job, Lacey. Mac said not to let you out of my sight. Because that's when it always happens."

She glared at him. "When what always happens?"

"You know, the killer, the scoop, whatever. I live to serve. You're stuck with me."

"Knock yourself out, Trujillo."

Before they could board, all passengers were required to have their photographs taken "for security," which was simply a clever way to create personalized souvenir photos to hawk after the riverboat ride. There was no obligation to buy them, but few tourists could resist.

"They get you coming and going," Vic said.

"Good, because I want proof this really happened." Lacey realized it was the first time they would have their photo taken together, so she smiled brightly for the camera. They boarded the ship, followed by Trujillo, and climbed the green painted steps to the mid deck. They listened as the tour guide drew their attention to points of interest over the boat's PA system. The riverboat headed upstream toward the Chalmette Battlefield, where Andrew Jackson fought and won the Battle of New Orleans with the help of the sexy pirate Jean Lafitte. Trujillo went in search of the bar on the upper deck, no doubt looking for cute blondes to try his killer smile on.

"Alone at last," Lacey said. "Only a hundred strangers. And Tony. Kiss me, you fool."

Vic obliged her with a kiss. "At least that idiot Griffin didn't follow us here. And where's Stella?" He rubbed Lacey's weary shoulders, kneading knots she didn't know she had.

"She said she was sleeping in. Did she leave the bar with one of Turtledove's cousins last night? I lost track of her. Maybe she's soothing Nigel's bruised ego."

"You could always soothe my ego." Vic grinned at her. "How about a drink? I'll go find that bar Tony was looking for."

"Something tall and cold, darling. Lemonade maybe?"

Lacey gazed up at him and smiled as he disappeared in the crowd of tourists. As she looked toward the upper deck, something else caught her eye: the profile of a woman wearing large sunglasses. The sweep of her hair looked familiar. Very familiar. The woman turned and looked the other way. And as far as Lacey knew, this woman had no business in New Orleans or on the *Steamship Natchez.* It couldn't possibly be a coincidence.

Lacey climbed quickly up the stairs. She must have been only a few seconds behind Vic, but he was nowhere to be seen. She reached the aft upper deck of the steamship, overlooking the huge red paddlewheel that moved the ship, chopping the surface of the Mississippi with a strong, steady rhythm. She walked slowly now, looking for Vic or Trujillo and scanning female faces carefully, expecting to see the face of the woman who must have killed Magda. But it was her scent that announced her presence. Hovering on the air was her perfume, *Forêt de Rose.* The skin on the back of Lacey's neck prickled and fear did a tap dance on her spine.

"Hello, Miss Smithsonian. Small world, isn't it?"

Lacey wheeled around to the melodious accented voice behind her. "Natalija Krumina. Traveling again so soon?"

Natalija laughed, displaying her nice even teeth. "You're no dummy, Smithsonian. You're smarter than I thought."

"It's the secret weapon of reporters everywhere. So, did you enjoy France?"

"Not so much as I had hoped. You kept me so busy." Natalija leaned against the railing, her hands jammed into her skirt pockets. "I didn't mean for you to see me today, but since you did, we have things to discuss. Like the corset. Where is it?"

"A corset?" Lacey asked, making her eyes go wide. "If you wanted a corset, Magda could have made you one. I thought it was a Fabergé egg you were looking for. Or was that just a story to hook Gregor Kepelov?"

"Didn't take much to hook Gregor. But you are wasting my time. The corset."

"So you know all about the corset?"

"Why deny it?" Something pinned to Natalija's white blouse glittered in the sunlight. Lacey recognized the gaudy pin that Magda had loved. The piece of costume jewelry she was so attached to. She wore it with everything. Natalija had pretended to Broadway Lamont that she could hardly remember the pin. *Everyone lies about it,* Lacey realized, *so it must be valuable.*

"Magda's jewelry," Lacey said. "You said that was just an ugly old broach."

"I was making a joke. Romanov emeralds and sapphires and rubies, set in platinum. How could that be ugly? And it is old, that part is true." Natalija removed her right hand from her blue denim skirt pocket and let her fingers stroke the pin. "The corset wasn't the only thing her grandfather stole. I suppose this was something that fit easily into the lining of a soldier's cap."

"You stole it," Lacey said.

"From whom is it stolen, Lacey Smithsonian? From Magda? From her grandfather? From the Romanovs? Or from the peasants who mined the stones and never enjoyed a full belly in all their lives for all their hard work? It was stolen a long time ago. But it's mine now." Natalija touched the pin again as if to make sure it was still there.

"So you did kill Magda." Tears sprang to Lacey's eyes. "For that? A lousy pin?"

"So sentimental over an old lady. She is just a newspaper story to you."

"No, she was my friend, and yours. How could you do it?"

"It was easy." Natalija showed no remorse. "A child could have done it."

"You stabbed her."

"Yes, a couple of times, but the blade was short." Natalija smiled like a cat, her almond-shaped eyes turned up at the corners. " 'Die, you old bitch!' That's what I said to her." She seemed to relish the memory.

I think I'm going to be sick, Lacey thought. She was looking desperately around for Vic when Natalija suddenly flicked out a small pearl-handled knife. She held it in her left hand and smiled, as if she were simply showing Lacey another piece of jewelry. Lacey took a breath and tried to control her stomach. *Keep her talking.*

"How did you know there was a Romanov corset?"

"Magda was not the only one with family secrets. Drosmis Berzins was my great-grandfather."

"Your great-grandfather?" Lacey absorbed the information. "Drosmis?"

"He talked about it all the time, the corset, how he helped his friend steal it, the awful thing he did, the wages of sin, the shame, blah blah blah. My family all thought he had lost his mind way back in Ekaterinburg. I was only a child, but I believed him. The old bastard! All those years as a tailor and he died with next to nothing. He'd given it all away. All he left was half a torn note and that led me to Magda, and her grandfather's diary. And this broach. She said it was costume junk. I knew better."

"Why kill her?"

"She wouldn't tell me where the corset was. Old gargoyle." Natalija's eyes were wild and hard.

"So you tried to make it look like a robbery?"

"No, I was mad! Furious! She wouldn't tell me, so I dumped

out all the cheap costume jewelry on her, then I opened the cabinet, all those chains, ropes of fake jewels, all junk. 'Dummy,' she yells at me, as if I thought that junk was Romanov. Dummy?! I am a 'dummy,' she says? I am no one's dummy! She laughed at me. So then I stabbed her." Natalija shrugged, an eloquently expressive motion. Lacey thought it would pass for French. "I was going to stab her anyway."

"But you already poisoned the wine," Lacey said, aware that Natalija could try to stab her at any moment. The blade was still in the woman's left hand, drooping casually. *Why must there always be knives?* she thought miserably. *I hate knives!*

"No, no, no, I *drugged* the wine," Natalija corrected her, as if Lacey had been taking poor notes. "I *poisoned* the dagger. You can't be sure you'll hit an artery, you know, and all that blood! So distressing. 'Bloody stitch, all get rich,' eh? But who wants so much blood all over the shop? So hard to get blood out of good clothing. With poison, you only have to nick the skin."

"Why kill her before you got the information?"

"The old cow wasn't going to tell me. She hated me. All she said was, 'Dummy, dummy, dummy!' I'm glad she's dead," Natalija said. Her eyes glittered dangerously. "Now, tell me where it is."

"I don't know where it is."

"You're lying. You came all the way here, you must know."

"Your great-grandfather Drosmis Berzins made sure no one would ever find it," Lacey said as the woman moved slowly toward her, her knife hand twitching. *Not working! Change tactics!* Lacey retreated and tried another tack. "But maybe if we work together, Natalija, we'll figure it out. We'll go over all the clues together, find the missing piece, maybe something Drosmis said or left you. That torn half of the note? What if we could find the other half—"

"You're a liar. You think I'm a dummy too. You want it all for yourself."

"Wait a minute, Natalija." *Where the hell was Vic?* Lacey didn't want to scream or do anything that would set her off. "What do you think will happen if—"

"I think I'll be happy when you're dead." The woman lunged at her, but Lacey dodged out of the way.

"How can you be happy when you don't have the corset?"

"I was happy when Magda was dead. Why not the same with you?" Natalija had a very weird smile, Lacey decided.

"But I know where it is," Lacey said, making it up as she went along, almost as if she worked for DeadFed. "You're no dummy, Natalija, half the jewels are better than none—"

Natalija sneered, making her beautiful face ugly. "Why does everyone lie to me?" She lunged at Lacey again with her knife. The only weapon Lacey had was her shoulder bag, laden with her usual reporter's tools, but she swung it like a mace and knocked the blade from Natalija's hand. It clattered across the deck and over the edge. *Please don't let it be poisoned,* she thought, *and stick some innocent tourist on the lower deck.*

Angry at losing her sleek little pearl-handled blade, Natalija yelped and body-slammed Lacey, throwing both of them to the deck with a resounding thud. "What are you doing, you idiot?" Lacey screamed. "Vic! Where are you?"

"You won't tell me where the corset is, so I'm going to kill you! With my bare hands!" Natalija had a mad gleam in her eyes and she certainly looked like she could do the job. But they were both momentarily distracted by the sound of Vic's voice somewhere on the lower deck.

"Lacey! What the hell—? Where are you?"

"Vic! Up here! Help!" Lacey managed to shout while trying to roll away from Natalija. The madwoman was trying to climb on top of Lacey and grab her throat.

Vic came racing up the stairs and slammed head on into Kepelov, running down the deck toward the two women. At least Lacey thought it was Kepelov from her vantage point on her back with Natalija clawing at her. Then suddenly the two men were trading punches and one of them fell to the floor. He staggered back up and they went at it again, and then they were both rolling on the deck, fists thrashing furiously.

Lacey threw Natalija off long enough to scoot away from her and back up against the railing. She tried not to worry about Vic: He apparently had his hands full too. What on earth was Kepelov doing here? Natalija dived for Lacey's throat again. Lacey pried her hands from her throat and bit one as hard as she could, then she kicked her off and rolled away. Natalija slunk across the deck, sucking her wounded finger.

"Lying bitch!" Natalija cried. "I'm going to kill you."

Lacey managed to grab onto the railing and pull herself up by one hand, directly above the huge red paddle wheel steadily slapping the water with its long, flat blades. The roar was deafening.

Dazed, Lacey shook her head. Vic seemed to be punching the hell out of Kepelov, but Kepelov was still standing. Natalija coiled like a cobra, nursing her injured hand, eyeing Lacey venomously. Lacey leaned back against the railing and tried to catch her breath. She watched Natalija warily as the woman crouched across the deck from her.

Lacey looked over at Vic. He shoved an exhausted Kepelov to the deck and then raised his head to look at her. He shouted. "Lacey! Look out!"

Lacey glanced down. Natalija uncoiled and sprang at her in a running leap. Somewhere nearby a woman screamed. Lacey instinctively hit the deck and clung to the bottom railing. She saw sudden fear in Natalija's eyes as the woman realized too late she had miscalculated, that a body in motion stays in motion. Natalija Krumina hurled herself over the railing where Lacey had just stood, clawing at it, unable to catch herself. She screamed as she fell, and the heavy thud as her body hit one hard red paddle and then the next seemed to repeat and repeat, until the paddle wheel plowed her down, under the muddy waters of the Mississippi, and she disappeared beneath the riverboat's churning wake. Her screams stopped, but the sound echoed on in Lacey's head.

Vic abandoned Kepelov and ran to Lacey, lifting her up and holding her so hard she could hardly breathe. "My God, Lacey, I think my heart stopped when she came at you," he whispered. He held her tight as they leaned over the railing to look for the woman in the river. They never saw her again.

Kepelov's nose and lip were bleeding and his clothes were torn and dirty, Lacey saw as he stumbled up to them. Vic lifted a weary fist at him, but he held up his hands in surrender. "No more, no more! I wasn't going to hurt her. Not Smithsonian," he said. He turned back to Vic. "Why did you stop me, Donovan? I was after that scheming bitch Natalija Krumina!" He pointed at the river. "She's the one who shot me." Vic unclenched his fist and clasped Kepelov's shoulder.

Trujillo strolled around the corner of the deck, a drink in his hand and a pretty blonde on his arm. He stopped dead in his tracks.

"Oh, man! What did I miss? Mac's gonna kill me, isn't he?"

Chapter 39

Lacey didn't quite know why she invited *everyone*, including Kepelov and Griffin and Stella and Trujillo, to the Passion Flowers boutique on Royal Street the next day.

Maybe she wanted a sense of symmetry for her story, or possibly to suppress the men's raging testosterone levels in that excessively girly dress shop, or maybe she was tired of being stalked and this might end it once and for all. But she invited them all, even the jewel thief and the ex-spy. Turtledove's cousins tracked them down, and they promised to behave, even when she explained over and over that not only was there no Fabergé egg to find, there might very well be nothing at all. She took the precaution of enlisting Turtledove and his cousins to stand guard over the Russian and the Brit, not to mention the excitable Stella, while Lacey made one last search for the corset.

Nicole Demaine was gracious and pleased that her shop would merit a prominent mention in a story that might go around the country, even the world. With some gravity she read aloud the note from the crypt for the assembled group, while Trujillo took photographs. And on behalf of her mother, Madeline Demaine, she was delighted to turn over to Lacey Smithsonian and *The Eye Street Observer* Lacey's prime suspect: the antique dressmaker's dummy that had been on display in her shop for decades.

Lacey had realized where she had to look when she finally stopped shaking from the deadly encounter with Natalija, and they had made their statements to the police. She waited to tell Vic until they were finally alone. He said it was ridiculous, it wasn't logical. How could she be sure? She told him she wasn't sure of anything, and it didn't make any logical sense, just intuitive sense. But finding Magda's note hidden in her corset told her to keep looking for the truth hidden inside. Magda had shed a drop of her blood to wish Lacey luck. And now she kept hearing two dead women saying the same word over and over, Magda and Natalija, both of them descended from the two Latvian soldiers who had stolen the corset in Ekaterinburg long ago. They were both saying the word "dummy."

Nicole brought a step stool and lifted the dummy down from the ledge near the ceiling, where it had been keeping company with antique hatboxes and other forgotten decor. She set it on a low table in the center of the shop, which she closed for the occasion, and whisked off decades of dust with a feather duster. She stepped back and nodded to Lacey. *Prick a finger for me, Magda, wherever you are,* Lacey thought.

Lacey examined the dressmaker's dummy carefully. Nicole Demaine had supplied her with a pair of thin white cotton gloves to wear. The cloth covering the dummy had aged to a deep ivory, smudged with dust, rust-stained around the metal neck plate, but it was intact, its front seams straight and neat. But on the back of the dummy Lacey saw a jagged seam, crudely sewn. *"Secrets between the stitches,"* she said to herself, *that's what Magda wrote inside my corset.*

With trembling fingers, Lacey opened the jagged seam with a seam ripper borrowed from Nicole. She slipped her gloved hand inside the dummy and felt a flat wad of some material. She drew it out slowly while the others held their breath. It was heavy. The material was folded over and stiff with age and heavily stained. Lacey carefully unfolded it: It was a small corset. It would fit a very small-boned young woman, perhaps a teenager. There was a hush of expectant silence. She wondered what color the corset was originally, perhaps even pure white, in a finely woven cotton or linen with a quilted covering. Now it was aged a dark yellow, smeared and spattered with the brown of long-dried blood, its laces cut. The corset was torn and gashed, some of the rips mended by hand with irregular patches of a rougher homespun material. Some were loose, their stitches brittle with age. The darkest brown stains seemed to radiate from beneath the largest patches.

Lacey delicately lifted one of the loose patches with the seam ripper to expose a long gash through which something gleamed. She turned the corset toward the light. It flashed brilliantly, and someone gasped. Through the gash Lacey saw large diamonds set in platinum, perhaps a bracelet or a necklace. It was dazzling.

"Holy cow, Lacey," Stella blurted out, "what the hell is it?"

"A treasure, a dream, a nightmare," Lacey said. "Or all those things." She lifted another loose patch: More diamonds glittered in the shop lights. And then rubies. Vic gave a low whistle.

"My God," Kepelov said slowly, "it can't be real, can it?" He reached out to touch it, but Turtledove cleared his throat gently. He pulled his hand back. "But the corsets don't exist. They were all cut apart and the jewels were taken by the Bolsheviks."

"Nothing's real till you bloody find it, mate," Griffin said. "The Romanovs' bones didn't exist either. And then they dug 'em up a few years back."

"This is incredible! It belongs to Russia," Kepelov proclaimed. "To the Russian people."

"Ha! Finders, keepers, mate. But just wait till the live Romanovs hear about this."

"I feel an international incident coming on," Lacey said. Vic hired Turtledove and his cousins on the spot to provide security all the way back to Washington.

Lacey let everyone gaze at the corset and its contents, under Vic and Turtledove's watchful eyes. She and Trujillo took endless photographs. Nicole posed with the dummy and the corset, a little breathless, and then Lacey, and then Stella too. Lacey called Mac at *The Eye* and listened to him laugh and yell for someone to get the presses ready for a special edition. She even called Brooke at her law office and listened to her squeal with joy. She let everyone in the little dress shop marvel and wonder and speculate and talk. And talk and talk.

Finally she put the corset in an archival document box lined with acid-free paper and the dummy in a similar but larger box. Handling them again would be a job for experts in historical garment conservation, and in Romanov jewels. And probably international diplomacy.

"Isn't it funny," Nicole Demaine said to Lacey as she packed it all up. "I wanted to get rid of that dusty old thing years ago, but Mother would never let me. She said it brought her good luck."

"Your mother was the only one," Lacey said. "It's brought everyone else bad luck." *Including Magda Rousseau,* Lacey thought. *But Magda brought me good luck. Maybe this will break the chain.*

Vic held her close. "What about us, dragon-slayer? We never get enough time, do we? Well, this is your lucky day. You just proved it. So come on, make a wish. I'll make it come true."

Lacey looked at Vic, wondering. She thought perhaps they were both finally making the same wish. But then she shook her head, reluctantly.

"This dragon-slayer has to write a big story, fly home, and bake a cake for Thanksgiving, remember?" She sighed. "Will you help me, Vic?"

Vic kissed her and picked her up and spun her around until she laughed and begged him to stop. "Let's go home and bake that cake, sweetheart. I'm all yours."

"Good to know, cowboy." She kissed him again, and she kissed him so he'd never forget it. "Now we just have to tell that to your mother."